Diane Nielsen was born and raised in Nebraska. She has been entertaining others with her stories since the age of nine.

Besides her passion for writing, Diane loves spending time with her two sons, rock hunting and the Nebraska Cornhuskers.

This is Diane's second published book, from the Guardian Series.

Other Books Published by author Diane Nielsen:

"WISH ME DEAD"
Book #1 in The Guardian Series

Dark Whispers

* Book Two in The Guardian Series *

DIANE NIELSEN

Order this book online at www.trafford.com
or email orders@trafford.com

Most Trafford titles are also available at major online book retailers.

Printed in the United States of America.

ISBN: 978-1-4669-7608-5 (sc)
ISBN: 978-1-4669-7607-8 (hc)
ISBN: 978-1-4669-7609-2 (e)

Library of Congress Control Number: 2013900469

Trafford rev. 02/04/2013

www.trafford.com

North America & international
toll-free: 1 888 232 4444 (USA & Canada)
phone: 250 383 6864 ♦ fax: 812 355 4082

DEDICATION

This book is dedicated to three people: To Lori Borchert my web master and cover creator, for all the work you do. You are a wonderful friend. To my agent/manager Christine Sigg, you are tireless and most excellent at what you do. And to Erin Heilbrun the gifted artist who creates book covers and posters for me. Your talent is envied. Thank you all!!!

Prologue

The powerful Dark Being known as Roman dipped and swayed before the roaring flame known to the Dark minions as "The Inferno of Torment." Unlike the "Window to the World" the Immortal Guardians used to watch over their human charges, this portal enabled the Dark to spy on those same mortals, seeking traits that they could exploit and nurture until their souls fell from the path destiny had written for them at birth, tumbling down into the darkness never to see the light again. Their turned souls became the army that Roman commanded in bringing pain, chaos and death to earth. His army had become bloated with its numbers, and Roman worked hard to make sure the current trend of enrollment did not lessen.

The Inferno of Torment was not the comforting flames of campfires or even the flames that danced and warmed in fireplaces, but instead it was an awful beast that gave off an icy chill and sucked all the light it could reach into its belly that was always hungry, never satisfied. It craved the failings of mortals and grew monstrous when wars were fought, lives were taken, and deceit was faithfully practiced. Roman and the Dark minions had fed its hunger, until it now reached high enough to tickle the under belly of the sky with its greedy tongues of fire.

The Guardians, led by the mighty Saul, beat back the flame with every soul they rescued, every human led back to the path written for it, every disaster averted. But the times were in Roman's favor as mankind grew more violent and greedy in the bid to gain power, fame and fortune.

Roman and Saul had done battle over mortal souls more times than either of them could count, but Roman had never quite been able to put an end to his most powerful foe, his counterpart and equal from the light.

Today Roman undulated slowly in front of the flame, seeming to be nothing more than a sinister wisp of smoke, but he was not watching the mortals. Today he was after a way to poke at his rival again. So he chose to spy on Saul and another Immortal, Jeannicca, as they stood before The Window to the World, discussing the upcoming troubles that two of their charges would be facing. But Roman stopped his movements as he listened and to his delight detected jealousy and rivalry coming from the female Guardian. He could see how she envied Saul, his power, and how she aimed for that power for herself and craved the adoration of her peers.

Roman could not believe his good fortune in finding this juicy tidbit, and it took very little thinking for him to come up with a plan to use it to his advantage. The golden beauty of this second Immortal would be a feather in his cap if he could use her to get to Saul and work against him to throw destiny for two humans into turmoil. All he had to do was send in one of his Dark forces to take over Jeannicca, and he, himself, would do the rest. It would be fatal to the one possessing the Guardian if Saul was to discover its treachery, but Roman was not worried about that. He cared not that his army would be less one. After all there were hundreds waiting to take its place.

Roman danced and twisted with glee as he celebrated his good luck, and knew that his time would be coming soon when all it would take from him was whispers, dark whispers, and lives would be influenced and his flame would be fed.

Fed with murder.

Chapter 1

Balthazar Marcus Hix sat like a Nordic God, golden skin, rippling muscles, flowing blonde hair, deep blue eyes, and a face that could only be described as sinfully beautiful, while his subjects made merry all around him. Well, not exactly like a god. His subjects were his team mates and friends that were celebrating their victory over the neighboring town's over twenty men's basketball team, and his throne was a bar stool. His beer sat before him untouched, his mind focused on something far from this place. His eyes looked off into the distance, but did not see the far wall paneled in dark wood hosting a scarred dart board, not the wall surrounding it, having as many holes as the board itself, nor the posters taped to it of various athletes doing whatever it took to earn the beer at the finish line. Pictures of big breasted women, wearing very little clothes, and promising all sorts of delights if you only chose their liquor to drink, lined other walls as if they were wall paper, leaving no room for anything else to distract the drinker. Drink, drink, drink was the message, and most who came into The Nineteenth Hole followed it to the letter.

It was the local sports bar of the want-to-be jocks that were out of school and too old or not good enough to make college and pro teams. The ones still trying to hold on to their youth and popularity by playing the sports they had left behind in high school and or college. They stood in groups, reliving the game and bragging about their amazing feats as if every shot they had made had taken a super human effort, sure that only because of their herculean effort was the game won. Each made themselves seem larger than life. As the beer flowed and backs were slapped, the tales became more outrageous until an observer would not have recognized the game they were talking about as the same game they had witnessed.

Through it all, Balthazar, known to his friends and coworkers as Hix, sat on the fringes, not feeling like joining in, his 6 foot 6 frame lounging seemingly without a care at the bar as he nursed his one beer all night until it was flat and warm. He gave no heed to the women that sidled up to him, touching his arm and trying their best to gain his attention. Each hoping they would be the lucky one to finally bring him to the altar, if only he would give them a chance to show him how wonderful they were. But each left after only a few moments, getting grunts and half smiles from the hunk who was happier sitting by himself and thinking. He had troubles.

The game had pushed them to the back of his mind for a time, but with no distractions, they came blasting back, to sit in vivid color, front and center, daring him to try and ignore them.

At 28, Hix was at a point in his life were he figured he had the world at his feet. He worked in construction and was happy making things with his hands. He had learned the business from the ground up, starting when he was in high school with a week end job cleaning up at work sites, until he was where he was today, master of his craft and confident in his abilities. He loved working outdoors, and the physical part of his work kept him in rock hard shape, his body honed to perfection, tanned from the sun and gorgeous.

He had never had a problem getting dates or handling the women he did date. He let each of them know that there was nothing permanent or even serious in the time they spent together. He always figured he was young and did not want to settle down. He wanted to have fun and enjoy all that life had to offer.

Because of his looks and his outgoing ways, things had come to him easily. He never had to work at what he wanted. He treated everyone as a friend and had a heart the size of Texas, when it came to being generous with his money. If he had it and someone in need came to him, he gave it. He was by no means a push over, and no one ever took him as such.

He really was deep down good, and tried to be fair and equal with everyone. His friends numbered many.

So how could this have happened to him? He sat there going over and over his life, finding all the good he had done, pondering his luck with friends and family. So, why him? Why did he deserve to be punished now?

His mother, Sarah, had taught him, with a kind and loving hand, to believe in Karma and in what goes around comes around. So, he had been ever mindful to be good and treat everyone as he wanted to be treated. At the thought of his mother, Hix squirmed on the stool. He was going to have to talk to her, soon. He had the sinking feeling in his stomach that she was going to be disappointed in him, and he did not want to hurt her. What should he say to her? How to break the news to her was one of the problems he was trying to figure out, sitting here in self-imposed isolation. His mind felt like a hamster going round and round on its little hamster wheel, never getting anywhere no matter how hard or how fast it went.

Hix was brought out of his musing when the stool beside him was pulled out and Andy, his best friend, plopped down to join him. They had been best friends since grade school, being considered Mutt and Jeff ever since he could remember. Him being tall, athletic and good looking, Andy being a good 8 inches shorter, average when it came to looks and more of a book worm then a jock. No matter their differences they had bonded and became fast friends ever since the day Andy's family had moved to town and Andy had joined Hix's class. In the here and now, Andy draped an arm over his buddy's shoulders and gave him a pat.

"Hey man," he said, his voice coming out slightly slurred with a puff of beer breath. "What are you doing sitting here all by yourself? This is a celebration you know. We won!"

Hix spared him a glance and a half smile as he said "Yeah, I know. You did really good tonight bro. It was definitely your night."

Andy pushed out his chest at his friend's praise. To have someone like Hix say he did good, and mean it, was great for his ego. He knew he was no jock, but he liked to join in and play with his buddy. Most times he stayed in the shadows, never having been able to compete on Hix's level, but tonight he really had done well and he deserved the praise "Thanks man," he said, taking a drink of his beer and setting the glass on the bar next to the warm, flat one already there. "You okay?" he asked, not looking at his friend. "You seem kind of quiet tonight. I mean, you don't have to tell me, but I'm here if you need me."

Hix was surprised and warmed by the insight and thoughtfulness of his friend. He smiled, looked over at Andy and gave him a friendly elbow in the ribs. "Thanks for asking, Andy. There are just some things on my mind that I've got to figure out myself. Nothing for you to worry about though." Hix added, trying to reassure himself, as well as his friend.

Andy nodded his head in male understanding. Sometimes a guy just needed to think and figure out life on his own. But he had offered and, if he was needed, he would be there. "Okay man," Andy said, rising a little unsteady on his feet. He turned to rejoin the rest of the team then turned back to ask, "Hey Hix, where is that hot girlfriend of yours? Abby wasn't there tonight"

"Home," Hix said, stiffening up. "She's home."

Andy nodded once again and moved off to mix with the rowdy bunch near the bar.

To himself, Hix thought, "Yeah, she's home. Home planning a wedding. Mine."

Chapter 2

Abigale Jewel Mathews was hot. Andy had been right on that score. She was 5 feet 10 inches tall, in her stocking feet, and had long honey-gold hair that hung in soft, fluffy waves past her shoulders. Her eyes were a deep, dark brown, with shards of gold in them, her brows a darker shade of brown than her hair. Her lashes were not necessarily thick, but when makeup, in the form of mascara, was added they were excessively long, leaving many women thinking cattily that they must be fake, or just wishing theirs were as beautiful. Her cheeks still had the blush of youth riding upon them, and her mouth was slightly wide and inclined to smile rather than pout. She had been modeling since she was in her early teens, but unlike many of those in her profession, she did not look like she was in desperate need of a sandwich, so thin that she would propel herself across a room just by farting. She worked with women like that, and shuddered when, in the dressing rooms, they took off their clothes and had arms like sticks with no definition to them and legs that looked even worse, all knees, feet and no shape. Their stomachs may have been flat but they had no breasts, unless they had them augmented, and their rears looked like plucked chicken asses.

Abigale's body had curves that were all female. She spent an hour a day in the gym to make sure she stayed toned and fit. She was only 22, but as her mother always said, it was never too early to exercise and learn to eat right. This included lots of fruits, vegetables and fresh water instead of sodas. On occasion she indulged herself with a big, juicy burger and fries, with no guilt or throwing up involved.

Her mother, Cathy, had acted as her manager when she was young, pushing her into taking many jobs that Abby had not wanted to do.

She'd wanted to be a normal teenager and not a super model, her name a household word. When she turned 18, she'd cut the apron strings and gotten herself a manager that did not make all the decisions for her, but listened to what she wanted.

In four short years, she'd earned enough money that she could live comfortably for the rest of her life, just by using the interest her savings accounts earned. Now, she only worked when she chose to and, because of this, her demand in the market had gone up. Businesses considered themselves very lucky if they could get Abigale Jewel Mathews to do a shoot for them. She demanded and got top dollar for the use of her face and figure, saving most of what she earned. She'd never fallen into the drug and alcohol scenes. She didn't party every night, or even every weekend, preferring to spend time at home, in her apartment with her cat, Sidney, a big bundle of orange fur with a bad attitude.

She liked to watch TV and she was addicted to movies, watching her favorites over and over again. Depending on her mood, she watched horror movies, loving to get the crap scared out of her, but finding it hard to find good, scary ones. She watched funny shows when she was feeling down and romantic movies when she was lonely. She even watched cartoons, finding they made her forget her worries and feel like a kid again, just when she needed it the most. She had her favorite TV shows on each night of the week, and thanked the Gods for her DVR when she was not home to catch a new episode. Modern technology was a wonderful thing.

Abby had three very close friends that, when she wanted to go out or spend some time just talking, she could call on for support. They had all, at one time or another, together and separate, tried to talk her into changing her lifestyle. They urged her to go out more, socialize more, and date more. She patiently listened to their concerns but, in the end, she'd gently told them that she was happy with her life just the way it was, but glad to have friends who cared. They would shake their heads and sigh, never admitting defeat, but knowing when to back off and give it a rest. Watching Abby's reaction to her mother's nagging and constant demand for money, gave them a clue of how stubborn she could be when she was pushed. Abby had a face you could read like an open book and her friends recognized the darkening eyes, raised eyebrow, and tightening of her lips as a dead give-away to back off or change the subject. But once in a while they chalked up a victory and got her to go out and have a girl's night with them.

Such had been the case three months ago in late winter. It had snowed every day for two weeks, leaving the town of Winston, Nebraska, pretty as a Christmas card. But the streets were as dead as a Saturday afternoon when the Huskers were playing on TV. Staring out the window at the peaceful scene, Abby felt the urge to get out of the house for a while.

Seeming to sense her need, Kendall had called saying, "Hey girl, Tonia, Mary and I are going to The Nineteenth Hole to get a bite to eat and maybe play some pool. Care to join us?"

Abby had readily agreed to bundle up and meet them there, dropping the phone and heading to the bathroom to shower and change. It was an hour and a half later that Abby had walked through the doors and spotted her friends in the dimly lit, smoky room. They sat in a booth in the far corner, their coats heaped in a pile at one end, and a pitcher of strawberry margaritas in the middle of the table, her glass already filled and waiting for her.

Abby's smile had been huge and immediate as she spotted them and headed in their direction, looking neither right nor left. She unzipped her coat and pealed it off, as her jean-clad legs ate up the distance across the scarred wooden floor. The black, cable-knit sweater she'd chosen to wear was a perfect frame for her golden hair, as she shook it out after pulling off her stocking hat, letting it fall to her shoulders and down her back in silken glory.

The bar that Friday night was filled with a variety of people, families out for a burger, couples on dates, and single men and women hoping to hook up with Mr. or Ms. Right before the night was over. It was still early in the evening so the atmosphere was one of playfulness and fun, not having progressed to the sloshed and desperate that would prevail towards closing time.

As Abby made her way across the floor, conversations ceased and all eyes tracked her progress. Men because of her beauty and women because of the competition she would pose. Lust rose in the hearts and minds of the guys, both single and attached, while envy, despair and jealousy could be seen in the faces of the women present. Abby paid no attention to the stir she was causing, as she kept her eyes on her friends and made straight for them. She tossed her coat on top of the others and slid in beside her best buds, lifted her drink, and took a sip before letting her eyes, full of merriment, circle the table.

"Hi ladies," she said. Bumping shoulders with Kendall, and letting her eyes speak for her, giving her friend thanks for pulling her out for a night of girl-fun that was much needed. Kendall returned the bump with one of her own and winked before lifting her glass to her friends and waiting for them to do the same.

"To friends," she said, clinking her glass with the others.

"To best friends," said Mary as she touched her glass all around.

"To us," said Tonia joining in.

"To my friends," Abby chimed in, "I love you all."

It had been almost a month since they had all gotten together, usually meeting at one of their apartments. Being cooped up because of the snow had brought out the need for a change of scenery, so gossip and catching up was the order of business and the Nineteenth Hole was the venue of choice. Leaning their arms on the table and bending their heads in close, they got down to business.

Chapter 3

Hix had spent a grueling week in and out of the cold, working on a house he was helping to build. It was going to be huge and would belong to a local businessman that had money to burn and needed another home like he needed another hole in his head. But hey, who was he to say what the guy spent his money on. It kept him in work and he was happy doing what he loved. Hix took pride in his work, completing each project as if it was going to be his own home, each detail turned to perfection.

But damn, he thought, it had been cold. No matter how many layers of clothes he put on, the wind had cut into him like a knife, digging in all the way to his bones. He'd gone home each night beat and in need of a hot shower to thaw out. Tonight had been no different. He'd gone home, stripped down to his chilled skin, and stepped into a steaming hot shower, letting the heat loosen up his cold, tired muscles.

He had planned on a quiet night at home, kicking back in front of the TV with a big bowl of homemade chili his mom had brought over the night before. He smiled at the thought and his stomach agreed with his choice as it growled in anticipation. His mom was always doing things like that for him, bringing treats over she had made and knew he would enjoy.

He loved his mother and he was not afraid to show it, although it might not be considered cool to do so. He didn't care. He remembered how she had struggled to give him what he needed as he grew up, being a single mother and having a job that did not pay all that well. So when he had gotten this job, one that paid him good money, he made sure she did not want for anything, giving back a little of what she'd given him all those years. They were close, and Hix couldn't even imagine his life without her loving and caring presence in it. He had taken a lot of ribbing from his friends as he grew up, making sure to never leave the house or hang up the phone without saying "I love you" to her. That was okay with him. Life was short and he didn't want to wake up one day and find her gone, regretting not having told her he loved and appreciated her. His friends had finally gotten used to his behavior, and Hix liked to think a little of his attitude had even rubbed off on some of them.

The guys he hung with were, all in all, a pretty good bunch. They drank a little, sometimes too much, but there were no drugs, no guns, no gangs, and no crimes committed. They were true, and stuck by you when times were hard and problems cropped up. Everyone in town knew that where Hix was, you could also find Andy, his best friend. Not far behind and completing the set were the identical twins, Josh and Dylan. All four had grown up together and become fast friends from the very beginning. They weren't all that much alike, but tight just the same.

Andy, as everyone knew, was average in height, average in looks and average at sports. He was kind of average at everything, except computers. He was a whiz, and had a pretty good job doing what he loved, just like Hix. But different.

Josh and Dylan were more like Hix, in that they had been jocks in high school and still liked to play just for the fun of it. Either one could have gone to college on a football or basketball scholarship, but neither one had. They were missing that competitive edge. Laid back and easy going were good words to describe them both. They worked on the family farm with their father, and knew more about raising cattle and corn than anyone else in the state. They had green thumbs when it came to plants and soft hearts when it came to their livestock. The calving barns were kept cleaner than most of the homes around town, and because of the attention they paid to their cattle and crops, they made good money while doing what they loved. Just like Hix. But different.

All four were single and all four had no trouble getting dates with women that for the moment held their fancy. None of the four were in a hurry to settle down, and tended to hang out together, whether they were seeing someone or not. Usually, not doing a lot, just hanging out. It was a guy thing that most women did not get, and most did not like, preferring that their man chose to spend more time with them instead of their buddies. Needless to say, the fighting this generated was not worth the effort, so relationships usually ended before they could get anywhere near serious.

Hix got out of the shower and dried off, donning an old pair of flannel lounging pants and a comfortable Husker shirt that had seen better days. He had just stuck his head into the refrigerator to pull out the anticipated chili, when there was a heavy knocking at his door. Eying the chili and trying to decide if he should answer the door occupied his mind for a full 5 seconds, before the pounding on the door came again. Heaving a sigh, he went to the door in his bare feet. He knew, before he opened it, who was on the other side. He was right.

As the door swung open, three male bodies tumbled in like young puppies, all vying for the chance to be first. Hix stood at the door shaking his head and shivering, as cold air followed the trio in before he could slam it closed. By the time he had followed them into his living room, the three had formed a line and were facing him with slight frowns on their faces. "Dude, are you in your jammies?" Dylan asked, letting his eyes wander up and down his barefoot friend.

Hix shrugged his shoulders and walked past his friends, heading for the kitchen and his supper. "I just got home," he explained over his shoulder, "and I hadn't planned on going out again. So, yeah, I guess you could say I'm in my jammies."

"Where are you going?" asked Andy, trailing behind Hix as he made his way into the kitchen.

"I'm going to make myself a bowl of the chili my mom brought over yesterday. Why?" asked Hix, stopping so suddenly that Andy ran into him, and Dylan into him and Josh into him.

"Chili?" all three asked at once.

"Is that your mom's chili?" Josh asked, wanting verification.

Hix smiled and stood in front of the fridge door. "There is only enough for one bowl, and as much as I like you guys and would give you the shirt off my back, I'm not sharing."

Three faces fell as they realized Hix really wasn't going to share his supper with them. Hix laughed at the sight of their sad Sam faces, then finally asked why they were there.

"We thought we would go to the Nineteenth Hole and grab some burgers and maybe play a little pool. None of us has to work tomorrow so we came to pick you up and drag you with us," Dylan supplied for the trio of intruders. "Get dressed, man," he said, turning to re-enter the living room and plopping onto the couch to wait for Hix.

Hix really did not want to go out into the cold again, but knew it would be hopeless to say no to his friends. They would just harass him until he couldn't stand it anymore, and he'd end up going anyway. "Give me five," he said and went into the bedroom to drag on a pair of jeans that were soft with age and a bulky sweater that was heavy and warm. Sitting on the edge of the bed, he pulled on a thick pair of socks and a warm, dry pair of work boots. He grabbed a heavy parka out of the closet by the door, put it on, and zipped it shut.

"Ready," he said, as he waited by the door for his friends to get off the couch and join him.

They all trouped out into the cold and piled into Josh's pickup.

"Christ," Hix said through clenched teeth, feeling the cold bite at him again, "turn the damned heater on, man."

Flashing a grin at Hix in the rear view mirror, Josh complied. Hix settled back against the seat and wondered if he was getting sick or something, because he had a feeling that he really should not be doing this tonight. Something felt off, not quite right. Hunching his shoulders and burying his nose in his coat, he let his friend drive him towards the bar and, unbeknownst to him, his destiny.

Chapter 4

Hix and his band of merry men arrived at the bar. Stepping out of the pickup onto the sidewalk, they made a mad dash for the door before the wind could carry them away to Kansas. The gust at his back felt more like a hand shoving him inside. Hix twitched his shoulders trying to dispel the feeling.

All four stood just inside the door as it slammed with finality. They shook the snow from their coats and hair, while stomping it from their boots. The air that greeted them was warm and the scents it carried were like old friends to them, familiar and comfortable.

Hix headed into the room looking for an open table, almost stopping when he heard a low, gravely voice bitching about the cold air that they had let in. Still moving, he turned his head toward the voice, his eyes falling on four rather dirty men seated just inside the door. They all had long, crusty beards, were wearing overalls that looked like they hadn't seen the inside of a washer since winter had started, and boots that were caked with mud and something unidentifiable. It was probably manure, judging by the faint smell of cows that seemed to radiate from the area of their table.

"Damn pretty boys," the one nearest the door grumbled "must have been born in a barn. Don't know how to close a door after they get in?"

"Trying to freeze the rest of us out?" another complained.

"I hate pretty boys," the third one chimed in with a nasty sneer on his face.

"Shut up and drink your beer," the fourth man said, not looking up. If he had, he would have seen that it was his comment that had stayed

Hix from coming over to the table and making them apologize for their rudeness.

At the man's comment, Hix continued on and found an empty table, shrugged out of his coat, hung it on the back of his chair, and sat down. All four had just barely settled into their chairs before the waitress, Kate, came over, tray in hand, swinging her hips, to take their orders and get in a bit of flirting.

"This table," she thought to herself, *"housed the hottest guys she had seen since landing in this small town."* "Yummy," she whispered under her breath as she approached. Maybe she could get some action from one of them after closing tonight. Liking the looks of the big blonde giant of a man, she stopped behind and a little to the side of his chair, letting her breasts, that were straining against her white tee shirt, graze his shoulder. A little rubbing, she figured, never hurt anyone. Just enough to peak his interest of course.

"Hey boys," she drawled, her accent telling them she was not from the area. "What's your pleasure tonight?" she asked her voice dripping with innuendo.

Hix knew he was in for some ribbing after she left because none of the guys would look him in the eye, seeming very interested in their menus and wearing identical smirks on their faces. They seemed to have lost the power of speech, so Hix figured they were going to leave the ordering to him.

Hix leaned slightly forward in his chair and turned to face the person attached to the boob that had been resting against his shoulder. His eyes traveled up the body clothed in a tight tee shirt and tighter blue jeans. "Not bad," he thought to himself, a little plump but he preferred a little meat on the bones of his women. When he got to the face he swallowed once before smiling at "Kate", as her name tag announced.

She wasn't ugly, just wore enough make up that Hix figured she had applied it with a putty knife. Her hair was dark and piled high on top of her head, giving her another 6 inches, if any. Her eyes were blue, and heavily outlined with black liner. Her smile was suggestive and aimed right at him.

"Hi, Kate," Hix said, "you must be new in town."

"I just moved in about a week ago," she said, preening to herself that he had noticed her as a fresh face in Winston.

"Well, welcome," he said. "I'm Hix, this is Andy, Josh, and Dylan," he said pointing to the trio, who were forced to look up at Hix's introductions and unspoken invitation to be polite to the waitress. They all murmured a greeting, then quickly glanced back at their menus, still smothering their silly grins that threatened to escape at any minute.

"I think we are going to have four of your House burgers, medium well, with fries and a pitcher of tap beer with four glasses," Hix told Kate as he closed his menu.

Kate made notes on her order pad, then removed the menus from the hands of the four hunks. "I'll be right back with the beer," she said, hugging the menus to her chest and pressing upward so that her breasts were the center of attention. "Like you said," she continued, "my name is Kate and *I'll* be taking care of you tonight. If you need anything at all, you just let me know," she winked, the undisguised innuendo again heavy in her words.

"Thanks," Hix said with a polite smile, "we will."

When she was out of earshot, Hix turned to the table and looked at each of his friends with a sober face and raised eyebrows. "She's new in town, you guys be nice."

For three seconds there was dead silence as Andy, Josh, and Dylan suppressed the smart assed remarks they itched to deliver. Each knew that Hix was a good guy and polite to everyone, giving them the benefit of the doubt when they first met.

Letting out a sigh, Dylan flopped back in his chair and shook his head. "Okay," he said, "but if you figure you don't need a ride home tonight, just let us know."

Hix made a swipe at him and all four laughed as they shared the joke.

Kate brought their mugs and pitcher of beer, pouring each of them the first glass, and the evening got under way. The conversation was lively, the four of them discussing sports and what had happened to each of them during the week. The burgers came and were devoured with relish, before the men turned their attention toward the two pool tables set up in the middle of the room.

Several guys milled around the green felt tables, ques sending the colored balls popping against each other, then one by one into the pockets, until the field of green was, once again, all that was visible.

Hix grabbed a couple of quarters from his pocket and placed them on the side of one of the tables, indicating his intention of being the next contender. Going back to his table, he turned his chair around, straddling it as he watched the players and their styles, planning his strategy for when he came up next. He planned on winning and, with the way he and his friends played, they should be able to hold the table for the rest of the night. Hix waited till the game was over, then rose from his chair and made his way to the pool table. He gathered his money, and was about to put it in the slots, when he felt a hand land heavily on his shoulder, stopping him.

"I'm next, pretty boy," a voice he recognized ground out.

Hix closed his eyes for a second and sighed. All his life, guys smaller than him had tried to take him on, just to prove they were the toughest. Most of the time he was able to talk them down, but a couple of times things had gotten out of hand, with the end result being Hix walking out, while the other guy was carried.

Opening his eyes he looked over at his friends. They had all quieted, reading in Hix's expression what was about to happen. Three chairs were quietly pushed back and three able bodies, with muscles bunched, waited and watched. Hix gave a slight nod of his head and turned to face the man attached to the hand on his shoulder. He recognized him as one of the guys who'd made comments about them when they'd first walked in.

The man still had on his dirty overalls, but they were now unzipped down the front, revealing a slight paunch under a plaid work shirt. The eyes that met Hix's were red and watery, showing him that the man had consumed more than a little beer tonight. He wore a stocking hat over his greasy hair, which was long enough that it poked out from beneath the hat around his whisker-stubbled chin. The man stood a good foot shorter than Hix, coming just to his shoulders.

"No, I think it's my turn," Hix said in a non-threatening voice, looking down on the man and pushing the hand from his shoulder. "I had my money up next."

"So what?" the drunk belched the words in Hix's face, as bad breath and spittle threatened to make Hix lose the burger he'd just consumed. "I called next game a long time ago."

Hix took a half a step backwards, putting a little distance between himself and the drunk then looked at the winner of the last game for confirmation, receiving a shrug and then a negative shake of his head. Not wanting trouble, Hix shrugged his shoulders and placed his money back on the side of the table for the next game.

He turned to go back to his chair, but was stopped as the drunk, seeming to have a death wish on a cold night uttered one word at Hix's retreating back. "Pussy!" the man spat out.

Hix stopped in his tracks, closed his eyes, clenched and unclenched his fists at his sides. He rolled his head on his shoulders and then turned to face the man. "Look mister," he said, "I don't know what your problem is, but I'm just here to have a little fun, so let's just drop it." He didn't raise his voice but his meaning was clear.

As Hix spoke the three dirt bags from the drunk's table got up and stood behind their friend. Hix wasn't the least bit intimidated, feeling the presence of his friends who'd come to stand at his back. The bar became quiet and all eyes focused on the eight men squaring off. The air thickened with tension as fists clenched, each side waiting to see who was going to make the first move.

Just as the drunk pulled his arm back to throw a punch, Kate stepped into the middle of the testosterone. Placing her hand on the drunk's chest she pushed him back and said in her southern drawl, "Come on now. We don't want any trouble here. You boys look like you've had enough for the night, so you 'all get your things and head out."

She was firm but friendly as she continued, "You boys are welcome back here anytime, but tonight you've had enough."

A full three seconds passed before the fourth guy at the table grabbed the neck of his cocky friend. "Come on Jack, she's right, let's call it a night." He put his arm around his friend's shoulder and steered him toward the door. The other two men followed close behind.

Jack glared at Hix as he and his friends moved toward the door. "I could have taken him Bob. I could have taken him."

"Sure you could, buddy," Bob said, patting his friend on the shoulder and throwing a slightly apologetic look over his shoulder towards Hix as he ushered his buddies out the door.

As the door closed behind the men, Hix relaxed and took a step back. "Sorry about that, Kate," he told the waitress. "We usually don't have that kind of trouble around here."

Kate smiled and shrugged one shoulder, saying matter-of-factly, "I've calmed down a lot worse than him. I think you're up next, sugar" she said, pointing toward the pool table and winking at Hix as she left to go get an order waiting at the bar.

Hix smiled after her swaying hips, thinking that Kate was quite a woman. Turning, he put his money in the slot, sending it home to release the balls. The mood lightened as he racked them up, and the game got underway. For about an hour Hix ran the table. Then, getting tired of pool, he gave it over to Josh and Dylan and returned to their table.

Kicking back a chair, he sat, propping his jean clad, muscular leg on an empty chair across from him. Tipping back his head, he took a long cool pull from his beer and settled in to watch the crowd. He was relaxed and having a good time, laughing at something Andy had said, when a sudden chill ran up his spine, caused by the opening of the door as someone made their way in from the cold night into the warm, noisy bar. Hix let his gaze wander toward the door, as in walked a dream.

Chapter 5

Hix felt his mouth go dry and the muscles of his gut clench as he, and every other guy in the bar, watched the woman walk with confidence across the room and seat herself at a table with three other "lookers". He had noticed the other three earlier, and had listened to his buddies make comments about how good looking they all were. Definitely worth a second and maybe even a third glance. There was one with pitch black hair, one with medium brown, one with golden blonde and now, one with the color of warm honey. With her arrival the set was now complete.

Hix sat up straighter in his chair and rested his forearms on the table in front of him. He glanced over at his friends who were still playing pool, smirking as he watched each one of them drooling at the femininity gathered in one lucky spot in the Nineteenth Hole. Then, as if some dam had been let loose, about seven hands went up, all male, summoning Kate to their table. He knew that every man attached to one of those arms would be sending drinks over to the table where the new arrival sat with her friends. If the drinks were accepted, the lucky buyer would have an excuse to approach and get an introduction. Hix wasn't going to be one of them.

He relaxed back into his chair and watched as Kate took the orders. Rather than taking seven pitchers of free margaritas to the table, she made a list, then she went to the table where the women sat. She bent over and Hix could hear her telling the ladies that they had more drinks coming than they could drink in one night. As Kate pointed them out, the ladies made eye contact with each man, giving them polite smiles. When Kate had finished with the list, the girl with the black hair, Kendall, told her, "thank all of the gentlemen for their kind offers but, even though the offers were appreciated, they couldn't possibly drink all that much."

Kate shrugged her shoulders as she walked away, thinking the ladies were crazy not to take advantage of all the male attention coming their way. Didn't they know it wasn't just a matter of how much they drank, but also a way to get better acquainted with some of the finer male specimens in the bar? She had to admit though, that the women didn't appear to be snobs or think they were better than the crowd in the bar. "To each their own," she always said. She moved about the crowded barroom delivering the bad news to the eager men.

Their faces fell as Kate delivered the news that the drinks had been rejected. She made sure, however, to tell each guy that the girls had said thanks, just not at this time. Most, Hix knew, would take the news and shrug, going back to whatever they had been doing. But he also knew that a couple of the guys would not give up easily, and were likely to cause problems by the end of the evening if the table of hotties stayed that long.

He mentally shrugged it off and brought his attention back to his own friends as they came to the table, pool sticks in hand, to drink from their frosty beer mugs. Setting down his glass, Dylan made a small motion with his head towards the table in the corner, and said to no one in particular, "Not bad, huh?"

Andy and Josh nodded in appreciative agreement, while Hix just sat there, looking at his friends with an air of indifference. For some unknown reason, he didn't want to be one of the crowd that was falling over themselves to hook-up with one of the women. "Why don't we see if we can buy them a drink and then maybe join us at our table?" Andy suggested.

Josh shook his head saying, "Nah, not yet. Let's wait for the feeding frenzy to die down. Look around," he gestured across the room, "most of these guys look like sharks after a side of bloody beef that has been dropped into their midst."

The men all nodded their heads in agreement at the wisdom of this strategy. Setting their beer back on the table, Dylan, Josh and Andy returned to the pool table to finish their game. Hix sat alone, musing, trying to figure out what it was that felt off to him.

He had never had a problem picking up women in a bar. It was a lot like gambling to him. When you picked up a girl in a bar, you took your chances on what she would be like under all that perfume and lipstick. She may be someone who'd want to sit and share a couple of drinks with you, talking about the weather and the state of the world, before you spun her around the dance floor a couple of times, writing down her number at the end of the evening. Maybe you'd call her, maybe not. Then there was always a chance you'd meet one who liked drinking more than she liked anything else, and she'd end up dancing to Bon Jovi on the top of a table with half her clothes off by the end of the night. Same went for women who came into a bar to meet men. You could spot them a mile away, the way they made eye contact and smiled in a suggestive way, letting a guy know she could be his if he had the balls to ask. You rolled the dice.

Maybe, Hix thought, he was feeling this way because all four of the women who were seated across the room were just too damn beautiful. The really good-looking ones were usually high maintenance princesses who could suck a man dry if he let them. They usually demanded lots of time and money be spent on them, while taking all the attention for granted.

Hell, Hix even remembered dating one girl who was so pretty his eyes had watered every time he looked at her. One day, she had showed him her driver's license, trying to prove that she could take a good picture even when everyone else's looked like a mug shot. Hix had gotten the surprise of his life. In the picture this particular girl had been wearing a tiara. Hix had gaped at the thing and asked her if she had worn it on a dare, but her response had been stiff and snotty when she informed him, "No it was the way she saw herself." Hix had given her back the license and walked out the door, never looking back. Since that day he'd steered clear of the drop-dead gorgeous ones. Maybe that was the reason he was reluctant to chase the four at the table in the corner. They all definitely fell into that category.

Hix shelved the problem for the time being and sat back to enjoy the activities around him. Two local women were involved in a lively game of darts, and both were finding it hard to hit the board. They didn't seem to care, as they laughed and had fun adding holes to the already scarred corkboard wall surrounding the dart board.

A couple of kids had bummed a few quarters from their parents and were plugging them into the jukebox. Soon the place would be rocking to music that would probably make the older crowd cringe.

There were a few high school boys at the foosball table, looking intent while playing as if it were the super bowl instead of a bar game. He remembered being one of them back when he was in school, trying to impress his date by slamming home the final ball, then beating his chest to prove he was the king. Kid stuff. Not harmful, just kind of a rite of passage that everyone goes through. Hix looked around and smiled. He knew many of the faces in the bar tonight and he liked most of them. He liked his town. It was small enough that you knew your neighbors and trusted them to watch your house when you weren't home. But then again, it was still big enough that you had a WalMart, a shopping mall, movie theater, convenience stores, and a couple of car dealerships. It was all just right by his way of thinking.

He could have gone traveling with a big construction company, moving from town to town, job-site to job-site, but he had decided to stay close to home, and was happy that he had. He looked around and realized that he was okay with his life at the moment.

Hix was brought out of his musings when the two Carson brothers got into a wrestling spat. Their tempers were as fiery as their red hair. The fight was short-lived, however, as Kate walked up with a pitcher of ice water and dumped it over their heads. Then she proceeded to hand each of them a mop and told them if they wanted to stay, they had to clean up the mess and leave the rough stuff outside. "Yup," he thought, "she was going to fit in just fine."

Hix pretty much stayed at his table all night, enjoying the friends who stopped by to talk. Andy, Josh and Dylan had gotten tired of winning at pool, so they gave the table up and came to sit with him for a while. Eventually they got up and wandered around, visiting, joking and telling lies the way guys do and everyone seemed to be having a great time just hanging.

Along about eleven the crowd had thinned out. Most of the kids had left, either with their parents, or to go parking at the local make-out place called The Grove. It was actually just a thick stand of trees, but had been used by young lovers since before Hix was born. Those now left in the bar ranged from young couples, married or on dates, to old men and women who came out just to socialize and meet their friends. No one was messed up yet, that he could tell, so the air was festive and the mood happy.

Hix hadn't noticed the two guys who had tried to cause trouble earlier, until Josh came up behind him and rested his hand on his shoulder. Hix looked up, but Josh wasn't looking at him. Instead his eyes were focused across the room on the two jerks who were swaying on their feet in front of the table in the back. Things must not have been going the way they wanted because their voices were getting louder and the language harsher.

"Ah crap," Hix said as he rose to his feet, "some people were just too stupid to leave things alone and just have fun." Nodding his head at Josh, Hix faced the back and thought to himself, "it was time to take out the trash."

Chapter 6

Abby set her drink on the table and listened as each of her friends described, in detail, what had been going on in their lives over the last month. They were all complaining about being overworked and underpaid. Abby could relate to the overworked part, but modeling paid well and she was, to put it simply, loaded. None of her friends begrudged her the money she made, because they all knew that it came with a heavy price.

Although each of them had minor family issues, Abby was the one they felt sorry for. Having a controlling, money-hungry mother on her back, as she did, was by far worse than the simple sibling spats that cropped up in normal lives. No matter their differences or their problems, the four women around the table were friends for life.

Abby sat listening to the conversation, but her mind wandered as she looked from one face to another, all dear to her. Sitting across from her was Mary Olsen. Her hair hung in a straight silken sheet down her back and was the color of pale dawn, true blonde shot through with strands of gold. Her eyes were hazel, tending to change from green, to brown, to blue, depending on what she was wearing or the color of eye shadow she sparingly used. Mary owned and worked in the town's one and only gym/spa. Her business offered everything from workout equipment, complete with trainers, to facials, tanning beds, herbal wraps, and haircuts. Mary liked to pamper herself with manicures and pedicures, so she offered those to her clients as well. If a woman, or a man for that matter, wanted a little "me time" Mary's business, "It's All About Me", was the place to go. No one under the age of 16 was allowed in. Mary had a steady business helping people de-stress, as they snuck away from their everyday lives for an hour or two. Keeping her hand in the front of the business kept her 5'4" body in top condition. She was toned and tight, and took pride in looking good while promoting the benefits of exercise and taking care of your body.

Abby had done a lot of work for Mary, posing in posters and appearing in ads when her business was new, a mere two years ago. In return, Mary let Abby use her gym for her workouts, as well as a place she could go to refocus and recharge when her life got too hectic. Mary was a good friend, and Abby was very proud of her for what she had built with hard work and sweat.

Beside her, snuggled into the booth, was Tonia Marks. Tonia was the office manager of one of the local doctor's offices, Doctor Dean. While at work, her hair was pulled back into a thick, fat braid. The severe style did nothing to hide the rich tones of brown that blended together to shine with health and softness. Her jade green eyes held all the compassion in the world as she skillfully dealt with people, both the ones that worked under her and the patients coming into the office for help with their ailments. Abby knew it took someone very special to keep things running smoothly and on time, as well as being able to comfort a sick child. She had a smile for everyone, and Abby was sure that if there was a saint in their midst, it would be Tonia.

Tonight, with her hair down and her feet tucked under her, she looked much younger than her twenty two years. Smiling, laughing, and enjoying her friends, she exuded warmth and happiness. Tonia was the calm, rock-steady one of the group and each of them looked to her for grounding and solid advice. Abby loved her dearly.

Sitting right beside Abby was her best friend and confidant, Kendall Powell. Kendall was the manager of a local convenience store called "Snacks and Such" in which everything from fuel to yummy treats that, when eaten, went straight to your butt, could be found. Her staff loved her, and she was a favorite with her customers as well. She had great customer service skills, and more than one of the men who frequented her store were totally infatuated with her. Of course her looks were part of the attraction as well. Thick black hair that hung just past her shoulders, blue eyes that sparkled with the devil, and skin that, because of a slight touch of Italian ancestry, always glowed with color and health, made men flock to her like bees to honey. But Kendall was strong and knew what she wanted, and right now a man was not in the picture for her. She spent her time at the store or at her home that she had purchased, preferring to be alone than in a crowd. She smiled and joked with her regulars and was great in a crisis, but her eyes always held a touch of seriousness in their depths. She never really seemed to let go and relax. Abby used her as a sounding board when she had issues, because Kendall always had good advice for her.

Each one of the women around the table would have given their all for any one of the others, and they all knew this. It held them together like glue, making their connection strong and sure. Their friendships were solid.

Abby sat, chin propped in her hand, as she considered each one in turn. Funny, but none of them had been born in the town of Winston, Nebraska. It was an unlikely location to want to move to but, for whatever reason, each had left their place of birth and settled here. Destiny had wanted them together, and here they were, fitting together like pieces of a puzzle.

Abby lifted her glass, raised it slightly in a silent toast to the Gods that had brought them together then took a sip. "Thanks," she mouthed silently to the Fates, then brought her attention back to the table and her friends.

Kendall was telling a story about two young girls that had come into her station to fill up with gas. It seemed to be taking them a very long time to fill their car. Finally one of the two had come into the store, almost in tears, and asked for Kendall's help. It seemed that they were having trouble getting the gas to stay in their car. Kendall had grabbed her jacket and went out to the pumps to see if she could help. When she got to the car, she asked what the problem was. A young blonde girl told her that the gas kept bubbling out of the tank, and they didn't know what to do. Kendall had had to use all of her will power to keep her humor in check, telling the girls to turn the key on and see how full the tank was. Sure enough the car was full, thus the reason the gas kept leaking out of the tank.

As if on cue, groans sounded from the women around the table, followed by laughter, as each one agreed that blonde jokes had to come from somewhere, and youth was not all it was cracked up to be.

"OK," said Tonia, "since this seems to be the time for funny stories, I have one for you. Last week we had an older lady come in for a pap test and like usual she was instructed to empty her bladder. Well, no one knew that we were out of bathroom tissue in the restroom, and the lady was forced to use a tissue out of her purse to wipe off. She came back into the exam room, got up on the table and when the doctor came in to do the examination, he found a green stamp stuck to her, um, hair. Doc Dean came out and laughed until he cried, because he had wanted to ask her if she gave green stamps."

The women around the table, once again, erupted with laughter. The next few moments were spent with each one taking turns telling funny tales, until their sides were hurting from laughter.

"No more," Mary finally got out as she wiped her damp eyes. "I can't take any more. Besides," she said "I'm starved, let's order something to eat."

Everyone agreed and they spent the next few minutes going over the menu as they decided what to order. Seeming to read their minds, Kate came to their table, her pad and pencil in hand. Before they could tell her what they wanted to eat, she told them that they had offers for seven free pitchers of margaritas, from gentlemen around the barroom. Kate turned and pointed to each guy who had offered to buy the ladies a drink, saying, "One from that guy, that guy, that guy," and so on until she had pointed out each one.

Abby, Kendall, Mary, and Tonia followed Kate's finger as she pointed them out, smiling and nodding at each man in turn, until, with a huff of air, Kate finished and turned an eye to the women, waiting for them to let her know what to do.

Looking around the table, Kendall finally answered for the rest. "Please thank the gentlemen for their offers, Kate, but I think we still want to pass. What we really want is to order some food."

Each girl gave Kate her order, then settled back to talk and drink until their food arrived. Abby had been looking around the room while Kate pointed out the men who had ordered drinks for them. Her eyes settled on a table of four men sitting slightly off to the side who had not offered to buy them any drinks. She liked the looks of the big blonde guy at the table, and had felt a little tingle run down her back as she had watched him talking with his friends. Not that she was looking to be picked up by anyone, but from what she could see, he sure was pretty. *Later,* she thought, and once again joined in the conversation around her.

The food came and everyone sampled each other's menu choices, until all their plates and pitcher were empty. The evening was beginning to wear down as the hour approached midnight.

"I hate to be a party pooper," said Tonia, "but I have to get up and put in a half a day tomorrow."

"Yeah, me too," said Mary, but no one really made a move to get up.

"Tonight was good," said Kendall "and I don't know about you guys, but I needed to have a good laugh with friends." The four women clinked their empty glasses together in a toast to their friendship.

Abby had been about to comment, when she looked up and saw two guys standing by their table. Well, standing may not have been an accurate description of what they were doing. Swaying or staggering may have been better.

The ladies quieted as each became aware of the men. Four pairs of eyes were turned up to stare expectantly at the drunks.

"Can we help you guys?" Abby asked. Being the closest to them she got the full effect of their breaths, laden with alcohol and something that smelled like garlic. Not wanting to offend the pair, Abby refrained from moving back, but if there was anything that smelled worse than garlic breath, she didn't know what it was.

"We just thought you ladies looked awful lonely sitting here by yourselves so we thought we would come over and liven things up." The one speaking threw his arm around the shoulder of his friend, and seemed to be hanging on to keep himself upright.

"Thas right," said his friend with a slur to his words. "You ladies looks like you needs some fun over here." He wiggled his eyebrows and leered at the women who were looking at the pair without smiling.

"Actually, we were just leaving, guys. So thanks, but no thanks," Kendall replied. She arched an eyebrow and gave them a look that invited them to take off.

"Come on girls," the first said. "You don't know what you're missing. Why don't you just scoot your pretty ass over and let us sit down," he said to Abby as he reached out and tried to shove her over.

Abby's eyes turned stone cold and the golden shards in them turned to lightning, and she opened her mouth to let the two intruders know exactly where they could park their asses. But before she could get a word out, she heard a deep rumble from behind her, beating her to the draw.

"Billy," the voice said, "get your hand off the lady."

Chapter 7

Without turning around, Billy continued to shove at Abby, trying to make her scoot over so he could sit beside her. "Beat it," he slurred to the voice trying to move in on his action. "We were here first, go bug someone else."

Just then he over balanced, and would have fallen face first into Abby's lap if two strong hands had not grabbed him by the back of the shirt and the belt at his waist. He was picked up until his feet left the floor and, for a moment, he resembled a swimmer without the water. His arms and legs were moving like windmills in the air. He was set back on his feet with a jarring thump that had his head bobbing and his teeth rattling. His feet skated out from under him, as if he were on a pond of solid ice, before he gained his balance as best he could, being three sheets to the wind. Billy turned to confront the voice and ended up with his eyes staring smack dab into a chest that seemed a mile wide.

Standing only about 5'7", he had to tip his head back to let his eyes travel up, up, up until they met and were held by serious blue orbs. It took him a full 5 seconds before recognition set in. Being in an inebriated state, however, and not wanting to lose face in front of the ladies in the booth, Billy made the mistake of puffing out his chest and thinking he could take on the giant in front of him. "*Besides*," he thought "*it would be two to one*," and stupidly that sounded pretty good to him.

"Well now, Hix," he said, "I'm thinking we," jabbing a thumb at his friend, "Carl and I, were here first. We were just about to get to know these ladies, and we don't need your help in doing that, so go away." He turned his back on Hix like he'd taken care of things and fully expected Hix to turn around and go back to his table.

Hix rolled his eyes and shook his head. He knew that when dealing with a drunk, there was no getting around egos. They all thought they were 10 feet tall, bulletproof, and the most desirable person on earth. He'd known Billy and Carl most of his life, and they were usually pretty mellow. But then again, all you had to do was add alcohol and their personalities changed.

"Come on guys," Hix said "let's find you a ride home." He began to turn away when Billy grabbed his arm and hung on.

"We're not going home," Billy slurred. "And if you don't like it, we can take this outside. I think me and Carl can take you," he said, hitching up his pants, sticking out his chin, and squinting his eyes, trying to make Hix's image stop dancing.

Carl stepped up to his friend's side and, not being in much better shape than Billy, was all for going along with the idea of taking on Hix.

Timing was everything, as at that moment Josh stepped up to Hix's side and aimed a smile at the two banty roosters posturing in front of him. "Hey boys," he said "I heard you needed a ride home and Paul over there at the bar is heading that way now, and he's offered to give you a lift."

From the booth, four pair of eyes turned to look at the bar. Giggles were quickly stifled behind raised hands as the ladies spied a little man at the bar with no teeth, grinning from ear to ear as he waved a hand in their direction. They waved back before turning their attention back to the drama still going on in front of them.

All the fight had seemed to go out of the two smaller men, as they now faced not one big man, but two. True Josh was only 6'2", but that was still way more than they wanted to tackle along with the 6'6" giant.

"We were only trying to meet some pretty ladies, you know?" Billy grumbled at the floor.

"Well I'm sure you made quite an impression," Hix said putting his arm around Billy's thin shoulders. "Let's go get your coats and Paul will make sure you both get home safe."

Josh buddied up to Carl, but as he started to steer him away Carl turned back towards the booth with a smile and one last question. With hope in his voice, he looked at the women and asked to any and all of them, "Could I give you my phone number?"

The women looked at each other in silent agreement, and it was Tonia that finally said, "That would be nice, Carl."

The grin that filled Carl's face was bright and proud. He grabbed a wrinkled napkin from the next table to write on. Then he proceeded to move his hands over his shirt and pants pockets, as he was feeling himself up and down, frantically trying to find a pen to write with.

"Here," Abby offered handing him one from her bag. They watched as Carl leaned over the table and scribbled his name and phone number on the napkin.

"Have a safe trip home," chimed in Mary and Kendall, giving him a wave as Josh finally got him to head towards the door and his ride home.

Carl put on his coat, all the while telling everyone within ear shot that the ladies had taken his phone number. He was so proud. Josh and Hix stayed with the pair, firmly moving them towards the door. Then waiting while Carl and Billy turned one last time to wave to the girls. All four women raised their prettily manicured hands and waved back, sending the men home on cloud nine.

As the door closed behind the two, Hix and Josh turned back to the bar room. They were joined by Dylan and Andy, and the four men approached the table of women. They came to a stop and fanned out, taking up the whole front on the table.

Hix, locking eyes with Abby, said, "That was really nice of you, taking his number and all. They really aren't all that bad, and probably won't remember much in the morning, but thanks just the same."

"You're welcome, and thank you," said Abby, as she tilted her head back to meet clear blue eyes surrounded by long, thick black lashes. "It wasn't that big of a deal. We do appreciate your help. It could have gotten ugly, but thanks to you, it didn't, so no harm, no foul."

As Abby's eyes were held by Hix's, she got that same tingle down her spine and a jumpy feeling in the pit of her stomach. "I'm Abby," she said taking a chance, "and these are my friends, Mary, Tonia and Kendall."

As she finished the introductions, her hand was enveloped by Hix's as he gave it a shake, and she felt his linger a moment, hesitating to let go. When he finally did let go, he had to swallow hard at the spit that had pooled in his mouth. When he had touched her hand, he felt an electric shock go up his arm. You know the kind everyone in sappy movies always talks about.

"I'm Hix," he said coming back to reality and returning the favor of introductions, "and this is Josh, Dylan and Andy. We have a table over there and were just playing some pool. Would you ladies like to join us?" he asked.

Abby looked back at her friends, knowing that two of them had to work the next day. What she saw were three sets of slightly glazed eyes, each staring at one of the four men standing in front of them. With raised eyebrows and laughter in her eyes Abby jostled Kendall until she had her attention.

"Shall we?" she asked. Kendall looked at Tonia. Tonia in turned looked at Mary. Some unspoken signal, that the guys cannot see, passed between the females. Then, with a smile on her face and in her eyes, Abby turned to Hix and said, "Lead the way."

Hix and Josh waited by the booth as the girls slid out and collected their coats. Meanwhile, Dylan and Andy went in search of empty chairs and another table to pull up next to theirs. Everyone grabbed a seat and Kate came over to take their drink orders. She was surprised as each of them ordered a soda.

"OK," she said with a shrug, as she went to fill their order. Didn't they all know that alcohol was considered the social lubricant of choice? It loosened people up and made getting to know each other a little easier in the beginning. "*Whatever!*" she thought and brought the tray of drinks as asked.

Hix put quarters in a table and grabbed a stick. "Do you want to play doubles?" he asked Abby as he chalked up the tip.

"Sure, Mary and I will play you and . . . ?" she let the question hang in the air, her eyes roaming over the other three men until Andy jumped up saying, "Me. I'll play."

"OK," said Abby, "we'll break." She chose a que, chalked the tip, and handed it to her friend Mary for the break.

Hix and Andy had no problem with this and stood back, exchanging a glance of silent understanding that they would go easy on the girls so as not to embarrass them. They would even give them some tips if they needed them.

Mary leaned over the table, putting her muscle behind the break. She had the balls scattering and falling in holes as if they had magnets in them. The girls took turns making shots, and, in no time flat, had cleared the table of their balls, leaving a stunned pair of males holding their sticks.

Tonia and Kendall got up to join their friends, bumping knuckles, while Josh and Dylan joined their stunned friends at the other end of the felt.

Shaking his head, Dylan dug out more quarters and bent over to put them in the table for another game. With laughter and appreciation in his voice, he said, "Guys, I think we've just been hustled."

Chapter 8

The last two hours of the evening were spent in competition at the pool table. Hix and his friends soon found out that the girls were no slouches, and seemed to be taking a great deal of pleasure in kicking their butts.

After the third game, and the third defeat for the guys, Hix huddled them up, kind of like a coach with his players late in the 4th quarter. With a serious look on his face he said, "Look you guys, they may be all pretty and sweet looking, but we have to get our crap together and start playing some ball. I know we've all had it hammered into our brains that men are supposed to let women win, but right now we have to get over that mind set and start winning," he said, throwing a glance over his shoulder at the women who were giggling and high-fiving each other across the room.

Three heads nodded in agreement, fists knocked against each other, and a pact was formed. No more mister nice guys. It was time to regain a little of their masculinity. They broke huddle and headed for the pool table, a new determination in their attitude.

By this time all eyes in the bar were gathered around the pool tables watching the action. There were smirks on the faces of some of the men who had taken a beating at the hands of the four men competing, as the women continued to come out on top. Others watched, partly because of the beauty of the women and the handsomeness of the men, but after the newness of that wore off, they watched for the competition.

While the men regrouped to talk and figure out a strategy, all four women headed towards the bathroom. When the door closed behind them Abby looked at each of her pals and as if on cue laughter erupted.

"Did you see the look on their faces?" Kendall got out between giggles. "They looked as if they just found out there was no Santa Claus."

More laughter peeled out as each hit the stalls, then stopped in front of the mirror to check their faces, hair, and to do a little fluffing.

Tonia cocked her head and aired a question. "Should we ease up on them a little? Men have such fragile egos after all."

Each of them took a moment to consider and all agreed in unison, to the tune of more laughter, "No."

"They're going to step up their game, so we need to just keep on going the way we have been," Mary stated in a more serious voice.

"Agreed," said Abby.

Mary finished in the mirror and turned to face the room. "Is it just me, or are those four guys the best looking you've ever seen?"

"Yummy," agreed Kendall.

"I have a feeling this night is going to be lucky for all of us," Mary wiggled her eyebrows. "I kind of like Dylan, and I'm getting vibes that he likes me, too. So I call dibs on him."

"I want Josh," Kendall hurriedly chimed in, staking her claim on one of the four men.

"I get Andy," chimed in Tonia with a gleam in her eye.

"So that leaves Hix for you?" Mary said, turning a questioning look toward Abby.

Again Abby's stomach jumped at the thought of Hix and his blonde good looks.

"I think I can live with that," Abby said, trying to sound as if it were no big deal.

"Okay ladies," Kendall said, turning from the mirror and exchanging a look of conspiracy with the other girls, "let's go see if we can't stir up a little something besides pool balls?"

They exited the ladie's room and were met with four identical puzzled gazes. "What's up?" Abby asked Hix, as she moved to stand beside the blonde hunk.

"We were just wondering why women always go to the bathroom in groups?" he said honestly.

Abby shrugged her shoulders at the age-old question, and took the que from his hand. "We do that so we can talk about you men. Want to be my partner?" she asked with a challenge in her eyes.

Hix's heart beat a little faster as he wondered if there was a double meaning to her question. He decided on the spot, that either way, the answer would be yes.

When last call was given, the men and women had paired up into couples, just as the women had predicted. They all decided to decline the last round of drinks offered, and the ladies returned to the table to gather their coats and began getting ready to brave the freezing cold that awaited them outside the warm bar room.

Hix moved to help Abby with her coat, stepping back as she zipped and buttoned herself into it. Pulling her knit cap over her honey blonde hair, and pulling on her gloves, she finally faced Hix. "Thanks for tonight," she said, looking up into his handsome face. "I think I can speak for all of us, when I say we had a good time." She looked at her friends, who were smiling and laughing with the other three men.

"Maybe we can do this again, just you and I?" Hix returned, looking into her eyes as he stuffed his hands into his front pockets before they did something she wasn't ready for. He wanted to reach out and snuggle her coat under her chin and tuck the stray strand of honey back inside the cap. He wanted to bend down and rest his lips against hers and find out if they tasted as sweet as they looked. Not a good idea when you just met someone, he told himself.

Hix's usual style would have had him draping his arm around the girl's shoulders and walking her out to her car. He would then give her a few hot kisses, get her number so he could set something up in a week or so, then see how things went. But tonight was different. Tonight he felt unsure and awkward, kind of like he was back in high school asking out his first date. His hands were sweating and his mouth was dry. He took comfort in the fact that Abby seemed just as nervous and unsure of how to end the evening as he did.

"Would it be too soon for me to ask for your phone number?" he finally asked, after standing in front of her, silently staring for what seemed like an eternity.

Abby looked him straight in the eye as a ghost of a smile creased the corners of the mouth Hix wanted. "Tell you what, how about if I get your number, and I give you a call?" she asked, turning the tables on Hix with little effort.

Hix hid his surprise, but not before Abby had seen the raising of his eyebrows and the widening of his eyes. Hix reached for his wallet and withdrew a piece of paper. On it he wrote his name and his phone number, before handing it over to Abby.

"What if I had said no?" he asked her, trying to figure out whether she was just toying with him, or if she was really going to call him at all.

She smiled up at him, her eyes half-closed, letting the look smolder and heat until Hix was as hot as a July night on the plains. Then she slipped the piece of paper inside her glove, trying to hide the fact that it seemed to burn against her palm. She curled her fingers into a fist and moved closer to the blonde god. Her eyes rested on his lips and she let her tongue come out and moisten her lower lip before raising her warm brown eyes to meet his.

Hix held his breath, anticipating a kiss but was disappointed as she stood up on tiptoes and whispered in his ear, "See you around, Hix," and headed for the door.

As the door closed behind the women, Hix noticed the bar seemed a little darker, emptier, like the air had been let out of a balloon. Finding no reason to stay any longer, he grabbed his coat and exited the bar, followed by Andy, Josh and Dylan.

Silently they got into the pickup, each deep in their own thoughts. As they waited for the engine to warm up against the bitter cold, and the heater to start pumping out warmth, Hix turned to his buddies and asked if any of them had gotten phone numbers from the other ladies. They all shook their heads no, then each went back to their silence, wondering if they were going to be hearing from the girls, or were going to be just left hanging. It did not occur to any of them that this was exactly the way most women felt when they gave their numbers to a guy and had to wait for them to call.

Josh drove to Hix's place first. Hix thanked his friends for braving the stormy night with him and promised to get in touch with them in a few days. He jumped out of the warm pickup and landed in a snowdrift up to his knees. Slamming the door and waving, he made his way to his door and let himself in.

He took off his coat, shaking the snow from the collar and shoulders, as he hung it on the coat rack behind the door. He pulled off his snow-covered boots, leaving them on the rug to dry. Rubbing his hands together, he walked to his favorite recliner and plopped down in it, reaching for the TV remote and pushed the buttons for the weather channel. He thought he'd catch an update on the snowstorm before hitting the sack. As he reached for the remote, his eyes were drawn to the phone beside it on the end table. Hix's gaze zeroed in on the instrument which could bring him one step closer to the beautiful lady he had met tonight. The realization that his willpower was about to be put to the test hit him as under his breath he said, "RING."

Chapter 9

Almost two weeks had gone by since the night Abby and Hix had met in the bar, and still she hadn't gotten up the courage to call him. Oh she wanted to, but kept coming up with excuses that kept her from picking up the phone. She'd been tied up for a few days on a shoot. When she'd gotten home, she cleaned her apartment from top to bottom, which managed to take her two days and left her too exhausted for anything else. After she'd recovered from her cleaning spree, she found herself pacing back and forth in her living room, passing the phone a thousand times, trying to work up the courage to pick up the stupid thing and use the number Hix had given her.

The paper was wrinkled and worn from all of the times she had picked it up from where it lay beside her phone, holding it in her hands, memorizing the numbers, before she flung it back down to the table. Why, she asked herself a thousand times, couldn't she just call him? She wanted to. He was good looking, funny, easy to be around, and she was totally attracted to him. So why did she have this feeling that this was going to be the biggest decision of her life?

She knew why, but didn't want to think about it. She pushed the answer to the back of her mind a dozen times a day, until finally she could ignore it no longer. He was going to be the one. The one man that would rock her world and change it forever. Did she want that? Was she ready for that? What if he didn't feel the same way? What if they went out and she became just another ex in his life? Could she handle that?

Abby paced her apartment as the questions kept coming at her, never seeming to give her any peace. She realized she'd even been avoiding her friends. Each of them had already been out at least once with their guys from that night, and literally gushed about them each time they'd spoken to Abby. She'd heard the question and concern in their voices each time she had told them that, no, she had not called Hix yet. Only Kendall had been bold enough to ask her what she was waiting for. And only Kendall had been told her deepest, darkest fears and feelings.

But Abby had not gotten any sympathy from her friend. Instead she was told how Hix had Andy, Josh and Dylan trying to find out from the girls why Abby hadn't called him yet. Then Kendall had flat out told her that Hix was very interested and she should get off the pot and ask him out, saying, "Guys like him don't just grow on trees and fall into your life every day, so stop stalling and take a chance."

Abby had hung up the phone, a little miffed at her friend for not siding with her and making her feel like a coward instead.

The end of winter was coming, and so was the end of the day, as Abby stood in her front window and stared out at the fading light. Her mind didn't register that lately the days had been warmer and the snow was melting, leaving the ground dark from the moisture. Nor the fact that although the breeze had a wicked bite to it, the sun was warm and inviting, if you stood in a sheltered area, soaking clear to your bones with heat that hinted of the warmer months to come. Nope, Abby was deep in thought and remained at her window until the glare from the street lights coming on brought her back to the present.

Squaring her shoulders, she pulled the hem of her comfy old sweat shirt down and turned to face the phone on the table beside her couch. The distance seemed to grow with each passing second until the room seemed to be a mile long. Closing her eyes to the trickery, she shook her head, took a deep breath and opened them again. The phone sat just a few feet away and Abby moved, heart pounding, towards it. She sat stiffly on the edge of the couch and rested her hands on her knees in front of her. She was going to call Hix, right now. But what should she say?

"Hello you gorgeous hunk of a man, you. This is Abby, the chicken. I'm sorry I haven't called you before but I was busy hiding in my house, scared of I don't know what. I was wondering if you were going to be busy this weekend. If not, would you consider going out with me?"

Abby grabbed a pillow from beside her, covered her face with it, and let out a frustrated scream deep into its fluffy softness. When she had no breath left and her face felt hot from the pillow, she flung the muffler aside. Taking the plunge, she grabbed up the phone, dialed the numbers, not needing the paper as she knew the sequence by heart, held her breath and waited.

The phone rang once, twice, three times, and just as Abby let out her breath trying to decide if she was disappointed or not, a deep male voice poured warmth into her waiting ear, sending goose bumps rushing up from her toes until they reached her hair and made each follicle tingle and rise.

"Hello?" the voice said twice before Abby collected her wits enough to answer back.

"Hix?" she asked tentatively.

"Yes," came the cautious reply. "Who's this?"

"This is Abby, Abby Mathews. We met a couple of weeks ago in a bar. Well, we didn't just meet, we played pool for a couple of hours. Is this a bad time to call? If it is I could call back later, if it's a bad time that is. If not I was just wondering if you would like to meet me for dinner, or a movie, or dinner and a movie, or something else if you don't like dinner and a movie?" Abby knew she sounded like a blithering idiot, but she couldn't seem to stop the words from gushing out of her mouth like a raging river during flood season.

Her tongue was dry and wanted to stick to the roof of her mouth, while her hand was gripping the phone so tight that her knuckles were white. She had it pressed so tight to her ear that the post of her earring was jabbing into her neck. She tried to swallow, but she had no spit to wet her mouth and throat, so her voice came out husky and slightly gravelly and breathless, to say the least.

"Oh for God's sake," she thought. She was a super model. Her picture was in every country in the world. She had met famous people, and had been pursued by men since she was sixteen years old. But, she realized, this was the first time she had ever asked one for a date. Her words slowed. Then stopped as she heard a soft chuckling coming across the line.

Hix had almost given up hope of having the honey haired, dark eyed beauty call him, but was delighted when he recognized the voice coming through the phone as hers. Her nervousness reached across the distance and pinched at his heart, as he discovered that women went through exactly what men did when they asked out a guy for the first time. No matter how many times you did it, the first time was always filled with stress, uncertainty, and the fear of rejection.

"Hey, Abby," he said in a low, deep voice. "I didn't think you were going to call. How have you been?" He kept his voice low and soothing, trying to calm her and get her to relax while she talked to him. They exchanged small talk for several minutes, before Hix could sense that she was almost back to her sane self again.

Finally Hix brought the conversation back to the reason Abby had called him. "And by the way, yes, I would love to go out with you. Dinner and a movie sounds really good to me. How about this coming Saturday night?" he asked hopefully. "Did you have any place in particular you wanted to go to?"

"No," Abby replied. "I actually hadn't thought that far ahead," she admitted with a smile in her voice. "Do you have any suggestions?"

Hix took a moment to think and finally said, "How about The Greasy Spoon? They have good burgers, salads and sandwiches. Even some passable Mexican dishes."

"That would be great," Abby sighed, relieved that the decision had been made for her. "I don't know what is playing at the movies, but we can find out and decide over dinner if we want to go."

"Sounds good to me," Hix agreed. Getting ready to hang up, Hix added one more comment that had Abby's butterflies stirring again. "Hey Abby," he said his voice low and rich, "thanks for calling. I was really hoping you would."

"My pleasure," she said, her voice pitched low and dark with promises. "I'll see you on Saturday."

"Bye," he whispered and hung up the phone.

Abby lowered the phone to the table, letting out a deep sigh as she slowly melted, sliding off the couch, and landed in a puddle on the floor.

Chapter 10

As Saturday drew closer, Abby began to rifle through her closets looking for just the right "look" for her date with Hix. She had fancy dresses and outfits from her photo shoots, but she didn't think fancy was the look she wanted. On the other hand, she didn't want to look like she just came in from the barn. Feeling frustrated, Abby finally broke down and called Kendall to come over and help with her dilemma.

When her doorbell rang, Abby pulled the door open, grabbed Kendall and yanked her into the apartment, before slamming the door quickly behind her. While Kendall shed her coat and scarf, she got a good look at her friend. She noticed the flushed face, bright eyes, and the slight wringing of her hands. Jeez she had it bad! Playing dumb, Kendall walked into the living room and dropped onto the couch.

"What's up?" she asked Abby, who remained standing in front of her.

"I need some help," Abby started. "I'm going out with Hix on Saturday and I can't figure out what to wear. Help me," she pleaded as she pulled Kendall to her feet and almost dragged her to stand before the open closet.

With eyebrows raised and head cocked, Kendall considered her friend. She had seen Abby get ready for dates with some of the biggest stars and richest men, but she had never seen her so worked up and nervous before.

"Okay," she said, turning her attention to the tunnel of clothes before her. "First of all, where are you going?"

"Um, somewhere called the Greasy Spoon," Abby replied already head and shoulders into her clothes.

She didn't see Kendall's raised eyebrows or speculating look. For all the foul images the name brought to mind, the Greasy Spoon was one of the best places in town to go. It had excellent food, great atmosphere, and was clean and well cared for. Most of the locals went there for anniversaries, birthdays, celebrations, and many engagements were staged there. Not bad for a first date she decided, and was happy for her friend. Kendall started going through the hangers one by one, deciding she needed more information.

"What time is he picking you up?" she asked.

Abby stopped what she was doing and said with a look of confusion, "I don't know."

"Better find out," Kendall advised, as she continued into the closet.

As if by ESP, the phone began to ring. Abby almost let it go to voice mail, but then on the fifth ring she grabbed it up. Anchoring it between her shoulder and chin she absently said, "Hello?"

"Abby?" came the deep voice she had dreamt about. The clothes she'd been holding fell from her hands and a wide grin spread over her face as Abby recognized and drank in the richness of Hix's voice.

"Hey Hix," she purred. "This is a surprise. What's up?"

On his end, Hix tipped his hard hat back on his head and leaned back against a half-finished kitchen counter he was working on. "I got your number from my caller ID and I had a break, so I thought I'd call and fill in the blanks for Saturday night. If I picked you up at about 5:30 we'd have plenty of time to eat and still be able to take in a movie. That work for you?" he asked, letting his eyes close half way as her image floated before him.

"That sounds great," Abby replied, meeting Kendall's questioning gaze with a raised finger.

"I'll need your address," Hix said, as he got out a pencil and paper to write it down.

"That might be a good idea," Abby said, as a giggle slipped out of her smiling lips. She promptly rattled it off and Hix recognized it as one of the nicer places he had had a hand in building. The rooms were big, the carpets plush and the smallest room in the place was the large walk in closet that his bedroom at home would fit into.

"Okay," said Hix, "I'll see you Saturday, at 5:30. It was nice to hear your voice," he said, his own voice lowering until it rolled over and through Abby.

"Mmmmm," was all Abby said.

The single sound had Hix picturing her lying in his arms, just having made love, with the same sound coming from her throat. Swallowing hard, he said, "Goodbye." in the same smooth, deep voice that had Abby melting on the other end of the line. Hix hung up and quickly took a deep breath through his nose to pull his run-away imagination back under control.

The time would come when they made love. He knew it. He felt it all the way to his soul. AND it scared the hell out of him! He had never felt this strongly about a woman before, and certainly not one he had never even been out with yet. "One more day" he thought out loud. "One more day until he would see her again." He wondered if it was a bad thing to wish your life away but he did. He wanted it to be Saturday afternoon right now.

Hix took a deep breath and put ideas of Abby away for now. Break was over and he could not afford to be distracted. He could get hurt. But tonight he thought, tonight he could dream all he wanted.

Abby stood for a few seconds after Hix had hung up just holding the phone and smiling. Kendall watched her and could not resist teasing her just a little.

"I take it that was Hix?" she asked, looking at Abby from the corner of her eye.

"Mmmm," was all Abby said.

Kendall stopped what she was doing and crossed her arms as she faced her friend. "Are you having an orgasm?" she asked.

Abby was snapped back to reality as if she had been doused by a glass of cold water. Laughing at and with Kendall, Abby looked at her friend with the devil gleaming out from her sparkling eyes.

"Bite me," she said, as she got back to the business of dressing herself.

For the next hour both Abby and Kendall looked at and discarded outfit after outfit, not finding the one that jumped out at them and screamed, "P*ick me! Pick me!*" It wasn't until the bed was full of clothes and the floor was littered with every color of the rainbow, that Kendall emerged holding what she thought was perfect.

"This!" she said triumphantly, "Wear this."

Abby turned to look at Kendall's find. She took the hangers, turned and held the garments up in front of her at the mirror. The wine red cashmere sweater was thick enough to be warm, but not big enough to be bulky. The color made her hair gleam and added depth to her dark eyes. The rounded neckline exposed her soft, smooth neck but kept her other assets a mystery. Outlining but not showing all. It was as soft as butter and Abby knew Hix would rub his hands up and down her arms, wondering if her skin was as soft and warm as the material covering them. Abby held up the black pants to look at the outfit as a whole. They were long and hugged her hips, but had stove pipe legs that made her legs seem a mile long. Since they were long, Abby would have to wear her heeled boots to keep them from dragging on the floor. If she pulled her hair up softly and maybe left a few strands loose to brush her cheeks and neck she figured she would not be too dressed up or too casual.

Meeting Kendall's eyes in the mirror, Abby nodded her head and said, "Perfect. I owe you."

Kendall sat down on the bed, right on top of Abby's clothes. Grabbing a handful, she held them up to her saying, "I think you should go through these as you put them back and give some to the donation house down on Main Street."

"I like that idea," agreed Abby, "but not right this minute. Come on, "she said hanging up their find and heading for the door, "I'm hungry and I think the least I can do to thank you for helping me is feed you."

Kendall bounced up from the bed and followed her friend out the door. "I won't argue with that," she said and followed Abby down the hall, grabbing her coat and sliding her arms into it as they walked out the door.

Abby kept up her end of the conversation as she and Kendall ate homemade soup and drank tea at a local diner. As the dishes were finally cleared away, Abby grabbed Kendall's hand and gave it a hard squeeze. "Good friends are hard to come by, I know, and I just want to say thanks for being mine."

Kendall squeezed back and nodded her head. "Same here," she said. "Now let go of my hand before we give the gossips something to talk about."

Abby grinned and did as she was told. But not before the clicking and whirring of a cell phone camera across the room had gotten the whole thing. A smile crossed his face and dollar signs danced before the sleaze balls' eyes.

Chapter 11

Saturday finally came and Abby woke up rearing to go. No lying in bed and dreaming before she got up for the day. No groaning and wishing for 15 more minutes like the days when her life was governed by that annoying little alarm clock telling her to get her butt up and get to work. Not today. Today was a present and she couldn't wait to open it.

Throwing the covers off her legs, she swung her feet over the side of the bed and let them slide to the floor. Brrr! The chill of the hardwood floor could jumpstart just about anyone fresh out of sleep, and had Abby running on tiptoes into the bathroom, where she sunk her toes into the plush cream rug that lie before the bathroom vanity. Looking into the mirror, she studied the face staring back at her. It had bright expectant eyes, soft pink cheeks that still held the blush of sleep, and was framed by tousled golden hair, which she quickly pulled back from her face. As if sharing a secret with an old friend, Abby was inclined to smile at the image staring back at her, and did not hold back.

Today was going to be a good day. In fact she decided it was going to be the start to the rest of her life. She'd had this feeling ever since she met Hix over two weeks ago. He was going to play a very important part in her life and she just knew it was going to be good.

Abby slipped her arms into her favorite robe, a soft flannel one that had been like a second skin to her since she was in high school. She slipped her bare feet snuggly into her fuzzy black slippers, and made her way to the kitchen. She opened the refrigerator and began taking out the ingredients for her favorite morning treat, a yogurt smoothie. She made it with fresh strawberries, low fat vanilla yogurt, skim milk, and a tablespoon of vanilla frappucinno to make it rich and creamy. She added the ingredients to her blender and watched as the whirling blades turned the concoction into a smooth pink liquid. Then she added a cup of crushed ice from the refrigerator and hit the liquefy button. The grinding noise started out loud and finally settled into a purr as the smoothie reached perfection. Abby poured the thick drink into a large plastic mug from the local S 'n S, added a straw and took her first sip. Perfection! This was her ritual every morning and she craved it as much as a coffee addict craved his caffeine first thing in the morning.

While she sipped her breakfast, not too fast or she'd end up with a brain freeze, she settled into her favorite oversized pillowy chair by the window, tucked her feet up under her, and took her first look at the day outside.

The sun shone brilliant through the trees as it made its way up over the horizon. The snow, almost sensing its end was near, lay in dirty brown hills up against the fences, the corners of the yards and parking lots, clinging to life against the heat of the sun and wind that threatened to melt it away by nightfall.

The heat of the sun coming through the window felt good on Abby's face and bare arms. She closed her eyes and turned her face towards it, relaxing under the blanket of warmth that curled around her. She sipped her breakfast and stayed where she was even after her drink was empty, not wanting to move just yet, acting like a cat sunning itself after a cold winter's night. When she had taken her fill of the moment, Abby said a silent thank you for simple pleasures, rose to her feet, and went to the kitchen sink. She hand washed her dishes and put them back in the cupboard.

Mentally placing a check mark beside the first thing on her list of what she wanted to accomplish in preparation for her date tonight, she headed for the bathroom to take a long hot bath. She pulled her hair into a knot on top of her head and fastened it with a simple clip. She let her robe pool at her feet as she ran the tub with steaming hot water and added some of her favorite bath salts, the kind that fizz like an Alka

Seltzer when they hit the water and leave it a pastel color, reminding Abby of coloring Easter eggs when she was a little girl.

As the tub filled, a dark musky smell rose with the steam, turning Abby's visions to those of her and Hix locked together in each other's arms, their slick bodies aching for fulfillment as they tried to melt into each other.

Lifting one shapely leg, she touched the water with her toe, before stepping in with both feet and settling her body in the steamy mix. Slipping into the water, Abby lay back and rested her head on the edge of the tub. The visions continued to swirl in her mind. What would it be like having Hix here beside her, tasting the warmth of his lips, feeling him follow the droplets of water as they ran down her body with his hands, his lips?

Realizing she was getting a little carried away, Abby brought her mind back to reality, picturing her and Hix out together as a couple. The combination of both their golden good looks would be startling to anyone who saw them. The cameras would love them. Abby was sure that photographers would fall over themselves and follow them everywhere to get shots as the "golden" couple fell in love.

Abby wasn't conceited or spoiled as she considered this, just accepting that it was a part of her life. Now and in the future. She was used to the paparazzi and the extents they would go to get pictures of those in the public eye, but she was sure Hix was not, so she was going to have to guide him, even shelter him, when they were out in public.

As she sank deeper into the scented tub, somewhere between sleep and wakefulness, Abby heard the doorbell ring. Stepping out onto the rug, she wrapped herself in a thick towel and fastened it by tucking one corner into a spot just below her collarbone. She walked to the front door and opened it, only to find Hix waiting for her on the other side.

He was bundled in a down parka, which he'd left open down the front, letting the sun's warmth inside the heavy jacket to warm his neck and chest. She could see the V-neck sweater he wore, peaking out of the opening in the jacket. She noticed how the deep blue color added to the brightness of his already intense blue eyes. The hint of crisp blond hair filled the V at the base of his throat and chest, and then disappeared to places only Abby's imagination could see.

His blonde hair teased his shoulders as it fell in soft waves around his neck and collar, making Abby want to run her fingers through it and see for herself if it was as it appeared, soft as silk and warm as melted butter.

Her eyes traveled lower to his waist and hips, and she sent up a silent heartfelt thanks to the Gods that he was not wearing a pair of baggy jeans that hung off his butt, only staying up as if by magic, and showing a good six inches of his multicolored boxer underwear. She'd always had a secret desire to walk up to a guy wearing those and give them a good yank, watching as they slipped the last inch, pooling around his ankles and exposing the skinny body underneath.

Instead, Hix wore 501 button-up Levis that hugged his hips and butt, and showed her the long muscles in his legs. He wore black boots with a buckle hugging each ankle, that managed to serve a dual purpose of keeping his feet dry and looking sexy as hell. A manly look that was giving Abby a feeling of delicious danger as she took him in. She liked what she saw. The slow smile that teased her face let Hix know she approved.

Hix stood still as her eyes ran over him, giving her time to get to know him, to want him. After a moment, not waiting for an invitation, he moved in through the doorway, bringing his body close to hers, almost touching, as she didn't budge for him to pass. The heat and electricity that jumped between the two of them was almost visible to the naked eye, so strong was the feeling, and had Hix needing to rid himself of the heavy jacket which surrounded him to the point of suffocation.

Having a little trouble breathing herself, Abby finally moved enough to let him into her home, letting out the breath she'd been holding since she'd laid eyes on him.

Hix gladly shrugged off his coat, giving Abby a view of his wide shoulders as he did so. He unconsciously pushed the arms of his sweater up until they bunched right below his elbows, giving her another piece of him to examine. His forearms, still holding a slight tan from working in the sun all summer, were solid with muscle and had a light covering of hair that glinted golden in the streaming sunlight. Abby swallowed hard and moved into the room to stand before Hix.

"Hi," she said with a shy smile, "you're early."

Unable to resist another minute, Hix closed the mere inches between them and wrapped his arms around her, pulling her close to him until she rested against his chest. She could smell the clean freshness of the outdoors on his skin and clothes and felt the coolness of the late February air that still clung to him.

"I waited as long as I could," Hix said in a low voice, having bent his head until his lips were almost touching the small shell of her ear. "I've thought about you for the last two weeks and I wanted to see if my memory was any good. I'd convinced myself that I couldn't possibly have remembered you right. No one could be that beautiful, that desirable," he whispered against her damp hair, wet tendrils having escaped to hang in moist ringlets on her neck.

Abby held herself perfectly still, feeling the vibrations of Hix's voice travel from his wide chest, to her body, and into her soul. She shivered with the deliciousness of the feeling and moved even closer to the man who held her so tight in his arms. She didn't just jump into bed with every man she went out with, and was very careful of her feelings, not wanting to get hurt. But standing here, wrapped in Hix's strong arms, all caution and inhibitions deserted her. Her senses went flying and scattered to the four winds. Her world shrank to the size of her living room and the two who occupied it.

Slowly she lifted her head from his chest and found herself reflected in blue eyes that burned with the promise of desire and passion, whether it was hers or his she was not sure of. His eyes held her captive, willing her to see the depth of his feelings, and promising pleasures that she could only have dreamt of before.

Lifting her lips, Abby gave her silent consent to Hix, and he took it, and her lips, with no hesitation. His kisses, at first, were soft and tentative, learning her taste and touch, then deepening only when he felt her desire as she pressed her mouth more firmly against his. Only then did she feel the fire inside him as he devoured her mouth, fogging her brain until she could think of nothing, feel nothing but him.

She felt as if she were floating, but realized he had picked her up in his strong arms, cradling her as if she was the most precious thing in his world.

"Which way, Abby?" he asked, holding her body as he held her eyes. Totally.

Abby answered his question with her eyes, showing him the way to her bed without speaking a word.

Hix did not hurry as he lifted Abby higher in his arms and carried her toward the shadowed bedroom, but he took his time, stopping many times along the way to continue his exploration of her mouth and to trail kisses along her ear and neck before continuing on towards their destination.

The curtains were still drawn and the dark added mystery to the events unfolding, as Hix brought Abby into the bedroom. He lowered her gently onto the bed, the shape of Abby still remaining in the rumpled sheets and comforter from the night before. Hix followed her onto the mattress, his weight covering her, his kisses and hands igniting fires on every inch of her body. Abby gave back as good as she got, running her hands beneath his sweater to his hardened shoulders and back, then around to tangle in the soft hair of his muscular chest and stomach.

When Abby thought she could stand no more, Hix levered himself off of the bed and took with him, in one sensual motion, the towel that had covered her. She lay there bare to his gaze, but felt no shame or shyness.

Instead, she gave him only a moment before she came to her knees before him on the bed and slowly began the process of exposing his body to her hungry eyes. With fingers that were slow and deliberate she peeled off the sweater, letting her hands run the length of his torso before she let them lower to the buttons of his jeans that had become tight, and in the way.

Hix stilled her hands as he removed his boots, and then stood back up before her, wearing nothing but the jeans that Abby wanted off. He took her hands in his and guided them back to his body, his eyes closing and his head tipping back as Abby took one selfish moment for herself, exploring the hair that lightly covered his chest, tapering to a fine line that dipped into his pants. She followed that line with her fingertips, then, reaching the barrier of his jeans, whose top button had come unfastened and beckoned mischievously to her, deliberately ran a nail up and down his torso, teasing them both by delaying the final exposure.

Looking at the beautiful man before her, seemingly filled with desire for her, Abby wanted to give Hix something that no other woman had ever given him. She wasn't sure she knew what that was. Having nothing to go on but her instincts and her desire for the man standing beside her bed, Abby decided that she'd made them both wait long enough as she settled her forehead against his chest and opened the buttons of his jeans.

She slid her hands in around his hips, pushing the unwanted garment down around his knees, where he could finally finish the job of removing them by stepping out of them and leaving them in a pile on the floor. With one quick motion he shed his boxers and joined her on the bed.

As much as Abby burned for Hix to make love with her, and he could feel her need, he burned with the need to know every inch of her, taste every inch of her, and make her want him so much that she would forget every other lover before him. Want no other lover but him. He played her body until her brain was nothing but a pile of mush, and she could do nothing but whimper and beg him never to stop.

Hix shook with the effort of holding back, giving her all the pleasure he could until he could deny himself no longer. Sliding up and over her body, he joined himself with her, making them one. He felt her gasp against his neck and the goose bumps that rose felt like needles to his sensitive skin. He marveled at the way he fit with her, like no other he had known.

Bracing his hands beside her face, Hix whispered low and deep. "Open your eyes Abby. Look at me. I need you to know it's me filling you, loving you. Please."

Abby opened her eyes. She felt as if she had been drugged by Hix's love making. Abby arched her back, striving to take all of Hix in and, in doing so, felt herself begin to topple over the edge of her passion.

"Now," she said to Hix. "Now!"

Abby came up sputtering as her head had slipped under the water, filling her nose and making her gasp for breath. She flailed her arms until she found the edge of the tub, and panting, hung onto the edge for dear life. She looked around the bathroom as her senses slowly returned.

Realizing where she was and what had just happened, Abby groaned and closed her eyes. Bending forward, she lowered her head until she felt the cool tub on her fevered brow. A low growl started deep in her chest as she raised her face to the ceiling and roared out her frustration, "YOU'VE GOT TO BE KIDDING!"

Chapter 12

Hix slowly opened his eyes as the sun made its way over the eastern horizon. Its pale warmth did little to dispel the cold from the night before. It would be hours yet until the earth heated and the day warmed up to the predicted high of 40 degrees. A heat wave compared to the frigid temps that had moved in and settled for the last few weeks. Almost shirt sleeve weather, he thought.

Thoughts of the weather didn't occupy his mind for long, as he remembered today was Saturday, and in less than 12 hours he was going to see Abby again. A tingle of anticipation ran through his body at the thought of finally getting to see her up close and personal again. He'd had to make do with the memories of her from that first night for the past two weeks, wondering if she was going to call him or if she was just plain not interested. More than once he had considered asking Andy or one of the others to see if they could get her number from one of her friends, but had held back, not wanting to press her or appear that he was stalking her.

Hix lay for a few minutes more, enjoying the warmth under his blankets. It was the weekend after all, and he didn't have anywhere to be for several more hours. Saturday was one of the two days he got to sleep in and not worry about work. He didn't care if it was considered unmanly not to want to leap out of bed, pound his chest and drop down to the floor to do 100 push-ups to start his day. Today he just burrowed down into the covers until only the top of his head was visible, closed his deep sapphire blue eyes, smiling at the decadence of sleeping late, and drifted into a state somewhere between sleep and wakefulness.

It was almost an hour later, the sinful hour of nine, before Hix woke and felt like starting the day. Stretching under the covers until his bones cracked and his muscles protested, Hix twisted and turned until he'd worked out all of the kinks of sleep. Giving one more jaw cracking yawn, he flipped back the covers and crawled out of bed.

The coolness of the room had Hix, who slept in only a pair of boxers, grabbing for his favorite NU tee shirt which was lying across the bottom of the bed. Pulling it over his head, he made his way to the bathroom, took care of business, splashed some cold water on his face, and looked at his image in the mirror. He ran his fingers through his tousled hair and across the stubble that had cropped up on his chin and cheeks while he slept, assessing the damages of a good night's sleep. Just as he pulled his shaving cream out of the medicine chest, his stomach gave a long, low growl, and he decided that taming his hunger was going to have to come before beautifying the beast.

He hurried to the kitchen, a new purpose to his slow start, and began the process of, as his mother called it, raiding the refrigerator. Sticking his head into the cold treasure chest, he emerged with a wide smile and a cold slice of pizza for breakfast. Holding the pizza between his front teeth, Hix grabbed a can of soda to wash it down with, pulled the tab, and listened to the hissing sound as the carbonation rushed to the small opening in the top of the can.

Pizza in one hand, soda in the other, Hix kicked the refrigerator door closed, and made his way into the living room. He plopped down on the couch, and propped his feet up on the coffee table in front of him. He loved pizza for breakfast, and always ordered extra so he could have leftovers the next morning. After all, he considered pizza and soda two of the four major food groups. He polished off his first slice, then jumped up and grabbed another one from the frig before settling back on the couch and turning on the TV. He flipped to his favorite cartoon channel and prepared to enjoy his day off.

Hix always told his friends that he was just a big kid at heart, which was why he never grew tired of watching cartoons. Lately he had been having a hard time finding ones he liked, as most of the new ones were drawn in another country and were boring and of no entertainment value. So it was not long before, having surfed all the channels, he grew restless and turned the set off.

Stretching his long muscular legs before him he hauled himself off the couch and made his way back to his bedroom. Deciding to leave his grooming until later in the afternoon, Hix pulled on a pair of Nike wind pants and running shoes, ran a comb through his hair, brushed his teeth, and called it good. He grabbed the bag of dirty clothes from the hamper stand in the corner by the tub, his keys from the top of the dresser, threw a heavy wind jacket over his t-shirt, and headed out the door.

Even though Hix had a washer and dryer at his place, he liked to take his clothes over to his mother, Sarah's, house. It had become a Saturday morning ritual for mother and son. They spent the morning visiting while the washer performed miracles on his smelly socks and work clothes. They both enjoyed this time together. They only lived about a mile apart, so in no time he was pulling up at her door.

Hix put his pickup in park and gunned the engine once to let the deep growl of power announce his arrival. He got out and hoisted the bag over his shoulder and made his way to the back door of the small, but neat, two bedroom house he had grown up in.

Remembering to stomp his feet clear of moisture and wipe them on the outside mat, Hix opened the door to the warmth and fragrance of cinnamon rolls that, if he knew his mom, were fresh from the oven.

"Hi Mom," Hix grinned, as he shut the door behind him and dropped his sack of laundry. By the time he had taken off his coat and hung it up, Sarah was at his side, waiting for the big bear hug she knew was coming. Hix didn't disappoint her as he bent down and wrapped his arms around her to give her a squeeze of affection. Her 5 foot 4 inch body all but disappeared for a moment before she was released to stand back and gaze up into her son's face.

They were mother and son but also best friends, having had only each other to rely on when Hix was growing up. Sarah loved her son, and every time she looked at him she was thankful he had turned out to be such a good man. He had good friends, a good job, and didn't get into trouble by drinking too much or fighting. She felt a little glint of pride every time she saw him, knowing that she had done the best job she could molding this young man into someone people respected.

"Hi back," she replied, a smile on her face and in her voice. "You're just in time for fresh rolls. Come in and sit down, Santa," she laughed, "and bring your bag with you."

Hix dumped the dirty clothes on the floor by the washer and began to sort the clothes into piles of whites and darks, towels and jeans. He grabbed the pile of jeans and stuffed them into the wash tub, squirted a little laundry detergent on top of the whole mess and turned the dial to heavy. The water poured into the washer as Hix closed the lid and settled himself at the kitchen table, almost drooling as Sarah sat a plate covered by a large gooey cinnamon roll in front of him.

"Milk or pop?" she asked, heading for the refrigerator to get him something to wash down the roll.

"Pop," he said, around a mouth of warm gooiness.

Sarah shook her head, but sat the can in front of him anyway. "You're here early today." she said, with a raised eyebrow. "What's up?"

"Nothing," Hix replied, finishing the first roll and looking towards the plate piled high in the middle of the table. Sarah nudged it toward him and took a seat beside him to watch as he dove into the second one, a look of dreamy satisfaction on his face. "Oh mom, you're the best," he said and she grinned at his pleasure.

"I know," she said with a sassy smile, then settled back and waited for him to finish so she could find out what was on his mind.

When he had licked the last drop of frosting from his fingers, and wiped the crumbs from his mouth, he grinned at the small, female version of himself and said with smug satisfaction in his voice, "You spoil me, Mom. I hope you know how much I appreciate you."

Sarah smiled softly at his praise and got up to put fabric softener in the washer. She stopped behind Hix's chair, put her arms around his neck, and rested her chin on the top of his head. She didn't need to say anything the gesture telling him how much she loved him. He squeezed her hands in return before she pulled away and made her way into the laundry room.

"So," she said, coming back to the table and sitting down, "how was your week?"

She propped her elbows on the table and cupped her chin in her palms as she waited for his answer.

"Good," he said and commenced to tell her about the progress they were making on the house he was working on. She noticed how his face took on a glow as he described the work in detail. Sarah was pleased that Hix liked his job. So many young people just worked to pay the bills and didn't really enjoy what they were doing. For Hix it was a passion. He'd started building things when he was just a little boy and had never stopped.

Sarah knew Hix had a reason for coming over so early and would get around to it when he was ready. So until then, she'd let him talk until he ran out of things to say and got down to the nitty gritty of his visit. It didn't take him long before he sat forward, leaned his elbows on the table and spilled what he'd been holding inside.

"I've got a date tonight, Mom," he finally said, as a mixture of seriousness and expectation ran across his handsome features.

"You've had dates before," his mother said, leaning forward and looking into her son's eyes for answers.

"This one might be different," he said, blushing just a little as he revealed one more piece of the puzzle.

Sarah raised an eyebrow and waited for him to continue.

"Her name is Abby, Abby Mathews. She lives here in Winston, but she's not from around here." He paused and looked his mom in the eye saying, "She's a model."

"And?" Sarah prompted, as he said nothing else.

"I have a feeling about her," Hix admitted soberly. "She might be special. I thought so the minute I saw her."

Sarah had known the day would come, the day when all mothers were replaced by lovers. The day when her son would find a woman to fill that special place in his heart. The place that, up until this moment, had been reserved for her. Sarah saw the truth in her son's face and, sitting back with a smile on her face, she opened up her heart and let him go. She knew he wouldn't go far but the time had come.

Chapter 13

Hix stayed with his mother most of the day, doing his laundry, helping her fix a door jam that was loose, and pulling out the bar-b-q grill and making them burgers when lunchtime rolled around. They'd teased and laughed their way through the day, leaving Hix feeling relaxed, and happy that he had been blessed with such a great mom.

As mid-afternoon rolled around, Hix decided he'd better pack up his clean laundry and head back to his place. He noticed that the freshly washed laundry bag of clean clothes smelled a whole lot better than it had when he'd arrived, as he took a moment to bury his face in a still-warm sweatshirt fresh from the dryer before stuffing it into the bag with the rest of his things.

He plopped the bag by the door, pulled on his shoes and coat, and turned to fold his mom in another bear hug. Sarah hugged him back, kissing his cheek and whispered, "Good luck sweetie," as she waved him out the door.

Hix made his way down the sidewalk he cleared of the last of the snow earlier today to his truck. Stowing the clothes inside and turning on the engine, he turned and threw a smile over his shoulder calling out, "Thanks, mom, I'll give you a call tomorrow and let you know how things went."

Sarah nodded as she waved good-bye to her son, waiting in the doorway until he had backed out into the street and drove out of sight. She moved back inside the house and closed the door. The house felt empty and a little too quiet after his exit, but she was used to living alone, and the feeling didn't last long.

Grabbing a mug from the cupboard, Sarah poured herself a cup of coffee and made her way into the room she used as an office. She'd decided to do a little research on her son's latest interest. She settled into the leather office chair and booted up her computer, smiling at the information available at her finger tips with modern technology. When she was growing up, the only way her parents had access to information on one of her prospective boyfriends was to call a friend or neighbor on the phone and see if they'd heard anything about them. This way was much more reliable, when it worked, which it did unless the power went out.

Sarah typed Abigale Mathews, model, in the *Google* search line and watched as a list of possible sites filled her screen. She clicked on the first one on the list and watched as a picture of a beautiful young woman filled her screen. Sarah raised her eyebrows in appreciation as she scrolled down several pages of pictures, each one showing a honey haired, brown-eyed beauty smiling into the camera as she represented various product lines. In one she lay across the hood of a fancy red sports car, dressed in a sequined evening gown. In another her head was slightly tipped back as she sprayed perfume on her bare neck from a bottle of very expensive perfume. Another must have been a swimsuit or vacation ad, as she was scantily clad in a two-piece swimsuit and standing on a sandy beach, as the waves of the ocean lapped around her tanned ankles. The message in each was clear, "I am beautiful and you can be too" (if only you buy this product). In all of them Abigale Mathews looked very comfortable in her skin.

Sarah had no problem with the young woman's profession, or the fact that she was gorgeous. She just didn't want Hix to get hurt by becoming involved with someone who obviously lived such a different lifestyle. Studying the young woman's face, Sarah pictured the two of them together. Both were young, healthy, beautiful individuals, but together they would be incomparable. They would definitely cause heads to turn if they went out in public together. Sarah hoped with all her heart, for her son's sake, that Abigale Mathews was as beautiful on the inside as she was on the outside.

Having satisfied her curiosity, Sarah closed her computer and sat back in her chair, staring into space and nibbling on her finger nail. Hix had said he had a feeling about this one from the first moment he met her. Sarah also had a feeling, but she was sure it was not the same one Hix was having, as she felt a worm of doubt slowly working its way into her mind and into her heart, telling her of misfortune to come.

Sarah had good instincts and usually followed them without question, but this time it was not her choice to make. She would not tell Hix her feelings of dread. She would not interfere, but would watch and protect if she could. Hix was all the family she had and, like a tigress, she would come out with claws bared and teeth sharp if the moment called for it. No one hurt her family. Not without consequences.

Chapter 14

Pulling away from his mom's house, Hix decided to take a short drive around town and see how everything and everyone had fared through the latest weather. With a critical contractor's eye, he looked over the houses and rooftops as he idled down each block. He made quick notes of houses that would be in need of repairs when the cold weather finally decided to take its leave. He noted areas where shingles had blown off in the fierce winds that had accompanied the snow, fences that had succumbed to its weight and were leaning over long after it had melted into the ground, and driveways that had been cracked or broken under the weight of heavy tractors pushing the snow onto vacant lots and lawns. Maybe he could pick up a few side jobs this spring, saving the residents some money and making himself a little extra cash. Everyone knew he was good at what he did and that he charged a fair price for his efforts.

After about an hour of driving around, Hix glanced at his watch, and decided it was time to head home and get ready for his date with Abby. His stomach did a little flip-flop and his heart picked up speed at the thought, letting him know that tonight was indeed going to be special.

Pulling into his driveway, he cut the engine, grabbed the bag of laundry, threw it over his shoulder, and headed inside. Having been taught well by his mother, Hix immediately put his clean clothes away in dresser drawers and closet, before trying to decide what to wear for his big date. Looking through his closet, Hix silently thanked his mom, again. Because of her, there were several nice button-up shirts with actual collars and sweaters to match, mixed in with his abundance of screen-printed tees and sports sweatshirts. He pulled a sky blue shirt and his favorite snowy-white sweater off the hangers, deciding they would do nicely for the occasion. He put both on the bed and pulled his newest jeans from the dresser, adding them to the pile. Feeling satisfied with his choices, Hix made his way into the bathroom to shower and shave.

He took extra time washing and conditioning his hair. He liked it long and always kept it clean and soft. The new style of having it so short you were almost bald was something he had never bought into. From his experiences, he knew ladies liked something to play with and hang on to. Besides, he thought standing in front of the mirror, he liked the way he looked and was not too worried about anyone else's opinion.

He lathered his face and took care to make sure it was cleared of all stubble before giving a satisfied nod to his reflection in the mirror. As a finishing touch, Hix splashed a generous amount of cologne on his cheeks, neck, and bare chest. His favorite was a subtle, woodsy smelling concoction.

Dropping his towel, Hix strode to the bed and pulled on his boxers and his favorite jeans that fit his muscular legs like a glove. He drew his arms into the sleeves of the soft blue shirt, buttoned it over his muscular chest, and tucked it into his jeans. He smiled, noticing the smell of dryer sheets as he pulled his favorite sweater over his head. Finally, he pulled on a pair of socks and stepped into his black boots. Standing in front of the mirror, Hix checked to make sure everything was buttoned and zipped. Satisfied that all was where it was supposed to be, he called it good and made his way to the kitchen.

He grabbed a soda from the frig and tipped his head back, as he took a long draw from the can. Glancing at his wristwatch, Hix decided he had waited as long as he could. He was not an impatient man, but today he wanted to be somewhere else and with someone special, so he grabbed his parka and headed for the door.

He drove slowly to eat up a little more time, but arrived at Abby's door a good half hour earlier than they had arranged. Maybe she'd give him points for eagerness. Hix stepped out of his truck and made his way up the walk. Standing before the closed door, Hix ran his hands down the front of his jeans, trying to dry them of the nervous moisture that had sprung up despite the cold air, fussed with his hair a little, and swallowed hard, before finally lifting his hand to knock twice.

He was surprised when Abby opened the door before his hand had made it all the way to his side. Eager as he was to begin their evening, she'd heard him pull up and had rushed to the door to stand waiting. "To hell with being coy and making him wait at the door," she thought.

Abby looked at Hix, standing on her stoop waiting for her to invite him in, and was relieved when she noticed he was not wearing a blue sweater. If he had, she would have had to believe that her dream had actually been a premonition, and she was not sure she could have handled that. Her eyes traveled over him appreciatively, taking in the soft waves of his hair, the sparkle in his eyes, and the shy smile he gave her as she looked at him for the first time since they had met.

Hix, in turn, looked at Abby, framed in her doorway, and more than liked what he saw. She was dressed in black slacks that accentuated the shape of her long legs, a deep red sweater that made him want to bury his face in it to feel its softness and warmth, and knee-high black boots that brought her almost eye-to-eye with him.

"Wow," was all he could get past the lump that had lodged in his throat.

Abby's grin widened and her eyes gleamed as she stepped aside, motioning with her hand for him to come inside.

Hix made his feet move, as he entered her home for the first time. Turning to face her as she closed the door behind them both, he spread his hands out at his sides.

"I couldn't wait any longer. I hope it's not an inconvenience, my being early?" Hix groaned inwardly at the stiff way his words had sounded. She was going to think he was an idiot and regret having to spend an evening with him.

"Not at all," she replied with a smile, flattered that he couldn't wait to start their date. "Come in and sit down, while I grab my coat," she said as she moved toward a door down the hallway. Probably her bedroom, he thought to himself.

Hix made his way to the living room, which was just off the entryway, and sat rather stiffly on the edge of the couch. He felt like he was picking up his prom date, his stomach was all tied up in knots. "*Man,*" Hix told himself, *"you have to get a grip or she is going to think I'm some kind of bumbling virgin on his first date.*

Abby stepped into her room, let out a deep breath, and put both palms to her cheeks. They felt flushed to her, which a quick peek in the mirror above her dresser confirmed. She waved her hands in front of her face trying to cool down and get control of herself. He was better looking than she remembered and her memory had been pretty good, or so she thought. AND he smelled good enough to eat! Grabbing a long black coat from her closet, she blew out a deep breath, and walked back to the living room where Hix, the man in her dreams, waited.

"I'm ready," she said out loud, while thinking to herself, "boy am I," as Hix held the coat while she slipped her arms into the sleeves and drew it around her body, hiding its details from the hungry eyes that seemed to scald her where ever they touched.

Holding out her hand, she grasped his much bigger, work roughened, manly one and led the way back to the door. Hix reached around her to open the door, and Abby took the opportunity to fill her lungs with his scent. Not only the cologne, but also the maleness lurking underneath. Warm, rich and arousing. Abby could see herself slamming the door, pushing Hix up against it, grabbing fists full of that luscious hair and planting a kiss on his lips that would fry his brain. She almost ran out the door trying to out distance the fantasies that were so foreign to her. She needed to get control and start acting like a human being instead of a cat on the prowl.

Hix closed the door and waited until he heard the lock catch before he followed Abby down the walk to where his pickup waited. He opened her door and held out a hand to help her into the truck, noticing her perfume as she leaned on his arm and lifted herself into the vehicle.

Closing her door, he inhaled a long breath of cold air to clear his head, as he walked in long strides to the other side of the truck. Climbing in, he turned the key and the engine purred to life. The air coming out of the heater was still warm and soon they were driving toward the restaurant in the close, cozy cab.

The drive to the restaurant was filled with attempts at small talk, mixed with long periods of silence. The two seemed awkward with each other in the confined space. Hix told himself that he wanted to wait until they were at the restaurant, sitting across from each other, before he really started to get to know his date. When they finally pulled into the busy parking lot, Hix parked and shut the engine off, still gripping the steering wheel with both hands and dropping his forehead onto his knuckles. Abby shrank back against her door and waited for him to speak. Maybe he'd changed his mind and he wanted to turn the truck around and take her home before this evening went any further.

Then, raising his head, Hix broke the silence, saying, "I have to apologize to you, Abby. I don't know what's wrong with me tonight. I'm not usually this nervous, and God knows I never have trouble saying what's on my mind, but tonight I feel like I'm on my first date and don't know where to begin with you." From her side of the pickup, she gave a little smile at his confession of nerves.

He raised his head and let out a great sigh before turning in his seat to fully face the young woman who was silently thankful that she wasn't the only one who was nervous tonight.

"I've spent all week thinking about tonight, and about you. I don't know why I'm acting the way I am. I could care less about the weather, but I can't seem to put two intelligent words together to save my life." He looked totally helpless as he confessed to her, "The only sane thing that has come out of my mouth is the, WOW, that came out when I first saw you. You look great!" Hix said shaking his head and smiling at Abby across the pickup seat as she fidgeted with her hands in her lap. "I've had this feeling that tonight was really going to be special. I hope

I haven't blown that. If you want me to take you home right now, I'd understand."

Abby slowly relaxed as she let herself gaze into the honest blue of his eyes.

She'd wondered where the fun, happy guy that she had spent a few hours with had disappeared to. The Hix driving to the restaurant had been stiff and uncomfortable in her presence and she, in turn, had withdrawn into herself until only a polite shell remained behind. Watching him now she could see the embarrassment and the agony on his face, even though he tried to hide it. She too had been anticipating tonight, and wasn't about to give up so easily on the man sitting so apologetic beside her.

Abby took a chance and reached out her hand, leaving it half way between them on the seat, until Hix tentatively reached out and took it in his. Abby gripped the larger, calloused hand he offered, and felt the zing all the way to her heart as their skin made and held contact.

"Hi Hix," she said, her voice low and sexy as hell. "I've looked forward to being with you tonight too, and I'm really looking forward to getting to know you better." She looked him straight in the eye as she continued, "I think you're right, there is going to be something special between us." Their eyes met and locked. "So, if you agree, let's start this date from this moment." He nodded and smiled as she dropped her eyes to their joined hands.

"You look really good, by the way," she said looking up, her head cocked at a flirtatious angle, "and smell even better," she added, low and easy. "How about we go in and get something to eat? I'm starved."

Hix didn't want to let her go, but was beyond glad that she was willing to give the evening another chance. Give him another chance to make a first impression. He raised her hand to his lips, barely touching them to her creamy skin.

"Hi, Abby," he said back to her, squeezing her hand one last time before he let her go. He grabbed the door handle and almost ran around the pickup to open her door. "Let's go," he said, a confident smile on his lips. "I'm starved, too," he said, the innuendo heavy in his words as he took her hand to help her down.

Abby chuckled soft and low before she nodded her head saying, "I think there's some food inside with our name on it. We can have dessert later."

Two much more relaxed people made their way, hand in hand, into the restaurant, and towards their destiny.

Chapter 15

Hix and Abby were guided to a comfortable booth beside a huge fireplace, complete with a roaring fire. The heat from the fireplace, which was big enough to park a small car in, felt delicious to Abby and Hix, as they settled into the booth to enjoy the fire, the food, and each other. Abby ordered a halibut steak and steamed vegetables, while Hix opted for the house special, a large cut of prime rib and a baked potato, smothered in butter and sour cream.

As the two talked and ate, Hix watched the flicker of firelight play across the beautiful face across from him. One moment her features were illuminated by the flicker of firelight and the next they were shadowed and mysterious. His fingers itched to follow the paths it illuminated, tracing her skin until he was as familiar with it as he was with his own. But he refrained. Instead, he listened, he talked, and he laughed, and before he knew it, two hours had passed, his stomach was full, and it was time for them to leave for the movies.

Hix laid a handsome tip on the table and handed the check and his credit card to their waiter. Standing beside the booth as Abby scooted across the leather, Hix held out her coat for her. She turned her back to him and he lifted her hair as she slipped her arms into the sleeves. For an instant, Hix breathed in the scent of her hair, fresh and clean, with just a hint of the perfume she had lightly sprayed on before he had arrived. He resisted the urge to bury his face in the soft tresses and wrap his arms around her waist, as she bared her neck while she lowered her head, leaving the fine, soft hairs on the nape of her neck vulnerable to his wandering kisses. He breathed a little easier when her hair dropped and she stepped away from him, fastening the front of her coat, and pulling on her gloves.

Neither Hix nor Abby had paid much attention to the eyes that followed them throughout the evening, or the heads that came together to talk about the young couple so into each other by the fire. They willingly acknowledged the smiles from the well-wishers, said hello to a few friends, and were oblivious to the glares of envy as they made their way to the door, where Hix retrieved his credit card and grabbed a mint and a toothpick from the dish by the cash register.

They walked close together, Hix guiding Abby's elbow, as they made their way to the pickup. Hix held Abby's hand as she stepped up into the vehicle, then closed her door. He made his way around to the driver's side and climbed in beside her. The engine had not entirely cooled down during their time in the restaurant, and in a few minutes Hix turned the fan on low, letting the heat slowly build, taking the chill from the cab. They drove to the one movie theater the town boasted of, where they had their choice of a comedy or action flick. Wanting to keep the mood light and not wanting to have to think too hard or pay too close attention to a plot, they chose the comedy.

It proved to be a particularly good movie, and they laughed along with the others in the theater, getting into the show and its characters. As the movie progressed, so did Hix and Abby's friendship. Their hands, that had lain idle at the beginning of the movie, found their way into each other, thumbs rubbing in circles, becoming familiar, getting the first touch and feel of each other's warmth and skin. Her's soft, warm, and smooth. His tougher, work hardened, and generating greater heat to warm her cool fingers. Gripping tighter as they shared a moment of laughter, and falling still as scenes of romance were played out on the larger than life screen. Each wondered what the end of the evening would bring.

As the credits rolled across the screen, Hix released Abby's hand, got up and again helped her on with her coat, letting his hands linger on her slim shoulders, giving them a slight squeeze when the task was finished.

He grabbed his coat and shrugged into it, as they moved with the rest of the crowd up the aisle and out onto the street. The air was cold and clouds of moist air followed them as they made their way to his vehicle, where they sat huddled until the heater began to take the crispness out of the air. Abby's nose showed a slight pinkness as it emerged from the folds of her coat daring to brave winter's lingering kiss.

"How about stopping for a quick cup of something warm?" Hix asked as he backed out onto the street, heading nowhere in particular.

"That sounds wonderful," Abby agreed with a tiny shiver, not wanting the evening to end just yet.

Hix drove them to a small diner, where they sat shoulder to shoulder, over cups of hot chocolate piled high with whipped cream, talking about the movie, laughing over the particularly funny parts, and keeping the conversation easy and light. An hour passed as they sat talking and looking into each other's eyes, sharing stories about themselves as they got to know each other.

Hix told Abby about growing up in Winston, the pride showing in his eyes and face as he spoke about his mother and the job he loved. He literally radiated happiness as he talked of his life, and Abby felt a stirring of jealousy at the love he had shared, and still did, with his mother and friends. He had grown up knowing he was loved because of who he was and not because of how he looked or the pay check he could deliver. Abby had never known a man to speak so openly of family and love without being embarrassed or self-conscious, so she listened more than she talked, letting Hix's memories paint a picture of everyday life in a small town and a close knit family. Most people would have given anything to have what they thought was Abby's life, but Abby would give anything to have what the normal family had. What Hix had. Support, understanding and truly unconditional love.

When it came her turn to talk, Abby spoke of growing up under the pressure of her mother's "guidance", the constant travel, and hard work involved in being a model. Hix watched the shadows and ghosts move over Abby's face as she talked of the hard work and trials of a job that everyone thought was just glamor. She became more serious as she talked of her mother and the relationship they shared. Reading between the lines, Hix realized that most of Abby's career was her mother trying to live her life through her daughter. Getting the money and fame she had dreamt of by pushing and controlling, until Abby had put her foot down and gotten a new manager. He couldn't imagine having that kind of relationship with his mother, and wanted to fold Abby into his arms and hold her until the smile came back into her eyes.

As the hour grew late, Hix grudgingly admitted it was time to get Abby home. He paid the tab and, once again, escorted Abby to her waiting chariot. He drove slowly as they made the short trip to her home and pulled up to her door step. He left the engine idling and turned to face Abby across the seat. "I had a really good time tonight," he said shyly, as he picked up her hand and enclosed it in his bigger one. He again felt a tingling feeling travel up his arm at the contact with her.

"Me too," she said, letting her fingers curl around and hold onto his.

"Is this something you would consider doing again?" he asked in a deep whisper, as he inched closer to her lips.

"Yes, please and thank you," she said, smiling as she moved slowly to meet him half-way. "I would love to see you again."

"How about tomorrow?" Hix asked, still moving towards his goal. "And the next day and the next?"

Abby laughed, as her eyes shone with the new found knowledge that Hix seemed to want to be with her as much as she wanted to be with him. No lone ranger here, she thought. She pulled her hand free from Hix's, and before he could protest, placed both hands along his lean checks so near to hers. She applied a slight pressure that brought his face willingly to hers, before she laid her lips lightly on his.

The kiss was feather light, but filled with the energy that had been building between them all night. Neither felt the need to hurry it into something deeper. Their lips lightly touched and nibbled each other's, exploring, getting to know the taste, the texture and what brought pleasure to the other. Slow and soft, their hands resting on each other's faces and necks, the time stretched out and seemed to stand still for the two young people beginning the journey of love.

Hix let his hand move to the back of her neck, applying a slight pressure, asking her to come closer.

Abby felt the request, but pulled back slightly as if to say, not yet, with her actions. Hix understood, and though he wanted nothing more than to hold her close until it would not be possible to find where one started and the other ended. He let her ease back, and watched as she slowly opened her eyes. Dark brown and flecked with gold, they told Hix that she felt the same heat and attraction that he did, going all soft and dreamy with the kisses they had shared.

Abby ran the pink tip of her tongue over her lips, taking the last lingering taste of Hix into her mouth. Memorizing his taste and storing that information for later inspection.

Hix brought his fingertips to her face and traced the smooth skin over her flushed cheekbones. "Can I call you tomorrow after work?" he asked, his voice low and intimate.

"I'd like that," she whispered, before moving back to her side of the seat. She gave him one last smoky look, before opening her door as she prepared to get out of the truck.

Hix hurriedly moved to open his door in an attempt to come around and help her out of the vehicle, but she laid a hand on his arm. "Stay," she said. "It's cold outside and I'm just going to dash into the house."

Hix would rather have walked her to the door and stole another good night kiss.

But knowing that they would have more time together soon, much more time, would have to satisfy them for now. He turned his body towards her and took one more "greedy" look at her before she ended their evening.

"Night, Hix," she said, stepping out of the vehicle. She closed the door and dashed up the sidewalk to her door. At the door, she turned one last time and waved to him before going inside and shutting the door between them.

Hix sat staring at the closed door for a moment before he eased away from the curb. His insides were on fire and he felt shaky and weak in the knees. His brain was fuzzy around the edges and his arms felt empty without her. "Not for long," he vowed. "Not for long."

Chapter 16

Abby closed and locked the door, before she allowed her legs to give out as she slid to the floor. Her knees were weak and her body was vibrating with an energy she'd never felt before. She didn't bother to take off her coat or remove her shoes, just sat there enjoying the deliciousness of the new feelings running through her. Feelings of total giddiness, new discovery, anticipation, and new beginnings washed over her. If she'd read correctly the signals Hix had been giving her all night, he was as happy with her as she was with him.

Letting one more little shiver travel up her body, Abby got up from the floor and made her way to the hall closet where she hung up her coat. She had just closed the closet door, when her phone began to ring. Grabbing it from the cradle, she quickly answered it without looking at the caller ID, feeling sure it was Hix wanting to tell her good night one more time. With a smile on her face, and an added hint of huskiness and mystery in her voice, she answered "Hello."

But the voice coming across the phone line was not Hix. Instead Abby felt like she had been blasted with icy cold water when she heard the familiar, disapproving tones of her mother, Cathy Mathews.

"Hello, Abby," she said, her voice cool and catty. "I know it's late there, but I figured you'd still be up."

"What can I do for you, mother?" Abby asked, rubbing a hand across her forehead as she made her way into the living room to sit on the edge of the sofa.

"Can't a mother call her daughter just to talk?" Cathy asked.

"It's late," Abby replied not wanting to play the cat and mouse game with her mother that most of her calls entailed. "What's the real reason you called?" Abby let the silence drag out for a moment waiting for her mother to speak. She knew that whatever the reason for the call, it would not be good. If she was not mistaken, her mother was about to drop a bomb shell on her. Abby didn't have long to wait, as her mother finally began to speak, almost bursting with the need to relate her news.

"You could have called me with your news, instead of letting me find out through "The Rag", you know. I am your mother, after all," Cathy Mathews scolded her daughter.

"I never read "The Rag", as you well know mother, so why don't you tell me what they said this time," Abby rolled her eyes and settled on the couch, prepared for another long, tiring lecture from her mother on her unbecoming public behavior.

"The Rag" was a weekly publication that delighted in reporting "news" about famous people, most of the time with a slant on the trashy side. More than once, they had run stories, or as they called them *scoops,* about Abby, including hinting that she'd had plastic surgery and lypo suction, to her being an operative of the CIA. All crap. Abby had learned a long time ago to ignore the garbage they printed. But not so for her mother. Cathy seemed to eat up every written word, and Abby had even suspected her mother of feeding some of the trash to their reporters, just to get her daughter's name in print. "I always knew there was something different about you, and now I know what it is," Abby's mother taunted her daughter.

"Get to the point, mom," Abby said, a familiar tiredness beginning to take hold of her voice and her body.

"You're gay," Cathy finally crowed, not being able to hide the malicious glee in her voice. Abby sat with her mouth open as her mother rushed on, her words almost incoherent as she imparted her news and berated her daughter all at once. "There was a very damaging picture of you and a dark-haired female holding hands at a restaurant in that little crap hole you call home. Now I know why you moved to Nebraska, for God's sake. It was to be with your girlfriend, wasn't it, Abby? You thought you could keep your dirty little secret out in the boonies, but you've been found out. Now I have been totally humiliated in front of all my friends, in front of the whole world, in fact. You could have warned me, so I would've been prepared when the news hit, but no. Instead you thought of no one but yourself, as usual, and I had to find out in the most despicable way possible. A reporter called me to get my response and I was absolutely speechless, in shock. I, of course, ran right out to buy a paper, and there you were. The picture was grainy and dark, but it was obvious that you were having a rendezvous of a romantic nature. With another woman! What were you thinking, Abby? You should have known better than to be caught like that in public. Your image is everything, remember? I would like to think I at least taught you enough to be discrete about your affairs, but it is now obvious to me that this is not the case. Well?" Cathy demanded. "Don't you have anything to say for yourself? No explanation, no excuse to give me for your behavior? What should I tell the press when they hound me for confirmation? That my daughter is a tramp that has wounded her loving mother with her dark secrets and her failure to share her life with me?"

Abby's emotions had run from disbelief, to the hilarity of the situation, to anger, as she let her mother moan and groan for another few minutes. Finally having had all she could take of her mother's ridiculous accusations, Abby let go with her own tirade of words.

"Enough mom! We both know why you called. It was just to dump on me and try to make me feel guilty and sorry for you. Well, it's not going to work this time. I am NOT gay, and the picture you are talking about was me and a friend having a simple conversation and nothing else. She's my best friend, that's all. I have no idea how it got in that paper or even who took it, but I will not defend spending time with my friends to you or anyone else. I really do not give a rat's patooty about your humiliation! So, say what you want to make yourself look better or to generate what sympathy you think you need. I'll live my life as I see fit, and to hell with you and everyone else! Now, I am going to hang up and go to bed, as I've had a long day. AND it was a good one, by the way, because I had a date tonight, with a man I might add, who just might turn out to be someone special to me," Abby said, finally running out of steam.

"Really?" Cathy said, jumping on Abby's slip about her date. "What is his name? What does he do? Does he live in that dump you call a town, too? Oh, of course he does, you're not smart enough to hook up with someone of importance and on the same level as you are. I'm not taking the blame for your behavior and your choices." Cathy started to work her way to a full blown snit again, but Abby had heard it all before and did not want to hear it all again.

"I'm hanging up now, mother," she said, talking over her mother. "Good night." And with that she hung up, silencing her mother's voice once and for all, or so she wished. Abby dropped the phone on the coffee table and sat still for a moment trying to get her emotions under control. How come, she thought for the thousandth time, she couldn't have a loving, caring mother like everyone else she knew? Was it too much to ask for a little bit of normalcy?

Abby was exhausted. She was tired of dealing with the same issues and going over the same questions in her head. "Not tonight" she thought. "Not tonight!" She got up off the couch and went into her bedroom, stripped down to nothing, and crawled under the covers to huddle there, alone and empty. She desperately searched her mind and her heart for something happy to calm her down and let her sleep.

An image of Hix rose up as he looked tonight, strong, handsome, warm and sensitive, all wrapped up in a delicious package. As Abby began to relive the evening she relaxed, and inch by inch began to uncurl her body until she was laying calm and relaxed in her big bed, her arms thrown up over her head on the pillow.

Hix was what she needed, she decided right then and there, and Hix was what she was going to have. Whatever it took, she was going to get what she wanted.

Soon.

Chapter 17

Hix waited until Abby was safely inside and the door closed, before he pulled away from the curb to head home. It was still early enough that, if he had wanted to, he could have stopped for a beer at one of the bars in town, but tonight he didn't feel like it. He wanted to go home and relive the events of tonight.

Pulling into the driveway, he parked his pickup and, ignoring the cold, slowly made his way to his front door. His hand on the knob, he stopped and turned around to look at his street, his town, in the late winter moonlight. Everything seemed brighter, clearer, newer, to him than he ever remembered it being before. He had looked at this same view day after day, but felt like he'd never really seen it until this moment. Maybe it was because he was feeling happy and at peace. He was content with his life and now it seemed that he had found a woman he wanted to share it with him. It sure felt that way to him.

He turned the idea over in his head and tried to imagine what it would be like to come home to a warm house and a loving woman each night. Come home to Abby. None of the warning bells that had pealed before when he had tried on the idea of settling down went off in his head. He did not have an issue with commitment, but he'd had the feeling that something was off, just not right with each woman he had gotten close to. He guessed everyone was looking for that someone who was perfect for them, and had to try on a lot of fits before they found the right one. That was life. He wasn't in a hurry, he had time. He could feel it. Time to make sure that this was what they both wanted. He didn't want to rush Abby into changing her life for him.

A slight frown marred his brow as he thought of the differences in their lifestyles. His was laid back, filled with a contentment to live and work in the small town he had grown up in. Hers was one of glamor and wealth that allowed her to live and travel anywhere she wanted, any time. Would she be happy to put down roots and make a life with him, he wondered? Doubt wiggled its way into his happiness and took root there, dampening his view through rose colored glasses.

He hunched his shoulders and dug his hands into his coat pockets, finally feeling the chill of the air around him. The cold breeze, that had been always present, finally penetrated his senses as it burrowed icy fingers down his collar and nipped at his ears. It fluffed his hair and sent it swirling around his head, dancing to the tune of some unheard strummer, lifting and twirling before it came to rest, leaving his golden tresses tousled and wildly beautiful.

Hix shook the hair out of his eyes and finally turned to enter his house. The warmth reached out to greet him and wrapped its arms around him as he came in and closed the door. He took off his coat and, as always, headed into the kitchen to get a snack before relaxing to some music in the living room. He grabbed an ever present can of soda and a handful of his mom's homemade cookies, before making his way back into the living room, where he pulled one of his favorite CD's, mellow tunes by Bob Segar, from his stack of music and plugged it into the CD player. Kicking back, he brought his feet up and rested them on the coffee table, relaxing as the music filled the room and his senses.

He slowly munched his way through heaven, dusting the crumbs from his hands when he was finished. Then he picked up the phone to call his mom. He knew it was late but he had told her he would let her know how things went on his date and he just couldn't wait until morning. The phone rang twice before he heard the voice of his childhood answer and ask if everything was okay. He had not meant to alarm her, and wasted no time in assuring her he was well, and he had only called to talk to her.

Sarah took off her glasses she only wore to read, it was hell getting old, and sank a little lower in her bed where she had been reading, getting more comfortable as she prepared to listen to her son.

Hix began talking, telling his mother how the night had started out with him sounding like a stiff bore, making her laugh at the colorful way he described his awkwardness. Even as a small child Hix had been able to tell a story in such a way that the listener was transported into the story with him, feeling like they had been there witnessing the events first hand. Tonight was no different, and Sarah listened intently, not only to the words, but to the tone of her son's voice, feeling his moods change and his feelings grow as the night and his tale went on.

When he got to the part where he had been thinking about the differences in his and Abby's life styles, Sarah sat a little higher in the bed and fussed with the covers. She knew he was going to ask for her advice, and that he wanted her to tell him that everything was going to be alright. But she didn't think she could give him those assurances. He was right to have doubts and she told him so.

"You have to look at everything," she told him, giving him the weight of her wisdom from years lived. "You and Abby are from very different worlds. The question is, can you make it work if you both want to?" she asked him. "Are you willing to work and compromise when those differences come up? Will she be willing to do the same? You know," she said softly, "you don't have to have all of the answers right now. You can't plan your future after one night, and any plan has to include Abby as well. There are two in every relationship, so both of you must have input. Just be happy with the way things turned out tonight, and give tomorrow a chance when it gets here. You have a lot to offer any woman, Hix, and I'm not just saying that because I'm your mother either," she teased. "Just be yourself from the start. No pretenses, no deceptions. Let her see you as you are, and ask the same of her, so you both have a true picture of what you're getting into. That's the best advice I can offer you sweetie."

Hix listened and took everything his mother told him to heart. She had never given him bad advice, and he trusted her to be honest with him. Looking over at the clock, Hix saw that it was going on two o'clock, so he let his mother go with a "*good night, thank you mom,*" and an "*I love you,*" before hanging up. He lay the phone down and got up from the couch to go to bed.

He took his clothes off, putting them in the hamper before crawling into bed with nothing but his traditional boxers on. As he closed his eyes he saw Abby as the fire light had framed her tonight. Beautiful and warm, soft and sweet. He had liked what he saw, and knew he wanted to see more. Could she be the one for him? Would she be the one for him?

He rolled over onto his side, but before he dropped into the land of slumber he again thought about his mother's words. "You are young and have all the time in the world to find out," her words whispered through his mind. He knew she was right, but all the same, he hoped that tomorrow would get there in a hurry. He clamped down on his feelings of impatience, willing himself to sleep. He had heard that love, like life, was like a roller coaster ride, with its ups and downs, and Hix was finally ready to take that ride.

"All aboard," he thought, smiling as he drifted away. Ticket in hand he took his seat and, with hands in the air, screaming from fear and delight, he left the platform and disappeared from sight.

Chapter 18

For Abby, the next month passed by in a blur of work and happiness. She had landed a new contract, being named "the face" for a new line of cosmetics and perfumes. She spent her days being made up every way possible for the ad campaign. She went home every night tired, but knowing that if she didn't get to see Hix, she would at least get to hear his voice over the phone, as neither of them seemed to be able to go a day without reaching out to the other. Abby turned down party invitations and girls nights out with her friends so that her weekends were free to spend with Hix. She was getting to know him and loving every minute of it. Their time was spent going to movies, eating out, taking turns making a quiet dinner at their homes and just spending time snuggling and kissing in front of the TV. Each night, as the hour grew late, they parted with heated kisses and reluctance, only to sleep in their own beds, alone.

It wasn't that they weren't attracted to each other, just the opposite in fact. Abby wanted Hix so bad she could taste him. She didn't know why he wasn't willing to sleep with her. She had sent out all the signals, dressing in every sexy thing she owned, giving him long, hot looks, and even going so far as to run her nails up and down his thighs when they were making out on the couch at home. But nothing had prompted him to lose control and take her, as she wanted him to. She knew that he wanted her, she'd felt his body react, seen the way he looked at her, and felt his desires as he kissed her with heat and passion. But so far it hadn't gone any further than that.

Kendall had grilled Abby as to how good Hix was, but Abby played coy, not wanting to have to admit to her friend that she could not entice him into intimacy.

The tabloids had gotten wind of the pair, snapping photos of the couple walking down the street holding hands or sitting in a restaurant, their heads close together as they fed each other bits of food from their plates with their fingers.The paparazzi loved the way they looked together, both tall, toned and good looking and, despite the short time they had been dating, they had become the darlings of the gossip magazines, being toasted as the hot new couple of the year, speculation running rampant as to what their future held in store.

Abby had asked Hix how he felt about seeing their faces pasted on the tabloid magazines, as they passed through the checkout line at the grocery store. Hix had only shrugged his broad shoulders, saying that as long as it didn't interfere with their lives, they could print what they wanted. He didn't put much stock in the tabloid articles and had spent very little time reading them. Abby warned him that not everything printed in them was good or true and that sometimes innocent actions were twisted and lies printed. Hix just smiled at her and said, "I'll deal with it if the time ever comes."

Abby just shook her head. Hix had no idea what was coming, but as long as she did, things would work out.

After seeing the pictures of her and Hix, Abby's mother had stopped grilling her about being gay and now only asked questions about the two of them. Knowing her mother would run right to the press with anything she revealed, Abby gave her the same information that she gave the papers, that they had just started dating and so far were happy together.

Abby was pretty sure that it had been her mother who had come up with the cutesy nickname of Baligale (Balthazar and Abigale), that the papers were so insistent on using for hot couples. "*How damn dumb can you get?*" Abby had thought the first time she had seen it. Her mother had gushed that it was cute and they were cute. Abby had found the whole conversation with her mother *not cute*. It was just irritating to have to listen to her claim what a great couple they were one minute and then how Hix was just after her for her money the next. Abby wanted to pull her hair out by its lovely roots by the time the most recent call was over.

Instead, she had put on some workout clothes and taken her frustrations out on the tread mill in her spare bedroom, not stopping until the sweat had run from her body and her mood had gone from crap to good.

Still breathing hard, Abby stripped off her wet clothes and got into a lukewarm shower to cool down and rinse off. It was Friday and she was tingling with the now usual anticipation of seeing Hix in a few hours. Maybe tonight was going to be the night that all her waiting and imagining would come to an end.

With thoughts of Hix pouring over her, along with the water, Abby added some of her favorite shower gel to a soft pink loofah and lathered her body. She took her time shaving her legs, making sure they were smooth as a baby's bottom, imagining Hix's hands gliding over the silkiness she had prepared for him. Next she poured a generous portion of her favorite shampoo in her palm and worked it through the long wet tresses hanging over her bare shoulders and back. Standing under the rain of water, she rinsed out the shampoo and then added a handful of conditioner to her hair, making sure it was conditioned to buttery softness before, once again, she tipped her head back until the water ran clear from her hair.

Stepping out from under the water, Abby grabbed a thick towel and patted the moisture from her body before winding it turban-style over her freshly washed hair. She smoothed her favorite lotion over her entire body, making it soft and enticing, before stepping into a pair of skimpy black panties and a matching bra. Standing before the mirror, she put on her makeup, using just enough to give her skin a soft dewy glow. Pulling the towel from her hair, she tipped her head down and blew it dry until it was full and shone with a rich luster. She flipped her head up, pleased that it fell in natural waves, not needing further fussing to achieve the look she was going for, soft and sultry. When the mirror told her she was perfect, she finished by adding a spritz of her favorite perfume behind her ears, at her wrists, over her breasts, and behind her knees

Going to her closet, Abby pulled on a pair of black jeans and black sweater, which made her honey golden hair shine like the sun. She stepped into black boots and attached a pair of silver and black hoops to her ears. She put on a chunky silver bracelet-watch and a necklace to match. Satisfied with the image that greeted her in the full-length mirror, Abby went to the living room to wait the few minutes until Hix arrived.

She turned on the TV set, mostly for noise, but stopped to listen when she heard her name mentioned by the skinny fake blonde who was hosting the show.

"Rumor has it that super model Abby Mathews is having a bit of trouble reeling in the man she currently has her sights set on, hunky construction worker Balthazar Hix. Inside sources tell us that although the two practically live in each other's pockets, there haven't been any early morning breakfasts as of yet for the couple. Up until now, men have fallen all over themselves to get to the aloof Abby Mathews, giving her whatever she wanted, when she wanted it, in an attempt to land the golden beauty. Not so with Hix, who seems to be playing hard to get, or maybe he's just not that interested in the current darling of the media. This reporter wonders if the great Abby Mathews is finally losing her touch." With a final wink to the camera the reporter went on to the next story, leaving Abby standing with her mouth pressed in a grim line and her knuckles white on the hapless remote.

In one angry motion, Abby turned off the set and tossed the remote on the couch. She paced the length of the room twice before the red she was seeing began to fade.

"What would that anorexic cow know about relationships anyway?" Abby fumed. "*She probably hadn't had a man touch her since her father bounced her on his knee as a baby.*" Abby had learned a long time ago not to listen to

the gossips, but this one had hit home, bringing her fears out into the open. Maybe Hix didn't want her. Maybe he just wanted to be friends. Maybe there was something wrong with him that made it impossible for him to perform. Maybe he was gay!

Abby worried her fingernail as she paced, forming a plan to get what she wanted from Hix, while silencing the rumors. Abby had never been the most patient of people and when she wanted things, she wanted them now. So, with a squaring of her shoulders and a flick of her silky hair, she decided that tonight was going to be the night. She was going to get Hix into her bed if she had to get him drunk and tie him to the bed posts. She knew they would be good together, even going so far as to think they were meant for each other. Now all she had to do was convince Hix of it.

Losing her touch my butt, Abby thought as she heard Hix pull into her driveway. She gave her reflection one last look in the mirror hanging in the hallway, before going to the door to let her prey in. Tonight she was going on the hunt, and by morning's first light she was going to silence her critics and have Hix right where she wanted him.

Exclusively hers.

Chapter 19

Hix had also spent the last month in a haze of happiness. He loved spending time with Abby and couldn't seem to be able to get enough of her. He spent every spare minute he had with her. He had even given up boy's night out so they could have a couple more hours together. They talked and laughed together, as if they had known each other all their lives, meshing like well-oiled gears.

Although their jobs pulled them apart during the day time hours, they spent their evenings relaxing and getting to know each other's likes and dislikes, seeing if they had any interests in common.

As far as Hix could tell, they were as far apart in most areas as the north and south poles. He liked to hang with his friends and family and enjoyed the outdoors. Abby liked to stay home, avoided her family, and stayed out of the sun to protect her skin. Hix knew her looks were her lively hood, but he still couldn't see how a few rays of sun would ruin her career.

He got ribbed by his friends and co-workers about the hottie he was hooked up with. They shook their heads and teasingly clapping him on the back when reporters showed up to disrupt work and the flow of his life. He laughed good-naturedly when a picture of him from last summer, bare chested and bronzed from the sun, had appeared in a magazine with the caption, "It's easy to see how the Thor look alike, Balthazar Hix has captured the attention of super model Abby Mathews. Having the golden good looks and the body of a God, Hix better watch out, as insiders say Abby is out for his heart as well as his body."

He took it all in stride with no complaints and would have endured much, much more just to have Abby by his side. He had never considered himself to have been in love before, but he was feeling pretty sure that he'd fallen in love with Abby, almost from the first moment he'd seen her. Even though it had only been a month, and Hix was still not a 100% sure, he trusted his instincts and they were telling him that this was the real deal.

He had held himself in check when it came to jumping into bed with her. He didn't want it to be just sex with her. He wanted to wait until they were sure of their feelings. Then he wanted to make love to her, with her. He didn't want to ruin what they'd begun to build by jumping the gun and rushing together just because they could.

He wanted her, though. It took all the strength he had to walk away from her and return to his home alone after a date with her. He knew she felt the same way by the way she looked at him and the small touches she grazed across his skin. She could make his mouth go dry and his knees turn to water with just a look from those rich brown eyes. Some of the guys he worked with called him "whipped." All Hix could do was smile, a deep growl coming from his throat and say, "Oh yeah."

Hix liked to remember little things she'd said, gestures she'd made that gave him insights into what kind of person Abby was. Like the time they had been eating at a local café when a tall, good looking young man had come up to their table and asked Abby to sign a poster he had of her. As she signed the poster, the young man had told her that he wanted to break into the modeling business, but didn't know how to start.

Abby had sat back in her chair, seriously looked him up and down, and told him that although he had the looks to be a model, the big holes in his ears, the ones kids nowadays thought were so cool that looked like something out of National Geographic, would keep him from being in front of the cameras.

The boy had been devastated, but Abby had told him the truth as gently as she could. No sponsor wanted a body covered in tattoos, piercings, and holes in ear lobes big enough to hang a fence post through them. Unless he was willing to have surgery to correct the damage a bad decision had created, she didn't see him becoming a model.

The boy had left with his fingers tugging at his earlobes. His dreams of modeling were dashed for the moment, but he was still smiling just for having had a conversation with Abby Mathews.

Abby had shown compassion by not brushing off her fan and by giving bad news with warmth, a smile, and a suggestion on where to go from there. Hix liked the way she handled herself and his feelings for her had grown a little more that night.

Hix whistled as he gathered up his gear and stowed it in the back of his pickup. His week was over and he had all weekend to spend with Abby. His plans for tonight consisted of taking her to meet his mother. The three of them would have dinner at his mom's house. His mother had insisted on cooking the meal instead of letting Hix take them all out to eat. And since Hix, along with half the town, loved the way she cooked, he had agreed readily to her suggestion.

On his way home, Hix stopped at the local florists and picked up two bunches of flowers. He chose an arrangement of six red roses for Abby, and one of spring flowers for his mother's table. He actually liked giving flowers to his mom. He loved seeing Sarah's cheeks blush slightly as she always smiled, showing her appreciation for his love and thoughtfulness. He wanted to include Abby in the gesture. He hadn't gotten her flowers yet and wanted to see both the women he cared about happy. Hix sat the vases in a box to stabilize them. He smiled to himself as he drove home to shower and shave for his evening with his two favorite girls.

Hix let the steamy water revitalize his tired muscles as he lathered his hair and body. Stepping from the shower he wound a towel loosely around his lean hips and applied shaving cream to his jaw. He took care in shaving, thinking of Abby's soft skin as he kissed her. He patted his cheeks with a clean smelling aftershave and added a splash of cologne to his bare chest and neck.

Letting the towel slip to the floor he strode to the closet and dressed, as always, in a button down shirt, under a light-weight sweater, and jeans. He pulled on his black boots and his watch, running his fingers through his still damp hair.

Taking one last look in the bedroom mirror, he was satisfied with his appearance. Hix grabbed a jacket and his keys. He nearly ran down the walk, anticipation apparent in every step, and he jumped into his truck. It only took him a few minutes to get to Abby's house. He gave a quick glance in the rear view mirror, smiled and nodded his head at his own reflection. He carefully took the bouquet of roses in the vase from the box and headed for her front door.

It always gave him a tingle in his gut when Abby opened the door, almost immediately after his knock, and he was greeted with a smile and a kiss that left him dizzy and breathless. It was like she was standing on the other side of the door, waiting for him, as eager as he was to begin their evening together. He loved it.

Tonight he anticipated no less, as the door opened and he got that first look at *his girl*. She was beautiful, dressed all in black and her hair shone like spun gold. Hix was about to hand Abby the flowers, which he had concealed behind his back, when she grabbed the collar of his coat, pulled him inside the house, and planted a kiss on his mouth that made his toes curl and his lips burn.

Hix felt something different in the kiss this time.There was a demand behind the fire this time. It was hotter, stronger, and he felt need mixed with passion.When Abby pulled back to let him breathe, Hix opened his eyes and saw his reflection in the jewel bright orbs before him. Something was different tonight.The woman before him was different. She was still soft and beautiful, but he could see there was purpose and resolve in her face as she slowly came back into focus before him.

Hix blinked his eyes and remembered the flowers he held in his hand, surprised he had not dropped them while under the spell of her kiss. "Hi baby," he got out, sounding rough and gravelly. "I missed you too," he said extending the bouquet with a slow smile.

Abby took the flowers, burying her nose in the blooms for a brief moment before setting them on a table inside the door. Drawing Hix completely inside, she shut the door with a snap that sounded like a gun shot.

"I have a surprise for you tonight," Hix said, as he allowed himself to be led by the hand into the living room.

"I have one for you, too," Abby said, turning to face Hix. She ran her hands slowly under his sweater, pulling the hem of his shirt from inside the waist band of his jeans as she looked deep into his eyes.

Hix swallowed hard, as her intentions of a surprise for him became clear. Pulling her hands out from under his shirt, Hix held them firmly to his chest, as he told her of his plans before things went too far.

"My mother has invited us over for dinner tonight," he said and watched as Abby froze, her eyes narrowing and her nostrils flaring as her plans were brought to an abrupt, screeching halt. "We only have to stay for a couple of hours, but she would like to meet you, and I would like you to meet her, too babe."

Abby wanted to hiss out her frustration, but she lowered her eyes before Hix could see the irritation in them. She pulled her hands out of his and gave him a bright smile, that didn't quite reach her eyes, and nodded her head.

"That sounds great," she said, as she turned to get her coat and purse from the closet.

Hix saw and felt her disappointment, but knew it was too late to call his mother and cancel their dinner. He wanted the two women in his life to meet and hoped Abby could put her plans on hold for a couple of hours.

Abby shoved her arms into her coat, buttoned it up and, taking Hix by the hand, led him to the door. "I'm ready," she said. She let Hix go out the door before she turned back to lock it, muttering one word under her breath, "Shit."

Chapter 20

The ride to Sarah's house was short. Hix tried his best to alleviate the tension in the cab of the pickup, making small talk as he tried to put Abby at ease. Pulling into the driveway, Hix cut the engine and turned to Abby, placing his hand on her forearm before she could get out.

"I'm sorry to spring this on you and ruin the plans you had for the evening. I just wanted you both to meet and I didn't think before accepting my mother's invitation for the both of us." he apologized, sincerity in his voice and his eyes.

Abby raised her downcast eyes, until they were met and held by Hix's honest blue orbs gazing hopefully at her. She let out a sigh of defeat, realizing she just couldn't stay mad at the man beside her. He looked so contrite and sorrowful that Abby gave in and let a smile steal onto her face and into her eyes.

Raising a hand she cupped his cheek and let her thumb stroke the soft skin beside his eye. "It's okay," she said, her voice coming out soft and quiet. "I was just taken by surprise that's all. My plans for the evening haven't changed, they're just postponed," she said, letting the fire inside her body show in her deep brown eyes, as the golden flecks danced with promise.

Hix swallowed hard and had second thoughts about spending the evening with his mother. But, as he turned his head to place a warm kiss in the palm that touched his cheek, he reined in his needs and got himself under control. He held Abby's hand to his face for one more second before releasing it, exiting his door and walking around to the passenger side of the pickup. He let the crisp, cool evening air clear his befuddled head before opening her door. They walked together to the side door of the small house where he had grown up.

Slipping his arm around Abby he tucked her protectively under his arm and waited for the door to be opened. Within seconds the knob turned and the door was held open in welcome, as Abby and Sarah met for the first time. Hix guided Abby inside and let the door close before releasing her and gathering his mother in for the hug that was their usual greeting for each other.

"Hi mom," he said, a smile on his face and in his voice.

"Hi yourself," replied Sarah Hix.

Then, releasing his mother, Hix turned to Abby and gently pulled her toward his mother. "Mom, I would like you to meet Abby Mathews," he said proudly. He grasped his mom's elbow as he pulled the two women towards each other. "Abby, this is my mother, Sarah Hix," he said, looking into Abby's face for her reaction.

Abby and Sarah faced each other for the first time, a tentative smile on each pair of lips. When Abby held out her hand for a shake, Sarah gently pushed it aside as she gathered the young woman in for a warm, welcoming hug.

It felt strange to Abby to have a mother's arms around her that asked nothing in return. The kiss that Sarah placed on her cheek actually reached the skin, and was not left hanging in mid-air.

Stepping back Abby dropped her arms as she said, "It's so nice to meet you, Mrs. Hix." Her smile was reflected in her eyes, sincere and warm.

"Call me Sarah, please," came the welcoming sincere response. "Come in, come in," Sarah said, and waved them to the kitchen as she collected coats and hung them up on hooks behind the door, brushing off Hix's hands as he tried to help.

Hix grabbed Abby's hand as Sarah led the way into the kitchen where mouth-watering smells drifted from pots and pans bubbling on the stove. Pulling out chairs around the table, Sarah motioned for them to sit while she went to the fridge and got them each a glass of cold raspberry lemonade. Placing the glasses before them on the table, Sarah stopped and looked at Abby in confusion.

"I'm sorry," she said, "Is this okay? I have regular sodas or diet ones if you prefer."

In response, Abby lifted the cold glass and took a long drink. Its iciness cooled her throat and moistened her tongue, which seemed to be stuck to the roof of her mouth.

"This is great, Sarah. Mmm," she said, taking another long draw on the glass of lemonade.

The tension quickly left Sarah's face and form as she gave Abby's hand a squeeze as she went to gather plates and flatware from the cupboards.

"Let me help, mom" Hix said, but he was waved back into his chair as she set the table for the dinner that was almost done.

"How is it outside?" Sarah asked as she made quick work of the chores and then took a chair herself. She was anxious to get to know her son's friend better.

"I think spring is finally here," Hix said. Hix smiled and began to fill his mother in on his upcoming projects he had planned once the cold weather finally decided to give it up for good. The friendly banter between mother and son was strange to Abby, but she found she liked the ease with which they treated each other. The love and respect Hix showed to his mother gave her a warm feeling in her stomach, and a glimpse of how things would be in their home when they had children. The old saying, "You can always tell how a man will treat his wife by the way he treats his mother," came to her.

Abby sat a little straighter in her chair as what she had just been thinking hit her. She was a bit surprised where her thoughts had taken her. She was actually thinking of a future with Hix. Not just the near future, but the future far enough away that there would be children coming and going from their house.

"Is everything alright, Abby?" Sarah asked, with a look of concern on her face. The girl looked like she had just got the scare of her life.

"F-fine," stuttered Abby, "I was just lost in thought there for a minute."

At that moment, the timer on the stove sounded and Sarah announced, "Well, there we are, dinner is done. No Hix, you don't have to help," she said as Hix rose from the table to help her with the food in the oven.

Hix sidestepped her protests, as he opened the oven door, lifted the roaster out and placed it on top of the stove. A warm rush of heat filled the room as the oven door lay open, relinquishing its aromatic treasure. Careful not to scald his nose that was seeking more of what lay hidden in the pan, Hix pulled the lid from the roaster and watched a burst of steam rise to the ceiling. He tipped his head back, closed his eyes, and took in the scent of the delicious food that lay within.

Sarah took control, pushing him gently aside as she placed two large forks under the roast pork and lifted it onto a serving platter. She placed carrots and onions around it, creating a beautiful garnish to the lightly browned meat, then poured a rich brown gravy over the whole contents. She pulled baked potatoes, wrapped in tin foil, from the oven with a large, cheerful colored oven mitt, and placed them in a basket on the table beside the meat tray. Turning back to the stove, Sarah picked up the steaming kettle of green beans, drained the water from them, poured them into a serving bowl, placed a pat of butter in their middle to melt, and brought them to the table. Opening the refrigerator, she retrieved three frosty bowls of crisp salad, along with a variety of salad dressings, and placed them on the three colorful placemats on the table. She pulled a bowl of sour cream, round balls of butter, and a dish of strawberry jam from the frig, and placed them in the center of the table beside the crystal salt and pepper shakers. Lastly, Sarah took fresh bread from the oven, sliced it into thick slabs, and piled a plate high with the fragrant fare.

Taking one last look to make sure she hadn't forgotten anything, Sarah took her seat at the head of the table and motioned for them to dig in.

"Is this okay?" Sarah asked Abby, looking over the meal and thinking that she had tried to make things even a model could eat while still watching her figure. The salads were big and the vegetables were not swimming with any fattening coverings like cream of mushroom soup or cheese sauce. The meat was lean and tender and if Abby chose to skip the carb-filled potato and fresh bread, that was fine with Sarah. Left over baked potatoes always made great hash browns the next day.

Abby smiled gratefully and assured Sarah, "This is a wonderful meal. Its all so amazing and smells so wonderful," Abby said, a smile still lighting up her face.

Everything was more than fine. Trying a little of everything, she found the flavors were better than she had ever eaten. She didn't indulge in the dessert, which consisted of strawberries over ice cream, but finished off her meal with a cup of coffee. It was just as delicious as the food. Sarah was an artist in the kitchen.

Throughout dinner the conversation flowed easily, with Sarah making a point of including Abby and explaining things that were brought up that she wouldn't know about. She noticed that Abby and Hix were comfortable touching each other, exchanging little caresses often, and with almost no thought that their attention to each other would be uncomfortable for Sarah, and it wasn't.

When they had all finished eating, Hix shooed his mother into the living room, insisting that he and Abby would do the dishes since she had cooked. Sarah could hear giggling and a few squeals mixed in with the sounds of dishes being hand wash and dried. When the two had finally joined her they were both smiling, rosy cheeked, and damp from a soap fight that had broken out as they washed the dishes.

Sarah just shook her head and smiled to herself as she watched them plop down in front of the TV, ready to watch a movie Hix had pulled from his jacket pocket. It was a new action flick that had been released on video just that week. All three lost themselves in the plot, arguing playfully as to who was the killer, and how it was going to come out in the end.

Sarah couldn't help but notice the love in her son's eyes every time he looked at Abby. She also saw the "hunger" when Abby returned his gaze. The evening came to an end when the movie was over. The hour was late but it was a very enjoyable evening.

Hix helped Abby on with her coat, before turning and enveloping his mother in another bear hug. "Thanks for everything mom. Everything was great." he said, kissing her cheek.

Sarah smiled, "You're welcome sweetie," she said and returned his gesture of love and gratitude for the evening.

Abby and Sarah also exchanged a heartfelt hug, "It was so nice to meet you Sarah, and yes, thank you so much for the wonderful meal and great company at the movie." Abby said, smiling sweetly at Sarah.

"My pleasure, dear. I am very glad that we finally got to meet each other." Sarah said with warm sincerity. "I hope we will see more of each other soon," she said, holding Abby's hand and then gave her a big hug.

Sarah could tell the young couple were quite happy together as she watched Hix and Abby step out of the cozy warmth of the house into the chilly evening and make their way down the walk, arm in arm. They got into the pickup and drove off, waving goodbye as they left.

Sarah stood waving from the door until the pickup was out of sight, before going inside and closing the door. She locked the door and turned off the lights in the kitchen and living room, preparing to watch a little TV in bed.

Sarah made her way into the bathroom adjacent to her bedroom, stripped off her clothes, washed her face, slathering on an age-defying concoction that cost a fortune, and brushed her hair and teeth. Standing before the mirror, she took a moment to examine her reflection. She was still an attractive woman, even at 53. Most people thought she was younger than her age. She attributed this to her daily romp on the treadmill, plenty of sleep, and her contentment with her life. Pulling on her favorite pajamas, an over-sized t-shirt and flannel pants, she moved into the bedroom, where she fluffed the pillows before crawling into bed and pulling the covers up under her arms.

Sarah lay back, turned on the late night news but paid little attention to it as she let her mind replay the events of the evening. She realized she was satisfied with the outcome. She had gotten to meet the woman in her son's life, and she was able to watch them together. They appeared happy and content with each other and, if all was as it appeared on the surface, she had no worries.

Cracking one last jaw popping yawn, Sarah turned off the TV, turned the knob on the lamp beside the bed and the room was engulfed in blackness, as she snuggled down into her bed.

Before she went to sleep, the gentle mother of the giant of a boy sent one last thought winging its way to the beautiful girl she had just met. "*Don't hurt him,*" she thought. "*Don't make me have to protect him from you. He's still mine, for now, and I won't let you do him harm. Know this, if you hurt him, I will repay you in spades for his pain. I never get even, I get ahead! Amen.*"

Chapter 21

Hix drove the short distance to Abby's house, holding her hand and feeling her warmth beside him. He pulled up to the curb in front of her home and shut off the engine. Turning in the seat, he gathered her body in his arms, holding her close to his heart before finding her waiting lips with his. The night was quiet with only the sound of their breathing interrupting the stillness. Hix pulled back with reluctance and opened his door to go around and open hers. They made the trip to her door in silence, arms wrapped around each other, their steps in unison.

At the door Hix turned her once again to face him and settled his lips on hers. This time they met with hunger, need and, reluctantly, farewell. As he ended the kiss and steeled himself to leave, Hix was only mildly surprised when Abby cupped his face with both hands and, resting her forehead against his, whispered low and sweet, "Don't go, Hix. Not tonight. Stay with me. Please?" she gently pleaded.

Hix knew this was coming. He had felt it all night, and was powerless to deny them both what they wanted. Nodding his head only once, Hix allowed himself to be led, by the hand, inside where the outside world was shut out with the closing of the door. It was dark and still inside, but neither of them needed a light to show them the way, as they walked side by side to the bedroom.

They took off their coats and laid them gently over the back of a chair before they faced each other in the shadowed darkness. Shadows moved across the walls as the breeze stirred the bare trees outside the window. They moved slowly, one step closer to each other, until they met at the foot of the wide bed that loomed in anticipation of the event to come.

Hix drew Abby into his arms, pressing her body to his until they touched from shoulders to knees, getting as close as they could with only the barrier of their clothing between them. The kisses they shared where soft and fleeting, as they let their senses find the way that their eyes could not see. Hix felt Abby's hands move to his waist, as again they found their way under his sweater and pulled the shirt from his waistband. He let her hands explore his body that was open to her. He held his breath as she feathered touches from his shoulders all the way down his back. He moved his arms as she nudged them aside so she could move to his chest and his flat stomach, feeling his muscles jump every time her fingers met his flesh.

"Take off your sweater," Abby said, her mouth wanting to follow where her hands had been. Hix grabbed the bottom of the sweater and, in one swift move, pulled it up and over his head, letting it drop where he stood, forgotten as soon as it left his fingers.

Abby took over as she slowly unbuttoned his shirt, finally getting to touch and kiss the flesh she had ached for, for what seemed like forever. She splayed her fingers across the rippling muscles of his chest and stomach, lightly skimming over his nipples and coming to rest just above his jeans as she circled his belly-button with her thumbnail. Her lips took over where her fingers had been, as she placed little kisses on his hot skin.

Hix let his hands rest on her shoulders until he could stay still no longer. With his shirt open down the front, he lifted his hands to pull the comb from her thick hair, letting it pour through his hands like a waterfall of the richest honey. He buried his hands in the softness then gently tugged her hair, tipping her head back before finding her lips with his.

Abby melted into the hard body in front of her and, slipping her hands to Hix's back, used her nails to lightly rake him from shoulder to waist. Hix sucked in his breath and felt as if an electric current had been unleashed in his body, making him arch his back and freeze him where he stood.

Abby laughed deep in her throat at the power she had over her soon-to-be lover's body. She ran her teeth over the chest that seemed to take up her whole field of vision, tasting the maleness and feeling the mat of hair that covered it. Not holding back, she rubbed her cheek back and forth over the softness and parted the light furring to find and nip the male nipples, running her lips and tongue over them in turn until they hardened with her attention.

Hix, again, held still for as long as he could, before letting his hands mimic the path and actions Abby's had practiced on him. Her sweater proved no protection as he urged it up her body and over her head, until it joined his, a forgotten lump added to the pile on the floor. Hix let his eyes drink in the shadowed outline of her breasts in a black, lacy bra that held them, as he wanted to, before lightly tracing the edges with his fingertips, taking his time removing the sexy scrap of fabric before adding it to the growing pile of clothing on the floor. Replacing the cloth with his hands, he used his thumbs to coax the peaks to hardness and let her know the feel of his hands.

Pulling back from his grasp, Abby bent at the waist to remove her shoes. She smiled to herself as she straightened to see Hix doing the same. She wanted nothing to interrupt the final unveiling of their bodies.

As Hix straightened he slipped his arms from his open shirt and let it fall where it would. It was another addition to the pile of their clothing on the bedroom floor.

Abby moved closer to him. She stood straight and tall, unashamed in her partial nakedness. She raised one hand and then the other, letting them meet at the buttons of his jeans that would prove the final obstacle to be eliminated. She undid one button at a time, touching each inch of skin as it was exposed.

While his jeans hung open, waiting to be lowered, Hix again followed her actions and, with painstaking slowness, pushed hers down, following their path with his hands until he knelt at her feet. Hix grasped each slim leg, as she stepped out of her last piece of clothing, running his strong male hands up the full length of her silky legs, then back down, before standing up.

Wanting to be rid of the garment that separated them, Abby pushed his jeans down as far as she could reach and then, hooking a toe in a belt loop, drug them to the carpet with her foot. With a moan, she wrapped her arms around his neck, pressing their bodies at long last together with nothing between them.

His body felt like a furnace against hers, heating and burning where they touched, warming her cool skin until she felt the same heat run through her, fusing them together from head to toe. Hix buried his head in her shoulder, kissing the skin on the side of her neck, while his hands learned the curve of her back and the firmness at its end. Hix lifted her up, and with murmured urgings, had her legs wrapped around his waist holding her by her legs before lowering her until he rested at her opening.

"Now Hix, please, now," Abby begged to have her ache satisfied and her body joined to his in the most intimate way.

And he gave her what she asked for, meeting her halfway, until he was fully encased in her softness, making her moan with the feeling of completion. Hix moved to the bed and lowered them both to the mattress, holding his weight off her as he moved with her, sending them both, this first time, over the edge, tumbling into the well of love.

Chapter 22

Their first night together passed on wings, as Abby and Hix explored and learned each other's bodies, wants, and needs. "*Touch me here,*" and "*Yes, like that,*" were heard frequently, mixed with sighs of contentment. Their bodies fit together like nothing either had felt or had before. Making love once had not been enough. Neither one was even interested in sleep, but willing and ready participants in the games of pleasure. Sometimes moving as fast as an avalanche down a mountainside, sometimes going as slow as the waves that lazily roll onto a beach, they made love well into the morning hours, before falling into an exhausted sleep.

The bright spring sun had long since made its presence known before Hix woke enough to slit his eyes and look around. He didn't wake up wondering where he was or who he was with. He knew exactly where he was, right where he wanted to be, and who he was with, Abby Mathews. His love.

Hix moved his head and found that he was lying on Abby's hair as it streamed across his pillow. It felt like the warmest satin under his cheek, as Hix breathed in its clean fragrance and buried his face in its richness. They lay spooned, his front to her back, and Hix found his hand grasping the upper arm Abby laid on, holding on to her even in sleep. It was rare that he woke with a woman in his arms, but this time Hix could only think that this was right and felt that it was meant to be.

Hix lay still for a few minutes, enjoying the feel of each breath his lover took. He wanted to wallow selfishly in the feeling and knowledge of her, but it became apparent he would have to rise soon and take care of personal business.

Slowly unwinding himself from Abby, he rose from the bed and made his way to the bathroom, where he took care of business. Hix then decided, while he was there, he would jump in the shower and rinse off.

Closing the door quietly but firmly, he turned on the water before easing under the stream to enjoy the feel of the hot water coursing over his skin. Hix poured some of Abby's shampoo in his hand and lathered it through his long hair, grinning as he made himself smell just like her. He had just rinsed the conditioner out of his hair, and was preparing to step out, when he heard the door open. Before he knew what was happening, the shower door opened and a slim leg stepped into the shower stall, followed by a beautiful, naked Abby, cheeks still rosy from sleep and her hair wildly mussed by his greedy hands.

"Hi baby," she said, her voice husky from lack of use. "Mind if I join you?" she asked teasingly, knowing by the look in his eyes she was welcome.

Hix did not have to think twice as he wrapped his arms around her. He turned them both so the water was running warm down her back, wetting her hair as it clung to her shoulders. Showering was the last thing on either of their minds, as soapy hands followed curves and valleys, sliding with ease and purpose, before pressing against the shower wall and diving head long into warm wetness that had nothing to do with water.

When the water had run cold, they finally turned off the shower and stepped out onto the plush rug that covered the tile. They dried each other's bodies, before putting on only the most necessary clothes. Abby opted for the shirt Hix had worn the night before. She wanted to have his smell surrounding her. It hung to her knees, but having left the top three buttons open, she gave Hix teasing glimpses of her body, as she prepared a breakfast of fruits and yogurt for herself, and eggs and French toast for him. Hix stood, leaning up against the counter, watching her, clad only in a pair of white boxer briefs that left little to the imagination.

Not bothering with the table, they took the food into the bedroom and, sitting cross legged in the middle of the rumpled bed, they ate, tasting from each other's plates and making slow, sweet love for dessert.

Hours later, leaving Hix drowsy and content in the bed, Abby gathered the dishes together and brought them to the kitchen, putting them in the dishwasher for later washing. Walking back through the bedroom, she smiled at her gorgeous man as he reached out a hand, inviting her to again join him in their nest of love.

"In a minute," she said, as she giggled her way in to the bathroom. Closing the door, she leaned her hands on the counter and studied her reflection in the wide mirror over the sink. She liked what she saw. She saw a woman soft and tousled, fresh from her lover's arms. Her eyes sparkled, her cheeks were rose petal pink, and her mouth was full and bruised from his kisses.

She grabbed her toothbrush, scrubbed her teeth, splashed cold water over her face, and found her brush to tame her wild hair. She dabbed bits of lotion on her face and body, wanting to look her best before going back to join Hix in bed.

Abby liked the way she felt when she was with him and daydreamed about sharing the rest of her life with Hix as her husband. Rousing from her daydream, she continued smiling as she opened a drawer and got out her daily vitamins and other supplements. Downing them all with a glass of water, Abby stopped as she held her packet of birth control pills in her hand. Turning them over and over in her hand, Abby gave much consideration to taking her daily dose. She felt sure that she and Hix were going to be a couple for a long time to come, and it just figured that they would want children to complete their family. She knew that their babies would be beautiful, with the combined genes of their parents. Money for their future would be no problem, as she had tons and Hix could dabble in his construction career. She imagined the pictures that would grace the magazines with her and Hix carrying their baby, or maybe pushing a stroller as they walked the streets of New York during breaks in her work. They would have one boy and one girl she decided. The names could wait until the time came that they were needed.

The future looked bright to Abby, and she could see no draw backs at all. Abby lay the pills on the counter and finished getting herself ready. She puttered around straightening up the towels and even took out an extra one and hung it on the bar so Hix would feel at home. She found a spare toothbrush and hung it beside hers, finally laying out an extra wash cloth, completing the preparations to share her home. Of course they would live here. It was newer and roomier than his place. Eventually they would get a house of their own.

Abby liked the plans she was making, and had no doubt that Hix would go along with whatever she wanted. They were in love, and Abby hugged herself with the new feeling that fit like a glove. She had had a few boyfriends before, but nothing had given her the feelings she was experiencing with Hix.

Once more she picked up the flat of birth control pills. She looked from it to her reflection in the mirror. Pursing her mouth in determination, Abby went to the toilet and, lifting the lid, popped them out one by one into the water. When she finished with the last one, she reached out with a steady hand and flushed, watching as her past swirled around and around the bowl before her, disappearing into the sewer. Putting the empty container in the bottom of the trash, she covered it up, before standing up straight and once more looking into the mirror. She looked herself straight in the eye and silently convinced her reflection that what she was planning was for the good of both their futures.

She wanted Hix, and she was going to get him, one way or another.

Chapter 23

The next few months flew by for Hix, bringing not only the milder temperatures of spring, but also a deepening love for Abby and contentment for their situation. They spent all of their time together and, although it was not official, they were pretty much living together at Abby's place.

Hix had a few moments of unease at this arrangement, but Abby seemed to be just fine sharing her space, never having brought up the fact that she was paying all of the bills. Hix had, however, brought up the subject, wanting to contribute his share towards the household bills.

Abby had waved him off with a flick of her hand saying, "This is my place and the bills have to be paid whether you're here or not."

Hix was more than a little uncomfortable, feeling like a kept man but he hid his objections to the arrangement, telling himself that things would change if and when they made the move towards permanency. But every time she sat down at her desk to write out the checks, his ego was bit, and he would sit in silence stinging with each scratch of her pen. It became a matter of stupid pride he knew, but he could not, and would not sit by for one more month and feel like a sponge, as the rags had called him in one of the few articles he had read.

Hix remembered Abby telling him that they tended to put their own spin on what little they knew to sell more papers, but that still didn't erase the bad taste that lingered in his mouth from the barbs aimed at him. "*A common construction worker*" they had called him. "*A user of Abby's generosity and wealth. Trading sex for a fancy place to live and hoping for more money in his pockets.*"

Hix had seen red when he finished the article and had crumpled it into a ball, intending to throw it away. But instead he hesitated, smoothing it back out and carrying it in his back pocket as he went to talk over his hurt with the one person he could trust.

Sarah had opened the door to her son, and with one look into his eyes, she had opened the door wide as she drew him inside. She could see she needed to offer him a safe haven and a sounding board for his frustrations.

He told her about the article then sat quietly at her side as she read it for herself, not once but twice. Picking up every double meaning and hidden innuendo the story held. Sarah folded the paper neatly before putting it aside and turning to face her son.

"There is no truth to this trash and you know it, right?" she demanded.

Hix lifted his eyes to meet hers and she saw the misery he was feeling pour out of him, threatening to drown her with its magnitude.

"I raised you to be a caring, loving man, generous with you time, your love and your money. Not once have you failed me or shamed me with your actions. What are you going to do about this?" she asked, sitting back as she crossed her arms and waited for his answer.

Hix took a long, deep breath, gave himself a mental shake, and drug himself out of his self-imposed shame. "I know what they wrote isn't true," he answered, his voice coming out soft and low, "but you should see how the old ladies in the store and on the street look at me. They act like I'm some low-life, taking advantage of a poor, little orphan girl for my own gains."

"Friends know the truth," Sarah said with conviction, surprised her strong son could be so intimidated by all of this. "I repeat, Hix, what are you going to do about this?" she asked, not willing to let the question be buried or ignored.

"I have a few ideas," Hix said. "What I'd like to do is to start building a house for us, Abby and me," he said, glancing through his lashes for his mom's reaction to this before he continued. "I've been working on plans for a house for years, tweaking them to incorporate all the things I've liked in the houses I've worked on." His voice took on an excited tone as he continued. "There's a piece of land just outside of town that I could build on. It has some really pretty trees and the creek runs through the back of the property. The house would be perfect there and I can get the land cheap right now," Hix finished.

"What are you waiting for?" Sarah asked as she watched Hix talk about his future, regaining the gleam in his eyes as he did so. This was something close to his heart and important to him, she could see it all over him. And it was a good idea, with or without Abby. She knew that the house would be beautiful, that her son would pour all of himself into it.

"Should I talk to Abby before starting anything?" he asked, looking at his mother sitting beside him, giving him her unconditional support and unfailing advice.

"Why not get the land and the project started then make it a surprise for her." Sarah suggested. "It would be a very romantic gesture for any girl. You can make it very special if you just put a little thought into it," she smiled at her son. "Is it a question of money?" she asked, "Because if it is, I have a little saved up, and you could have it to get started if you need to."

Hix shook his head, "No," he said, amazed at the love and generosity of his mother. "I've saved up all the money I've earned doing odd jobs over the years, and have more than enough to buy the land and get a good loan for the rest." he said with more confidence returning to his voice.

Sarah sat quietly, watching as Hix rolled the idea over in his mind, puzzling it out, then coming to a decision.

"I'm going to call on the land as soon as I get home," he finally said out loud. He smiled at his mother, feeling much better having talked to her and having a direction for his future. Picking up her hand that was lying in her lap, Hix gave it a squeeze and kept it in his much larger, work hardened one.

"Thanks, mom," he said, his heart in his eyes. "You always make things better. I love you."

Sarah stroked the hair from his face with her free hand, letting it rest for just a moment along his cheek. The same cheek she had washed and kissed for all the years of his life. "You're a good man, Balthazar, don't ever forget that, or let anyone make you doubt it," she said, her eyes taking on a sheen from the pride she felt for her son and the depth of her feelings. "Now, it's time for me to get to bed, and you to go home and get some sleep." Sarah rose to her small height, feeling dwarfed by her son, as he too stood with her and walked towards the kitchen.

Hix shrugged on his coat, turning at the door to give his mother one last hug before he walked out into the night.

Sarah watched as he made his way to his truck, got in and, with a wave of his hand, drove out of sight. Closing the door, she leaned against it, finally letting the anger at the hurt her son had unnecessarily had to deal with come to the surface. She wanted to get her hands around the throat of the person responsible for his pain, and teach them a lesson they would not soon forget, about printing lies. That they had accused him of trying to get at Abby's money, was just stupid!

Thinking hard as she made her way into the bedroom, Sarah tried to come up with a way to help, without interfering and making the matter worse. "*What if she gave a statement to a reporter at the paper, without giving her name,*" she thought? She could tell them that she was a close friend of the pair, confirming that they were happy and that there was no question of Hix being after any money. It was a true love match. That was one option, but she was reluctant to do even that.

Maybe she should just let it ride, hoping the whole thing fizzled itself out when the next bit of scandal came along. "*Yeah, that's what she should do,*" she decided, but she didn't like that choice at all. It went against every motherly instinct she had, to let her son go through this and have his good name smeared by some shitty little, glory hungry rag reporter. She wanted the record set straight and she wanted it to happen now!

Sarah changed out of her clothes and washed her face with short angry motions, taking out her frustrations on her face until it was pink from her efforts. Staring at her reflection in the mirror, Sarah played out all the scenarios in her head, until she was dizzy from just thinking about the whole mess.

"Damn," the word slipped through her lips. With a shake of her head she blew out a breath, sending her lower lip outward in a huff of anger. This would not have happened if Hix had not met and fell for the beautiful model, Abby Mathews. Still, it was not fair to blame her for what was printed. And Hix was happier than she had ever seen him. Why couldn't he have just met a nice local girl and been just as happy?

Turning out the bathroom light she made her way into her bedroom and crawled under the covers. She fussed with the bedding until she was comfortable, then reached over to turn off the bedside lamp, leaving the room in a darkness that was only broken by dim rays from the street light down the block which managed to sneak in around the curtains pulled across the windows.

As her eyes began to close, a single thought snuck into her consciousness, making her sit straight up in bed. *Cathy Mathews!* Sarah knew without a doubt that Abby's mother was the leak to the press. She didn't know how she knew, but she did. This woman was the cause of her son's pain.

Sarah lay back against the pillows as a smile that was hard around the edges pulled at her lips. Cathy was a publicity whore that wanted to keep her daughter in the public eye. Little did she know that Sarah was a mother that would fight like a tiger to protect her own child. She would not allow this whack job to interfere with the happiness of her son and his love. How could she care so little for her own daughter? Sarah was sure she was right and wouldn't stand for interference, even if she was Abby's mother. She was stepping out of bounds and someone needed to reign her in before she did damage to Hix' and Abby's future that couldn't be repaired.

The longer Sarah knew Abby the more she respected her. She couldn't believe a mother could work so hard at making her child's life so miserable. It appeared that the only goal Cathy had was to create havoc in Abby's life. She should have been protecting her daughter from the trash in the rag publications, but instead she was apparently working overtime to create as much trash talk as she could. Didn't she realize this would just make Abby unhappy? Didn't she want her daughter's love and respect?

Now she was involving Hix in her crappy messes and Sarah wouldn't tolerate it. She had come to love Abby for her good heart and the happiness she brought to Hix's life. Cathy had no right to interfere in that happiness. Sarah could see that she would have to be the one to give Abby the love and protection she didn't get from this poor excuse of a mother. Sarah was willing to give them both the protection they deserved

Whoever said that hell hath no fury like a woman scorned, hadn't been up against a mother fighting for her child's happiness. As Sarah rolled onto her side and prepared, once again, to sleep, her final thought before closing her eyes was, "*hell had better clear a path because there was steamroller coming, and its name was MOM!*"

Chapter 24

The next week was a busy one for Hix. The spring-like weather had everyone wanting to get started on projects they had been waiting on all winter. His cell phone never seemed to quit ringing as he took orders for a bedroom addition for a new baby, a privacy fence around a new patio he would frame and pour, a new roof and siding on a renovation project, were among many calls he received. The list got bigger every day and would keep Hix busy for most of the summer.

He managed to save his evenings for Abby, sharing intimate dinners and cuddling on the sofa, as they continued to get to know each other. Hix found himself falling deeper and deeper in love with her, making it seem all the more urgent that he get the ball rolling on the purchase of the land he had his eye and heart set on for their dream home.

The price was going to be cheaper than he thought, as he and the owner had struck a deal. It was agreed that half of the purchase price would be bartered for work that needed to be done around the old farmer's barns and house. Hix had even agreed to fix some fences that needed repair. So, by the time the haggling had been completed, both parties figured they had gotten a good deal, signed on the dotted line, and the land now officially belonged to Hix.

Hix's next step was a trip to the local bank, where he had been doing business since he was a kid. He applied for a construction loan for the house he was itching to build. His good reputation and financial responsibility made this a breeze. Everything was falling into place. Hix couldn't wait to surprise Abby with his dream. He could only hope it would become hers too.

On Friday night Hix finished work and hurried home to shower and change, having made plans to break the news to Abby this very night. He had ordered a special picnic dinner from the local deli, and tucked a chilled bottle of champagne into the basket, along with two wine glasses, so they could celebrate after he presented her with his news. He dug a big, soft blanket out of his linen closet, for them to spread out on the ground where their house would stand.

Satisfied that he hadn't forgotten anything, Hix loaded everything into his pickup, and headed to get his girl. As he drove to Abby's house Hix glanced up at the clear blue sky and smiled. The weather had cooperated, going from winter to summer in just a few short weeks. This was nothing unusual when it came to the state of Nebraska. Spring and fall were two seasons that, if you blinked, you missed them. He whistled along with the radio and even sang with a couple of songs he knew the words to, as he drove with his window down enjoying the cool air.

Pulling up in front of Abby's place, he got out, and with a spring to his step, covered the short distance to her door in a few strides. He knocked on the door, which she opened before his knuckles had lifted from the wooden surface. He immediately grabbed Abby up in his arms and swung her around as he planted a hot kiss on her laughing mouth.

"What's got into you tonight?" she asked, giggling happily. "Since when did you revert back to knocking before you come in?"

"I'm not coming in," Hix replied, his own eyes dancing with secrets she could not yet understand. "You're coming out!"

Abby arched her lovely brows as she gazed into the now familiar eyes above her. "I am, am I?" she asked. "What are you up to?"

"Come with me," Hix pulled her towards him as he began backing down the walk. "I've got something special to tell you and to show you."

Unable to resist his plea and his smile, Abby dashed back in the door, grabbed a jacket and shut the door behind her as she gave herself over to the infectious joy of her lover. They hurried down the walk, hand in hand. Hix opened the door to the truck and gave Abby a hand up, before jogging around the vehicle, anxious to get to his destination.

Once inside the cab, Abby snuggled up next to Hix. They told each other about their days like a couple of old married people. Hix didn't think much about it when Abby told him she also had a surprise for him, but refused to tell him what it was. She wanted to wait until later in the evening, so as not to up spur or spoil his surprise.

Abby gazed out the window as they drove, watching the scenery change from small town neighborhoods to open fields. She wondered where they were going as they left the town behind and sped down the highway.

She didn't have long to wonder, when about five miles down the road, Hix turned on the blinker and steered the truck onto a rutted dirt road. Maybe road was a generous term. It was more like a path filled with washboards and holes that had Abby bouncing up and down in her seat before they finally came to a stop.

As far as Abby could tell they were in the middle of someone's pasture. As far as the eye could see there was nothing but tall grass, with the exception of two lonely trees in the distance to break the scenery. For the most part, the pasture appeared to be a straw colored yellow, as the grasses were just beginning to turn green and, to her way of thinking, nothing to write home to mother about.

Turning to Hix with a question in her eyes, Abby watched him as he got out and came around to open her door.

"Come on!" Hix said excitedly, as he grabbed her hand and walked with her out into the grass. They walked for about a hundred yards, before he stopped and stood looking out into the distance at something Abby could not see.

He slipped his arm around her shoulders and hugged her against his side for just a few seconds before turning to her. He placed his hands on her shoulders, letting them run up and down her arms, before grabbing her hands and holding them tight.

"Look around, Abby." Hix said. "What do you think?"

"About what?" Abby asked, as she let her eyes roam the flat plains in front of her, seeing nothing special that she should be focusing on.

Hix dropped her hands and moved to stand behind her, wrapping his arms around her and resting his cheek against hers. "This is ours, Abby," he said. "I bought this land to build a house for us on."

Abby was glad her back was to Hix, as her mouth fell open and her eyes grew round in disbelief. *Oh my god,* she thought, *this is way out in the boonies. No stores within walking distance, no places to eat and no neighbors.* Luckily she didn't have to answer, as Hix continued explaining to Abby how he had bought the land and was going to build them a home.

He went on to paint her a picture of his dream, their dream, with words. Abby could hear the pride and excitement in each word that he uttered. He was so happy, that it was a while before he became silent. He put his chin on the top of her head and squeezed her shoulders, asking her, "What do you think about the surprise?"

Abby took a few moments to collect her thoughts, trying to calm herself after the shock of Hix's surprise. Because she cared too much for Hix, and didn't want to put a damper on his dreams, she swallowed her doubts. After all, lots of rich and famous people had houses or, as they called them, estates in the country. So, she told herself, having Hix build a home for them out in the country could be a good thing.

Abby let out her breath and pasted a smile on her face, before she turned and put her arms around Hix's neck. "I think this is a wonderful idea," she said, pulling his head down so she could reach his lips and rest hers against his. "You've been busy, haven't you?" she said between the butterfly kisses she was raining over his face and neck.

Hix laughed into her neck, picking her off her feet and swinging her around in circles, happiness beaming from him for all to see. He felt larger than life at having achieved his dream and having someone special to share it with.

He let go of Abby and hurried back to the truck for the rest of his surprise. Abby stood alone on the spot watching as he lifted a picnic basket from the truck bed. He carried it back through the grass then spread a soft red plaid blanket at her feet. He set the picnic basket on the blanket and with Abby's help, spread out the food and poured the champagne into the two glasses he'd stashed in the basket. They settled onto the blanket, and enjoyed their first meal in their soon-to-be dining room.

Everything tasted better, the air smelled sweeter, and the wine went straight to his head, as Hix looked with the pride of ownership on the land around him. His land. No. Their land.

With his hunger sated, Hix turned to Abby, noticing how the setting sun created a glow around her. It made her look like a golden angel. He wanted to capture this moment for all time, to remember her sitting just as she was, relaxed, happy and his.

Reaching out his hand, Hix tucked a stray strand of her honey blonde hair behind her ear, and let his hand delve under the thick mass until he felt her neck. With a little pressure he drew her to him and lost himself in the sweetness of her kisses and the softness of her arms.

"Make love with me, Abby. Here, now, out in the open, under the stars. Just you and me here where our future will be," he said softly, his voice just above a whisper.

Caught up in the magic of the moment, Abby couldn't have denied Hix's desires any more than she could have denied herself the air she breathed.

The two lovers took their time taking off each other's clothes, exposing their eager flesh to the sunset, the moon rising and the first stars of the night and to waiting hands and mouths, before they came together as one and danced to a rhythm as old as time and as unique to them as each day's dawn.

She's the one, Hix thought, feeling that there could never be a more perfect moment if he lived to be 100.

He's the one, Abby thought, as they lay fused together, so close not even the breeze that rustled through the grass could worm its way between them.

Pulling Abby's head to rest on his damp shoulder, Hix stroked her hair over and over, loving the feel of the silken tresses as they passed through his fingers. As they lay there, gazing up at the clearness of the sky, Hix felt his heart overflow with the feelings of rightness, and he knew without a doubt that this was only the first of a life time of nights they would spend together in this special place. Looking up into the sea of stars above them, Hix placed Abby's hand over his heart, and with a voice barely louder than a whisper, yet carrying the power of thunder, Hix turned his world and Abby's upside down with one statement.

The words broke out of him, refusing to be held back any longer. "I love you, Abby. Oh god, I love you!"

Chapter 25

Abby was floored by the plans Hix was making for them. He had totally taken her by surprise with his announcement. Going over the evening in her mind, she realized she had mixed emotions about the whole thing. On one hand she had to admit they were exciting plans. Still, it seemed to her she'd had no input or say in their future. There would be a future, Abby was sure of that. After all, no one bought land and planned to build a house for you, with you, if they weren't planning to spend the rest of their life with you. Did they? Was this the way they proposed in Nebraska, large gestures instead of simple words?

This realization had Abby's heart beating fast and joy running through her veins, like a swollen stream after a summer rain, swift and boiling as it carried away her past and left only room for the future with Hix. She tucked away her doubts and let herself be carried away by Hix's enthusiasm, enjoying their picnic under the stars.

Mother Nature had cooperated by giving them a warm evening, clear skies and more stars than Abby had ever seen. The twinkling lights filled the sky as far as the eye could see. The awe of falling stars, as they streaked across the heavens, only lasting for a split second before taking their wonder with them, had Abby and Hix casting fervent wishes through closed eyes. Hix wishing with all his heart for everything to go as he planned, to make the future bright, and fill it full of love and joy. Abby wishing for success in her career and happiness for herself and Hix.

After casting her wish skyward, Abby turned her head and opened her eyes.

Hix lay on the blanket next to her, with nothing to cover him but the blanket of stars. Twining her fingers with his, Abby asked, "What did you wish for?"

Hix turned his head slowly toward her, until he was facing her, just inches from her own face. Abby was struck by how beautiful he was in the starlight. The shadows on his face left mystery and darkness vying with the dim starlight. In his eyes Abby could see all the way to his soul, feeling the goodness of him wash over her, surrounding her like a cocoon of dark velvet. Abby's breath caught in her throat and a rush of feelings passed through her body like a bolt of lightning, leaving her nerves tingling and raw, sensitive to the merest touch.

Hix's answer, so low and sweet, was that she make love with him under the night sky. Giving in willingly to his wish, Abby had no will to deny him what she knew would be a memory they would cherish throughout their lives. And she was right.

Hix took his time, drawing out every moment, every touch, until Abby thought she would fly apart to join the stars, as he guided her to the peak and joined her in the long slow slide back to reality. She lay snuggled close to his side as her breathing returned to normal, only to have it taken away as Hix declared his love for her in an achingly emotional voice.

Like a sponge she absorbed it all and gave it back to him. "I love you, too," she whispered, rising up on her elbow to lay her hand along his smooth, masculine cheek. She looked into his eyes and fell into the dark depths as she lowered her head to kiss his lips and drink her fill, like a bee drinking the sweet nectar from a spring flower. Each sip was more sweet and satisfying than the last. His kisses becoming her addiction of choice, his touches more necessary than the air she needed to live.

Abby and Hix lay naked atop the blanket. They were in no hurry to leave this place they had christened with their love, until the chill of the evening finally chased them back into their clothes.

With one last squeeze of Abby's shoulder, Hix reluctantly rose from the blanket and began gathering the remnants of their picnic, placing everything neatly inside the basket, and closing the lid. He held his hand out and pulled Abby to her full height, gathering her tightly against him. Hix stole one more heart-stopping kiss from her lips, before taking her hand and leading the way back to his pickup.

Stowing the basket and handing Abby inside, he walked around the front, taking his time, enjoying the whisper of the grasses against his jeans clad legs. They seemed to be whispering words of welcome with each pass his legs made through their masses. "*Welcome home*," they murmured. "*We'll be waiting for you to come back*."

Hix knew it was his imagination that heard the words of welcome, but he gathered them into his heart and held them there, letting them take root and flourish in the fertile ground of his wishes and desires.

Getting into the cab, Hix started the motor and made a wide loop back to the rutted road that lead back to the highway. Driving with one hand, he let his other find and hold Abby's slim fingers, keeping them connected as they made the short trip back to town. She sat close to him, her hair brushing his shoulder. Her scent filled his nostrils until he thought he would run off the road.

They pulled up in front of Abby's house and Hix turned off the motor, leaving a deep silence that drummed against their ears. They sat still, not wanting to move or disturb the moment. Each listening to their own and each other's hearts beating and the sound of breathing as they savored the memory of the evening.

Hix finally gave himself a slight shake and turned to Abby, his love. With the happenings of the evening, he just remembered she had said she had a surprise of her own, Hix apologized, "Sorry for taking up the whole evening with my plans." He raised his hand and gently brushed the hair from her cheek, "What about your surprise?"

Abby turned her head, looking into Hix's eyes. She was prepared to rock Hix's world for the second time that night. "I got a job in New York. It's big, huge in fact. I'll be modeling for a major designer when they present their new spring line to the major retailers. There'll be a photo shoot following the show with layouts in all the top fashion magazines, maybe even a cover or two! This is a dream come true, and I want you to come with me, baby," she said as she gripped his hand in her excitement. "The job will take about two weeks. Just think Hix, two weeks in New York together, seeing all the sights, dining at all the fine restaurants, enjoying the night life of the City. I want to show you my world. I can hardly wait!" she oozed the enthusiasm of a little girl with her first Barbie doll.

"That's great," Hix said, trying to swallow his lack of enthusiasm and the uneasy feeling that had taken a grip on his throat and his heart. He felt like someone was choking the life from his dreams at her words. "I can't possibly come with you, though, not now. Spring is the busiest season for contractors. I have months of work booked, people are depending on me. Besides, I need to get started on our house," he explained to a stricken Abby. Had she forgotten so soon that he was going to do the construction himself?

"Oh," Abby said, dropping her eyes to try to hide the disappointment she was feeling at Hix's refusal to accompany her. "Do you really need to work?" she asked. "I mean, I have been meaning to talk to you about that." She paused before she landed her second punch of the evening, "I have all the money we will ever need, and the money I'm earning in the next two weeks will more than pay for a company to come in and build our house," she told him, her voice gaining enthusiasm as she tried to find a way that they both could have what they wanted.

"You could supervise, or whatever, and get it just the way you want it." She looked questioningly at him as she continued, "I don't mean to sound like I'm bragging, but I have enough money to make all this happen. A lot of money." She paused, not able to see his shell-shocked face, before she finished. "There really is no need for you to be putting in all these long hours when we could travel and be together all the time. What do you say, baby, please?" she asked, as she landed her final blow for the knock-out.

At Hix's silence, Abby tried, with no luck, to read his expression in the dark cab, but all she could see were shadows as he remained still beside her. "Hix, what are you thinking?" she asked hesitantly. She was very aware of his silence.

Hix beat down the sharp retort that wanted to come out of his mouth. A retort that said he had no intention of being a kept man, or thought of as a sponge, just hanging onto Abby for her money.

The seconds ticked by, with neither one making a sound. Finally Hix felt he'd gotten himself under control enough to talk to Abby without blowing a gasket as he politely answered her.

"I thank you for the offer Abby," he said stiffly, "but I have always earned my own way. I don't know how to be any other way. I can earn my keep and make enough money to take care of myself and you too, believe it or not. I could pay for our house to be built, but that's not the point. I want to build it myself, to pour my labor and my love into something just for us," he said with passion in his voice. He paused before he continued in a more business-like voice, "That's not to say that you will not be able to help, with the work or the money that goes into building it, if you so choose. But it's going to have to be a fifty-fifty deal with us, or it's just not going to work."

It was Abby's turn to sit in silence. She could feel the blood creep up her neck and into her cheeks until they felt like they were on fire. She was thankful for the cover of darkness in the cab of the pickup, as she fought to control her disappointment. Her offer to share her success, money, and time with him had just been thrown back in her face. Crap, he acted like it was an insult, her generosity. *"Fine,"* she thought to herself, *"let him work himself to the bone."* She would NOT give up her life style or her job to stay in this small town, eventually drying up and dying of boredom.

"I did not mean to insult you, you know," she said quiet, but hard. "I have to go to New York. It's very important to me," she stated matter-of-factly. "So, I guess I'll call you when I get back and we can see where we stand," she said.

With that, she leaned over and kissed the cheek she had caressed so lovingly just a few hours before. "I've got to go in and pack," she said, feeling tears begin to sting her eyes at the stiffness of her lover beside her.

Hix let her go, watching as she hurried to exit the truck cab and made her way to the front door and entered without looking back. How had things gotten so off-track between them? Only an hour before they had confessed their love to each other, making plans for their future together.

With a lump the size of Texas in his throat, and the will of a junkie in dry-out, he let her go. He reluctantly pulled away from the curb and drove slowly as he made the drive to his home alone. Although it was a short distance to his house it seemed forever.

As he entered and gazed around the familiar surroundings, they felt empty and foreign to him. He closed the door at his back and leaned against it. He closed his eyes as he tipped his head back until it knocked hollowly against the wood of the door at his back. "*What happens now*?" he wondered.

Feeling helpless to do anything else, he came to the conclusion that he would give her the two weeks away to think, and he would do some thinking of his own. When she got back, maybe they would be able to sit down and talk like two reasonable adults. Hopefully the time apart would bring things back to normal between them. It had to, he was sure of it. They had just gotten started and he had no intention of giving up on them before they'd had a chance to see how far this thing between them could go. Every relationship has issues and they would work this out. At least that is what he told himself as he crawled into his cold bed alone.

Hix realized he was tired to the bone, feeling like a truck had just run over him, not once but twice. *"Love,"* he thought as he closed his eyes looking for sleep. "*What a pain in the ass.*"

Chapter 26

Saul stood beside the bed of his human. Even in sleep, a mar was visible on Hix's handsome brow. "*How had things gotten so messed up?*" he wondered. The relationship had been going along pretty much as planned. There had been a couple of times that Saul had had to direct the course of events as they began to stray from the path that was written, but nothing too serious, until now. Saul could see the work he had done begin to unravel.

He went over their last night in his mind, satisfied with the course of events right up until the end, when Abby had told Hix she was leaving for New York for a couple of weeks for a job and wanted him to go with her. Instead of Hix saying he had work to do and could not go this time, and Abby understanding, there had been hurt feelings and resentment on both their parts. They should have spent the days until Abby's departure together, with Hix driving her to the airport, and sending her off with sweet kisses and promises of each missing the other before she boarded. Instead they were now each in their own bed, anger and confusion coming between them.

Why had Hix become so angry and hurt that Abby thought he could just drop everything and follow her to New York? Why had Abby been so unfeeling of Hix's work, and brought up the fact she had more money than either of them could spend in this lifetime? It had unmanned Hix, and things had gone south from there. Still Saul could not figure out what had happened. It was as if there were outside influences at work.

Saul floated back and forth across Hix's bedroom and peered into his dreams. Saul was seeking answers to the situation. Hix was dreaming about Abby, but the dream was not a happy one, filled with thoughts of love as it should be when a couple is in love. Instead it was filled with anxiety and loneliness.

Not good, Saul decided. Not good at all. Once again stopping at the foot of the bed and watching Hix as he slept, Saul gave a sigh and mentally rolled up his sleeves. He figured he had two human weeks to work the kinks out of the mix so destiny could have its way when the couple reunited.

Before he faded away, Saul made up his mind to enlist some help in getting the situation back in order. It was time to bring in Jeannicca.

Chapter 27

Jeannicca also stood at the foot of the bed of her human, a smile on her face that was so beautiful it almost hurt to look at her. She was very pleased with the way things were going. It had taken only a little nudge from her to make Abby begin to have doubts about merging her life with Hix's. Hix was not good enough for Abby, Jeannicca had decided, and she needed to work fast and quiet to get the results she wanted and what she felt her human deserved.

Jeannicca looked down on the sleeping Abby, seeing the beauty and the potential for greatness that was hers for the taking. "*Poor stupid mortal,*" she thought, "*you do not need to have a construction worker from a small hick town in Nebraska hanging around your neck, dragging you down.*" Abby was capable of getting anything and anyone she wanted. Jeannicca had made it her job to make sure Abby realized what she would be giving up if she continued on the path she was taking.

So far Jennicca had been able to stay out of Saul's way. She had remained undetected as she worked the situation to her advantage. She had even gone so far as to nudge Hix towards feelings of reluctance and commitment issues, but Saul had been there to get Hix back on track with his feelings for Abby with every attempt at interference she had tried so far. Not to worry. She had never been one to give up easily and now was not the time to start.

Jennicca bent over the bed, almost nose to nose with her mortal, as she peered into the dreams that were taking place behind Abby's beautiful closed eyelids. Abby's dreams were filled with loneliness and hopes for a tearful reunion with Hix when she returned from New York.

"I don't think so," the Guardian thought. With little effort, she replaced the dream with one of glamour and excitement where Abby was a high-paid model in New York. In the dream, Abby was sought after by all the right people, fawned over and admired everywhere she went. She had little trouble getting everything she wanted in life, just by snapping her fingers.

"Now that was a dream," Jeannicca thought as she stood erect and dusted her hands together in appreciation of a deed well done. So far she had bested Saul without him even suspecting. But she was pretty sure that the time when the gloves would come off and they would fight to see who would have the final say in destiny's plan for their charges would come.

Jeannicca didn't like to lose. The word wasn't even in her vocabulary, and she was prepared to use everything in her arsenal to get her way. She was going to be the one on top this time. Everyone in their realm would know it was she that had bested the mighty Saul.

The lovely smile of before, was replaced with a sneer, and she was not so beautiful anymore. Her softness of before had been replaced with a sinister demeanor, and anyone would have been smart to steer clear of her.

"It's my turn to shine," Jeannicca thought as she began to fade out.*" It's my turn, and Saul better not try to stop me!"*

Chapter 28

Abby awoke with a start! There was no drifting slowly up from the deep, dark pillows of sleep. Not this time. This time she jerked awake with a feeling that someone was watching her. Something was not right.

Memories came back in a rush, as she remembered her parting with Hix the night before. Her heart pinched, and she allowed one little mewling sound to sneek out before she covered her mouth and hung her head. "*Were they over?*" she wondered.

Abby didn't know what she felt or wanted at this point. She had told Hix, only last night, that she loved him. Now here she was, as dawn made its way into her room, her arms empty and her heart heavy. Or was that really what she was feeling?

In one corner of her mind she felt relief at not having the burden of a man in her life. She didn't have to worry about making breakfast, doing the washing, cooking or anything else having a partner entailed. If she decided not to take a bath today no one would be here to see her hair spiked up from sleep, smell her bad morning breath, or want her to get up if she didn't want to. That's what her mind was telling her, but her heart was sending a different message that she could not ignore.

It wept for the feel of his arms around her, and his heat surrounding her under the pile of soft blankets. It wanted his soft kisses that told her she was special to him. It ached for his hands on her body, bringing her to full wakefulness, as only he could. That's what her heart wanted. But then her mind butted in and told her to get her head out of the clouds and get her ass moving, before she missed her plane.

She had packed last night, trying to burn off some of the extra energy she had been left with in the wake of her hurt and anger. All she had to do was shower, dress, and walk out the door.

Abby flipped the blankets over and climbed out of her bed, feeling like she was at least thirty years old. Almost ready for a walker! Picking up the clothes that she had laid out last night, Abby made her way into the shower. She took her time soaping, washing, conditioning, and shaving, until her head was clear and she felt more like herself again. She was now ready for a new adventure!

She stood naked in front of the mirror, wiping the sweat from the glass that her hot shower had conjured. As she brought herself into focus, she looked at herself from head to where the counter cut her off from sight. She was pleased with the reflection staring back at her. She was as close to perfect as she could be. Never having had the urge to do such an examination before, her actions kind of surprised her. It had her shaking her head in puzzlement. She certainly wasn't herself today.

Walking back into her bedroom, she drug on her clothes, casual for her flight. She made her bed so everything was in order for her return. She looked at the clock, finding she still had an hour before she had to leave. She turned on the TV for noise and distraction. Flipping through the channels, her finger froze when she saw a picture of herself and Hix together. *"Ignore it,"* she told herself, but as if her hand had a mind of its own, the volume was turned up until the reporter's sultry female voice filled every nook and cranny of her home.

"In the small town of Winston, Nebraska, not everything seems to be peachy as we can see in this picture of beauty Abby Mathews and her hunk of a guy, Balthazar Hix as they walk down a street in the small town. No holding hands and no kissing that we are used to seeing from the couple. Instead Hix seems to be focusing on a dark haired beauty coming out of a gas station on his right. Well, well, maybe the golden Abby has some competition for Hix's attention. One golden and fair, the other dark and mysterious. Which one will Hix choose? Stay tuned and see," she said, smiling cattily.

Abby rolled her eyes at the TV as she recognized her best friend Kendall coming out of her store. She remembered the day well. They had been out walking the town when they had run into Kendall, and stopped for a chat before going on their way. "*As if Kendall was any competition or even wanted Hix*," Abby thought. Just another twisted version of the truth from the news hungry press. "*Wasn't there any place on this earth that they couldn't get to? No privacy?*" Abby wondered.

Abby clicked off the set and flung down the remote, deciding she would rather wait at the airport than sit around in her empty apartment, alone and thinking. Grabbing her bags and purse, she hit the door before she could change her mind. Loading her car and heading out, Abby rolled down the window and let the fresh warm air comb her hair, lifting it off her neck and sending it in a wild dance around her face as she put miles between her and the town that held her heart's desire.

Maybe she should make a quick stop at Hix's place and see if they could repair the rift that had sprung up last night between the two of them.

"Don't look back," a voice in her head said. "*Keep going. It will do him good to wonder about you while you are in New York.*"

Abby's hands tightened around the steering wheel and she lowered her foot on the gas pedal without even meaning to. The engine growled as it picked up speed, and she shot down the road, leaving the town of Winston just a speck in her rearview mirror.

The airport was in the next town, some forty miles away, but it didn't take long to cover the distance. As Abby parked her car, she was surprised to find herself already at her destination. She didn't remember getting there. She'd been consumed by the war going on between her heart and her head. She felt tired from being pulled in two directions at once.

Peeling her hands from around the wheel, she turned the engine off and sat for just a second in the dead silence of the parking structure. "*Might as well get this over with*," she said to herself, as she opened the door and got out. She hauled her bags to the curb, and then made the trip inside the small terminal to check her luggage and wait for her flight.

She grabbed a diet pop and a book that was supposed to be the hottest one at the moment. She lowered herself into a hard chair, where she waited impatiently for the call to board her plane.

She passed the time with the book on her lap, not understanding the words she read, just passing time. The call finally came to board, and Abby snapped her book closed, grabbed her purse and drink, and got in line to board her flight.

She made it past the heavily made up flight attendant and walked down the long lonely tunnel to her escape. Locating her seat, she plopped down. Having been the first to board, she knew there would be a short wait. Abby passed the time looking out the window at the activity going on under her plane. The shuddering of the plane's cabin finally brought her back to reality. She sat patiently listening as the captain announced over the speaker system that take off was but a moment away.

Abby always loved watching the ground fly by as the wheels gathered speed and the craft became a bullet rocketing off into the vast beyond. A small smile played around her lovely mouth as the ground became a blur, and she was pressed against her seat with the force of takeoff.

Abby was on her way to the big city. She was silently hoping that she would be busy enough to have no time to brood about her personal life. She wanted a break. No, she needed a break. She would take this time to relax and pull things back into perspective. That sounded good to her.

Abby settled into her seat and placed a pair of earphones over her delicate ears, focusing on the movie just starting on the screen in front of her. She had no way of knowing that a lone figure was standing, with legs braced and hands pressed against the terminal window, watching the plane as it lifted off the ground.

She did not hear the deep male voice calling her name as if to bring her back by sheer will alone. She did not see the anguish burning in the tired eyes of her lover as he broke apart with her leaving, feeling as if a major part of his soul was being ripped out and left wondering if it was ever coming back. She did not know that he watched until the dark dot in the sky, that was her plane, disappeared from sight and then lowered his forehead until it rested on the cool glass.

"Two weeks," Hix thought, feeling the time stretch out in front of him. Fourteen days, 336 hours without her. He could make it, couldn't he? After that, and not a second more, he would move heaven and hell to get to her and bring her back.

"You have two weeks," he murmured, raising his eyes to the spot where his love had disappeared from his sight. "*Come back to me Abby,*" he sent a silent plea to her, heart connecting to heart." *I'll be waiting.*"

Chapter 29

Hix stood with his head against the cool glass as he watched Abby's plane fade from sight. He had waited too long to get to the airport. His stupid pride hadn't let him leave sooner, as he argued back and forth with himself. He'd told himself that it was she who was being unreasonable. Couldn't she see how it would look and how he would feel, being kept by her, living off of her money, not working as he had all his life? He had told himself that if he just waited, she would come to him, and they would make things right before she left for New York.

As Hix waited at his home to hear from Abby before she left for New York, the minutes ticked slowly by. It seemed time went on forever. He finally realized that he was the one that would have to make the first move. He had jumped into his truck and set the wheels on fire, flying down the highway trying to make it to the airport before she boarded a plane that would take her out of his life. He screeched to a stop in front of the airport terminal and, leaving his truck half-way up the curb, ran through the terminal like O. J. Simpson, only to find he was just minutes too late.

He'd wanted to take her in his arms and kiss her senseless, until she promised to come back to him, to miss him until she did, and to say again that she loved him. He'd wanted to tell her that she took his heart with her and that he would not be complete until she returned. Too late! Too late to say any of it, and to show her he was in love with her for always.

Hix hated that he stood there with his heart breaking, his knees shaking and his gutt rolling with fear, but he couldn't move. He was sure he would still be here, in this very spot when Abby came back, not having been able to move until she was back by his side.

"Since when have I turned into such a whipped man?" he wondered. *"Is this what love does to a man?"* He fought against the pain and the hurt, but it was a losing battle. He had been caught and held fast by the love he felt for Abby, and there wasn't anything he could do about it.

As he stood by the window, Hix felt a warm sensation start at his shoulder, work its way into his back, then continue through the rest of his body until he began to relax. He could feel some of the pain and fear melting away under the warming tide. He braced his hands and pushed back from the window, and as he did he thought he caught a flash of light off to his right in the glass. In the blink of an eye it was gone, leaving Hix to wonder what it was, if anything at all.

Hix squared his shoulders and, turning with intent, walked out of the terminal.

"I'll be okay," he kept telling himself. He knew, without knowing how, that he was right.

He would keep busy for the next two weeks, working until he dropped each night, too tired to dream. She would call him, he would call her, and they would talk things out.

They would make up, and not come up for air for a week when she returned.

"She will return," he thought positively. "She will come back and we will be stronger for this time apart."

Hix made his way back to his truck, and heaved himself inside. He scrubbed a hand over his face before turning the ignition and pointing the truck towards home.

"Not yet," a voice in his head said, "*you need to make a stop before leaving town.*"

"A stop?" Hix wondered. What the hell was he thinking? Talking to himself? Hearing voices in his head? First he had turned into a weenie, and now he was nuts. "*Great!"* he sneered to himself in disgust. *"Let's just sit here and have a break down, why don't we!"*

"Not yet," the voice in his head repeated.

"Why not?" Hix asked himself.

"There is an errand you have to do first. Turn here," the voice said, "*left, now*."

Hix obeyed without thinking twice, and it was only after he had parked his truck and looked around, that he realized where he was. "*Oh hell*," he thought "*I'm not ready for this yet.*" He reached out his hand to turn the key, but stopped a mere inch from his goal.

"We are just looking," the voice said. "*You've thought about this before,"* it continued. "*It won't hurt to just look. It will help pass the time. You do not want to go home yet anyhow, do you?"* the voice nagged at him.

"If it will get you to shut up, then I guess I can spare a few minutes of my life," Hix muttered to the unseen voice.

He got out of his truck, reluctantly, and walked with dragging steps to the door of the shop. He hesitated a moment, before he felt what seemed like a shove from behind, propelling him forward, as he stumbled through the door.

The overhead bell tinkled merrily as he entered, and only stopped when he let the door slide shut behind him.

"May I help you?" a soft female voice asked, causing Hix to jerk in surprise.

"Uh, no," he stuttered, "I'm just looking. Well not really even looking." he babbled senselessly. "I just stopped in for a quick peek around."

"Talk about feeling like a bull in a china shop," Hix thought as he focused his attention on the glass cases lining the four walls of the shop. He felt as if he was holding his breath as he made a quick tour of the square, not really even looking at the twinkling gems in the cases then, finally coming to stand on the other side of the door. He panted, as if he had just run a race. Sweat was running like ants down his back, and he wanted to twitch his shoulders to make the creepy feeling go away.

The young red head that had spoken to him upon entering stood silently by, watching him make a half-running circuit of the room, before stopping at the door. She didn't need to be a mind-reader to figure out what this good looking man was here for. She knew, beyond a doubt, that this was not really where he wanted to be. The way he was acting, told her she was going to have to help him along if he was ever going to be able to move from the spot he now seemed rooted to.

"Are you looking for a gift?" she asked, trying to draw the man out, and help him relax.

"No," came a choked reply.

When nothing else came from the delicious mouth, Lacey, as her name tag read, took pity on the guy and nodded her head as she accepted the role of the leader in this twosome.

"My name is Lacey," she said, and held out her hand, waiting patiently for Hix to take it.

Swallowing over the lump in his throat, Hix finally got out his name and shook the hand presented to him.

"Come with me," Lacey said, and led the way to a chair in the corner of the room towards the back. "Have a seat," she said, pointing to the comfortable looking chair. Going behind the counter, she busied herself, removing a black velvet cloth and placing it with care on the counter between herself and Hix. Looking into the scared eyes across from her, she reached under the counter and selected three breathtakingly beautiful diamond rings, which she laid upon the black velvet cloth. The contrast between the sparkling white gems and the jet black cloth was enough to take a man's breath away, at least apparently Hix's, as he sucked in air at the sight before him.

She let the silence stretch out as she watched Hix's eyes grow to the size of saucers. Lacey smiled as she realized he seemed to be holding his breath, again.

"Is this what you came in to look at?" she asked, taking pity on the scared male across from her, not making him voice what he obviously couldn't get past the lump that had grown in his throat when he entered the door of the shop.

"I don't know," he choked out, "I think so. How did you know?" he asked, his eyes flashing up to meet hers, as a small giggle escaped her tightly compressed lips.

"If I may say so, Hix," she said, her bright green eyes dancing with mirth, "if you get any whiter you will be able to pass as a ghost." At her comment, his skin changed from a deathly pale color to a bright red.

Lacey placed her hand over his and patted it like a mother would a small child. "It's been my experience that when a guy walks in here alone, scared to death, this is the cause. Have you asked her yet?" she wanted to know.

"No. No I just stopped in on a whim," he replied. "A*nd because the little voice in my head told me to,"* he thought to himself.

"If you're just shopping around on your own for now, relax," she said. "There's no pressure, no dead line, and no one will be the wiser if you change your mind about popping the question."

Hix felt his shoulders sag in relief. What she said made sense, and with the pressure off his shoulders he was able to breathe again. This didn't mean anything he told himself. There was no harm in just looking for possible future reference.

Hix gave Lacey the first real smile since walking in the door, and she almost had to wipe her chin. *"Judas priest on a pony, he was hot!"* she thought to herself, and it was her turn to swallow over a lump in her throat.

Hix spent the next fifteen minutes asking questions about the different types of rings available. He was pretty sure he'd need to build a couple more houses to afford a ring that would appeal to a girl like Abby.

When he got up to leave, he shook her hand again, this time meaning it when he told her, "Thank you," and walked out the door.

Lacey felt her hand tingle where he'd touched her skin, and closing her fist around the feeling, held it up to her chest. She stood in the front window and watched Hix get in his truck and drive away, giving her a small wave as he did. After he was out of sight, she moved to the small office in the back of the store, rummaged around in her desk drawers until she found the paper she was looking for. It was one of those tabloid rags that stared at you as you waited in the checkout line of the supermarket.

Lacey thumbed to the back of the paper and placed her red-polished fingernail over it. She picked up the phone from the desk and dialed the number. As she waited for her connection, she sat back and crossed her feet on top of the desk. She didn't have long to wait, as a voice came on the line and asked the nature of her business.

"I want to talk to one of your reporters," she said, looking at her nails as she did. "I've got a juicy tip for you, what you guys call a scoop. So put someone big on the line, someone with clout, and get ready to say thank you with lots of zeros."

Chapter 30

Hix drove at a more sedate speed as he headed for home alone, or so he thought. He had no idea that he had a passenger sitting right beside him, one that he could not see, but who was there none the less.

Saul rode easy in the seat, enjoying the wind coming in through the open window beside his human charge. It had been a long day for him. First, trying to get Hix to go after Abby then taking away some of the pain and loneliness that had swamped this man, and finally getting him to stop and look at jewelry as he considered the future he wanted with his love.

It had seemed harder than it should have been to Saul. As the miles flew by, the Guardian tried to puzzle out the mystery of the reluctance and stubbornness of his mortal. Something nagged at the edge of his brain, seeming to be just beyond his comprehension. He needed a more quiet and still place to ponder the situation, but he stayed where he was until Hix pulled into his driveway and killed the motor.

Saul sat with Hix as the stillness closed in around them, and waited, still, until Hix drew in a deep breath, and finally made a move to get out of the truck. Wanting to make sure things would be alright until he returned, and that Hix got a good night sleep, Saul floated, unseen, behind Hix. Saul kept an eye on him as he let himself into his house. Saul stayed with Hix for the rest of the day until he was in bed, the lights out, and his breathing became slow and deep, before he was satisfied that he was not needed for the moment. Giving one gentle push, Saul formed the dreams that filled Hix's sleeping head. Thoughts of the home he was going to build, and the great satisfaction that would be gained by making his plans become reality. No unhappiness was allowed in.

Satisfied, Saul prepared to leave. "Sleep well," he said to an unhearing and unaware Hix. "Tomorrow will be different. You'll be one day closer to your goal."

Saul began to fade away. As he did he sent out feelers trying to locate Jeannicca. "There you are," he said to no one, "I think it's time we talked."

With that he left Hix in the sweet arms of slumber. He had a meeting to go to and the way things had gone today, he was late.

Chapter 31

Jeannicca hung around the jewelry shop until the twit had done everything the young Guardian had asked of her. "*It really was so simple to manipulate these humans,*" she thought, amused as she glided around the cases looking at the shiny baubles they held. If she wore these trinkets, which she didn't, she might have thought some of them quite beautiful. They sparkled and shone brighter than any star in the night sky. They made colors dance on the walls with the movement of the wearer, and people even killed for them. "*How strange,*" the beautiful being thought. Humans fought and killed over things that didn't matter, and yet didn't over things that did. "*What a backwards race,*" she mused.

Even with all of the help the Guardians gave, they could not direct the course of destiny. Man still stumbled his way through, often making a mess of things, when only a gentle nudge in the right direction by a Guardian could have brought peace and harmony to an otherwise chaotic world. But then again, what fun would that be for the Guardians or the humans? A little chaos once in a while kept the blood flowing and the adrenalin high.

Jeannicca was quite pleased with her day's work. She had gotten Abby on a plane heading away from Hix. She had been able to make Hix reluctant to think of a future with Abby, and she had gotten Lacey to twist the truth of Hix's window shopping to the press. That ought to embarrass and anger Abby further, adding strain to their budding relationship. A few more tweaks and things should fall apart quickly, leaving their futures a blank slate for her to rewrite.

"Good job," she told herself, getting ready to check in on her charge.

As she began to fade out, Jeannicca was stopped by a tingle she felt in her head. Saul was trying to contact her. So she paused, deciding what to do. Should she ignore his summons or answer and see what he wanted, as if she didn't already know. Saul was no dummy. He was probably very aware that something was off with their two humans.

Shrugging her winged shoulders, Jeannicca decided to meet with the mighty Saul, and see if she could fool him a little longer into thinking they were working together to bring about the changes needed to fulfill what destiny had written. "After all" she thought, smiling to herself, "humans were not the only ones that she could make dance to her tune."

Closing her eyes, she sent her thoughts to her opponent in this game of chess. "I am here Saul. What can I do for you?"

"We must meet," Saul replied in her head.

"Yes, okay. I was just going to look in on my charges. So I will meet you at the Window to the World, shortly." she replied.

"Very well, thank you Jeannicca," came Saul's answer.

Jeannicca broke the connection, opened her eyes and allowed one small, sly smile to curve her lovely mouth before arranging her face into a mask of serenity mixed with curiosity. If she were human she would have been an actress, playing a part came easy to her and she had been doing it forever.

Taking one moment to run her hands through her hair, arrange the folds of her clothing and fluff her awe inspiring wings, she felt ready to face anything. Counting to ten, a trick she learned from the humans, she made Saul wait for just a little longer. After all, she rationalized, all is fair in love and war. Love for the humans and war for her and Saul.

Chapter 32

Jeannicca finally appeared at the Window to the World. As she stood behind the great and awe-inspiring Saul, she took a moment to study this Guardian that had proved himself one of the best, trying, as she often did, to figure out why that was.

He was tall in form, as well as presence, radiating power from every part of his being. Was it this aura that made him successful with his charges? Was it his compassion that one could see shining from those dark and lovely eyes? Or was it just that he cared, more than the other Immortals, what happened to his human charges?

"Nonsense," Jeannicca thought, "*I am as good as he is or ever will be.*" The only difference was that she liked to bend the rules, tweaking the path of destiny until it bowed, but did not break. She saw no harm in getting the best for her humans and, in turn for herself. After all, if they did well, she looked good. And she liked looking good. Receiving praise from her peers was what she was all about, what she existed for.

Now she found herself working alongside Saul, her rival, to guide two humans along life's path. It wasn't surprising that she found herself at odds with the great being before her. Saul wanted things to go the way they were written, she wanted better and more for her charge.

"How long," she wondered chewing on her lower lip, *"could she pull the wool over Saul's eyes, keep his attention elsewhere until she had gotten her way?"*

"Are you going to join me, Jeannicca?" Saul asked, mild irritation riding the edge of his deep voice. "Or are you going to continue to stand behind me staring or should I say plotting?"

"Whatever do you mean, Saul?" Jeannicca asked, all innocent and sweet. "I've just now arrived to meet with you, as you asked."

Saul turned to the other Immortal, impaling her where she stood with his dark gaze. "I know what you have been up to. Do not take me for a fool!" he growled, the words coming from deep within his chest. "Once again, you have been working against destiny, trying to break apart the two humans we were assigned to guide. I know this," Saul continued, not letting her speak, "because I have felt your interference. All the while I have not wanted to believe the facts that have been right before my blinded eyes. I have given you every chance to prove me wrong," he continued, "but the incident in the jewelry shop was more than I could ignore."

Seeing disbelief and denial in her expression, Saul stopped her before she could speak. "I stayed behind to watch what you did, or should I say, made the shop girl do, before I left." Jeannicca closed her lips and let him finish. "You will not be allowed to continue as Abby's Guardian. Effective immediately, I have been given the task of guiding both mortals until they have fulfilled their lives' paths. You are no longer needed here," he said, turning his back on the stunned immortal behind him.

"You can't do this," Jeannicca finally ground out. "You have no power to strip me of my charge," she said, her cheeks flaming red and her sea green eyes now black with anger.

"I do, and I have," Saul said, still not facing the anger he could feel rolling off her in waves at his back. "I have spoken to the Fates, and they agree with me. You will not be allowed to interfere with their plan any longer. As of this moment, they are reviewing your past performance in other cases, and will make a decision as to what you will be allowed to do in the future. It is out of our hands."

Jeannicca ground her teeth together and curled her hands into fists as she fought against the impotence she now felt. Her mind whirled faster than a tornado let loose to ride the flat plains, as she tried to decide how to handle this change of events.

She could play dumb and deny all knowledge of what Saul was talking about. *"No, that would not work,"* she quickly decided. He would ferret out her lie and be even angrier than he was now.

She could say that she had no idea her actions would cause problems or that she was innocent of deliberately trying to change destiny. Saul would not believe this, knowing she had been guiding humans almost as long as he had and that she would be aware of what was allowed and what was not.

Tossing her beautiful head, she decided that the only way to approach Saul was head on, admitting what she had done and explaining why she had done it. Surely he would be able to see reason and take back the complaint he had made to the Fates about her behavior.

Moving to stand in front of the great Immortal, she looked into his eyes with strength and determination.

"Yes," she said, her voice strong and sure, "I played with the destiny that was written for my charge. I want her to have the best life she could ever want. I want her to be happy and I don't believe Hix is the answer to her future. He does nothing for her, and will only cause her pain if they stay together. Is that so wrong?" she asked, daring Saul to disagree with her.

"It is not for you, or I, to decide what happens to the humans," Saul pointed out, not falling in with Jeannicca and her schemes as she hoped. "Have you forgotten our role as Guardians? Have you EVER followed the rules?"

"Rules are made to be broken!" she fired back at him. "Do what you will to me," she said, turning to show her back to the mighty Saul as he had done to her. "I will not feel sorry or apologize for my actions in the past, now, or in the future."

"I will be taking over the direction of both human lives from now on," Saul said. "You are to wait here until summoned."

Jeannicca only shrugged her shoulders and, with a flick of her fine head, tossed only one word in Saul's direction.

"Fine!" she snapped, and no more.

Saul let a small sigh escape his lips, feeling regret at the way things had turned out. Jeannicca had once been good, and it was a shame and a blow to all Immortals that one of their own would be punished.

Nodding his head with finality, Saul began to fade from her side. He now had to see if he could undo the damage caused by the unrepentant Immortal.

"Good luck," he said to the female Guardian, "I hope to see you again." With these final words he was gone.

Jeannicca felt a sense of emptiness when he was gone, but would not allow the feelings to show. She would hold her head up and take what was given to her with calmness and dignity. They could do what they wanted but she would have the last say, the last laugh, for she had a secret. A secret that only she knew.

"Not for long," she thought as she swayed to a tune playing in her head. *"Not a secret for long."*

Chapter 33

The two weeks it had taken to complete the photo shoot were almost up, and Abby wondered where the time had gone. It seemed like only yesterday that she had departed on a plane, leaving behind the rolling plains of Nebraska, and stepped into the high fashion glamour and glitz of the New York fashion scene.

The attention started as soon as Abby's feet had hit the airport terminal, where a driver with a sign bearing her name was waiting for her. She'd been escorted to a limo and settled into the soft luxurious leather interior, relaxing as she left the driving in the congested city to an expert. She rested her head against the seat and in no time at all she found herself stepping out in front of a luxurious hotel, her bags being whisked up to a suite that had been reserved just for her.

The suite was huge, with a hint of understated elegance. Colorful pillows were decoratively tossed on the butter-soft, cream-colored sofa, while an overstuffed chair welcomed her like a big hug, waiting to embrace her within its arms. She could picture herself sitting there with the new bestseller she'd tucked into her luggage, relaxing with a steaming cup of cappuccino after a long shoot. There was a large bouquet of fresh flowers in the center of the glass coffee table, filling the suite with their color and delicious fragrance. The room had a fireplace and a flat screen TV.

Abby felt at home as she moved through the suite with ease. She made her way through a set of French doors which opened into the suite's bedroom. In the center of the room was a huge bed with an overstuffed comforter and pillows sitting atop the mattress. Abby allowed herself a moment to sit on the edge of the bed, bouncing up and down a couple of times as she tested the mattress, before she lay back and allowed herself to relax into the plush bedding. It wasn't frilly, just luxurious and welcoming.

Looking around the room as she lay there, she saw a chaise lounge in one corner by a large window and a flat screen TV over the dresser opposite the bed. She picked up the remote from the nightstand beside the bed, and noticed a button marked draperies. She pushed the button and watched as the draperies on the wall behind the bed opened to reveal a breathtaking view of Central Park. Abby smiled in delight at this discovery.

Abby got up from the bed and moved toward the door which opened into the suite's bathroom, complete with a spa tub for guests that liked a long soak in a bubble bath. There were multiple jets on all the walls of the shower for those who preferred a standing massage. An array of soaps and lotions sat atop the marble vanity and a thick, plush robe hung on a hook on the back of the bathroom door.

Abby caught her image in the mirror as she looked about the room. A hint of sadness touched her eyes as she wondered to herself what Hix's reaction to a place like this would have been. But before she could feel sad and start missing him, the phone rang with the first of many invitations.

She'd been able to get away with declining that first night, claiming jet lag, opting to enjoy a light dinner in her room, a hot bath, and a heavenly night's sleep in the big bed. After that, no excuse she could think up saved her from the dinners, parties and outings her co-workers had planned while she was in town. She knew what to expect.

Her days were filled with long hours of costume and make-up changes, as she posed in some of the most glamorous clothes she'd ever seen. They all seemed to be made for her and the camera loved her.

It was hard work for Abby, as she went from getting blown around by wind machines in the studio, to freezing her butt off on the beach and in the surf that had not yet warmed to match the spring temps. Every day her face was made up and her body dressed to ooze sex and desire.

Abby did her part as she pimped the line of clothing and cosmetics that some well-known actress was launching. "Wear this, and you can look like me! Get any man or woman you want, and be rich and famous!" was the line they were selling. "*Just by buying this crap*," Abby thought to herself.

At first she had loved the attention she received, especially by the actress. But as always, it began to wear on her and by the end of the shoot she was tired and just wanted to go home. GO Home to Hix!

They had spoken on the phone almost every day she'd been in New York, and seemed to be on the right track again. Hix told her he loved and missed her, and she in turn let him know that she loved him, and wanted to be in his arms instead of half way across the country in a strange hotel room. Each call had brought them closer together, missing each other more, not wanting to hang up and face their big beds alone at night.

Abby's dreams, each night, were filled with scenarios of their reunion. The moment when the two of them would see each other and race into waiting arms, exchanging kisses that were hot and urgent. Their bodies pressed tightly together, and their patience thin with staring eyes and the lack of privacy. Hearts racing, matching their hurried steps, they would flee to a more intimate setting to be together and end the forced celibacy the distance had caused. Each morning she had opened her eyes, frustrated to realize it was only a dream, and she was still time and distance away from her lover.

This morning was no different, except it brought her one day closer to living her dream. One more day to get through, one more night to endure, and she would feel Hix's strong arms around her for real. Anticipation curled in her belly and made her hands shake slightly this morning as she showered, taking a moment to let her hands run over her body where she wanted Hix's to be.

Slick and soapy, they made her skin tingle as she closed her eyes half-way and remembered the feel of the work roughened grip and glide that was unique to Hix. Leaning her head against the wall she almost moaned in frustration, wanting Hix with her, now. She was not sure what she had done to anger the Gods, to be punished this way, but punishment it was, torture for sure.

She rinsed off, then reached up and turned off the jets of hot water. Getting out of the steamy shower, she toweled off, and prepared for her last day of work.

She was to be "dressed to the nines" today, in an array of evening gowns from all the top designers as she was photographed applying expensive perfume to her lovely throat and behind a jewel bedazzled earlobe. Any girl would feel like Cinderella, but Abby just wanted the day to be over.

Pasting on a smile, she greeted the young woman who would apply the evening make up at 9 a.m. in the morning, and the one who would dress her in the gowns, shimmering on a rack in the order they would be worn. Both women found their jobs made easy by Abby's natural beauty. She needed no extra work to cover flaws for the camera, and the clothes hugged her perfect body like a second skin, needing no pins or tape to make them fit.

An hour later, Abby emerged from her dressing room with her hair a silken fall down her back. A long black dress swept the floor as she walked. The deep V neckline open to her waist, revealed tantalizing glimpses of soft rounded breasts with each step taken. The workers on the set stopped their conversations as she walked past, taking a moment to appreciate the stunning woman in their midst.

This particular set would have her posing on a dark balcony, with city lights shining off in the distance. Her hair would be gently blowing back from her face, which would hold a look of hot passion, her eyes dark promises, as she waited for her man to join her. The breeze would mold the dress to her body, and the overall look would make men drool and women want to be her. They would want the romance and love she was waiting for.

Abby knew all she had to do was conjure up Hix in her mind, and she would do her part, achieve the perfect look of wanting, waiting, and passion. Abby moved to take her place on the set and, as she did, she heard a voice from her past.

"Hello, Abby," a familiar male voice said. A dark head came out from behind the lights that had been set up, and Abby recognized the hottest photographer in the business walking towards her.

Max Swift had been on a few of Abby's previous jobs, and a mild flirtation had developed between the two of them. Max had made it clear that he wanted more, but Abby had not been interested, holding him at arm's length. Working with Max was not a problem for Abby. She was sure Max would make the final product so tempting that everyone would want some. She looked good, but Max would make her stunning.

"Hi, Max," Abby replied back, a smile on her face. "Nice to see you again."

The two clasped hands as Max did a full body check and gave a low whistle of appreciation. "You look good!" he said, nodding his head in appreciation. A mischievous smile lit his face as he released her hand and asked, "You ready?" He picked up the first of many cameras he would use during the day and stepped back a few steps, bringing the camera to his eye.

"Sure." she said with confidence, "Let's do this."

The day flew by, with Abby changing clothes every hour to match different photo sets that had been arranged for the shoot. The only thing that didn't change was her inspiration. As instructions to look dreamy, look sexy, look passionate, look hungry, were thrown at her. All she had to do was to think of Hix, over and over. He was her true inspiration and she had never looked better.

In the last set Abby, being dressed in a silky night gown on a bed of rose petals the color of fresh blood, was directed to "*look like you have just had the best sex of your life.*" Not hard to do, Abby thought as she smiled sensually for the camera.

Abby pictured Hix above her, the stars at his back, the warm breeze blanketing them, and the love they had shared that last night in Nebraska, Abby laid back and let her memory take her away from this place. The look that came over her face, as the camera whirred, was not what Max asked for. Instead of hunger satisfied, and limbs limp from completion, she wore a look of love, soft, warm, sweet, and what every man wanted, waited for, and wished to see. It was the look of Love that would last a life time.

Max snapped shot after shot, telling Abby how great she was, how perfect she was, how beautiful she was. When he was done, Max lowered the camera and wiped the sweat from his face. Damn she had made him hot! Hot for her!

Max had been to bed with some of the most beautiful women of the world, all grateful and, if he had to say so himself, terribly satisfied to have been chosen by him. But not Abby. She eluded him and always turned down his advances. Stubbornly he acknowledged that he wanted her, and by God, he was going to have her.

Planning his attack, Max loaded his cameras in their cases. Placing his hands on his hips, he turned to the crew and said, "Drinks in one hour at the C Note, I'm buying." Cheers went up from the crew and everyone hurried to get the work done so the partying could begin.

Abby knew the bar Max had mentioned, having been there a time or two herself. It was dark, and always packed with the young and beautiful crowd. Hard Rock and Metal were the choice of music, making grinding second nature to those who chose to get on the dance floor.

Max was standing before Abby, blocking her way to the dressing rooms. "You're coming aren't you?" he asked, a challenge in his voice, a dare in his dark eyes.

Abby thought it over for a minute. It would be a way to pass the hours until she could get on a plane to return home. She would not have to sit in her hotel room wishing the time would go faster, being impatient for the next day.

"Why not." she said, with a flip of her honey blonde hair and a flash of her perfect white, teeth. "I'll go for a little while."

Max grabbed her arm and walked with her to the dressing room. "I'll give you a lift," he said, leaving her at the door. "Don't be long."

Winking at her, he turned away and walked with quick strides to gather his things.

'Step one,' he thought. rubbing his hands down his thighs before reaching into his pocket to pull out a small pill case. Looking around he made sure no one was watching before he popped the lid and counted the pills inside. '*We're good,*' he thought.

It never hurt to have an ace in the hole to make things turn out the way you wanted. And tonight he wanted.

Chapter 34

Hix had spent the better part of the last two weeks running his construction company during the day, and working on his dream house at night and on the weekends. Even though he put in full days at his business, he always had enough energy to work on the house when he and the crew quit for the day. He would work well into the night, losing track of time as he saw the house taking shape before him. Only until he was ready to drop with exhaustion, would he finally quit for the night. Weekends found him up at the break of dawn, working nonstop until after the sun had painted the western sky with nature's purest golds, pinks and purples. Only when the chill of the late spring air drove him inside for the day, did he reluctantly stop.

He tried to keep busy, hoping to keep thoughts of Abby from his mind, but she managed to intrude no matter what he did. No matter how tired he was, or how determined he was to bury his thoughts and his feelings for her, they were still there. The worst times came when he lay down at night in his lonely bed. Then there was no stopping the memories and longing from swamping him like a tsunami making land. Their power was more than he had the strength to hold off.

Yes, nighttime was the worst, but even during the day he found himself lost in thoughts of her, and would shake himself back to awareness only to find he had been running a hand along a piece of warm smooth wood as if it was part of her he held. He cringed inside and out when he thought of the ribbing he would take if any of his co-workers would have seen him. "*Boy did he have it bad*!"

Hix spent time with his mother, going over his plans for the house and even took her out to the country and showed her the progress he was making. Her sound advice, of giving them both, he and Abby, this time apart to see what would happen and how each of them would feel when she returned, grounded his thoughts. He let the wisdom of his mother's words sink in and even welcomed her help doing some of the smaller jobs, as they labored to make his dream a reality. She kept him sane, when he wanted nothing more than to jump on a plane and go grab Abby like the cavemen of long ago. "*Me man. You my woman. Let's go share my cave.*"

More than once Sarah had taken food out to the new house site and made Hix stop to eat. He had no thoughts of things like eating. He was focused on getting the foundation poured and the walls ready to be raised. But Sarah was not going to let him make himself sick just to build a house. It would be there waiting for his hands even if he dared to take a few moments to fuel his body, rest his mind, and take a few deep breaths.

Every day Hix stood back and viewed his progress before going home. It was coming along just fine. By the time Abby came home she would be able to see just what he had in mind for their family. He had no doubts that she would love it as he did and be sure that this was the place to spend her life with him.

When Abby had first left for New York, Hix had had doubts about their future or if there was even going to be a future, like in the jewelry store. But lately such thoughts were being replaced by the certainty that all things would work out between them. They would mesh their lives together. Hix's mother had said that they were moving too fast, and he should slow down and take his time. It was the one time that Hix could remember that he was not going to listen to her advice.

Sarah had cautioned him about the differences in their life styles, their family backgrounds, and their overall values. But Hix didn't care. He wanted Abby by his side, and the rest would work itself out.

Hix straightened his back and stretched to relieve the soreness that had settled across his shoulders. He had put in a full day's work, before driving out to work on their new house before the darkness chased him away.

Tonight the dark had come sooner, or at least it seemed so to Hix. As he looked around his property, his eyes raised to view the western sky. His brows lowered as he scanned the horizon. The buildup of storm clouds was thick and heavy, blotting out the sun and causing Hix's senses to sharpen to the possibility of danger. It finally sank in that the air had become thick and still, and the rumbling he heard was not from his empty stomach, but from the thunder and lightning coming his way. It Was Coming Fast!

He stood there only a moment, just long enough to take in the boiling of the skies. He recognized the greenish black tint to the clouds, and the rotation found in the angry midst of the belly of the beast charging his way.

Hix flew to gather up his tools and secure the lumber he had stacked on the ground before the storm hit and created havoc at the site. He was almost finished when the first wave of viciously cold wind hit him, making his hair fly behind him like a golden banner. *"Hail?"* he thought, as he finished cleaning up. The wind was cold because it was coming off of hail. Not good! From the looks of the sky and the feel of the wind, the town was in for some nasty weather tonight.

Just as Hix dove into his truck, the sky opened up and water gushed down in sheets, making it impossible for him to see out of the windshield. He turned on the wipers, cranking them on high, but they didn't stand a chance against the down pour that came pouring down from up above. Hix had no choice but to wait out the weather in his truck. He didn't like being out in the open, no trees or garage to give him shelter from the rain, or the hail if it decided to beat down on him.

No sooner had the thought entered his mind, when he heard the first heavy thump of the icy balls as they hit his windshield. It wasn't as bad as it could have been. The hail, averaging only marble size and not too heavy. The hail splattered into mush as it connected with the hard glass. He wouldn't have to worry about dents in his pickup from this one.

As Hix sat trying to see out of his windshield, suddenly it was as if someone had turned off a faucet. No rain fell and the hail stopped along with it. The air, as Hix climbed out of his truck, was still, and so heavy it was hard to breath. The small hairs at the back of his neck stood straight up, as he whipped his head around and looked up at the sky.

In horror, he watched a funnel drop from the clouds and snake its way towards the ground. It was big, black, and made the ground debris fly in a circle before it touched down.

"Tornado!" Hix ground out to no one but himself. His gaze darted everywhere at once trying to find a ditch or indentation in the flat prairie to take shelter in.

"Of course," he thought. The basement he had just finished was close by. He made a mad dash for safety and jumped into the concrete hole, driving his back against the wall directly in the twister's path.

He watched above him as dirt, trash, boards, weeds, and everything else, twisted by with enough power to cut through any object in their path like a hot knife through butter. Including human flesh! He stayed crouched down expecting to see his truck fly by on its way to Kansas any minute. But he didn't.

Though the air was almost sucked from his body and the sky was thick with debris, the twister did not find his hiding place. Its path had taken it to the south and before long Hix was able to climb the stairs and peak over the edge to see the back end of the funnel racing off to parts unknown.

When he was sure it was safe, he came all the way out of the basement. He stood where his drive way would be and observed the damage. His mouth fell open and a cold sweat ran down his back. It was as if a large bowl had been placed over his ground, leaving the rest unprotected. He saw big clumps of dirt that still clung to tree roots all around him, but the trees on his land had not been touched. Nothing had. Something had protected him and sheltered his dream from destruction.

"Maybe it's time to give thanks to the Gods," Hix thought, swallowing hard. That was the only explanations he could come up with for not having his property destroyed.

Backing away slowly, he reached his truck and climbed in, deciding not to push his luck and get out of there. Off in the distance he watched as the funnel finally left the ground and fell apart in the air, becoming only wisps of clouds no longer posing any danger.

Hix cranked the truck's engine to life and spun away with a spray of dirt and mud. He headed back to the highway and turned toward town as fast as he could. Once on the main road, he lifted a hand from the steering wheel and wiped a trail of sweat from his forehead. "I'v*e been saved,*" he thought. He could have died out there in the storm that had crept up on him while he worked.

His first thought was to go to his mom's house as he got back to town but decided not to since he saw that there was no major damage in town. Just some leaves knocked off the trees by the hail and a little trash blown around by the wind. He let out a big sigh of relief and turned his truck towards home.

"It just wasn't my time," he thought. *" Not today. Thank the Gods, not today!"*

Chapter 35

Saul let his hands fall to his sides. He had cupped them around Hix and his property just before the tornado had hit. He had deflected the tornado and turned its path away from his mortal, saving his life. Saul was certain that Hix would have died in this sudden, violent storm of nature if he had not intervened. It was not in his destiny to die this way, or this day. So Saul, once again, knew that Jeannicca had interfered, trying to rid the world of his charge.

His eyes grew even darker, flashing with lightning, as he became aware of the trick she had already put in place before being stripped of her powers over Hix, his mortal, and Abby.

Saul closed his eyes and relayed his thoughts to Jeannicca. When he felt their minds connect, he let her feel what he thought of her weak attempt on Hix's life.

"Is that all you've got?" he asked, not expecting an answer to his sarcasm. "Don't you know that I will be watching over him and that I will not let you hurt him? You're attempt was weak. I would have expected much better from you." Saul said mockingly.

Not feeling or getting a response, Saul took in a deep breath then let it out, causing the clouds to race even faster across the sky. He began to fade but before he did laughter, carried on the wind, reached his ears and made his mighty wings snap out in a warrior's response to a threat.

"Beware," it said "I'm not done. We'll see who is weak when this is over. We shall see."

Chapter 36

Hix opened his eyes as the pale morning light was just beginning to creep into his bedroom. It brought with it the knowledge that today was the day his lover came back to him. He rolled over, looked at the bedside clock, and groaned. It was still fourteen hours until he could finally get his hands, and mouth, on Abby. It was barely over half a day but still it seemed like a lifetime to him.

'How bad was it,' he thought, 'that he was wishing his life away, wanting the hours to fly by as if by magic, giving him what he wanted?'

Taking a deep breath, Hix folded his arms behind his head and made himself stay in bed for a while longer. He decided he wasn't going to work on the house today. Instead he was going to clean himself up and give himself plenty of time to get to the airport. He wanted to be standing at the gate when Abby came off the plane, flowers in hand, as he welcomed her back home.

He'd make a trip to the store to get the fixings for a meal that he could have cooking in the Crockpot. It would be ready for them to eat when they got home. He wanted Abby all to himself so he planned a meal they could be in no hurry to eat, if other things came first.

Hix lay there, picturing in his mind the reunion that was coming closer every second. But, the events of the day before seeped in, pushing out the happy thoughts. The storm yesterday had rolled in with no warning, bringing a tornado that could have left his dreams in splinters. But his land had been protected by something or someone. That was the only way Hix could explain the devastation that had gone on around him, but left him nearly untouched.

As he lay there remembering, his muscles tensed and his skin tightened as his memory replayed the events of the day before. The feeling of fear, helplessness, and dread, as he waited for the storm to wipe out everything he'd worked so hard to build, came back to him. It sent shivers down his entire body.

His mind fast-forwarded to the moment he'd heard the pounding on his front door, and the way his mother's face looked as he opened it to her. She had been terrified, knowing that her son had been out at the site when the storm hit. Not knowing if he was okay or not, she'd driven like a mad woman across town, and had only started to breathe again when he opened the door. She'd gathered him into her arms, clutching him to make sure he was whole and safe. Assured that he was all in one piece, she'd smacked him smartly on the arm for having worried her nearly to death and for not thinking to call her and put her mind to rest.

"Damn it, Hix!" she'd said, her voice shaking slightly as her emotions were given free rein to pour out, "I've been worried sick wondering if you were out in the storm and if you were okay. Why didn't you call when you got home, or pull out that cell phone you always have with you and let me know you were not in danger?"

Hix stood in the door way rubbing his arm, peering at his mother's face. It had been white with fear when he'd opened the door, but had changed rapidly as red spots bloomed in her cheeks as she yelled at him. Looking up and down the block he'd finally opened the door wider and gently pulled her inside and closed it on the nosy neighbors that had come out on their porches, curious about the yelling that was going on.

Once the door was closed he led his mother to the couch, pushed her gently into its softness and sat beside her. First he apologized to her, "I'm sorry mom, I wasn't thinking. Well, I did think about coming to your house but didn't think there was any damage so I came home. I was soaked to the bone and needed to get home." Then he began, slowly, to tell her what had gone on out at the site. He held her hands gently as he continued. He left nothing out as he told her how he and the house had been spared.

As Hix talked, Sarah's face had gone from being angry, to concerned, to scared, all in the matter of minutes it took her son to tell his story.

"Show me," she had demanded, standing up and heading out the front door for the pickup in the driveway.

"It's getting dark, Mom," Hix said, as he rose to cut off her escape.

"It's still light enough!" she said, and gave him no more chance to argue as she swept out the door, marched to his vehicle, opened the passenger door, and planted her butt firmly in the seat. She'd shut the door and sat staring straight ahead, leaving no doubt as to her intentions.

Hix, knowing when to throw in the towel, locked the door and got in his truck. It only took a few moments to arrive at the site. As he stopped at the edge of the property and killed the motor, only dead silence remained in the cab of the pickup. They both had stared in stunned silence at the torn ground and the uprooted bushes that lay strewn about. Everywhere but on his land, just as he had told his mother.

Sarah had sat and took in the destruction on one hand and the normalcy on the other. She could almost see a line drawn on the ground, the difference was so apparent. After a few moments of total silence, she cleared her dry throat and turned in her seat to face her son.

"You have someone or something watching over you, you know. I think I'm looking at a miracle." she said matter of factly.

Hix squirmed a little in his seat, as the thought of something watching over his every move sank in. He didn't like it. He didn't need any help with his life, and shaking his head back and forth, he denied the possibility out loud. "I've been trying to make sense of it too, but all I came up with was 'Thanks to the Gods'," he told her.

Sarah took one more look around and said, "Hix, please take us back to town." which he did without arguing.

The rest of the night had gone by without the subject being brought up again by either of them, as Sarah stayed and cooked a meal for them both before heading home. Hix had watched her tail lights fade away and disappear before he closed the door and got ready for bed.

Not being really tired, despite the events of the day, he'd plumped up his pillows behind him and punched the remote to the TV. He surfed the channels, trying to find something to catch his interest until he could fall asleep, finally settling on a crime show. He'd let himself be pulled into the plot, watching until his eyes began to close and his body felt limp and relaxed. He turned off the set and snuggled under the covers, knowing that his last thoughts would be of Abby as he drifted off to sleep.

Hix wasn't wrong. He could feel her beside him. Her image was so vivid and clear. In his mind he pulled her close to him, drawing in her scent with each deep breath he took.

His last thought, before he let the whirlpool of deep sleep suck him down, was that maybe his mother was right. It seemed like the only explanation for what he had been through. If it was true, he only hoped that the same being would extend its protection to Abby, and let them have a long and happy life together.

Hix woke the next day before the sun had fully cleared the horizon. He lay for a moment thinking that this would be the last time he would have to wake without Abby by his side.

For a moment he let thoughts of yesterday events creep into his head but only for a moment before pushing the thoughts back into a corner of his mind, and firmly closed the door on them. He did not want anything to darken this day. Today Abby came home to him.

Hix couldn't stay still any longer, anxious for the day ahead. He jumped into a hot shower, taking extra care to use a bath gel that he knew Abby particularly liked. He donned a worn pair of jeans and a soft flannel shirt, yanked on his boots and jacket and headed to the store.

He picked up a pork loin roast, which he placed in the Crockpot, along with some tiny potatoes, carrots and pearl onions. He topped it all off with just the right amount of seasonings, placed the lid on and left it to cook until they were back home this evening. He'd stir up some gravy from the broth on the roast when they were ready to eat.

With time left on the clock until he had to leave for the airport, Hix paced the rooms of his apartment until he felt he would wear a hole in the carpet. Finally giving in to his urge to be closer to Abby, he drove to the airport. Feeling a little sheepish at his impatience, Hix strolled the concourse and visited the shops until he had looked at everything the building had to offer. There was nothing left for him to do except sit at the gate for the arrivals and wait until she came home. "Not long now," he thought. "Not long now."

Chapter 37

Sarah's night had not been so peaceful. She'd tossed and turned until the blankets were wrapped around her hips and hanging onto the floor. She woke tired and drawn from the dreams that had chased her into the deepest recesses of her sleep. They were still fresh in her mind as she opened her eyes and squinted against the golden glare of the sun that had been up for more than an hour before she was released from sleep's torturous arms.

Her first thought was to call Hix and make sure he was okay. But, knowing he would find her calling first thing in the morning because of some silly dreams strange, she didn't. Still, they bothered her.

Untangling herself from the bedding that clung to her hips like ropes tied to an anchor, she rose from her bed, not wanting to lie there any longer. With a heavy step, she headed towards the bathroom, where a hot shower was calling her name.

Turning on the light, she glanced at her reflection in the big mirror that hung over the sink. Doing a double-take, she paused and raised her hand slowly, touching her face as if it was a stranger's instead of the one she had been born with, and took for granted every day of her life. Until now.

Sarah couldn't remember all those lines, so deep and dark, in places she hadn't noticed until this morning. In fact she was sure she didn't have that many before going to bed last night. "*What was going on?*" she wondered to herself. She looked deep into the eyes in the mirror, as if trying to find answers to her worries in their depths. Something was not right, and that something was trying to hurt her son.

Sarah had seen evidence of this yesterday afternoon. The fading, late spring light had not been able to hide the facts that lay before her. The storm had come up out of nowhere and had tried its best to kill Hix. She felt it in her bones, the truth waiting there to be faced.

"But why?" she asked her reflection. Hix was a good man, who had never hurt anyone in his life.

"It's Abby," a tiny cold voice whispered in her ear.

Sarah slowly came to the realization that Hix had never had any problems, as far as she knew, until he started to see the beauty,

"That's right," the same cold voice encouraged, "*Abby is no good for your boy. He deserves someone who has the same values as he does. He needs someone who grew up in the area, who understands his life style. Not some model that lives to have her picture in the paper and her name on everyone's lips.*"

Hatred tried to take root in her heart, but Sarah braced herself on the rim of the sink and shook her head from side to side. "*No,*" she thought, *"this is not Abby's fault."* She makes Hix happy. Hadn't she seen firsthand the love that shone from his eyes when he talked about her, the pain their separation had caused him?

"Infatuation," the voice persisted," *lust, that's all it is."*

"Maybe," Sarah answered the voice out loud, causing herself to jump as the sound of her own voice startled her.

Sarah heard a hiss in her head, then the voice became quiet, letting the doubts it had planted in her mind fight to take root and flourish.

Instead of the shower she had meant to take, Sarah headed back to her bed, straightened the covers, and crawled back under them. Her head was fuzzy and confused, and she needed to sleep without dreaming before facing her day.

Lying still against the pillows, Sarah felt a comforting warmth creep into her chest and spread outward, until she was warm and relaxed. Her already tired eyes grew heavy as she slipped back into the land of slumber. This time there would be no bad dreams to keep her from the rest she needed.

The warmth made her feel safe and protected as she made her way deeper into sleep. "*Safe,*" she thought." *Keep my son safe. That's all that matters to me. Keep him safe.*"

"*Sleep now,*" the warmth that was in and around her seemed to be saying. "*Sleep now and worry no more.*"

Sarah let go, and sunk deep into slumber, like a rock dropped into a deep lake. Going deeper and deeper where no sound or light interrupted. No sound except a faint tinkling of laughter that, for the briefest blink in time, replaced the warmth with cold and dread.

"The battle's not over yet," it seemed to say. *"It's just beginning."*

Chapter 38

Saul hovered at the end of Hix's mother's bed, aiding her as she fell into a dreamless, much-needed sleep. He knew Jeannicca was still in the picture, even though she had been removed as Abby's Guardian, and strictly forbidden from interfering in destiny's path.

However, the problems he was encountering on Hix's behalf proved she had not heeded the instructions given to her by the Fates. Saul definitely had his hands full. First, protecting the home Hix was building from the tornado's rage and destruction. Now, helping Sarah fight the dreams planted in her mind that urged her to doubt and even hate Abby.

Saul remained at the foot of the bed for a moment longer, watching, making sure Sarah was resting undisturbed, before he began to fade.

He found himself hoping he was done with this situation, but doubted it, as he decided Jeannicca was evidently not going to give up easily. His great wings flexed and his dark eyes narrowed as he wondered what else she had planned for his humans. Only time would tell, he decided.

Disappearing from the room, Saul left to take care of his other charges he'd had to neglect lately.

It was only a moment before another Immortal took his place, floating at the end of the bed, staring at the woman who slept there. Only this one did not have her best interest at heart. This one wanted things to go wrong and had worked quietly to see that they did. Now, the need for secrecy was past, and her final plan was already in motion.

Jeannicca also flexed her lovely wings, but hers moved with excitement at the thought of what was coming, not with worry. She had been successful in keeping the mighty Saul's attention off of her true plan, sidetracking him with the other issues. The petty fight, the tornado, and the night of bad dreams had been only a smokescreen. She'd already put her master plan into play. It's true purpose about to be revealed. After this, she wouldn't have to do anything else, if she knew humans at all and she did. She could just sit back and let them destruct on their own.

If Jeannicca were human, she'd put on the popcorn, snuggle down in a big chair and watch the show. "*Yes,*" she thought, smiling to herself. This was going to be her big moment. The moment that she would beat Saul at his own game. Guiding humans. They were really just pawns for the Immortals after all, right?

With her last move in play, Jeannicca decided that this was going to be check and mate. Jeannicca One, Saul nothing. "*Damn I'm good,*" she mused. *"I'm really good!"* And Saul was going to be finding that out soon, very soon.

Fluffing her hair and gliding a hand over her clothing, Jeannicca preened for just a moment, basking in her own glory before deciding to take herself off and watch as the drama unfolded.

Today was going to be a good day, she decided, a very good day.

Chapter 39

Abby awoke slowly, not floating up prettily from the depths of slumber, but struggling as if she was trying to swim against a strong current. She fought her way back into her body and tried to open her eyes. They felt heavy and dry, as she lifted the lids a fraction of an inch to see if she still could. The meager light coming through a crack in the curtains stabbed them, driving pain as sharp as an ice pick into her brain. She lifted an arm to cover the offended orbs and groaned out loud. The effort left her shaking as if her appendage weighed a ton. Her voice came out low and gravelly, as her pain escaped her lips in a low moan.

"Crap!" she thought, *"What did I do last night?"*

She remembered changing clothes and heading with the crew to the C Note to celebrate the ending of the shoot. She had ridden with Max, no big deal, and then joined everyone at a big table to have a drink or two before going back to her hotel room to pack for the trip home today.

"Hix," she sighed, *"I get to see Hix today. Finally."* This thought alone had the power to bring a small smile to her lips and make her head ache just a little less with the anticipation.

"What had she drunk last night"? she wondered. Her body ached, her head hurt, and her stomach rolled with each thought, as if she had really tied one on. But even with her head pounding out a rock beat, she could not remember having drank more than a couple of glasses of wine. She remembered having the first glass brought to the table by a pretty waitress dressed like a hooker. *"Probably waiting for someone to discover her,"* Abby had thought. The evening had been fun. Everyone was more than happy to be able to let their hair down following a successful shoot,

mixing and mingling with ease. The booze flowed as if there was a never ending supply. It never failed to surprise Abby how much one person could drink and still remain upright. There were a lot of *happy* people at the C Note.

Abby had spent the evening talking, laughing and watching, as her coworkers partied. It wasn't that she had distanced herself from the fun. She just chose to remain a casual bystander, as they drank, danced, and raised hell around her.

She had other things on her mind, Hix to be exact. She let her mind wander over how they had left things. How they had made up during conversations on the phone, and how she wanted to be with him right now instead of this crowded bar. She felt restless and itchy, wanting to be home, not thousands of miles away.

The first glass of wine helped to calm the feelings, but had not erased them completely. Max had taken a seat beside her, taking advantage of the noise as an excuse to inch his chair closer to hers. He leaned in close every time he spoke to her, whispering bits of gossip and directing her attention to actions of the crew as they danced and mingled with each other. His arm had found its way to the back of her chair and his fingers frequently found a reason to touch her hair, her shoulder, or her back, letting her know he was interested.

Abby gave no indication that she knew it was there, or that she wanted more from him than the slight friendship that was already in place. Max had brought her another glass of wine when her first one had gotten low and warm.

Abby frowned slightly as she lay remembering how she had not drank much of it. She remembered the first few sips had left a slightly bitter taste in her mouth. She remembered Max asking her to dance, and that she had gotten up to join in the mass on the floor, figuring that if she danced once with him he would stop asking her. The beat had been fast and there had been no reason for them to touch. The music would be keeping them moving and apart.

The slight frown deepened as she remembered feeling off as she moved to the music. The people had started to swim and the colors blurred before the tempo slowed and Max had moved in. He was trying to gather her close for a more intimate dance. She had placed a hand on his chest, holding him off, and shaking her head no, before turning and making her way back to her seat.

She had taken a few more sips of her drink, trying to get a grip on her spinning head. But it hadn't helped. If anything it had gotten worse. Max had asked her if she was okay. She remembered telling him she thought she would call it a night, as she was not feeling well. He had put an arm around her waist and guided her towards the door, saying he would take her home in the limo they had come in.

She'd let him escort her to the door and out onto the street. She remembered the bright flashes of light as they waited for the car and then Max helping her into the back seat before the door closed and she was able to rest her head on the soft, cool seat.

Then she remembered no more. Try as she might, she could not raise the memory of her getting back to her hotel room, or into bed. Abby knew she was not much of a drinker, but blacking out had never happened to her before. Maybe it was time for a checkup. She'd get one when she got back home, she thought. Just to make sure everything was in order.

The loss of memory bothered Abby for a few more moments, and then with a mental shrug of her shoulders, she put it away until a later date. As she'd lain in bed remembering, her head had begun to feel better, her body less achy. Her stomach had settled down to a slight queasy feeling, so all in all, Abby figured she was now able to get up without falling down or throwing up.

She again cracked her eye lids and tested the waters. Things seemed to be better now. Abby opened them all the way and blinked as she stared at the ceiling. "*Wasn't the ceiling supposed to be white and not this beige brown? Oh well,*" she said to herself, "*not a big deal.*"

She stretched her arms above her head and glanced down her body as she did so. Stopping in mid arch, she lowered one arm to lift the blanket that covered her, and again her eye brows rose as she discovered her nakedness. Not that she never slept in the nude, but usually she wore at least a tee shirt, when not at home.

"I must have been a mess last night," she thought, hoping she had not done anything that would be spread all over the front of some rag paper.

Putting it from her mind, she again let her thoughts turn to Hix. Remembering how it was to wake up with him at her side. Yummy! "*Oh baby,"* she smiled to herself, "*ready or not I'm coming home tonight and we are not going to come up for air the rest of the weekend.*" With this thought swirling around her head like a happy swarm of summer bees, Abby threw her arms out wide.

Puzzlement stopped her happy musings, as her right arm came into contact with a hard lump in the bed. "*Maybe it was where she had shed her clothes the night before,*" she thought, and rolled over to take a look.

Her heart stopped and a scream rose in her throat, as she came face to face with the smirking, tousled form of a newly awakened Max. Abby's speechlessness lasted only a moment as she finally sat up with the sheet clutched to her chest.

"What are you doing in my room?" she ground out, anger making her cheeks flush a rosy becoming red.

Max reached out a hand to tuck a sleep tousled hank of honey blonde hair behind a small ear, but stopped short of his target as an actual growl came out of Abby's lovely throat, accompanied by a showing of her teeth, which threatened a very painful bite if he moved even an inch closer.

"I'm not in your room," Max said, as he let his arm fall to the bed. Male pride and gloating smeared all over his face, Max looked Abby straight in the eye and took great relish in saying, "Shit babe, you're in mine!"

Chapter 40

Max lay gloating as he watched the expressions crossing the face of the woman in his bed. The exquisite, the mouth-watering, the hard to get Abby Mathews. He'd finally gotten her into his bed.

Max hadn't been all that concerned at first when she had rejected his advances. After all, there were women lined up around the block begging for a chance to sleep with the famous photographer. He was sure that not all of them found him attractive, but had slept with him anyway on the outside chance that he would take their picture. The hopes that he would make their faces and bodies famous for a time, was a certainty they just couldn't pass up.

Max had a knack of taking pictures that spoke to the public. His eye for beauty was unfailing, both in pictures and women. He was not an unattractive man, but had learned that his talent with a camera made getting women to do his bidding all that much easier. He exploited it every chance he got. There was no challenge, no need to hunt. Except where Abby was concerned.

They had met a few years ago when she was just a fresh face among many that had tried out for a modeling job. He had been hired to take their pictures, then turn the photos over to the big-wigs to make their decision. They had chosen Abby.

She was just a teenager at the time and her face, beautiful with youth, had gotten only more beautiful as she entered her twenties. He had looked at the pictures of her lovely face, and had wanted her on the spot. But, much to his amazement, she had turned him down flat when he had suggested she come back to his apartment with him. Sure, she had been nice about it, but nothing he could say or offer changed her mind. He had never forgotten that moment. The moment when the "Great Max" had been denied.

Since that time their paths had crossed a few times. Each time he had tried to persuade her, to prove that he really could have any woman he wanted. But each time she had turned him down, leaving him hot and wanting as she drove off.

He had begun plotting ways to get her ever since a story had appeared in the press about how she had been able to resist his charms. She was unaffected by his power in the modeling industry. He had taken the article personally, and taken the ribbing from his friends and the snide comments from his enemies, to heart. No one embarrassed him. No one made him look like a fool.

It became a challenge to him. A challenge that he was going to win one way or the other. And, when he did, he vowed to splash it all over the rag papers. The beautiful Abby Mathews had finally bowed to his charms.

Last night had been the first opportunity he'd had to put his plan into action. A tiny voice had been whispering in his head since he had learned they were going to work together on this project. It had coached him in the specifics of what to do. Even how to get the little pills that would guarantee the success of their meeting. He had followed the voice in his head to a tee, and it had worked.

It had almost been too easy for Max to slip the tiny pill into Abby's glass of wine, and sit back until it took effect. He'd had to be patient until he saw her eyes become unfocused, and her movements visibly jerky. Then things had happened fast.

Max waited until she told him that she wanted to leave, then played the gallant gentleman, holding her close against him as they made their way from the club. He made sure they paused long enough for the cameras to record them leaving together, seemingly unable to keep their hands off each other.

Pictures could be deceiving. By looking at the shots, you could imagine almost anything. Now all he had to do was to make a few calls, anonymously of course, to get the captions just right. *Lovers at last,* he thought. Yeah, that sounded pretty good to him.

His musings were interrupted as Abby finally found her voice, and the questions and anger flew fast and freely.

"What happened last night?" she demanded. "What did you do?"

"It wasn't what *I* did," he responded, lying back with his hands under his head and a smug look on his face. "It was what we did."

"We didn't do anything!" she stated fiercly, a thread of panic underlying her statement.

"Didn't we?" he countered, his eyebrows raised and a knowing smile on his face. "Don't tell me you don't remember."

Abby pressed a shaking hand to her forehead, which pounded as she tried to recall the events that had led to her waking up in this perverts bed.

"I remember leaving the club, and then everything is a blank. Why?" she demanded.

"Why what?" he asked calmly.

"Why can't I remember? I wasn't drunk! I only had two glasses of wine. I didn't even finish the second one. What did you do?" Abby asked angrily, with a sense of dread in her voice.

"Abby," Max said, with fake disappointment in his voice, "you wound me. Why do you assume I did anything? It's obvious to me that you can't handle even two drinks, but that's not my fault. You seemed willing and able last night. I had no reason to think you didn't want sex as much as I did." Coming up on one elbow, he faced her anger, and reaching out a hand, again tried to touch her. "You were great, Abby," he said. "I knew we would be good together, but you surpassed even my wildest dreams."

"Shut up!" she said, her voice edging on hysteria as she slapped his hand away before it could come into contact with her skin. "You're lying! You've wanted this from the first time we met, and it hurt your fragile male ego when I said no, repeatedly. You are lying just to make yourself feel big. You're lying!" she shouted again. "Say it! Admit nothing happened!" she demanded.

Max looked at Abby's pale face and the desperation lurking in her dark eyes. "I'm not." he said with a smirk curving his mouth. "What's the big deal anyway? We are two consenting adults that just happened to have a romantic interlude."

"Bullshit!" she said, feeling her anger growing. "Nothing happened and you can't convince me any differently! I would remember something that revolting!" she shouted as her anger reached a boiling peak.

"Whatever it takes," Max said, looking like the cat that drank all the cream.

"Fuck you!" she said as she grabbed the sheet and rose from the bed. She tore the room apart looking for her clothes, finding pieces strewn around as if she had been in a hurry to get them off. Why couldn't she remember? With her arms loaded, she flew into the bathroom and slammed the door, locking it behind her. Abby couldn't face herself in the mirror, so dressing took only a moment before she was back in the bedroom, hurrying to gather up her coat and hand bag.

"You will NEVER make me believe anything happened," she shouted over her shoulder, hesitating in the door way. "I don't EVER want to see you again. Ever!" she shouted in disgust at his smug expression. She stopped herself from walking back over to him and doing bodily harm.

With that she walked out.

Max lay in the bed, running a hand over the place that was still warm from her body. He enjoyed his victory for a moment more, before rolling over and grabbing up his phone. He knew one of the reporters that had taken their picture last night, and he thought a call was in order. He got the number out of his address book, wrote it down then got up, deciding to make the call from a phone booth. After that, he decided, a stop at the corner coffee shop was in order, and then maybe he would treat himself to something useless and expensive.

Today was going to be a good day, he decided, a very good day.

Chapter 41

Abby made it all the way from Max's apartment to her hotel room before she fell on her knees, hung her head over the toilet bowl, and was violently sick. She stayed that way until she had nothing left inside her. Her hair was clinging to her sweaty cheeks and neck, her sides were aching, and her soul was sick with doubt.

"Nothing happened," she repeated over and over to herself, trying to make it true. Deep down she knew it wasn't something she was capable of, sober or drunk.

Abby had less confidence in Max, knowing what a womanizing, egotistical asshole he was. She'd been warned of his reputation when she first got into the business, by models that had gotten burned by him. She had wanted nothing to do with him.

Abby recalled how she'd felt his gaze moving up and down her body the very first time she'd been introduced to Max. She'd fought the urge to cover herself, not wanting to give him the satisfaction of knowing she was even aware of him, and refused his pathetic advances without a second thought. She had worked with a few men that had tweaked her interest, but never Max. She could not believe that, even if she had been drunk on her butt, she would ever consent to sleep with that pig.

Abby finally eased herself up off the bathroom floor. Wanting to rid herself of any remnants of the previous night, she pulled off the clothes she'd been wearing and threw them in a heap on the floor. She would not be packing them to take home, but would leave them for the hotel to do with what they wanted.

She stepped into the shower and turned the water on hot enough to make her skin turn bright red, and began to scrub at her body. She wanted to wash the bad memories away, and left not an inch unattended. She finally quit when her skin began to feel raw, and just stood under the hot water, letting it work its magic on her tired, aching muscles.

Finally she turned off the faucet and wrapped herself tightly in the big soft towel hanging outside the shower door. She, once again avoided the mirror, slowly making her way back to the bedroom to find some clothes to put on. She didn't want to walk anywhere naked. Even in the privacy of her own hotel room. She didn't want to be bare and vulnerable.

Abby dressed in her favorite pair of jeans, soft and comfy from so much wear. She topped them off with a bulky sweater in a rich bronze color. Covered from head to toe, she finally felt a small measure of comfort.

Moving around the room Abby began to fill her bags for the trip home. Her hands stilled as she thought of Hix. She had been keeping him out of her mind on purpose, but now his image came flooding in along with the question, what was she going to tell him? "Nothing," she said out loud, because nothing had happened, right?

A voice in her head shattered the small confidence she had built up that nothing had happened last night. "You wanted what happened last night," it said. "You wanted to feel his arms around you, to feel him over you, inside you. You wanted the hot sweaty sex he gave you."

"No!" Abby shouted with her hands covering her ears. "No, no, no! Shut up!" she snapped. Abby moaned, "Shut up and get out of my head. I have Hix. I only want Hix!"

The small voice seemed to grow as it attacked her where she was most vulnerable. "Do you honestly think Hix will want you when he finds out what you have done?" the voice nagged at her

"I didn't do anything!" she said again, sitting on the edge of the made-up bed. She rocked slowly back and forth with her arms wrapped around her middle, as if trying to keep the hurt out and protect her heart from the wound the words wanted to cause.

"He will turn his back on you and call you the slut that you are," the voice taunted.

"No, he would never do that. We love each other," Abby said out loud, continuing the conversation with the small voice.

"He isn't good enough for you," the voice said. "Hix isn't even on your level. He is a peon and last night proved that you are not ready to choose one man yet. Especially not Hix."

"Get out of my head!" Abby yelled to the empty room. She couldn't handle any more of this, feeling on the verge of flying apart. Then something happened.

One second she was almost mad with guilt and indecision. The next she felt a warmth moving through her being, creeping down her limbs, all the way to her finger tips and toes. She felt safe. Safe from what she wasn't sure, but safe none the less. The feeling wrapped her in a calming embrace. As Abby gave herself over to the feeling, her eyes no longer had the wild, near-mad look blazing from them. Her heart slowed its wild beating, until it thumped in her chest with a more normal rhythm.

Unless unquestionable proof was offered that she had sex with Max last night, she would not worry about it and she would say nothing to Hix. A story like that would only hurt him, and without just cause.

Feeling calmer than she had since entering the hotel room, Abby finished packing her bags. She called a cab, checked one more time to make sure she hadn't left anything behind and closed the door firmly behind her. Sighing deeply as she entered the elevator, she made her way down to the lobby just as the cab arrived. She settled in the backseat for the ride to the airport. She couldn't wait to be in Hix's strong, loving arms.

Thoughts of last night were locked away, not to be obsessed over. "Everything is going to be alright," she thought one last time. It had to be.

Arriving at the airport, Abby checked her luggage and boarded the plane without incident. Dropping into her seat, she rested her head against the headrest and closed her eyes. By the time the plane took off, she was lost in the cradle of dreamless sleep.

Chapter 42

Saul had felt Abby's pain as if it was his own. He'd felt her heart squeeze and her soul burn with it. He hadn't been able to come to her until she'd made it back to her hotel room, and was rocking on the bed in agony. Laying his hand on her shoulder he'd found his way into her mind and read the turmoil there. He also had felt another Immortal presence there with him. He knew who it was, what it was doing, and he felt rage.

He had given his charge the comfort he could, and had eased the burden of her pain and confusion with his reasoning and warmth. Giving her the peace she needed, Saul stayed with Abby until she slept, before moving away to begin his hunt for the cause of her distress.

His hair streamed out behind him as he swiftly travelled the heavens looking for Jeannicca. He gave vent to his anger with a mighty bellow, as he spied her sitting amongst the clouds trying to play the innocent. His eyes shot fire as he came to stand before her and confront her on her treachery.

"You were warned not to interfere again in the life of Abby Mathews!" he said, his breath burning her with the heat of his rage. The clouds boiled around them, fierce bolts of lightning flashed and mighty crashes of thunder rolled beneath their feet, as Jeannicca stood to face her foe.

"Why have you come to me in anger?" she said, a serene smile about her lips.

"Do not play me for a fool," Saul snarled. He felt no pity for her, even though he knew the sentence that he was about to deliver. The punishment was his to hand out. "Do not deny what you have done," he said, as she started to open her mouth to decry his accusations. "You have gone against the orders of the Fates. You have done so on more than one occasion since being told to step aside and to leave Abby alone. You have proven yourself unworthy of the title and responsibilities of an Immortal. From this moment forward you will no longer be known as an Immortal. You will reside no longer with the Immortals. You are stripped of the powers granted to the Immortals."

Immediately the lovely vision before Saul melted away. To Saul's surprise she was replaced with a twisted gnarled form of a Dark being. These beings existed to bring pain, destruction and despair to mankind.

"You may think you have won," it hissed, without cowering before the mightiest of Guardians, "but you cannot stop what has been put into motion. I win," it said in a voice that came out wet and foul, as black drool leaked from the hole that passed for its mouth. "All the powers of the Immortals cannot undo what has been done. I have defeated the one you call Jeannicca and taken her place without your kind's knowledge. She died with screams of pain in her throat. Victory is mine!" the Dark being gloated, daring Saul to deny it.

Saul did not hesitate, not giving the Dark being a chance to escape back to the shadows from whence it came. Instead he reached out with hands that sizzled with power, and grasped the form in front of him, letting his reined-in power have freedom to wrap around and consume the Dark in front of him. "The victory you claim is yet to be seen," Saul said as the Dark being twisted and screamed in the agony of its death. "Yes, victory may be yours but revenge is mine!" Saul's voice thundered. "Go to hell!"

Chapter 43

Abby fought her way back from sleep as the plane began its decent over the plains of her home state, Nebraska. Sitting up straighter in her seat, she ran a hand through her hair, wanting to be at least presentable when she stepped off of the plane and into Hix's waiting arms. Her sleep had been deep and healing, leaving her feeling calmer, like the last twenty four hours had been nothing but a bad dream.

The plane finally rolled to a stop and Abby stood with the rest of the passengers to collect the small bag she had carried on with her. She waited her turn to walk out the door, even though she wanted to elbow everyone aside and make a mad dash down the long tunnel. Taking a calming breath, she reined in her impatience, shifting from one foot to the other while waiting her turn. Finally it was her turn, and she was walking down the home stretch before the rolling in her stomach started again.

"What about last night?" a small voice in her head asked snidely. "He's going to know that something is wrong right away. It's written all over your face. Anyone can see it, even a country bumpkin from Nebraska."

Setting her lips in a hard line, Abby shook her head and kept walking. "*Not true,*" she thought. "I*t's not true! Everything will be fine. Just keep walking towards the light.*" she thought, "W*alk towards the light.*"

The light she aimed for was the end of the tunnel, and when she finally emerged into the waiting area she didn't have time to even look around before she was grabbed up by two strong arms and held close to the body she had been craving. She was almost crushed by Hix, before realizing she was holding on just as tightly. Wanting just as badly, needing the feel of him around her.

She took a deep breath and drew his scent into her body, loving every second of her homecoming. It felt so good to be holding each other, that Abby and Hix were not aware that the other passengers had to detour around them where they blocked the aisle. Abby didn't see the knowing looks or the smiles at their happiness that was out in the open for all to see. She had eyes only for Hix.

Just as she buried her face in his warm neck, a light flashed behind her closed eyelids. Abby was so happy that she couldn't even muster up the irritation at having their reunion captured by some photo putz on film. Caring about that would come later.

It was a long moment before Abby and Hix parted long enough and far enough to look each other in the eyes, smile and exchange a long kiss. A kiss that was inspired by separation, longing and finally, of intimacy to come.

Abby's lips felt almost bruised as she pulled back and smiled at Hix. "Hi," she breathed out, not having much air left to talk. "I missed you." She whispered quietly.

Hix swallowed the lump in his throat that was his emotions at finally having his world right again. "Hi baby," he said smiling with his eyes, as well as his beautiful mouth. He loosened one of his arms long enough to bring his hand up and burry it in her dark honey hair. "I missed you, too," he said, closing his eyes as he rested his forehead against hers.

Abby didn't want to move. She wanted to stay in this moment forever. Then she felt Hix back up a step and, with his arm securely around her back, he led the way to to the carousel to claim her luggage.

"Let's go home," he said, when they had collected everything.

Smiling hugely, Abby nodded her head once and stayed glued to Hix's side as they went to find his truck. Loading the bags into the back seat, Hix stole one more lingering kiss before he handed Abby in and shut the door. He walked around the hood and jumped in, not believing how good he felt, how happy that she was as glad to see him as he was to see her. He cranked over the motor, but before putting the truck in gear he turned his golden head to look at Abby.

"We have options," he said. At her quizzical look, he went on to explain. "If you like, we can get a hotel room for the night and have room service, or we could go out to dinner and then head home. You chose," he said, not wanting to rush her home and into bed where he wanted her badly.

That wasn't all he wanted from her or their relationship. He wanted her to know that she was special to him, and not just a roll in the sack. So he would let her slow it down if she needed a second to catch her breath.

"How about we go home, and later we can worry about something to eat?" she said innocently. "I've been staying in a hotel for the last two weeks, and all I want is to go home, now. Does that sound okay to you?" she asked, not wanting to be pushy. Waiting for his answer, she thought, maybe she'd just spoiled something he had planned, something else away from home? But one look into Hix's hot eyes told her he was fine doing as she asked. He did have plans, but a hotel was not a major factor in them.

"Home it is," Hix said, and headed the truck down the road. He kept Abby's slim fingers grasped in his much rougher grip, as he asked her how the shoot had gone, how her stay had been, and listened as she took him on an unfamiliar trip of her world.

She sounded fine, until she mentioned going out with the crew after the final shoot. That's when Hix detected something in her tone. A hesitation, a tightening of her voice, a twitch of her fingers as they tried to ball into a fist. He raised her hand to his lips and kissed away the tension, before sliding a look at her as he sped down the highway.

"What's wrong?" he asked giving her hand a shake to bring her attention back to him? He had lost her for a second, as she was looking back at an event he could not see.

"What's the matter?"

"Nothing," she said, "nothing."

Hix felt the lie, but didn't know how to make her talk if she didn't want to. Something had happened in New York, something not so good. He could feel it, he could tell. He wondered what it was, but decided he would not press for the information. She would tell him eventually. He was not going to let the little worm of fear ruin their evening together.

Pressing his foot down on the accelerator he made the truck growl with power and the speedometer rise fast. If he went fast enough, he thought, he could outrun the feelings that landed like a rock in his gut. "Don't borrow trouble," his mind told his heart. "She is here, with you and you should be thanking the Gods that she wants you."

"Mine!" he wanted to say out loud. "She's mine!" Why and to whom he did not know. Crazy, he called himself, as he drove with her at his side until his apartment came into view.

"I have something cooking, but if you want to go to your house I can just run in and shut it off first."

"No," Abby said, finally letting her hand fall from his. "This is just fine. Let's go inside."

She didn't have to tell Hix twice, as he turned off the motor and grabbed her bags. Abby jumped out of the truck and led the way up the walk, waiting only until Hix had unlocked and opened the door before she let herself go.

"Please," she whispered against his lips, his back pressed against the door. "Please don't make me wait any longer to have you. I need . . ." was all she got out before Hix dropped the suitcases, kicked the front door shut, and lifted her off her feet. Trying not to run, he made his way into the darkened bedroom and the soft blackness enfolded them.

"I'm starving," Hix growled against Abby's arched throat, "starving for you. But this isn't the way I had planned things. I don't want you to think that the only thing I want is sex. I don't."

"Hix," Abby said as she molded herself to him, "it's been so long. Please baby," she said softly, "please don't make me beg."

That was all the assurance Hix needed before he shut the door with his shoulder, and for a time forgot everything but her.

Chapter 44

Abby felt on fire as Hix slowly let her slide down the length of him, letting them both feel the other's body and the desire that made their dreams and imagining, while parted, pale in comparison. With hands that shook from anticipation, Abby began to tear at her sweater trying to get it off. She wanted it off now, so that she could feel his skin on hers. She stopped her struggles as she felt his warm hands on her shoulders. Raising her eyes she wondered why he had stopped.

"Oh God," she thought wildly, *"he knows, he suspects, I must be different somehow and he knows."* She had to meet his eyes when he moved his hands to either side of her face and raised it to his.

"Let me, Abby," he said, his voice coming out as the softest of whispers. Hix held her face trying to see behind her eyes into her mind. There was something different about Abby tonight. He could easily read the desire on her face, feel it in her hands, and taste it on her lips. But there was something else there too. The bite of desperation seemed to be underlying it all. Hix could taste the slight bitterness in her kisses, turning them darker, more demanding of his surrender.

"What is it, Abby," he asked, willing her to confide her secrets in him. "You can tell me anything, anything baby. You know that don't you?"

Abby searched his eyes, his face, trying to find the answer to the question of what would happen if she told him. Told him there was a chance she had slept with another man while in New York. Told him she could not remember but he had said so. Dare she take the chance of killing what they had only started to build? Her mind felt like a tornado had been unleashed in it, swirling her thoughts and emotions around until she was dizzy with the conflict. She did not want Max, she knew that with every fiber of her being, but she was not willing to lay the burden of her confession onto Hix's shoulders. Not now, maybe never.

"I've just missed you terribly," she said, lowering her lids to hide the lie her eyes could tell. "That's all. I've been without you for two whole weeks and it felt like years. I've just missed you." She raised her arms and wrapped them around the strong neck, pulling their bodies, once again, close and tight. She turned her face into his neck, bringing her mouth close enough to his ear so she could take the lobe into her mouth and wash it slowly with her tongue, bite it gently at first with her teeth, adding pressure as she continued. His taste was good on her tongue, a mixture of cologne, soap and his own sweat, uniquely his, but home to her.

With her first nip on his ear and her breath hot on his neck, Hix put aside his questions and forgot everything except the woman in his arms. He tipped his head slightly giving her more freedom and felt each touch as tingles shot though him, sending sparks from his head to his toes, raising goose bumps on his arms and legs, making him feel hard and powerful with her passion.

His warm hands found their way to the hem of her sweater, slipping underneath to find the skin of her back, smooth and hot. He let them wander up and down its length reacquainting his senses with the feel of her. The satin expanse satisfied for a short time, then he had to have more. He inched back from her and let his hands find their way to her flat smooth stomach, travel to the indentation that was her navel, letting his fingers circle it and dip into its bowl, until letting them rise to feel her ribs and more.

Hix felt the lace that covered her breasts, and knew that his touch was the reason they were puckered and hard, straining to fill his hands and mouth with no barrier between them.

Abby leaned into his hands, wanting him to remove the scrap of lace and let her feel his flesh. She moaned softly as he eased her back, and let his hands carry her sweater up and over her head, making her raise her arms so he could complete the task and toss the unwanted material into a dark corner, forgotten for a time.

He lowered his head and let his lips travel her smooth shoulders, never letting his hands rest as they fumbled slightly with the clasp that seemed to be a challenge and frustration to all men of the world. Abby wanted to help him, to hurry him but, as she made a move to reach behind her, she was stopped by a low growl and the suction of his mouth on her shoulder to keep her in place. It seemed to take forever before the fabric was swept from her body, satisfying them both.

Abby mirrored Hix's actions, but with more speed, as she removed the clothing from his upper body. At last she pressed her nakedness to his, moaning again as the soft hairs on his chest tickled and aroused her breasts more with each movement. Each slight twist of her body, each deliberate touch. Abby let her nails dig into the bunched muscles of the wide shoulders, as Hix lifted her up so her legs wrapped around his waist.

Before his waiting face was the feast he wanted. He took first one hard nipple and then the other into his mouth, gently pulling them deeper onto his tongue as he suckled at her breast in a rhythm that sent waves of molten warmth pouring through her to settle and dampen her in anticipation of his entry.

Abby loved the attention he was paying to her breasts, but she wanted more. She wiggled until Hix finally let her legs drop to the floor, dragging her nails down his chest, leaving pink lines from his shoulders to the top of his jeans, as he lowered her. As her lips kissed and traveled the wide expanse that was his chest, her hands slipped inside his waistband, loosening the buttons until the jeans gapped away from his erection that they could not hide. Her hand felt small and delicate as it traced the length, and finally wrapped around the hard shaft, squeezing and making it throb and jump with each small touch, each light caress.

It was Hix's turn to groan deep in his throat, as Abby made him her slave, willing to do anything, promise anything if only she would stop teasing him. Hix placed his hand over hers and deepened the pressure to give his body some relief, guiding her in the motions he desired.

Abby did not wait for Hix, but stepped back, and in one motion drew her jeans and panties down to her ankles and out of them. She moved back into Hix's waiting arms, and once again raised a leg up until Hix, bending slightly at the knees grasped her by her butt and lifted so she could wrap her long legs once more around his hips.

Abby felt his arms tremble and heard his heart beating like a bass drum, as she moved against the head that rose above the waist band of his underwear. Up and down, side to side. as she let the dampness from her body wet him, letting him know what she wanted.

Hix wanted to plunge into her and bury himself there until they became one, joined in their own dance of love, but he held back for a few moments longer. His hands almost met as they created a sling for Abby to rest in. But resting was not on his mind as he let his fingers slip inside the wet curls that stroked his shaft. He opened them wider and let his fingers tease and touch, until they found their way just inside her opening. His body shook once as her juices wet them both and he felt the heat almost burn him, so ready for him was she.

Abby sucked in her breath and pressed down harder onto Hix's hand, as she tried to make him go deeper, but no matter how she moved Hix would not let her ride his fingers when he wanted to be inside her. Abby reached down, panting, and drew Hix all the way out of his clothing, placing the tip of him just inside her. She moved trying to draw him deeper inside her, but could not budge him.

Hix finally let her have her way, as abruptly he lowered his hands, making her take him inside her in one fast slide. Abby flung back her head and screamed as she was filled all at once to bursting. She was open and vulnerable to Hix as he moved her up and down, controlling the pace, bringing her to the edge, only to stop and make them both wait.

Almost out of her mind, Abby clung to Hix. "Now," she begged. "Oh my God, Hix, now please."

Hix dropped her onto the bed and followed her down, never once slipping from her. As Abby hit the bed Hix was driven even deeper inside her, and she screamed with her release. Hix felt her tighten around him and then go liquid before he made one last plunge and joined her in heaven.

Chapter 45

Abby lay with her head snuggled under Hix's chin, her leg bent and riding his hips, letting her heart slow and her body cool in these first few moments after making love. Her hand lay limp on his chest, the fingertips barely moving as she gently played with the hairs that were damp and curling. She willed her mind to stay blank, resisting any thoughts that tried to disrupt her enjoyment of the moment. She could hear the deep thump of Hix's heart under her ear as it slowly returned to normal, slowing from the race it had been on.

A low rumble finally penetrated her haze and she opened her eyes to slits, trying to pinpoint its origin. It took her a moment and then she giggled as she figured out it was Hix's stomach that was making the noise. It was letting her know that the more pressing issues had been temporarily sated, and he was hungry for something other than her.

Pulling in a deep breath, Abby raised herself onto an elbow and looked at the handsome face above her. The eyes were still closed but the face was relaxed and a slight smile played around the corners of the mouth she still had the urge to kiss. Another growl rumbled from his belly, and with a giggle Abby lowered her lips to the spot, leaving small kisses, followed by one loud smooch, as she rubbed her nose in the soft line of hair that traveled downward and disappeared under the sheet lying low across his hips.

Hix's stomach muscles jumped and a trail of goose bumps bloomed in the wake of Abby's soft lips, placing whisper soft kisses across his belly. He lay still and let her rub her face in the hair that became sparser as she followed it under the sheets. He was more than willing to act as her playground, until his stomach emitted a rumble so loud it sounded like a backed up drain letting go, sucking all the standing water down in one big gulp.

Grabbing Abby by the upper arms, Hix pulled her up his body, letting her slide along his length until her lips were even with his. Looking into her eyes, Hix saw the lazy happiness and contentment in their depths. Locking gazes with her, he fell in, letting himself get lost in the beauty of those deep pools. The shadows that were there before had been quieted for now. He kissed them closed before one final growl of his stomach had them both giggling and flipping the sheets back.

"I'll take a quick shower and then, while you take one, I'll set the table and get the food ready," Hix said, rising and heading towards the bathroom.

"How about I join you and we save time and water?" Abby countered following close behind her lover, enjoying the view of his muscles laid bare for her. "*Yummy,*" she thought, reaching out a finger to trace the indentation down the center of his back.

Hix shivered in reaction to her touch and felt himself react to her unintentional invitation. As he stopped to turn and take her into his arms, his stomach gave the most disgusting growl yet.

Abby laughed, stood on her tiptoes and planted a lingering kiss to that delicious mouth, before shoving him the rest of the way to the bathroom.

"I get the message," she said, turning back to the room to retrieve one of her bags. She pulled out a pair of soft lounge pants and a t-shirt, both old friends of hers, and pulled them on as the water started in the other room. Abby went to straighten the bed, pausing for a moment to relive the most recent adventures she had found there. Pulling her mind back from its wanderings, she bent to straighten the rumpled sheets.

Just as she was giving the bed a final few pats, her phone began to ring on the bedside table. A frown formed on her lovely brow as she looked at the object which threatened to intrude on her perfect day. She let it ring a few more times, chewing on her bottom lip, as she debated whether she should answer it or let it ring. Finally, with a small huff, she picked it up, not bothering to check the caller ID before she hit the button to connect her to the person at the other end.

"Hello," she said, her voice coming out husky and sleepy, "Who is this?" Her fingers froze in the process of raking through her thick hair, the spit dried in her mouth, and her stomach clenched with sickness, as a male voice, all oily and slick, leaked like poison into her ear.

"Hello Abby," Max said, "Didn't you recognize my number on your caller ID? I'm crushed."

Without a second thought, Abby hung up on the bastard, promptly dropping the phone onto the bed and staring at it as if it were a snake coiled and ready to strike.

"This can't be happening!" she thought wildly, as the fear she had managed to forget came rushing back with twice the force. Her eyes opened wide in panic and she started to shake as the phone began to ring once again. She refused to answer it, willing it to silence, sending the message to Max that she wanted nothing to do with him.

She didn't hear the shower stop until Hix's voice came through the door. "Is that my phone baby?" he asked.

She jumped, feeling cold panic crawl through her body from her head all the way to her toes. She felt it fill her up until she wanted to puke with the bitterness of it. *"I can't let Hix find out,"* she thought. "N*ot now, not ever! It's all a lie anyway, all a lie!"*

"No honey," she managed to get out, "it was mine."

"How about you tell whoever it is not to bother you, or better yet just let them leave a message?" Hix suggested.

Abby lifted the phone from the bed and shut it off mid-ring. The silence that followed was deafening, until she opened the small drawer on the nightstand and dropped the phone in, closing the drawer with a small bang. "*That's good,*" she thought. "*I'll deal with this later when I'm alone, when I can handle it. Maybe the jerk will get the message and not call back.*"

Abby knew better though. She knew Max was going to make her life a living hell, leaching her happiness away one drop at a time. She was afraid he would never let her relax until she lost Hix.

Abby turned her back, searching for composure as the bathroom door opened and the warm fragrant air came rushing into the room. Soon, warm, strong arms wrapped around her waist, pulling her back against his wide chest, letting his lips find the side of her neck and nuzzle there.

Hix knew something was wrong the minute he touched her body, felt the stiffness there, the coldness of her hands as she gripped his forearm almost desperately. He lowered his lips to her neck, lending his breath and lips as comfort to her, warming her.

"What is it Abby?" he whispered low and deep.

For just a split second her nails dug into his skin with the panic she felt at his question.

"Nothing," she said, shaking her head, "nothing." She plastered a fake smile on her face and turned to wrap her arms tightly around his neck. "I'm just a little tired from the trip is all. I'll go jump in the shower, if you want to get started on the food. Then if you don't mind, we can crawl back into bed. I would really like to feel your arms around me. I've been craving your body next to mine as I fall asleep. Okay?"

Hix felt the half-truth in her words. He knew she had missed him and wanted to be held tonight, but he also knew, beyond the shadow of a doubt, that something was wrong. He couldn't fix it, if she wouldn't trust him and tell him what it was.

As her arms tightened around his neck, he increased the pressure, pulling her close, matching her grip. He felt shut out, but couldn't think of a way to convince her to tell him what was wrong even though he was sure it had to do with both of them.

"Okay," he said, after a moment. "You go relax in the shower, and by the time you get out supper will be ready." He kissed the top of her head.

Abby nodded her head and waited two more heartbeats before letting him go, heading towards the shower and closing the door behind her. She couldn't seem to get her clothes off fast enough. She couldn't get under the hot spray fast enough, scrub the foulness off fast enough, but she tried. When she was done, she lowered her head to rest on the wall and cried for what now would never be clean.

Chapter 46

Saul drew in a deep breath and sighed as he witnessed the pain Abby was going through. By eliminating Jeannicca, Abby's Guardian, and taking her place, The Dark had taken its time and messed destiny up but good. He searched his memory for signs he should have seen, but the foulness had done its job well. It had been sneaky enough to fool even him, one of the mightiest Guardians of all. He felt frustration run through him and could find no vent for the feeling.

Doing the only thing he could do, was allowed to do, Saul laid one of his beautiful hands on Abby's head and let the pain drain from her into him. He bit down in anger as he experienced the pain and fear of his charge. He replaced those feelings with ones of calm and assurance that everything would work out, and trapped the memories away in the back of Abby's mind. She would have to deal with them soon enough, but for now Saul would help her forget and enjoy this evening with Hix.

Tonight had to happen. It had been written. Saul was doing what he could to mend the course of Destiny, to assist in putting things back on track. Things that had happened were going to affect things that were to happen. He could see no way out of it.

Abby got out of the shower as Saul drifted in the corner, focusing his energy on the future and what was needed. He pulled himself back to the present as Abby wiped the steam from her shower off the mirror. He watched as the mortal looked deep into her own reflected eyes. He could read her mind as she fought to add her strength to his, securing the bindings that were keeping her fears at bay.

Pushing them further back into the darkness of her mind, she achieved a sense of calm as she lightly applied make-up and fluffed her hair, before opening the door to release the steam into the bedroom and going in search of Hix.

Saul did not follow to watch as the evening progressed. Instead he remained in the small room, pacing back and forth. He was trying to come up with a way to avoid what was to come. He went through a thousand different scenarios trying to make a round peg fit into a square hole, but he always came back to the same ending. Saul let his shoulders slump, for now, in defeat. He was far from finished as he began to disappear but, for now, he was going to have to let events play out until he could find a way to right this wrong.

This game was far from over he thought, far from over!

Chapter 47

Abby and Hix spent the evening totally absorbed in each other, feeding themselves and each other from their plates, often using their fingers, then licking the juices from the sensitive tips, looking deep into each other's eyes, promising more to come. They lingered over the food Hix had prepared, letting the anticipation build, teasing, until they could wait no longer.

They spent the night in each other's arms, making love without words, letting their hands and bodies tell their own tales. When sleep finally claimed them, the first rays of a new day were beginning to lighten the eastern sky. There was no hurry to awaken, and it was well past the mid-day mark when Hix stirred and cracked open his eyes.

Instantly he became aware of the body curled next to his. He knew exactly who it was and let a small smile curve his handsome lips with contentment, deep and satisfying. His hands wander gently, exploring the curves. He felt a need to memorize them before time ran out. "*Where had that thought come from,*" he wondered? "*They had all the time in the world, right?*"

An uneasy feeling settled over Hix. Like a mist, it rolled in, and there was nothing he could do to stop it. He remembered how Abby had been last night, almost desperate in her need for him. How the phone call had made her tense, and how she had escaped into the bathroom after lying to him and saying nothing was wrong. It had been a lie, and he knew it. Even now he wanted to wake her up and beg her to tell him what was wrong. He needed her to trust him to help and understand, listen and make it better for her, for them.

But he didn't wake her. He let her sleep and forget her troubles for the time being.

Hix slowly got out of bed trying, and succeeding for the most part, to not wake her up. He was going to go out and get breakfast for them, and have it waiting as a surprise when she opened her eyes. He pulled on a t-shirt and a pair of well-worn jeans, brushed his teeth, combed his hair, and softly crept out the door, closing it quietly behind him.

Hix hummed all the way to the store, and continued as he walked up and down the aisles. He filling his cart with fresh strawberries, cream cheese, bagels, donuts covered with chocolate and filled with creamy goodies. Yumm!

Hix made it to the check-out line still in a good mood until he, being next in the line, happened to look over towards the rag magazines. Instantly, the music died in his throat, cut off abruptly, as the muscles closed up tight, choking off everything except the air he needed to stay conscious. Time stood still and the everyday noises faded until he registered nothing and no one except the front page photo that seemed to grow until it left no room for anything else in his world.

He watched as a muscled arm reached out and grabbed one of the papers. He was mildly surprised to discover that the arm belonged to him, not having been conscious of wanting to touch the hideous paper, or of wanting to know what was written about the grainy imagine displayed in vivid color. He didn't know how long he stood there holding the paper, staring at it with unseeing eyes.

He was brought back to the present as a voice finally filtered in, the words finally making sense after being repeated several times.

"Hix, hey man, wake up," the young man behind the register said, while snapping his fingers almost under Hix's nose. "You're next, come on."

Hix recovered his composure and began piling his items on the moving belt until his cart was empty.

"You want that?" the kid asked, pointing to the paper Hix still held in his hand.

"What?" Hix asked, not getting what the boy was pointing at.

"If you want that, I'll have to scan it," the clerk said.

Hix finally looked down at his hand, and as much as he wanted to throw the paper on the floor and grind it under his heel, he couldn't bring himself to do it. Instead he handed it over to be scanned, and paid for his bags without saying a word. He loaded his arms with the bags and started to walk away.

"Have a good day," the boy said. Hix met his eyes before leaving, finding pity mixed with curiosity staring back at him.

"He knows," Hix thought, his gut clenching. Hell everyone in town knew he was seeing the hot model, Abby Mathews. He wondered what to say to ease the checker's discomfort. Nothing, he decided, nothing for now.

"You too," he said, his voice coming out rough and edgy. He headed straight out the door. He didn't stop to speak to anyone, or making eye contact. His just kept moving until he was safely inside his truck with the windows rolled up and the door locked. Only then did he take another look at the picture peeking out of the closest bag. He could see Abby looking back at him.

He couldn't help himself as he reached out and brought the paper up close to his face. He studied the woman in the picture, recognizing his lover, familiar but different. She was breathtakingly beautiful, but her eyes seemed to be wrong. They looked glazed, watery, and unfocused, and Hix thought he saw a spark of fear in their depths.

It took him staring at the photo a moment more, before his eyes finally left her face, to study the rest of the picture and the caption that was big and bold. ***Super* Model Parties Hard While Latest Boyfriend Stays Home**. Hix didn't recognize the guy in the picture, but it seemed like he was way too familiar with Abby. Much more than a normal friend would be.

He flipped the pages of the paper to find the story inside, slowly at first, then faster, until he finally found what he was looking for. There was a picture of himself and Abby walking down the street, holding hands and laughing. Then there was another picture of her and a man they called Max, leaving a club, hanging onto each other, looking very intimate. Abby had told Hix that there would be pictures and things written that he should not pay attention to. Such was the life of a celebrity and the never-ending fairytales spun by the papparazzi. But this story and pictures, coupled with the way Abby had been acting since she had gotten off of the plane, made the seed of doubt take root and flourish in his once trusting mind.

He read the article, not wanting to, but unable to stop himself. It was kind of like coming upon a car accident and not being able to look away from the horror. It seemed Max was the photographer on the shoot Abby had just completed. The story was pretty generic until the last paragraph, and the small picture that went with it—Abby leaving Max's hotel room early the next morning.

The air rushed out of Hix's lungs like he had just gotten sucker punched in the gut. Unexpected and hard! It hurt! Knowledge hurt! Hix didn't know what to do. So he stayed where he was until his mind was numb from thinking about it.

"Had Abby spent the night with this guy?" he wondered. "Why *would she do something like that*?"

Hix knew that they had something special, maybe not perfect, but it could be with time. He had to get Abby to tell him what happened. Maybe there was an explanation for everything, and he was just jumping to conclusions.

"Okay," he thought. "*Okay. I have to get home*."

He started the truck and drove slowly home, trying to figure out how to get the subject out in the open. He turned into his driveway and killed the engine, opened the door, and took all of the bags in one strong arm. He held the paper under his other arm. Then at the last moment, he threw it back on the seat and shut the door with enough force to rattle the windows. He would not bring that trash into his house. Not in his home!

Hix tried with all his might not to let his mind jump ahead. Taking his time, he walked slowly up the sidewalk and by the time he reached the front door he had almost gotten things under control. Hix wasn't a wimp and he hated having his happiness resting in another's hands. But that was exactly where it was at the moment, in a pair of beautiful soft hands. Would those hands hold strong, or would they let the happiness and future slip through to drift away on the breath of a wind called Fate? "Only time will tell," Hix thought as he reached for the knob to his door. Time would tell, and that time was now!

Chapter 48

Hix made it inside and had shut the door, before a soft half-asleep voice called from the open bedroom doorway.

"Hey baby, is that you?" Abby asked, her voice warm and rough from just waking up.

Hix cleared his throat and held his body stiff, willing himself not to rush to his lover and demand an explanation on the spot.

"Yea," he said, "I went out and got breakfast."

He heard a low purr in response, as he headed for the kitchen and the nearest counter. As he unloaded their feast, he realized he had no appetite left. If he hadn't gone to the store, he would be blissfully ignorant right now. They would have eaten in bed, licking the frosting from each other's fingers before making love, she still sleepy and warm from their nights slumber.

But he HAD gone out, and now his gut was in knots, wondering what the future held for them both.

He had just finished piling the donuts on a plate, when he felt slim arms creep around his chest and pull him back against the lush body he had not heard approach. Abby laid her cheek on his shoulder blade and breathed in the fresh scent that was Hix. His body was rock solid against her smooth cheek, and she nuzzled it with her nose for just a moment before letting go and squeezing herself between the counter and the body she was beginning to tingle for. Looping her hands around his neck she pulled his mouth down to hers, so she could satisfy her need to taste and share their first kiss of the day.

Hix tried to act normal, to push the awful doubts from his mind, but he could not. He kissed Abby, and as he did his arms wrapped themselves around her body, pulling it close to his, trying without conscious thought to absorb her into him. To make her his, and keep her all to himself. But again he could not.

After a moment Hix pulled back, and without meeting the beautiful eyes that had opened and were now searching his face, he reached behind her back and grabbed the plate of gooey goodies. He turned and headed towards the table, stopping to grab a jug of milk and two glasses, before placing everything on the table, pulling out a chair, and sitting down.

"Come sit down," he said, throwing the words over his shoulder without looking at Abby, not meeting her questioning eyes.

Abby padded over and took a chair opposite Hix without saying a word. She grabbed a donut from the pile and waited as Hix poured them each a glass of the icy cold milk. Absentmindedly she began to pick her meal apart, making a pile in her plate but putting nothing in her mouth.

Not a word was spoken between the two as they pretended to sate a hunger neither one felt. Hix, because of the knowledge he could not unlearn, and Abby because of the tension she could feel rolling off Hix like a thunder cloud building over the flat prairie, growing taller and more massive as time passed and it gathered speed.

Finally, being unable to stand it any longer, Abby leaned back in her chair and, with sticky fingers and a knot in her stomach, she found her voice enough to ask him, "What's wrong Hix? Has something happened? You've been quiet and withdrawn since you walked in the door. What happened? What is it? Did you have an accident on the way to get breakfast? Are you hurt, not feeling well?" she asked, one question quickly followed the other as she tried to get an answer from him.

Getting no response from the statue sitting across from her, Abby blew up and released her frustrations. "God damn it Hix, stop making me guess and just tell me what is going on!"

Hix finally raised eyes that were smoky blue with the emotions that were boiling inside him, and for the first time that day he looked into the deep pools that wanted reassurance from him that all was well. His mind was going a mile a minute, trying to bring the right words out, to get to the truth, to broach the subject that sat in his gut, mind and heart like a ball of poison growing with each passing second.

"Ask her," a voice in his mind urged. *"Just be a man and ask her."*

Hix cleared his throat and wiped his hands on the thighs of his jeans. They were cold and clammy with sweat. Like the sweat that was running down his back, in fear of the answers he needed to hear.

"Actually, Abby," he started in a rough voice, "I need to ask YOU what is wrong? Last night you were different. Something was bothering you when you got off the plane. I could feel it, see it, and when you got that phone call you ran for the bathroom, shutting me out before I could ask what was wrong. So, I'm asking you now, what is it?"

Abby pulled back and sat with her back stiff against her chair. "I don't know what you're talking about," she said, fear gripping her with cold, mean fingers. "I was just tired from working so hard and the flight back home. Nothing else."

Hix wanted to cry with the feelings of sadness that gripped him. She didn't trust him. His love didn't feel she could confide in him about what was wrong. He looked at her and even now he could see the fear in her eyes, making them dark and jittery. They looked everywhere but at him. Her fingers were clenched tight until the knuckles were white with the effort of deception.

Swallowing hard, Hix couldn't bring himself to say the words, so he took the coward's way out in exposing what he knew. "I left something for you on the seat of the pick up when I came in," he said, his voice barely above a whisper. "Could you go and get it?"

Abby let a frown settle on her brow, as she mulled over what could possibly be waiting for her out there. Maybe it was a welcome home trinket, she thought. Or maybe, she thought, her eyes glowing and her heart rate speeding up, maybe it was a ring, and Hix was just freaked out with the thought of asking her to marry him.

"Oh my God," she thought, letting the excitement rush through her. "That has to be why he was being so strange this morning." He was nervous. That's a typical man, wierding out when it came to making a commitment. Maybe she had been tense last night and he was unsure of her answer this morning. She remembered reading a story in a magazine about him shopping at a jewelry store while she had been in New York. He had been picking out a ring. Her ring! He wanted to marry her.

With a glowing smile on her face, Abby jumped up and hurried to the sink to rinse the stickiness from her hands, before stopping to place a kiss on Hix's cheek. "Of course, darling," she said, happiness surrounding her like the rays of the sun. "You have a surprise for me? You didn't have to do that, but thank you."

She pulled her silky robe together to belt it, and made a bee line for the door. She almost floated out to his truck, so happy with anticipation.

Hix got up and moved to the front window, not wanting to, but needing to see her reaction. He pulled aside the sheer curtain, watching as she skipped down the driveway until she got to the passenger side door and pulled it open. He watched as she looked around the cab, and could tell the instant her eyes fell on the paper he had left on the seat. He watched her stiffen and a small hand rise shakily to her throat.

She took a step backward and did not move. Hix watched as the light breeze lifted her hair and made it dance in the sun. She was beautiful, he thought, so beautiful.

Hix hadn't moved from the window, but he felt the earth move as it crumbled and cracked beneath his feet, and then he fell. All the way to hell.

Chapter 49

Abby opened the pickup door and searched the interior with one sweep of her eyes. She did not see a package, large or small, anywhere. She leaned in a little closer, taking her time as she looked, but still nothing.

The only thing out of place was a magazine on the seat. She was confused for only a second, before the picture on the front page captured her attention.

"No!" she thought wildly. "N*o this can't be happening!"*

Her legs began to shake as she took one step back. The distance did not help, as the damning photo remained before her. Her heart was slamming so hard against her ribs, that she lifted a shaking hand to her throat to keep it inside.

"Oh my God!" her mind screamed. "O*h my God! What am I going to tell Hix? He knows*."

The time for lies and denial were long past. The only thing she could do was tell him the truth and make him see that this was not what it appeared. Not as damning as the pictures made it out to be.

As Abby stood in the open door, her mind almost numb with shock, and feeling like she wanted to throw up, she became aware of a new feeling creeping through her. It invaded her body until the shock was pushed aside, having no room to live once the rage set in. It not only set in, it moved like a tidal wave from her head down to her toes. No part was left out of the white hot anger's path. Abby lowered her hand from her throat, no longer wanting to keep anything inside. She wanted it out. It was growing too fast and too big for her to keep inside. The anger felt good. It was much better than the fear of before.

Abby's heart had slowed its frantic pace until Abby could hear the deep, powerful BOOM, BOOM, BOOM, in her ears. She felt it in the fingers that no longer shook, but were now clenched until her nails dug into her palms and the knuckles showed white with the effort. Her eyes, that only moments before had been wide, were now narrowed until they were mere slits, barely showing pupils that had gone from soft brown to deep black with her rage. She saw RED! And she liked it. She fed on it, until she stood straight and tall, nostrils flared, and skin flushed.

"You bastard!" she said low, through clenched teeth. Her focus was narrowed, until the only thing in her vision was the hated image of Max. "You fucking, slimey, bastard! If you think I'm going to lose everything because of you then you better think again. Nothing happened that night. Nothing! I don't know why you are doing this, unless your fragile male ego can't take being shut down, but you're not going to ruin my life." She picked up the paper and crushed it into a wad, before turning and closing the pickup door. She made her way up the walk on bare feet, moving slow and deliberate, until she reached the front door.

Hix was not there to open it for her.

"Not a good sign," she thought, then opened the door herself and walked in, then she closed it with an angry, sharp crack. She let her eyes roam the room until she found Hix standing off to the side by the front window. He held the curtain to one side, letting Abby know he had been watching her. He had sent her out to be blind-sided by his little gift. Some of the anger she felt for Max was diverted. She felt deep annoyance at Hix's actions.

"You could have just asked," she said without preamble.

"You could have told me," he shot back, not willing to take the blame for the drama they now found themselves in.

Some of the anger of being pissed off she felt towards Hix drained away, but still no words found their way out of her mouth. She didn't know where to begin.

Hix finally let the curtain drop as he moved on stiff legs towards the couch and sat down on its edge. He swiveled his body towards Abby before he let his forearms rest on his knees.

"Sit down Abby," he invited. "We need to talk about this."

Abby let a couple of heartbeats pass before complying, and lowered herself to sit a hands breadth away from Hix. She wanted to stand up again and pace, but made herself remain where she was. She wanted Hix to see the truth in her eyes as she talked.

"We haven't been together that long, and I know we kind of had a fight before you left, but when you got off the plane I knew something was off. You seemed almost desperate, for lack of a better word. Your eyes had shadows in them, and I didn't know how to get you to tell me what was bothering you." Hix said, looking straight into the eyes that still had fire in them. He hoped this would be the opening of the door for her explanation.

Abby looked straight into the blue eyes beside her, before she let her eyes roam over the face that looked like a God's. Hix was as beautiful on the inside as he was on the outside. Abby knew that. He didn't seem to have any hidden secrets, and what you saw was what you got. Abby could put it off no longer. Taking a deep breath, she started her story at the beginning.

"Max was the first photographer to take my picture. He worked on my very first shoot, and a few since then. He has always tried to pick me up, right from the start, but I had heard about his reputation as a player, and not finding him attractive, I had no problem turning him down then, and every other time he hit on me. I think I was the only model that ever said no to him. Most of the girls did what he wanted, so he could further their careers. I didn't. If sleeping with him was the only way to get a job, then I didn't need one that bad. I heard that it made him mad, and that much more determined to get me."

"So much for the history lesson," Abby thought to herself. *"Now to the hard part."* "When I got to the shoot in New York, I found out that I would be working with Max again. It didn't bother me as I have never

changed my mind about how I feel about him. Good as a photographer, a real Pig as a man. Anyway, the shoot went fine, and on the last day everyone was happy with the way things had gone. When we wrapped it up, Max suggested everyone go to a club for a few drinks, bragged that he was buying. He offered me a ride to the club, so after I changed, we got in his car and met everyone at the club. I had one drink while I was sitting at the table with everyone. We were talking and just having a pretty good time. Some of them got up to dance, and Max asked if I wanted to. I said no. I was going to leave soon. I didn't want to dance with that ass anyway."

Abby paused her story, looking off as she remembered, "Max got up and went to the bar. When he came back, he'd brought me a fresh drink. I told him thanks, and had a couple of sips, just to be polite. I remember not too long after that, I started feeling funny. I was feeling kind of sick, so I got up to leave. Max walked me out, because I was feeling worse by the minute."

Abby stopped talking. Her mouth was bone dry as she remembered what came next. She got up and got a soda out of the fridge, "Do you want anything Hix?" she asked as she pulled a drink from the shelf. When he declined, she came back to resume her seat and her story.

"The next thing I remember, I was waking up the next day in bed with a ferocious sick headache. I lay there for a few minutes my eyes closed until the pain let up a little, then opened them, to find Max next to me. It wasn't my bed or my hotel room even. I don't know how I got there. Max said it was his hotel room and that we had had sex. I didn't, don't believe him. I wouldn't sleep with him, if he was the last man on earth," she said with desperate conviction in her voice. "I got my stuff and left."

"I've been beating myself up ever since, trying to remember, but I can't. There is nothing there." Abby turned full face to Hix and looked him in the eye. "I didn't sleep with him, no matter what he said. I can't remember, but I know I wouldn't do that. All I had been thinking about was getting back to you, being with you. Why would I do what he said, if all I wanted was you?" She wanted to reach out and touch him, but held back.

"I don't remember those pictures being taken, but I wasn't drunk, so why can't I remember?" Abby was hoping that Hix would have some answers that would make sense, but she could tell he was at a loss also.

"That's the whole story," Abby said, her shoulders slumping. A weight had been lifted with her confession, but she was no closer to the truth than before she had spilled her guts.

With the finish of the tale, silence stretched out, unbroken, as both Abby and Hix were lost in their own thoughts.

Abby's nerves were stretched to the breaking point, as she silently waited for Hix to say something.

She had just opened her mouth to ask Hix what he thought, what he was thinking when the silence was shattered by the ringing of her phone laying on the table. Reaching out a hand she was about to shut it off when the caller I D showed her the last person in the world she wanted to talk to.

Her horror must have shown on her face, for in the next second Hix had taken the phone and looked for himself at the display. Abby felt a chill race down her spine as the bright blue eyes that could look at her with such warmth turned as cold as ice and promised pain.

Without asking permission, Hix raised the phone to his ear, fury burning deep and black in his soul. It was time he thought. Time for a little fun.

Chapter 50

Max had waited a couple of days, giving Abby time to get home. Enough time for the pictures and story to hit the rag magazine that he had called with his "inside tip", and time for it to hit the stands. Time for her to have seen it and for her and her hicksville boyfriend to fight and break up. Now it was time for him to move in and get what he wanted. That long legged, honey blonde, cold model he had been sniffing around for too many years.

Max had tried other ways before this one to get her to have to rely on him for her modeling future, for success that would only come if she slept with him. He had made calls and cut her down, trying to get her blackballed from the industry, but he had always met with failure. Her reputation, first as a stunning girl, and now as a heart-stopping beautiful woman, had her firmly embedded in everyone's minds. She had been on too many shoots and had been too easy to work with for anyone to believe the lies he was trying to plant. He'd thought long and hard, trying to come up with a way to get her where he wanted her. And it had finally paid off.

It had been easy to get the pills that had made Abby appear drunk, leaving her with no memory of all that had happened afterwards, even though nothing had. No matter what he said that night, what he did, she would not give in. She kept turning away from him, whining about that damn boyfriend of hers back "home".

"Home my ass!" he thought. Max thought he knew Abby better than she knew herself, and knew that she would never be happy living in that small town where nothing happened and there was nothing to do.

Max had done some homework on that dirt hole she now called home, Winston, Nebraska. It was small, boring, and the last place on earth he would have moved to. But Abby had landed there. She had gathered friends around her and they gave her the companionship she should have gotten from him. He was what she needed, he knew her world and he fit in.

"Christ!" Max thought. "*What had she been thinking?"*

But he had been patient, and when he heard Abby had been chosen to be the new face of a company he did photography for, he knew his chance had come at last. She would not get away this time. He had given her every opportunity to come around on her own.

In New York, Max had watched her face, her eyes when they first met on the set, to see if she was secretly happy to see him. But he saw nothing as she had looked at him. He stared hard at her, trying to catch even the slightest warming of those big brown eyes, but nothing. He had hid his anger, the stuck up bitch, and worked with her all week long, telling her over and over, every day, that she was beautiful, perfect, and desirable. He kept sending her signals from behind the camera to let her know he was into her. But she had not responded.

Max had watched her when she was not on the set, seeing the far off look in her eyes and the slight downturn of her mouth, only coming alive when someone mentioned her giant of a boyfriend she had left back home. Her eyes sparkled and her cheeks blushed as she told everyone who would listen about Hix, until Max wanted to puke. By the end of the week Max was fed up with it. If he had had to hear one more time about Hix's long golden hair or his toned, hard body, or how his eyes could see into her soul, he was going to throw himself off of the first roof top he could find.

Judas priest on a pony! Max was sick of Abby thinking of Hix, missing him, wanting him. Max had given her one last chance at the club to be with him on her own, but she had refused to dance with him. He wanted to get her out on the floor where he could hold her close to his body and let her feel what she was missing. But, once again, she had refused. So he had placed the small pill in a drink for her, and watched as she sipped it, and felt excited as he watched her as it began to work.

In the end, she'd leaned on him as they walked out of the club, right into the flashing lights of the cameras outside. Max wanted Abby looking into those same cameras, as if she were ready to jump his bones right then and there.

Max had propped her up in the car and half carried her to his hotel room. Closing the door he was almost popping out of his pants as he helped her into the bedroom. He sat her on the bed and stood in front of her so she could not miss the evidence of his desire, as she was on eye level with his crotch. But she had just sat there and moaned. She kept asking for Hix to come take care of her.

Max had gotten her undressed and under the covers before joining her, tossing his clothes wherever in his hurry. But she still turned her back on him, and moved away when he placed his hands on her body, trying to arouse her until she shut up and gave in. Before he could force her, she had passed out.

Max had lain for a long time grinding his teeth in frustration, wanting nothing more than to just roll her over and do it. But in the end, his male pride had wanted her to be awake and looking into his eyes as he made her forget about Hix, and have her admit to him that he was the best.

"In the morning," he thought. He would wake up, she would be there, and he would finally have her where he wanted her.

He fell asleep, only to be awakened as the beauty beside him began to stir. He had watched the horror cover her face, as she found herself in his bed, naked and not knowing how she had gotten there.

Max had lied and told her they had had sex, but she'd left without believing him, or actually doing it with him. "*That was okay,*" Max had thought. He knew she would remember nothing, and it would be her word against his about what had happened the night before. He would give her a few days and then he would push her hard to believe they had had sex and she had loved it. He would have her running back to his arms by the time he was done. Max was sure Hix would not want her any more when he saw the picture and found out she had cheated on him the first chance she got.

Oh yes, Max had a plan, and the phone call today was the first step. He was going to remind her about that night until she could think of nothing else. Enough time had passed. As he reached for the phone, dialing her number, Max had a lazy smile on his face, anticipating her voice in his ear.

It rang once, twice, three times, before it was answered. But she did not say anything, so Max started.

"Hi baby," he said, his voice quiet and soft, going for sexy. "Miss me? I've been thinking of you. About the night we spent together. How you felt in my arms, under me, around me. How you tasted. Your mouth, your mouth is wonderful, and the things you can do with it has got me hard just thinking about it. You were wild that night. Wild and hot for me and what I could give you. You wanted it, wanted me, and I gave it to you every way you wanted it. You ate it up, baby, and wanted more. God baby, you wore me out."

Max heard nothing from the other end of the line except heavy breathing. He could see her face, see her hand gripping the phone as she sat and listened to him. Was Hix sitting right beside her or was she alone, having been dumped by the muscle bound ass from the boonies?

"Come on, baby," Max said, "talk to me. Tell me how much you missed me, how you've thought of me and wanted me. Tell me what you want me to do to you or what you want to do to me. I can hear you breathing. It's hot in my ear. I know you want me just by hearing the way your breaths are so heavy, deep, and hot. Come on, baby, talk dirty to me."

Instead of hearing Abby's sweet sexy voice in his ear, Max was greeted with a laugh, low, deep, and dripping with malice.

"I'd love to talk to you, Max," the voice said, "and I'm going to tell you exactly what I'm going to do to you . . ."

Chapter 51

Hix held the phone to his ear and said nothing as he waited for Max to begin speaking. He tried to stay relaxed, willing himself not to crush the small phone into tiny pieces. He wanted to keep an open mind and listen to what the man had to say before he said a word, but with each passing moment, each word that found his waiting ear, he fought a losing battle to not roar out his rage. It built inside him until the red hot anger turned into ice cold hate.

Hix was sure that Max was trying to be sexy and convincing. But all Hix heard was filth that was aimed at Abby. His Abby! From what Abby had told him, he was pretty sure of what Max had pulled to get Abby to his room and into his bed.

Hix may live in Nebraska but he was not born yesterday. He knew of the drugs that were written about in the papers, which were used to commit acts of violence against women. Hix would bet his life that Max had given some of these same drugs to Abby. And why? Because Abby had rejected him repeatedly. Some men had egos that were so fragile they could not take being rejected, not being in charge, not getting what they wanted. Evidently Max was one of these men. He had delusions of grandeur and used women that were weak or greedy for fame to get the sex he needed to feel important and superior.

Abby had been the only one to tell him no, which must have been a deep blow to his ego. Oh yeah, Hix knew what he had done. AND Hix had every intention of paying him back in spades, until he bled. Until the name of Abby Mathews was erased from his memory forever.

Hix waited until the wind bag had run out of air, and finally shut up long enough for him to speak. His mind was so full of what he wanted to say, he didn't know where to start. He wished he could see the look on Max's face when he learned who had been listening to his sickening tirade.

Hix closed his eyes for a second and took a long, deep breath before he started to laugh. Only it was not a laugh of pleasure or amusement. It was low and mean. He wanted to raise the hairs on the nape of the bastard's neck, and it worked. He could almost hear the gulp at the other end of the phone. Hix paused only a second before letting a little of his hatred out.

"As you probably know by now, Max," he said, quiet and calm, "this is not Abby. This is Hix, and I know what you did, Max," he said, almost spitting the name from his lips. "Abby told me what happened, what she remembers, and after listening to your speech, by the way, did you write that down, rehearse it before you called?" Hix asked, contempt dripping from every word, "Or maybe get it off a movie? No man with any balls would talk to a woman who hates him, let alone a woman he is trying to impress, the way you just did. You must not be able to get a woman unless you use your job, or in this case drugs, to get a little action. And, to top it off, you have to make up lies when even those means don't work. You still there, Max?" Hix asked. "You're not nearly as talkative now as you were earlier. Take your hand off your dick and listen close," Hix said, as he sat forward on the edge of the couch. "Abby told me what she remembers, that she believes nothing happened, and I believe her. Don't call her again. Don't even think about her, or I'll be paying you a visit. I won't sneak up on you either. You won't be able to miss me if I have to come to see you. You'll be able to tell I'm coming by the way I'm going to make the ground shake and the people scatter to get out of the way of the tidal wave of hurt coming at you, for you! And I had better not see any more pictures or read any more articles about you and her and your supposed hook up either. I bet those same papers would love to hear my side of the story about what happened. Then we could see how your career fairs. How many people do you think would hire you if they knew you used drugs on one of their favorite models to try to bed her?"

"You can't threaten me!" Max cut in. His voice was no longer low and suggestive. Now Hix could hear the fear and false bravado in it, as his tone had risen a good two octaves. "You have no power in my world!" Max said. "You can't hurt me, but I can hit you where it hurts, can't I? Big macho man doesn't like that his woman fell into bed with a better man as soon as she got out of his sight. Do you really think she was going to say, yes I slept with Max and I liked it? She was probably too afraid of you to tell you the truth. So don't try to threaten me and expect me to quake in my boots. Hell, they cost more than you make in a year, by the way. You don't scare me," he finished up.

Hix let one more deadly laugh come out before he hissed into the phone, "Remember what I said, Max. If you bother Abby again in person, on the phone, or in the press, I'll be coming to town to see you, and I promise, you won't like it. If you don't believe me, then leak something else to the press or make another phone call. But when you're done, you better start looking over your shoulder, because I'll be coming for you."

With that final warning hanging between them, Hix hung up.

Chapter 52

Abby didn't want to give the phone to Hix, but her numb fingers would not obey her. She was not fast enough and, in a second, the phone was in the big hands of Hix. She watched him as he looked at the name on the caller ID, and then, pressing the button, held it to his ear. She didn't want him to talk to Max. She didn't want him listening to his lies. They had to be lies. She couldn't believe anything else.

With every tick of the clock her heart beat faster, as she watched Hix listening without saying a word. She saw his grip tighten on the phone. She could see his eye lids lower slowly, until only a mere slit of fiery blue could be seen. She watched his face drain of color until it was pale, only to fill up with red a moment later. Abby watched his body tense until she was sure he was as hard as stone. Whatever was being said was making him angry. Beyond angry!

By the time Hix finally spoke, she was ready to fly apart with the tension in the room. At first she was shocked that Hix could be laughing while talking to the weasel Max, until it sunk in that the laugh was not good. Not good at all. It was cold and mean. It scared Abby. "What was being said?" she wondered again.

Then Hix started to speak. His words ran with venom and they dripped hate. They did not threaten but promised action and retaliation. He did not negotiate an end to the lies Max was telling, but demanded and told him exactly what would happen should he not stop. At times his mouth barely moved and, at others, his lips curled back from his teeth and Abby expected fangs to grow along with his anger.

What was he saying about drugs? Hix thought Max had used drugs on her? The idea had not occurred to Abby, but it made sense as she thought about it. Or was she so desperate to believe she had not done anything that she was willing to grasp at and hold tightly to any explanation offered to her? Abby watched and listened as Hix gave Max a final warning and then hung up.

He sat still for a long moment, before gently laying down the phone.

"Don't talk to him again, Abby," he said looking straight ahead. "Please?"

Abby could do no less than give him the assurances he asked for. "I hadn't planned on it. I'm sorry, Hix," she said, pent up tears of tension and guilt in her voice. "I'm sorry you got pulled into this mess. I didn't plan on something like this happening."

Hix finally moved to face Abby. She looked into his eyes and saw only understanding and love shining out at her. "Don't apologize for something that was not your fault. I do not blame you. The only thing I will ask of you regarding this matter is that you do not keep things from me. I can help if you let me. Don't try to handle things like this on your own. I will always be there for you, try to listen, and together we can find an answer to anything. Okay?"

Abby hadn't realized she had been crying until Hix gathered her close to his body and wiped the wetness from her face with hands that shook. They shook from seeing her in pain and regret. He knew he had caused some of it by not trusting her from the beginning.

"Don't cry honey," he said, hugging her tighter, tucking her head under his chin.

Abby cuddled close and drew strength from the strong body next to her. Hix was like a rock against her cheek, so Abby could not fully relax herself.

"What did he say, Hix?" she asked, not really wanting to know, but feeling he needed to talk about it to get it out and be done with it.

"Nothing," he said, not elaborating further.

"That's not true," Abby said, pulling away from him so she could look into his eyes. "I don't want this to come between us, and if we don't deal with it, it will always be there waiting for us."

Abby heard what she was saying, and knew it was true, but she did not want to talk about it now or ever. She wanted to forget this had ever happened, but she knew Hix had to get it out and be okay with it to trust her again.

"So, what did he say?" she asked again. She felt Hix tighten up a little more, but she waited until, with a sigh, he again pulled her to him and leaned back into the couch.

"He thought he was talking to you. He was pretty vulgar. He didn't tell me any more than you did, so I filled in the blanks myself. Abby, I think he used drugs on you. I know you heard what I said. I don't think this was you fault, or that you wanted this in any way. Let it go. I don't think we will be hearing from that bastard again. We better not," Hix said once again, letting the hate seep out to deepen his voice and darken his eyes.

They sat that way a while, huddled together each lost in thought. Finally, with a pat on her cute butt, Hix sat upright and said with forced brightness, "Come on sweetie. Let's get dressed and go for a walk around town. Or maybe a ride out to the house and putter around for a while."

Abby tucked her hair behind her ears and looked at Hix. She could see how hard he was trying not to let Max ruin their day.

"Okay," she said with a small smile. "Let's get ready and go for a ride to our house. I haven't seen what you've done lately. We can spend some time out there and maybe we can go get something to eat later. There's a new movie out, so maybe we can do the popcorn thing and a movie tonight. How does all that sound?"

Hix grinned at her and rose to his feet, pulling her with him. "That sounds great, baby. Go get dressed and I'll wrap up the donuts to take with."

Hix watched Abby walk into the bedroom without moving. When she disappeared from sight, he let his fists clench, felt his muscles cord, and shook with the effort it took to not throw his head back and vent his anger to the skies. He needed to put this out of his mind and behind him. After a few moments, he had mostly succeeded. Mostly. Try as he might, he could not fit all the anger and hate into the room in his mind and make the door shut. One small worm was left to crawl and creep around Hix's mind and soul. Hix felt tainted, dirty from just talking with Max. It was going to take a meeting face to face to rid him of Max forever.

Abby would have had reason to be scared if she could have seen Hix's face at the thought of what he wanted to do, what he would do to Max. Hix savored the thought of violence for one more instant, before hiding it as Abby came back to his side. As they walked out the door Hix's last thought was to Max.

"This isn't over yet!" his thoughts went out to Max. *"I still have a score to settle with you Max. And believe me I never get even, I get ahead."*

Chapter 53

The trip out to their new house didn't take very long. Hix and Abby passed the time in silence, speaking with their clasped hands as he drove, the tight squeezes showing that they were both aware of the other.

Hix pulled the truck up into the driveway and shut off the engine, before turning his head to take in Abby's reaction. It had been a while since she had visited the site, and a lot had changed. He studied her face, letting a smile creep onto his face and a warmth into his chest, as he felt pride at her reaction to his work.

After a moment, Hix got out and walked around to open the door for an eager Abby, as she slid out and hit the ground moving. Hix moved at a slower pace, and finally caught up to his lover as she stopped at the front door waiting for him. He reached around her and opened the door, letting her go in first then closing them into their soon to be home.

He took a second to breathe deep, loving the scent of new wood, new everything. He had spent every spare moment pouring his heart and soul into making a place for him and Abby to start a life together. Friends and neighbors had helped, but the ideas and designs were all his.

He tried to see it from Abby's eyes as he looked around. A big entryway with doors to the living room and dining area on each side, the kitchen, den, bathroom, and family room in the back. Large patio doors opened to the backyard that, next spring, he would sod and landscape. A big staircase led up to the second floor in front of him, curving around to the right and ending on a landing leading to three bedrooms and two bathrooms. He had left the painting and carpeting till last, waiting for

Abby to let him know what she wanted. He wanted her to have a hand in the color scheme, so she would be happy with her home.

He didn't say much as Abby moved from room to room, running her hands along the walls and peering into all the nooks and crannies. She opened closets and cupboards to eagerly look inside. Her tour finally ground to a halt as she entered the master bath off the main bedroom. Their bedroom. The bedroom itself was huge, with a walk-in closet and large windows to look out over the soon to be backyard. But the bathroom caught her eye.

Hix got out of the way, as Abby made a bee line to the doorway and stopped short at what she saw. One wall was mirrors, sinks, and storage closets, but the other was filled by a jetted bathtub large enough to fit a small army in. Abby stood for only a second, before getting in and stretching out. She lay with her head on the rim and her arms resting on the sides. A small sigh escaped her lips. Hix could picture her reclining in mountains of bubbles, hair piled on top of her head, moisture on her face, and him beside her.

When he had gone shopping for the tub, he knew this was the one the moment he saw it. Big enough for both of them at once to relax in, make love in, and play in.

Abby opened her eyes and looked straight into Hix's before she inched over, and with velvety eyes, invited him to join her.

Hix didn't hesitate, but crawled in to lay his large body down beside her. Abby did not hesitate in rolling over and lying full out on top of him. There was plenty of room.

"But why waste a golden opportunity to share a moment of passion with this beautiful man?" Abby thought.

She placed her hands on each side of his face and brought her lips to his, tasting the love he had for her there. The kiss they shared was sweet and slow, warm and soft. Neither felt the need to make it deeper yet. They were both enjoying the moment of their first kiss in their new home. Abby pulled back, opening her eyes to get lost in the smoky blues only inches from her.

"So, do you like everything?" Hix asked, waiting for her answer, not kidding himself. He wanted her approval, her excitement to match his own.

"You made a miracle. This place, our place, is a miracle. You are a miracle! You are magic!" Abby answered with a smile on her lips. Once again, she moved in for a kiss, but this time she had every intention of letting him know that she was overwhelmed with his efforts and loved what he had accomplished. "We're going to be happy here, aren't we?" she asked, wanting reassurance that they would continue, their love would endure.

"Yes," he vowed against her lips, "we are going to be happy here. This is for us and us alone. Right now this is a house, but we're going to make it a home, and fill it with laughter and love and our own family."

Hix filled his hands with hunks of Abby's soft tresses, angling her head to make her mouth more accessible to his. He wanted her here, now. He wanted to erase the ugly taste in his mouth and soul that the morning's events had left behind. He wanted Abby to have only good memories of her first time in their house, and to think of nothing but them and their future. He wanted nothing to come between them. He wanted a lot, he knew, but he was going to make it happen. He proceeded to give Abby what she wanted and needed. What he wanted and needed.

The silence of the house was broken by low mummers and soft sighs as they christened the house as new lovers and owners do. Still, memories of what he had learned that morning added a touch of desperation to his every move. "Mine," he repeated over and over in his mind, keeping time with his body's movements. "She's mine, she has to be mine."

When they lay panting, hearts racing, letting their bodies rest, Hix felt the difference in Abby. A small distance lay between them that hadn't been there before. Her hand did not move slowly over his skin, and her stillness worried him. He was at a loss as to what to do, so he wrapped his arms around her soft body and held on tight.

"I'll kill you, Max, you low life!" he thought. *" I'll see you burn in hell!"* The heart that beat like thunder under Abby's ear, thundered still, but now it thundered for revenge.

Chapter 54

Saul moved out of the bathroom doorway, as Hix crawled in to join Abby in the huge tub. He didn't need to see what was going to happen, he knew. He always knew. Sometimes he wished he didn't know all that he did, what had happened, what would happen. He felt the emotions that they felt and hurt for them. But he was not allowed to interfere, to change the parts he had the power to change. He had to let the future play out as it was written.

Saul moved through the house that Hix had built with his heart and soul. He saw ghostly images of the future, near and far. Saul could only hang his handsome head, the glorious wings on his back feeling like they weighed a ton, and his knowledge of the future weighing heavy on his Immortal heart.

Saul stopped his wanderings and lifted his hands to stare at the power that he could see pulsing from them. He could take the painful memories from their minds and let them love without doubt, using nothing but the very hands he held in front of his dark eyes. "*Just one touch.*" he thought, "*Just one small act to make two lives easier.*"

"But you won't." spoke a dark whisper in his mind *"You know the chaos that would be unleashed should you interfere."* Saul heard the Fates as they whispered in his ear, spoke to his mind, and heard the warning underlying the simple words that were uttered for him alone. He knew they were right, but it did not make the future any easier for him to watch. Saul lowered his hands to his sides and squared his shoulders, hoisting the burden he carried to a higher position. "I can carry this load." he thought. He had many times before, and would many times in the future. It was what he did, the only thing he did.

Saul felt the Fates retreat from his mind. They knew he would do the right thing. He was their champion, their mightiest. He wielded his power with care and compassion, but always within the boundaries set for his kind.

Saul turned and made his way back to the bathroom, finding his charges wrapped in each other's arms. He found their thoughts, and doing the only thing he could, took their pain and doubts into himself, letting them rest and love for a time in peace.

Chapter 55

The next few months flew by for Hix and Abby, as the finishing touches to the house were completed. Their belongings found their way into their new home little by little. It was no longer just a house, but a home for both of them.

Abby turned down all the jobs that had been offered to her, opting to stay home and be close to Hix. Try as she might, the memory of her last shoot and what had happened afterwards would not leave her mind. She'd buried it as far down in her subconscious as she could, but reminders and images cropped up when she least expected them, leaving her reeling and sick to her stomach. Her eyes that had once, not so long ago, been clear and bright, were now dull and haunted.

Since meeting Hix, Abby had let her friendships with Kendall, Mary, and Tonia slide to the background. But in the last month, she had begun calling them, and had even set up a lunch with them for the next week. She hoped seeing and talking to them would bring things back to the way they had been not so long ago. She needed someone to talk to besides Hix. She needed her girlfriends to help her carry the burden and give her some advice on what to do. Not that there was a lot to be done now, since Max had not tried to reach her after his talk with Hix.

Just the thought of it made Abby shiver, as the ugly memory of that day flooded her mind once again. It made her stomach roll to the point that she rushed into the bathroom to bring up her breakfast. Abby leaned with shaking arms on the sink, head down, gulping for breath. As she raised her head, her skin felt clammy, and she saw tendrils of hair clinging to her pale cheeks in the mirror. Her eyes were watery, and seemed too large for her face. She hardly recognized herself. Pale, thin, and ill looking was not a good look on her. It took a while, but with the magic of makeup, Abby emerged from the bathroom looking none the worse for wear. Only by looking deep into her eyes would one be able to tell all was not as it seemed.

The morning was still young. With Hix at work, Abby was left on her own to putter around the house, or not. Making a decision, Abby grabbed her phone and hit a familiar number, waiting as she heard the ring sound once and then twice. She did not realize she had been holding her breath, until she heard her best friend's voice come across the phone.

"This is Kendall, may I help you?" the friendly voice came to Abby's ear.

"Hey woman," Abby said, her voice shaking slightly with relief.

"Abby!" Kendall said happiness and excitement in her voice. "What's up?"

"Can you get away for a long lunch?" Abby asked, not beating around the bush.

Kendall thought for just a second before saying, "Sure. What time? I can leave for the rest of the day and we can have all the time you need."

Abby swallowed the lump in her throat, loving her friend for knowing what she needed without having to be asked. "Great!" Abby said, feeling better already. "Can I pick you up about eleven, and we can go have lunch somewhere?"

"Sounds good to me, sweetie. See you then." Kendall replied, a happy smile in her voice.

Abby heard the click as the line disconnected, but still held the phone to her ear a few seconds longer. Kendall was no longer there, but it still felt like a life line to Abby and she clung to it as long as she could.

The morning seemed to drag, until Abby could wait no longer. At ten-thirty, she grabbed her keys and purse and headed out the door. She tried to corral her thoughts on the drive to get her friend. She wanted to be able to lay everything out for Kendall in an orderly fashion.

The car had barely rolled to a stop before Kendall yanked the door open and made herself at home in the plush passenger seat. Clicking her seat belt into place, Kendall finally turned her head to look at her friend and was not happy with what she saw. Although Abby had taken care to give her face some color, she saw through all that. Kendall was no slouch when it came to seeing what was underneath what people were trying to hide.

"Well," Kendall said, "we need to find a place to eat, and you will eat. You look like all the rest of those skinny-ass models. Not a good look on you. If you turn to the side and stick out your tongue, you could pass for a zipper. Food," Kendall demanded, "Now!"

Abby sat for a second, stunned that everything she saw in the mirror, Kendall had picked up on.

"Hello to you, too," Abby said, with a slight tremor in her voice.

Kendall shot a look in Abby's direction, making up her mind in a flash. "Tell you what," she said in an off-handed manner, "let's head to my place and I can grab stuff out of the cupboards and throw something together for us. I'm pretty good at doing that if you remember."

"I remember," Abby replied, glad to be out of the public eye for their lunch. She felt on edge and about to break, and didn't relish having anyone see her fall apart. Because that was what was going to happen, she knew it. "That sounds perfect, but you don't have to cook, we can grab a pizza or something and take it to your place. How 'bout that?"

"Pizza it is," Kendall said, and sat back as the car began to roll.

Within the hour, loaded down with pizza and bread sticks, the two friends walked in the door of Kendall's small two-bedroom house. She closed it behind them, leaving the world, with its prying eyes, outside.

"Food first," Kendall said, as she headed to the table and dumped her packages. "I'll get some plates and paper towels, and you get something to drink from the fridge."

Abby did what she was told, grabbing two pops and cranking the lids off as she rejoined Kendall at the table.

Kendall laid out the food and glanced at Abby. "We are going to eat and talk about stupid things, like the weather while we do. After we get some food in you, you are going to tell me what's bothering you, everything. Okay?"

Abby could only nod her consent, and keep her eyes down while she put food on her plate. She fought for control, and finally finding it, followed her friend to the couch in the living room. Sitting down, she followed Kendall's example and dug in, even though she didn't have much of an appetite. She knew Kendall would nag her until she ate, and she had things to get off her chest.

So Abby followed the plan and ate while Kendall told her about what was going on in her own life. Same old stuff, but she had a way of telling it that had Abby laughing. Before Abby knew it, she had polished off two pieces of pepperoni pizza and a couple of breadsticks. For the first time in recent memory, Abby felt full and happy. Her muscles relaxed and her smile came back, bringing a sparkle to her eyes with it.

Kendall kept a sharp eye on her friend as she talked and ate. She could tell that whatever was coming was big. It didn't take a crystal ball to figure that one out. Swallowing her last mouthful, Kendall sat back on the couch, grabbed a pillow, and snuggled it up in her lap.

"I'm feeling pretty fat and sassy right about now," she said, waiting for Abby to sit back also. The smile fell from her face, and the blue eyes she pinned on Abby were hot and intense.

"Now, Abby," she said," tell me what's wrong, and don't leave anything out. I'll help, if you let me, even if it's just an ear for you. But my shoulders can carry a lot, so spill it. By the looks of you, when you get done I'm going to feel like kicking some ass. So let's get to it."

Chapter 56

Kendall watched as the color drained from her friend's face, leaving her skin pale and waxy. She sat in silence for a moment, letting Abby collect her thoughts, and then she pushed. "Well?" she said, not unkindly. "We're not moving until you tell me what's going on." She watched as Abby gathered her thoughts, emotions running rampant across her lovely face.

Abby's mouth was so dry she could not work up the spit to loosen her tongue from the roof of her mouth. Finally, she turned on the couch to face Kendall and began, haltingly, to tell her friend everything she was keeping bottled up inside. She too had grabbed a pillow to hold in front of her, but unlike Kendall, Abby had a death grip on hers, digging her nails in and holding on for dear life. If it had been a person, black and blue marks would have sprung up and stayed, giving evidence to her rolling emotions.

Her words came out in short bursts at first, low and quiet. But the more she talked the faster they came, until they flowed out of her mouth as if an invisible dam had been broken, churning and tumbling over each other, taking their poison with them.

Abby held nothing back. This was Kendall she was talking to, after all. It wasn't Hix, so Abby did not censor her words or her feelings. She did not have to put on a brave face for her.

She began by telling Kendall about the modeling job in New York, and the small fight she and Hix had gotten into right before she left. Not so bad. Then came the part about the "after the shoot" party and waking up in bed with Max, the scum bag, unable to remember anything about the previous night and how she had come to be where she was. Her voice held disgust and loathing, and she spat the words out fast, as if they were bitter on her tongue. And they were, ripping her soul to shreds as she tried to purge herself of the guilt she could not seem to get over.

Then came the part where Max gave her his version of what had happened, and her fleeing his apartment, wanting only to escape from the nightmare she'd woken up to.

She described the flight home and the reunion with Hix, before stopping for a gulp of her now flat pop. She made herself tell her friend about the pictures in the rag paper and how Hix had found out about them standing in line at a grocery store, instead of from her.

Almost finished now, Abby told Kendall how Hix had answered her phone, only to discover Max on the other end of the line. How he'd listened without a word, before telling Max never to call again, his voice dripping with unbridled hate and the promise of bodily harm if he didn't heed his warning.

Coming in on the final stretch, Abby told Kendall how things were between her and Hix now. "They seem pretty good on the surface," Abby said, meaning to leave it at that, but then continuing when Kendall's questioning look prompted her to elaborate.

"Well, I can't really speak for Hix but it's always with me," Abby confessed. "Sometimes I can go a whole day without it popping into my head, but then other days something reminds me and it eats at me until Hix gets home and I have something to distract me."

Giving a deep sigh, Abby flopped back against the arm of the couch, spent from telling her tale. She closed her eyes for a few seconds and just breathed in and out, waiting for Kendall to say something. As the silence stretched out, Abby began to get nervous and finally made herself open her eyes a mere slit to see her friend's reaction to all of it. But her eyes did not remain slits for long. As Kendall's face became clear, Abby's eyes flew open and she sat straight up.

"Kendall," she asked, "are you all right? What's wrong? Do you need something?"

"Oh yeah," Kendall ground out, "I need something all right. I need that Max's shriveled up, unmanly balls on a platter."

Abby hardly recognized her friend as she was now. Her face, which was usually soft and smiling, was hard as marble, pale with spots of fiery red straining her cheeks, and a grim line where her mouth had been only a few short minutes ago.

All this was alarming to Abby, but what alarmed her most were Kendall's eyes. Her eyes were no longer the beautiful blue everyone loved, but black holes that gave a glimpse of hell and its dark pits of pain.

"Kendall," Abby said, alarm in her voice. "Kendall, say something!"

Kendall's eyes focused on her friend beside her, and even registered the hand that was reaching out to her. But her mind was a million miles away, traveling down a road that she did not need company to navigate. It was not a familiar place for her, but one she was not going to turn back from. Abby needed her right now so she pulled off to the side and postponed her journey until she was alone and could plan. But she would not forget. Would not forget where she was and where she was going.

In her mind's eye Kendall could see a road sign in front of her. It read only one word, REVENGE.

"Oh yeah!" Kendall thought. She was going to be traveling this road, and she was going to make sure that at the end of her journey Max would be just a bloody little speed bump for having hurt her friend.

"Buckle up baby." Kendall thought. "We're going for a ride!"

Chapter 57

Kendall blinked only once as she brought her mind back to the present. "I'm here, Abby," she said, her voice sounding hoarse even to her own ears. "I'm fine."

"No you're not." Abby said. "I'm so sorry to dump all this on you, but I had to talk to someone and you were the first one that came to mind. Really, you're the only one. I know it's alot, but I need you right now."

Kendall watched as tears began to form in Abby's haunted eyes. She could see fear in them also. Kendall felt her temperature rise again and worked hard to slam a lid on her anger, to focus on being the friend that Abby needed. She was there to give advice, comfort, and reassurance. Not to blow her top and tell Abby that she was going to take care of that little pimple. And, if need be, get Hix to help her.

Kendall took Abby's hand and squeezed it tight in hers, trying to let her know that she was right to have confided in her. "I'll always be here for you, honey" she said, "just as you are always here for me when I need someone." Kendall gave Abby's hand a pat and put a smile on her lips, encouraging one in return. "*That's better,*" she thought.

"Okay," Kendall said out loud, "let me get all the facts straight and see if I have missed anything. One, you went on a photo shoot and the photographer was an asshole named Max, right?"

"Correct," Abby said with a nod.

"He's been after you for a while now, hasn't he?" Kendall asked.

"I guess so," Abby replied hesitantly. As Kendall raised one eyebrow and looked sternly at Abby, she confirmed Kendall's suspicions with a hesitant nod.

"Okay, yes," Abby admitted, with more conviction "ever since I got into the business."

Kendall shifted her position until she faced her pale-faced friend squarely. "Tell me one thing, Abby. Why are you letting this eat you up? Why do you even believe for one second that you have anything to feel bad about? Do you believe in any part of your being that anything happened? That you wanted anything to happen?"

With tears in her eyes, Abby reached for the warm hand of her friend. "I can't remember anything after the club, Kendall. I woke up in his bed, naked, and he was so smug and convincing when he told me what happened. I didn't remember! I want to believe that he was lying, but I can't say for sure. That's what's eating at me. Until I know for sure, it will always nag at me. How can I know for sure what happened, Kendall, tell me that? How can I know for sure?"

Kendall's heart broke for the pain she saw swirling up from the depths of the brown eyes, swimming with tears, begging her to say any words that would make it all go away. They pleaded with her to say something that would erase the uncertainty and doubt. Kendall rose to her feet and paced her living room, head down and hands on her hips. She had so many thoughts running around in her head, filling it up, that she needed to take a minute to get them in order.

She stopped to look out her front window, not really seeing outside but looking inward. With her back still to Abby, Kendall spoke in a low voice. "Not one thing you have said will ever make me believe you were at fault in what happened. I know you, Abby. I know how you work. Yes, I am your friend and that would tend to make anyone bias, but the whole thing stinks. It reeks of schemes and planning and underhanded dealings. None of that is you. It never has been. I have seen you and Hix together and listened to you talk about him. You light up when he walks into a room and I'm sure a small spat would not make you dump your feelings for him. I just can't swallow that you jumped into bed with another guy, and especially one that you have avoided ever since you met him."

Turning to face her friend, Kendall shoved her hands into her front pockets, took a deep breath and squared her shoulders. "I don't know what to say to ease your mind, but I wish I did. You have to settle this so you can move on, Abby. It may be tough love to say these things, but it's all I have. You could not have been a willing partner in the events that happened. I wish that I could give you some of my certainty that you are being used. But all I have are my feelings and my shoulders for you to dump on until you believe for yourself. You have great friends, true friends that will support you and have your back in good times and bad, so use us. We will help you any way we can, even if it is just with ears to listen or words to comfort. I love you, Abby. You know that. I probably haven't been much help to you today, but until I can do a little digging to answer a few questions that I have, it's all I've got."

Abby got up and moved to her friend. She wrapped her arms around her waist and laid her head on the shoulder offered. "Kendall you HAVE helped," Abby's muffled voice said. "Just talking to you has helped, believe me. See?" she said, false brightness in her voice as she backed up to show Kendall a pasted smile on her trembling lips.

Kendall wanted to shake her until she forced Abby to drop the fake brightness she wore just for her benefit. There was something more. Kendall saw it in the brown eyes that couldn't or wouldn't meet hers.

"What else, Abby?" she asked. "There's something else you haven't spilled yet, isn't there?"

At Abby's silence, Kendall did give her a slight shake. "Abby, what is it?" Kendall asked.

Abby took a deep, shuddering breath and let it out, before letting her eyes show the horror she felt.

"I'm pregnant, Kendall," she said, the words falling like vomit from her lips. "I'm pregnant! But who is the father?"

Chapter 58

Saul felt each word that Abby spoke, as if it were a hammer blow to his chest. The pain was deep and, if he were a mortal, each stroke would have taken his breath away, leaving him doubled over and gasping for his life. But, as an Immortal, he took each wave of pain and stood straight and tall, accepting her hurt as his own. Though it didn't stop him from raging at the course Abby's destiny was taking.

"Damn it!" he thought to himself. Just once he would like to be able to fix things in his charges' lives so they would not have to live through unbearable pain. But that wasn't his choice, his job. This time, right now, he couldn't even rest his hands on Abby and make her pain less. More bearable! He had to stand by and let her hurt, let her figure this out for herself, so she could go on with her life and find the strength to accept her own pre-written destiny.

Saul paced behind the couch where Abby and Kendall had just been sitting, where they were sharing Abby's story. He was not Kendall's Guardian, but he could feel her surprise, her confusion, and her rage as she heard her friend out, until the last confession froze her mind and her blood, leaving her incapable of thought and movement, alive but not.

Saul came to stand behind Abby's friend, and bent down to whisper in her ear. "Call your friends," he said. "Call her friends. Together you can give her the support she needs. Help her through this. Do not take this on by yourself. Call for help!"

Saul pulled back after planting the suggestion in Kendall's mind. Saul knew she would act and do the right thing by her friend. His presence did not even ripple the air in the room. He gave no clue that he was watching, but wanted to. He wanted to appear before Abby and let her know she was not alone, give her comfort and strength and let her know that all was as it was supposed to be in her life. The problems she now faced were neither ever-lasting nor insurmountable.

Saul whirled to the other side of the room, trying to contain the frustration he felt, trying to find a way to let it out. He unfurled his great wings until they filled the room, unseen by the humans inside. Always unseen. He tipped back his head and let his feelings escape in one long cleansing roar. The sound, unheard by human ears, and the power that flowed like bolts of lightning from his clenched hands, seemed to help calm the Guardian. He dropped his now heavy head onto his chest and folded his wings until they lay on his back again. He had made room once again inside himself to do the tasks assigned him. Right now Abby needed him to give her what help he could, what guidance he could.

"So little," Saul thought. An idea, whispered in a waiting ear, seemed to be a meager way to help his charge. But it was all he had to offer at the moment.

"I will return," Saul said to Abby, letting her feel a small measure of calm she attributed to the suggestion her friend gave about calling all their friends together. But Saul knew it was his reassurance of returning that gave Abby a small space to breathe.

"Hold on Abby!" he thought, barely a glimmer of his presence remaining. "*Hold on.*" And he was gone.

Chapter 59

Tonia and Mary had dropped what they were doing and responded to Kendall's 911 call without question. When a friend called in trouble you didn't ask questions. You just came. They had arrived, as if planned, at the same time and were standing on the door step looking at each other for answers. None were forth coming, as the door opened and Kendall ushered them in without a word.

The grim look on her lovely face stalled the questions each was dying to ask. When the door closed, Kendall led the way into the living room and the four friends were united, with only two knowing why.

"Thanks for coming," Kendall said, standing in front of the couch where they all had taken a seat.

"What gives?" Tonia asked, not wanting to waste time. She knew by Kendall's posture and the sound in her voice that something serious was going on.

Kendall looked at Abby, noticing that the small amount of color that had returned to her cheeks had once again drained from them. It was as if a plug was pulled while gravity took her peace of mind once more.

"I . . . ," Abby began, but could not go any farther. With her eyes she begged Kendall to tell her tale to Tonia and Mary.

"One of you spill. What's going on?" Mary demanded, not willing to be patient.

Kendall looked at Abby, once more, to see if she would change her mind, but could see she would not. So, with a squaring of her shoulders, Kendall retold Abby's story. Leaving out nothing, she went over all the gory details for her friends. She tried to relay the story without putting her feelings behind it. She wanted to allow Tonia and Mary to judge for themselves, to form their own opinions. But she couldn't. Disbelief, hurt, anger and rage bled through, as she got deeper into Abby's drama.

When Kendall got to the end, the news of the baby, her smile was grim as she watched both of their friend's faces freeze and pale. Even without posing the question Abby had earlier, Kendall could see the question hovering in the air that filled the room. But just as quickly, she saw the idea dismissed without credence as each came to the defense of their friend.

"Have you told Hix yet?" Tonia asked, looking Abby square in the eye.

"He'll ask you to marry him, you know," Mary said.

"Are you going to say yes?" Tonia chimed in again.

"Of course she will," Kendall added, seeing where her friends were going with the conversation.

There was more than one way to show support to a friend, and one was to show them a new direction to focus on. Not one of them had a single doubt that Hix would get down on one knee and ask Abby to be his wife, and give his name to the baby. After all, they believed, as one, that the baby was his.

Abby let her eyes travel to each of her friends. Mary's soft hazel eyes held unwavering support. Tonia's eyes of pure jade, showed concern and compassion. While Kendall's smoky blue ones showed the promise of revenge for her friend. Abby forced a small smile to curve her trembling lips and drew strength from these wonderful friends that had come to her aide.

"You guys are the best, you know," she said. "I don't know what I would do without all of you."

Simultaneously, three hands reached out to Abby, each touching her, giving her warmth and understanding.

"We will get through this together," Tonia said, looking to the others for their nods of consent. "We haven't had a big wedding in this town for a long time. We are going to make this one a fairy tale event." she said with a bright sparkle in her eyes.

"You're all so sure Hix will ask me to marry him," Abby said, doubt still visible in her voice and her brown eyes.

"Yes, of course he will," was the answer that came from the three friend's voices in perfect unison as one.

"There is another choice," Abby said, dropping her eyes to her clenched hands. "I don't have to have this baby. No one would ever know except you three."

"Could you live with that decision, Abby?" Mary asked, her eyebrows raised.

"All it would take to be sure is a DNA test after the baby's born, and all the questions would be put to rest. There isn't any question in my mind that the baby is Hix's, anyway," Tonia said.

"Not one of us here thinks any differently either. Max's rendition of the evening in New York is a bunch of shit and you know it, Abby!" Kendall said with fierce conviction in her voice that mirrored on her face. "Not that I'm trying to tell you what to do, but Hix and you have made a baby, and I know you both will love the crap out of it. The only question I see here is if you want to marry Hix. You don't have to, you know. People have babies without getting hitched all the time."

"I guess it will depend on if Hix asks or not," Abby said, still hesitant to consider everything would be all right.

"Okay, suppose he asks." Tonia said. "What would you say"?

The question hung in the silence that followed, as the three friends waited for an answer.

Abby's eyes finally picked up a small sparkle as she gave her first genuine smile of the afternoon. "I'd say yes," she replied, as the other women hooted out their approval.

"When are you going to tell him?" Mary asked.

"We have to make a plan," Tonia said. "Make a nice romantic evening out of it. Make it special!"

Tonia, Mary, and Abby scooted closer together on the sofa and put their heads together, throwing out ideas, then rejecting them. All were giggling together as they jumped in, whole heartedly, trying to get the setting just right. None of them noticed Kendall did not join in. None of them noticed the ice that grew in her smoky blue eyes until the smoke was gone and all that remained was cold fire. It was a fierce fire that she would bank and feed until she could get to New York and face Max. Make him pay for putting her friend through hell. Make him pay until the fire in her eyes and in her belly was let loose on him. Then she was going to sit back and watch him burn.

Chapter 60

Hix had worked like a dog all day. The owner of a new house he was building wanted some changes made, nothing major but still time consuming and stressful. He didn't really mind. After all, he'd been hired to build them their dream home, and he took great satisfaction in knowing they'd chosen him to make it all happen.

The crew had just knocked off for the day, jumping into their trucks and heading, balls to the walls, to the Nineteenth Hole for a cold one, or two, to wash away the dust and sweat of a long day of manual labor. Hix lifted the hem of his t-shirt, swiping at the dust and sweat mingling on his face, as he made his way to his truck. He pulled his work gloves out of the waistband of his jeans and tossed them onto the passenger seat, pulled himself into the cab, and started the engine. His arms rested on the steering wheel as he sat for a minute, relaxing and taking a few moments to enjoy the quiet. No hammers pounding, no saws buzzing, no voices shouting to be heard over the din, just blissful quiet.

Letting out a big sigh Hix threw the vehicle into gear and made for home. Man he was beat. What he wanted was a long, hot shower, then something quick but satisfying for dinner, followed by a short call to Abby, before turning in early for a little extra sleep. His body was craving some down time.

In no time at all he was parking his truck in the driveway and dragging his tired wagon to the front door. Once inside, he put his plan into action, peeling off clothes as he made his way from the front door to the bathroom, leaving a string of items to be picked up later. Turning the water on as hot as he could stand it, Hix stepped in and bowed his head under the much needed spray. His hands braced against the shower walls, he turned his shoulders to the hot spray, letting it massage his tired muscles. Right now, bliss was nothing more than a hot shower and some down time. Emptying his mind, he stayed under the water until it began to chill. Reluctantly he grabbed a towel and stepped out into the steamy bathroom, rubbing his body from head to toe. He pulled on a pair of sweats and a soft tee shirt, combed his hair without even looking in the mirror then headed in the direction on the kitchen, on the hunt for his dinner, which he had decided was going to be a frozen pizza and a cold beer.

Taking out the pizza and putting it in the oven, Hix popped the top on his beer and took a long, cold drink. Still craving heat for his tired body, he turned his back to the oven and leaned against the door. The heat felt good through his shirt, warming him into a state of calm. He leaned against the glass until it was time to take his dinner out of the oven and put it on a plate to eat.

Hix carried his plate, stacked high with steaming pieces of pizza, and his second beer, into the living room, where he made himself comfortable on the overstuffed sofa. He grabbed the remote and turned on the big-screen TV, flipping through the channels with one hand, while the other one guided the steaming pizza past his lips. Cheese trailed down his chin as he devoured slice after slice. In no time at all he had polished off the entire pie. Cleaning up the trash, Hix sat down again on the couch to do the next thing on his list. Call Abby.

It wasn't that he didn't want to see her, but tonight what he needed more than anything else was sleep. He was just going to have to be satisfied with hearing her voice over the phone. He dialed Abby's number and waited for her to answer. It only rang three times before the warmth of her voice poured into his ear. It traveled throughout his body, leaving him satisfied and relaxed like no shower or meal ever could.

"Hi baby," Hix said, in a low sexy voice, as he cradled the phone to his ear. A slow smile spread over his face as his eyelids lowered and his head fell back against the couch. "How was your day?" he asked, his voice low and deep.

"Pretty good," Abby replied. "Not much to tell really. How was yours?"

Hix filled her in on the extra work he'd finished, emphasizing how tired he was. "I probably won't be over tonight," he said, apologetically, "I need to get some extra sleep tonight, so I'm just gonna turn in when we get off the phone. Do you mind, baby?"

"No, that's okay," Abby assured him, disappointment heavy in her voice.

Hix heard something in her voice that had him sitting up a little straighter and holding the phone a little tighter. "What's wrong?" he asked.

"Nothing," she said, telling a lie that Hix could hear through the phone.

"No really." he said. "What is it?"

No matter how he asked or how he prodded, Abby insisted she was fine. Feeling sure there was something Abby wasn't willing to share with him, but too tired to play the game any further, Hix finally gave up, assuring Abby he would see her tomorrow night, and promising her as much of him as she could stand, as it was Friday and he had the whole weekend off.

After their goodbyes Hix laid the phone down and sat back against the cushions, a puzzled frown above his troubled eyes. Why wouldn't Abby tell him what was bothering her? Since she had never hidden anything from him before now, he wasn't sure what to do. He couldn't think of anything he'd done that would have upset her, so he was sure it wasn't about him.

"She's been acting off for a while now," a small voice in his head whispered. "Not her happy bubbly self, not her warm self, not her carefree self? What's different, Hix?" it asked. "What's changed?"

Hix shifted in his seat, trying to get a handle on what the voice was hinting at. "Nothing," he answered back in his head, the puzzled look deepening, "we've been just fine. Everything has been going great."

"Liar," it accused. "You know what's different. It's changed you, too. Always just under the surface, always waiting to creep out and sour your peace of mind. It's worse for Abby, and you know it. What is it?" the voice asked again. "What is different?"

Hix didn't want to think about it, but he couldn't keep the memory of it back in the dark corner where he had shoved it. It flooded his mind and lay in his belly like a rock. The scene when Abby had told him about what happened in New York, what happened with Max, was still fresh in his mind. It flashed before his eyes as if it were yesterday instead of a couple of months ago. He still felt the tensing of his muscles and tasted the bitterness of it on his tongue. "No," he thought "that can't be it. We are done with that! Over it! Finished!"

"No you're not," said the voice "or it would not come back to bite you in the ass when you least expect it."

"But I don't believe anything happened," Hix said. "I just don't believe it."

"If you had no doubts we would not be having this conversation," the voice stated. "You need to do something to get over this once and for all. Bury it and let it lie. Besides," the voice came back, "what makes you think this is the cause of Abby's distress?"

Hix knew it was. He felt it. He felt it every time he was with Abby. He saw it when he looked at Abby, when she thought he did not see. There were shadows in those eyes he had come to love. They lurked, were banked, but never really completely gone. The memory haunted Abby, so in turn it had haunted Hix. He could not completely let it go until Abby did.

"Of course," the voice came again, "I could be wrong. Maybe it's something totally different."

"Maybe," Hix thought, "but I don't think so."

"Well then," the voice whispered, "what are you going to do about it? What are you going to do about putting this to bed for both of you?"

"What can I do?" Hix asked. Frustration had him balling his fists and his heart pounding. "I should be able to give us both peace. But how?" Hix asked himself.

"You need a plan," the voice insisted.

"Yeah, like what?" Hix sneered, having many times traveled down this road of thought. He had no more hope of finding an answer this time than the times before.

"You know," the voice said. "You've already found the answer."

"I can't," Hix said, "I won't."

"Let me show you. Let me help you," the voice whispered slyly as it planted the seeds for action in Hix's tired mind.

Chapter 61

The Dark, that had destroyed Jeannicca and, in turn, had been destroyed by Saul, was not alone. It had many brethren. They numbered more than the Guardians. When one fell another was always ready to take its place. They had waited until Saul was busy, not looking, before unleashing another to worm its way into the mix of Hix and Abby's lives.

Dark Whispers and feelings of anger would be cultivated to bring an end to Destiny's path, to bring about pain and suffering and to feed their blackness with glee for having destroyed a human. Making mortals do the unthinkable to themselves and each other was why they existed. They fed off the chaos, and grew stronger with each victory achieved.

They badly wanted this one to succeed. The outcome would give them great strength, as more than one life would be ruined. Numerous lives hung in the balance, ripe for the taking.

The Dark beings that were left behind, waited and watched from the shadows as the chosen one, called Roman, twisted his way into the minds and hearts of the players in this drama. He took bites of souls along the way and consuming whole, others that were weak and willing. Blackness was what they were after, blackness where there once was light.

As they watched, they rejoiced as one, in the seeds of blackness that were being sown and rained hatred and revenge down on them to make them grow. Grow and grow until the time for the harvest was at hand. "Reap what we've sown," they chanted. "Reap what we've sown," they howled in anticipation, for Roman had sown death.

Chapter 62

Abby put the phone down, having said goodbye to Hix for the night. Feelings of disappointment warred with relief in her breast, as she thought of what she had planned for the evening. She had taken the advice of her friends and made plans to tell Hix the news of her pregnancy.

She'd spent the day setting the scene. She'd cleaned the house, placing scented candles throughout to make it look and smell inviting. She'd gone shopping for a meal she knew Hix enjoyed. Big fat steaks were, even now, sitting on the shelf in her refrigerator, waiting to be taken out and grilled to perfection. Two potatoes, one small and one man sized, were in the oven baking, with only an hour to go until they were to be taken out and served with whipped butter and mounds of sour cream. She had tossed vegetables together and placed the salads in bowels that would have been served cold and crisp for the first course. Fresh bread, bought from the bakery this morning, was waiting to be warmed and served up, with more butter melting into its fragrant softness. For dessert Abby had made a treat that Hix's mother had said was his favorite, hot cherry pie with ice cream on top.

Abby almost felt guilty preparing the menu and staging her house. She felt like she was fattening Hix up in anticipation of the kill, bribing him to be in a good mood and accepting her news with love and joy.

She had pictured him taking her into his arms and kissing her at the news of his upcoming fatherhood. Lifting her and carrying her into the bedroom to make love to her gently and with care, to seal the bond of their making a child. Then drifting to sleep in each other's arms after whispering their plans for the future quietly into the dark.

Hix probably would have asked her to marry him during those whispers, and she would have cried while saying yes to him. It was all so perfect in her mind, except for the worm of doubt she lived with every day, all day. "Would Hix bring it up?" she wondered. "No not Hix. He would have totally claimed the child as his and never voiced anything different to her."

But all her planning and her imaginings had been for naught. Hix was not coming over tonight. "Was he trying to pull away from her?" she wondered. "No," she thought, shaking her head. This wasn't the first time they had not spent a night seeing each other. After all, Hix worked hard and she knew there were many times he had come over when he should have just stayed home and rested. But tonight had been different, life changing in fact. Now her news would have to wait.

Should she tell him tomorrow? Maybe wait until later on, maybe Sunday night?

Abby didn't know if she could plan another night like tonight. It had taken all the courage she had and some she had borrowed from her friends, to have the guts to tell Hix. She lived with the fear that Hix would reject her or say the awful words that would destroy her, "Is the baby mine?"

She lived with the fear that the baby was Max's. That what he had said happened that awful night, was true. What would she do then? "No," she thought, "I can't think like that or I will go crazy. I'll fall apart and I'm not sure I could pull myself back together." She could not think about the 'what ifs.' Not now.

Abby went into the kitchen and turned the oven off. She took out the half baked potatoes and threw them into the trash. She had no desire to finish cooking them and then have to eat the small one by herself. She wrapped the steaks in plastic wrap to keep them fresh and put them back into the refrigerator to wait for Hix to come by. She looked at the salads. Even they didn't appeal to her, so she dumped them into the trash. She covered the pie and put the bread in a bag, squeezing the air from it and twisting it shut to keep it fresh. Looking around the kitchen she could see no evidence of the night she had planned.

Her appetite had left her. Abby turned the kitchen light off and went into the bedroom, planning to crawl into bed to watch TV until she drifted off to sleep. She took off her clothes and hung them up, pausing in front of the mirror to pose in the way expectant mothers do to see if her baby bump was showing yet. But her tummy was flat. She touched it, running her hands over and around it.

"Hi baby," she whispered. "I'm your mommy." There was no answering movement, of course, so she dropped her hands and pulled a big tee shirt over her head. She pulled the covers down on the bed and crawled in, making a warm cocoon with the blankets.

As if there was a magnet in her belly, her hands, again, found their way to rest on top of her child. She gave a deep sigh and tried to relax.

"What are you doing?" a soft whisper sounded in her head.

"What do you mean?" she asked, also in her head, her brows creasing at the question.

"You are pretending to love the baby inside you," the voice said.

"What?" she asked again, her eyes completely open and looking wildly around the room? Where was the voice coming from? Who was the voice coming from?

"We both know that you cannot really care for this baby as long as there is a question in your mind about who the father is." the voice taunted her.

"Hix is the father," she said, continuing the silent conversation she believed she was having with herself, her conscience, or something.

"Is he?" the whisper came again.

"Yes he is," she said firmly. "I believe he is."

"No," the whisper came again "because you want it to be true. Not because it is."

"You have no proof that he isn't," she accused her inner voice.

"Nine months, you know," it said "Nine months is what it will take for you to know for sure. "Until then the question will eat at you. It will bleed into your baby, making it wonder if it will be loved when it is born. It will shape its thinking, making it nervous and unhappy. Making you nervous and unhappy."

"Shut up!" Abby said, tears in her eyes. "Leave me alone!"

"You are alone," the voice kept picking at her. "You have no one to blame but yourself for this mess."

"That's not true," Abby hissed out.

"Oh that's right," it said, creeping around her mind "there is Max, right? He's a liar, no matter what he said. But, you don't remember do you? After all this time you still don't remember. Maybe what he said is true."

"It can't be!" Abby moaned, "It can't be!"

"What are you going to do about it?" the voice asked, seeming closer than before. "What are you going to do?"

"What can I do?" Abby asked, beginning to shake with emotions.

"Stop being a wimp!" the voice hissed in her ear. "Stop lying down and taking it!"

"There's nothing else I can do," Abby stated with little conviction.

"Yes there is," the voice said, as if sharing a secret.

"What?" Abby asked.

"You can make Max pay for the pain he has caused you. Make him pay for the lies he tells. Make it so he can never hurt you or anyone else again."

"I don't know how," Abby said, tears finally falling down her pale cheeks. "What can I do?"

"Make him pay," the voice sneered into her ear. "Make him pay!"

The tears stopped as Abby sat up higher in the bed. "How?" she asked, "Tell me how."

A chuckle echoed in her mind, and she shuddered at the sound of evil in its tone.

"Listen," it whispered, "listen and follow."

Abby did listen as the voice brought to light a plan she had forced to the back of her mind, but knew had been there all along. As she listened she grew calm, and a smile grew on her face.

"That's right," she said to the voice, "I like it."

The seed had been planted, and there was nothing to do now but wait for the reaping.

Chapter 63

Kendall had been the last of the friends to leave Abby the night before. The four friends had hashed out the details for a plan to tell Hix about the baby, while they fried and seasoned hamburger, chopped veggies, and shredded cheese preparing tacos for the group. Kendall stirred up margaritas for the girls, a virgin one for Abby, and they ate and drank while they devised the plan.

Bellies full, and everyone satisfied that the perfect plan had been hatched, Tonia and Mary rose to leave. Abby gathered them to her in a group hug, thanking them for their help and promising to call them with the results of her evening with Hix.

Kendall had then driven Abby home. She'd been in no hurry to let her friend out of her car, once they reached Abby's house. She was worried about Abby being by herself.

"Don't worry," Abby told her. "I am much better now that I have talked to all you guys and have a plan in place. I actually feel better than I have for a long time. I guess I needed to tell someone what was going on. I needed to have my friends behind me, supporting me."

Kendall reached across the seat and gave Abby a hug. Pulling back and pushing a stray hair behind Abby's ear, she said, "We are not behind you, silly, we are beside you."

Abby smiled as a single tear came to her eye. "I know you are," she said "and it means everything to me knowing I have all of you in my corner." With a final hug, she stepped out of the car and made her way to her door.

Kendall didn't leave until Abby made it all the way inside and the door closed behind her. As Kendall pulled away from the curb, she realized she wasn't ready to go home. Instead, she wanted to drive straight to Hix's house, beat on his door until he let her in, and demand to know what he was going to do about Max. Correction, what they were going to do about Max. She wanted in on the beat down she truly hoped Hix was planning.

She made it all the way to Hix's house, but at the last minute drove on by. There was no way to talk to Hix about this without giving Abby's "surprise" away. Kendall could not, and would not, do that to Abby. This was her news to share.

She took a deep breath and loosened her hands from their grip on the steering wheel. She hated to wait when she wanted something or something had to be done. She was a right now kind of girl. But hating to wait or not, she was going to have to give Abby and Hix their time together, and then go from there.

If she and the others were right, Hix would be asking their friend to marry him. Kendall hoped so, because that seemed to be what Abby wanted. They'd make a good couple, and their little one would be a knock out, Kendall was sure. But if the worst happened, and Hix denied being the father, then Kendall would be there for Abby to lean on. To help her friend do whatever it was she decided on.

Kendall felt the pressure between her shoulder blades begin to relax. She was feeling pretty good about the situation as she took a slow drive around town. She really liked the town. It was small, but still big enough to give people a variety of things to do. She had made many friends working at the convenience store, and was recognized when she went out. It felt good to be accepted and respected by the people in the town.

Kendall turned onto the street that led to her home. She didn't really want to go home yet, as she was feeling itchy, wired up and unsettled. She wanted to be doing something, but didn't know what. She pulled her car into her driveway and shut off the lights and the engine. The silence that followed was total and deep. Kendall still had her hands on the wheel as she sat and stared out the window. After a few moments she got antsy sitting there, so she got out and went inside.

It seemed empty, after just a short time ago being filled with four chatty females. Kendall turned on a lamp, letting the soft light guide her to the kitchen. She opened the fridge and looked inside, but wasn't hungry. She wandered from room to room, but nothing beckoned for her to settle there. "Damn," she thought to herself, "what's wrong with me tonight?

Going back into the living room she plopped down in her recliner and grabbed the remote, planning on watching a little TV.

"That's not what you want," a soft voice whispered in her head.

Kendall rolled her neck to get rid of the irritating voice, and again pointed the remote at the TV.

"Still not what you want," the voice snickered.

"What?" Kendall yelled out, throwing up her hands. "What do you want?"

"It's not what I want, but what you want," the voice said.

"What do you know about what I want?" she demanded, irritation oozing from her voice.

"I know," it replied. "Shall I tell you?"

Kendall wiggled her butt back into the chair and crossed her arms over her chest in a huff. "Well," she dared, "let's hear it."

The voice was quiet for a few heart beats before it began. Kendall had to strain to hear, so low were the whispers, but what she heard had her sitting up straight and leaning forward.

"You want revenge," the whisper began. "You want payback, not for you but for your friend. What that jerk, Max, did to her was the worst. Making her doubt herself and adding strain to her life. You want answers to the questions you all have. Am I right?"

Kendall thought for a moment and then hissed out, "Yes!"

"Well what are you going to do about it?" the voice asked growing louder."

"What can I do?" Kendall asked, frustrated.

"You know," it said, slyly. "You have been kicking things around in your head since the moment you heard Abby's story. Today made it worse, finding out she is pregnant."

"It's different when you plan to have a baby," Kendall insisted. "She is so young and hasn't really lived yet. It's not fair, not fair at all."

"You are so right," the voice agreed. "Poor Abby, she really doesn't have anyone but you to look out for her, does she?"

"She has Hix," Kendall said. "He is probably mad as hell about what happened."

"Not mad enough," the whisper hissed. "If he was really pissed and really cared he would have done something already, right?"

"I guess so," Kendall said, wanting to come to Hix's defense, but still finding merit with the logic of the whispers.

"You're going to go to Hix and ask him what he is planning, aren't you?" the voice continued questioning her.

"Yes," Kendall agreed.

"What if he is not willing to do anything? What then?" it taunted.

Kendall sat back, gripping the arms of her chair tightly until the muscles in her arms were taut and knotted.

"I don't know," she huffed, "I'm thinking."

"You know," the voice insisted in her ear. "You know what has to be done."

"It's wrong," Kendall said, shaking her head in denial, trying to dislodge the thoughts building in her head.

"No!" the voice almost shouted "Now it's fair and right. Max deserves everything he gets."

Kendall still resisted but, as the voice continued, she relaxed and began to see the light of reason. The whispering voice poked and prodded. It coaxed and stirred up anger, rage and hatred. It did its job and did it well.

When the voice finally quieted, Kendall sat back with new resolve and the Dark laughed, for it had once again planted the seeds of death.

Chapter 64

Abby woke early on Friday with thoughts of Hix, the baby, and what to do about all of it, fighting to be the first order of the day. She flipped a pillow over her head and groaned into its depths. "Just a few minutes peace," she thought, "just a few minutes."

A few minutes was all she allowed herself, as she tossed the pillow aside and found the courage to get out from under the warm covers to begin her day. The dawn had long since broken and the sun was well up as Abby's feet hit the floor. She tiptoed across the chilly surface into the bathroom to take care of her morning routine. Pondering what to do with her day, Abby showered, primped, and dressed before finally emerging from the bathroom and heading to the kitchen for breakfast.

Nothing jumped out at her yelling, "Eat me! Eat me!" as she stood before the cupboards and then the fridge trying to decide what, if anything, sounded good. Skipping meals when you were pregnant probably was not a good idea, even if you weren't hungry she thought, tapping her chin. She finally settled on two pieces of white toast slathered with a generous helping of strawberry jam, and a cold glass of milk to wash it all down. The wonderful smell of bread toasting and fresh strawberries made her tummy rumble, as she took her breakfast to the kitchen table and sat down to eat.

For not being hungry, she had no problem working her way through her breakfast, enjoying each bite to the fullest until her plate was clean and her glass was empty. Licking the last bit of sticky jelly from her fingertips, Abby felt satisfied and ready to face the day ahead. She rose and took the few dishes to the sink, quickly washing them and setting them in the drainer to dry.

Abby's apartment was just too small to let her thoughts have the room they needed to be sorted out, so she slipped on a light jacket and headed outside to take a walk and think. The morning was cool and bright as Abby made her way to the trail that wound its way through the small town. Walking with her head down and her thoughts whirling, she paid no attention to the scenic view and, without meaning to, soon found herself outside of Kendall's store.

Abby pulled the door open and went inside, the bell announcing her arrival to her friend. The door had barely finished closing before Kendall was at her side, grabbing her arm and steering her back outside for privacy.

"Well?" Kendall said. "What happened? I waited for a call this morning but nothing, so tell me. Good or bad? What did Hix say?" The questions came fast, with no break in between, leaving Abby no chance to answer.

"He didn't show up," Abby finally got out.

"What do you mean?" Kendall asked, surprise and worry on her face and in her voice.

"He called and said he was really tired and would see me tonight," Abby told her, looking closely at her friend to gage her reaction.

Kendall looked thoughtful for a moment, before nodding her head in approval. "Okay, so now what? Are you going to tell him tonight?" she asked her friend.

Abby jammed her hands into her jacket pockets and shrugged her shoulders. "I think I have to," she finally said. "I thought about waiting until Saturday or Sunday, but I don't think I could pull off being normal for that long. I mean," she hesitated, "I would probably fidget so much, Hix would wonder what the heck was going on."

"I think you're right," Kendall said, backing Abby's plan." "Just think of it as ripping off a band aid. If you do it quick, you won't spend time anticipating the worst. And the longer you leave it on the tougher it gets."

"I know," Abby said, smiling at her friend, "I know."

"Okay," Kendall said, slipping a supporting arm around Abby's shoulders. "Same goes for tomorrow or even tonight. Call when it's over. We all want to know what happens."

"You will be the first one I call," Abby promised. "But until then, can you call the others and tell them what is going on?" Abby implored Kendall. "I don't think I can take telling Tonia and Mary, until I have something definite for them."

"Sure, honey," Kendall said, "I'll take care of it. Just remember, tomorrow we all want to know what happened."

Abby gave her friend a quick peck on the cheek and, with a wave, headed back home. She was going to press rewind and, once again, prepare for an evening where she would come clean with Hix. Rip the band aid off, she thought. Just do it, tonight. Stop being such a chicken, she chided herself. Hix will understand and will still love you, and the baby. His baby.

Despite her newfound confidence, the same thought came sneaking back into her head, "Will he see it that way or not?"

Making it home with new resolve, Abby began preparing for the evening. Once again, she set the table with pretty dishes, putting flowers in the center for color and brightness. The steaks were still marinating in the refrigerator. All she really needed to do was wash the potatoes, put them in the oven, and toss the salad before Hix got there.

When she was finished in the kitchen, Abby went through the house, moving a pillow here and replacing a magazine there. She lit a scented candle, hoping to fill the room with a soothing scent and warm light. Needing noise, Abby turned on a CD before making her way into the bedroom.

She pulled a casual shirt and new pair of jeans from the closet and laid them on the bed. Staring at the sparkle-butt denims that had cost her a pretty penny, Abby realized that she wouldn't be fitting into them for much longer. "Crap!" she thought, letting out a sigh of resignation and mild disappointment. "Better wear them now before it was too late."

She moved to the bathroom and turned on the tap. Hot water spilled into the tub as Abby added her favorite bubbles and breathed in the wonderful scent filling the air, dark and mysterious. Oh what the hell, she thought and added a little more, making the amount of bubbles triple, and her soul smile.

She slid into the tub and spent an hour pampering herself, relaxing as much as she could before getting out and toweling dry. She blow-dried her hair into soft curls that lay around her shoulders and framed her face like rich waves of honey. She pulled on the clothes she'd lain out earlier, then put on just a touch of make up to bring out her eyes and give color to her cheeks. The final touch in her preparation was a small amount of perfume dabbed behind her ears and placed between her breasts. A girl could hope, couldn't she?

Straightening up the counter, Abby took one final look in the mirror and decided there was nothing more she could do but wait. The little clock on the wall showed she had about an hour until Hix showed up. Just enough time to get dinner ready.

Going back to the kitchen, Abby wrapped the potatoes in foil and put them in the oven. She sliced the bread and placed it in a napkin lined basket, wrapping it in the folds to keep it soft. She got the butter out of the refrigerator to soften, then stepped back to take in the scene. "All ready," she thought, with a satisfied smile. All that was missing was Hix.

Another look at the clock showed her that her wait was almost over. Just half an hour till the evening would begin.

Butterflies started in her stomach and her heart picked up speed. Her hands began to tremble and her cheeks paled. Suddenly Abby found herself making a bee line for the bathroom, where she proceeded to throw up.

Chapter 65

For Hix, the day couldn't pass quickly enough. Although he kept busy, thoughts of Abby kept creeping in. Something in her voice last night had left him with a nagging feeling that all was not right with them. He hated to have to wait until tonight to figure out what it was. "Maybe nothing," he thought. "No reason to buy trouble without a good reason. Just finish work and when you see her tonight you will know."

At the thought of seeing her, his heart sped up just a little and his breathing became just a little heavier. He liked the way just thinking of her affected him. He liked the way the first sight of her brought the sunshine into his day. Having her in his life gave each day a whole new meaning.

Even though he was beat last night, he still missed seeing her and holding her. When he woke this morning, his first thought was of Abby and the anticipation of having the whole weekend to themselves, had him jumping out of bed and whistling as he got ready for work.

Now the day was almost over and Hix knew anticipation sweet and deep. He was going to go home, grab a quick shower, and hustle his butt over to Abby's. If he hurried he could make it in half an hour or so. Hix put his tools away and cleaned his area so all would be ready for Monday. As he walked to his truck he waved off the invites to join the guys at the Nineteenth Hole for a few cold ones.

"Come on Hix," they implored, "one or two quick ones won't hurt. Your girlfriend will wait."

"Can't," Hix shot back with a big grin. "She can wait, but I can't."

He didn't care that he got ribbed about being whipped, that she was the boss of him, or that she had him all tied up. All he cared about was seeing her. He waved his hand in the air as he made his way to his truck. The door had barely closed before the engine turned over and dirt flew from his tires. The crew shook their heads collectively as they watched another one of their's bite the dust.

Hix wanted to floor it on the way home, but he kept his speed at the limit as he drove with one hand on the wheel and the other arm resting on the open window. The air felt good, cooling his body from the long day's work and making his hair fly madly around his face. He barely noticed. All his thoughts were focused on getting to Abby.

Pulling into his driveway, he jammed the truck into park and jumped out almost before the engine died. He kicked the door closed and his boots off as he headed straight into the bathroom to jump into the shower, a trail of clothes marking his path.

The hot water felt like an old friend, as it beat down on his skin. Taking one minute for himself, he closed his eyes and let it pour over his body, before soaping off and washing his hair. Satisfied he'd washed away all the day's sweat and grime, he shut the water off and toweled himself dry. He wiped the steam from the mirror and hung the wet towel over the shower rod before getting ready to shave.

He could have left the slight stubble on his cheeks and chin, but he didn't want Abby's soft cheeks to suffer because he'd been in too big a hurry. His hand was steady as he scrapped his skin clean. Looking in the mirror, Hix was satisfied with the results. He splashed on some aftershave and felt the rush it brought to his skin. After running a comb through his hair, he turned the blow dryer on it until most of the wetness had disappeared. He didn't see, as he combed his locks one last time, the way it shone with golden highlights, making him look sinfully handsome.

Back in the bedroom, he made his way to the closet and pulled out a pair of soft, denim jeans and a teal blue polo shirt. He drug on underwear, pulled the shirt over his head, and tucked the tails in when his jeans were in place.

As he sat to pull on socks and tennis shoes, Hix had a thought. Maybe he should put a few clothes in a small bag. He was probably going to spend the night, and maybe the whole weekend at Abby's. If he brought things with him, he wouldn't have to make a trip to his house to grab what he needed. Still Hix didn't want to assume anything.

His shoes tied, Hix rested his hands on his knees as he thought about this. He really didn't need to bring much, as a few of his things had already found their way over to Abby's and stayed. Just as a few of her things had been casually left at his place and found a home there. Finally he brought out a small gym bag and filled it with his toothbrush, underwear, socks, a fresh tee shirt, and one more pair of jeans. He could use Abby's shampoo and stuff like that, so those items he ignored.

Zipping up the bag, Hix carried it to the living room before heading into the kitchen to grab a pop for the road. Maybe two he thought and then, shrugging his shoulders, he grabbed the whole six pack and called it good. He opened one and took a long drink before bending down to sling the bags strap over his shoulder.

He only made it a step towards the door before a thought hit him like a truck.

"What if they lived together? What if they combined their homes and made it into one? After all, he was building them a house and they would live there together eventually. Why not sooner? Why not now?"

Hix dropped his bag and sat down on the couch. The idea crowded everything else from his mind as he turned it over and over, looking at it from every angle. He gulped down his pop as the age old reaction of men set in for a moment. He would lose his freedom. He would have to be home every night. He would have to ask permission or, at the very least, tell her he wasn't going to be right home when he wanted to go to the bar or out with the boys. How would that work out? Could he do that? Should he do that?

Hix took his time and thought, but all his objections were met with the same answer. He wanted Abby in his life and the thought of living with her now only brought happiness to him, not fear. He didn't care about the rest, he knew it for sure.

Rolling it around one more time, Hix got up and made his way to the small desk sitting in the corner. He pulled open a drawer and found what he was looking for. His spare door key. He could give it to Abby tonight and ask her if she would like to live with him. If she wanted them to live at her place, that was okay with Hix. He could take most of his stuff, or hers, out to their new house and store it there. It was going to end up there anyway, he reasoned.

Hix found his favorite Husker key chain and slipped the key on it. He brought it up to eye level and watched as the lone key spun slowly one way and then the other, mesmerizing him with the power it held. Bring happiness or not? Time would tell.

Bringing it back down, he put it in his front pocket. Yes indeed, he thought, picking up his bag and heading out the door, this was going to be a night to remember.

Chapter 66

Meanwhile, Saul had been preparing for this night, too. He'd taken care of a few minor problems his other charges had encountered, wanting to be able to concentrate on Hix and Abby tonight. He knew this was going to be a big one for both of them and he wanted to be nearby.

He arrived at Abby's side just in time to see her lose everything she had eaten that day. He watched as she got shakily to her feet and flushed the evidence down the toilet. He hovered as she brushed her teeth and fixed her make-up, trying to give color to her cheeks that were pale as moonlight.

He shook his head, wanting to stroke his hand over her soft hair and calm her worries. But he could not. All he could do was watch and wait, making sure everything went as written.

"Maybe," he thought, "maybe he could, just this once, calm her just a bit." Saul stilled and entered Abby's troubled thoughts. But what he found was not what he expected. Not all of it, anyway. He found the turmoil he'd expected, but buried deep in her mind, guarded against prying eyes, his eyes, something was hidden. "What is this?" he wondered?

He gently searched, but he could tell his hunting was giving Abby pain, as she rubbed her hands over her face and softly groaned. Saul withdrew from Abby's mind, but he knew he couldn't just let this go. He would wait until she slept to continue his search. He took the pain he'd caused Abby into himself, and watched as she relaxed again.

Saul moved from Abby's side to Hix's. He felt Hix's excitement and smiled. Things were okay here, he thought. He read Hix's intentions and, even though they were slightly off course from the written path, he let it go. There was nothing wrong with Hix's plan. It was just going to be altered slightly to fit the situation tonight.

As Saul began to withdraw from Hix, he again felt something strange. Similar to what he'd felt from Abby. There was something hidden and buried within Hix's mind, also.

Saul began to get that feeling. The feeling you get when something was about to go way wrong. But things were going to go wrong with help. Whose? Something had to have been at work while he was away. "What was it?" he wondered. "Who was it?"

There could be only one answer. It had to be the Dark. This puzzled Saul. He had defeated the darkness that had taken over the Guardian, Jeannicca. He had sent it screaming into hell, never to return. So who was this new one and how long had it been playing this game?

Saul's job had just gotten a thousand times harder and he knew that time was not on his side. He had to find the answers soon, before destiny was destroyed.

With the barriers he had felt from Abby and Hix, he was not sure that this time he could win. This time his opponent was one step ahead of him, with a plan that left no clues for Saul to follow.

Squaring his shoulders, Saul accepted the challenge. "Time to go to work," Saul thought as he faded away and, for his charges sake, he had to work fast.

Chapter 67

Hix rolled to a stop in front of Abby's place, grabbed his bag and his pop, he jumped out of his truck. He hit the auto-lock button on his keychain, not anticipating having to go out again tonight, and loped up the walk. He knocked once and waited, a little surprised that it took Abby a few seconds to open the door. She usually had the door open before he finished the first light rap.

Hix stepped inside and closed the door, slipping out of his jacket and dropping his bag and drinks before gathering Abby into his arms and leaning down for a kiss.

Abby rose up on her tiptoes and met Hix's smiling lips with her own. She kissed him, and wanted to go on kissing him until all their problems melted away. But no matter how she clung to the strong body before her, no matter that she put all her need into this one kiss, everything was still the same when they both came up for air.

Hix cocked an eyebrow, as he tried to read Abby's face. He'd felt the desperation in her kiss, the strength in which she held on to him. He knew something was off because rather than raising her eyes to meet his, she buried her head in his shoulder.

"Hi honey," he said, pouring warmth into her from those few words. "I missed you last night." he said, running his hands up and down her back in a soothing motion.

She allowed herself to be held in his arms for a few more moments before lowering herself back to her feet.

"I missed you too," she said, letting the first real smile she'd had in the last couple of days play about her lips.

Hix loosened his grip but didn't release his hold on Abby. Instead he let his arms rest in a loop around her waist and looked down into her face. "How was your day?" he asked, trying to get a clue as to what was wrong.

Instead of answering his question, Abby pulled back from the warm, strong body she had been leaning on and, smiling, said, "Come inside." She linked her fingers with his and led him into her home, letting the table setting and the smells coming from the kitchen tell him that she had planned a special dinner.

"Wow!" Hix said, spying her efforts. "What is the occasion?"

"No occasion," Abby replied, with a playful smile on her face. "I just thought we deserved a nice meal to start the weekend off right with. What do you think?"

Hix could smell the potatoes baking, along with fresh bread, and he guessed there was cherry pie in there too.

"This is great, honey," he told her, appreciation and approval in his voice. His stomach seemed to agree, as it decided to give a deep growl at that very moment, letting Abby know that he was hungry and would do justice to anything she put in front of him.

Laughing, Abby opened the refrigerator and pulled out the steaks.

"Would you mind firing up the grill and dropping these on for me?" she asked, turning so Hix could see what she was holding.

Hix felt his mouth water as he looked at the thick rib eye steaks on the platter. "Damn, woman," he said, leaning in for another kiss as he took the dish from her hands, "you're gonna spoil me."

Abby let go of the platter and laughed as Hix made a bee line for the back patio. Men sure were funny beings, she thought. Mention the word grill and they were off like a rocket traveling from their earthly realms straight into seventh heaven. Grilling was their territory, or so they thought, and women let them go right on believing it.

While Hix was monitoring the steaks, Abby pulled the fresh salads from the fridge and finished setting the table. She removed the bread from the oven and warmed butter for the soft insides of the loaf, before getting more butter for the potatoes and dishing up sour cream. Everything was ready for Hix to come back and join her.

With a few moments to kill, Abby felt her nerves begin to jump again. She wiped her damp hands on her jeans and fluffed her hair. She avoided going outside, thinking Hix would again ask what all this was for.

She wasn't sure how long she could hold her "surprise" in, without it spilling from her lips. She needed to tell Hix what was going on, but at the same time she was scared to death of his reaction. Later, she knew, would be better to drop her bomb on him Nerves always made her talkative and tonight she had a feeling she was going to be jabbering a mile a minute.

"Get a grip," she chided herself. She just had to calm down and try to enjoy Hix's company while they ate. Let them both enjoy the food. But where earlier Hix's stomach had growled with anticipation, Abby's was now tied in knots. Abby sent a silent prayer from her heart that for just a little while she be allowed to forget and enjoy the evening. At just that moment, Hix walked back in carrying the sizzling meat.

"These are ready if you are," he announced, pride at a job well done written all over his face.

"Let's eat then," Abby said, as she fetched the potatoes from the oven and placed one on each plate. Hix held her chair as she took her seat at the pretty table.

The conversation lagged as Hix gave his full attention to the meal on the table. He closed his eyes and let out a low moan of appreciation as he let himself take that first bite, the one he had been waiting for, for the last half hour. The steak melted on his tongue as did the potato, slathered with butter and sour cream. The salad was cold and crisp, topped with his favorite bacon ranch dressing. The bread was soft and hot, with just a hint of butter melted into its folds. Hix closed his eyes with every mouthful, almost knowing what heaven felt like.

Opening his eyes, he held out a hand and waited for Abby to place hers in it. He raised it to his smiling lips and kissed the back of it.

"Thanks, Abby," he said warmth fairly beaming from his eyes. "This is absolutely perfect. I don't know what I've done to deserve this, but I am one happy man." He gently kissed the back of her smooth hand one more time before letting it go and digging in once again.

Abby enjoyed watching Hix devour his food. He consumed it with pleasure, giving her a sense of accomplishment that she could feed her man at the end of his long day. Unlike Hix, Abby only picked at her meal, but tried to keep Hix from noticing by pushing the food from side to side and flattening it out to look like she had been eating all along. She just couldn't force food past the lump in her throat and the knot in her stomach.

"I can't finish this," she said to Hix, pointing to her barely touched steak, "Do you want it?"

Hix looked at her plate and, for just a beat, paused in his eating.

"No, baby," he said, his eyes on his own meal, "I've got enough here, thanks."

"I'll just put this away then," Abby said, rising from the table and taking her dishes to the kitchen.

Hix watched her go, again suspecting something was wrong. He had watched her play with her food instead of eating it, even though she thought she was fooling him. Sure her appetite was not as big as his, thank you very much, but she still usually ate more than she had tonight. Something wiggled at the back of Hix's brain. Some clue as to what was wrong, but he could not hold the thought long enough to grasp its meaning. It was almost there, but just out of reach.

Hix swallowed his last bite and moved to leave the table and see if Abby needed any help in the kitchen, but she came back before he had fully risen from his chair.

"Ta-da," she sang, as she carried in the pie and ice cream arranged on a tray.

"Wow!" Hix said again, "You really know how to get to me, don't you?"

Abby laughed and, unseen by Hix's eyes, crossed her fingers under the tray. "I hope so," she silently begged. "I hope so!"

Chapter 68

Saul surveyed the scene unfolding, having arrived at the same time as Hix. He felt Abby's nerves and fear, and he felt Hix's confusion and growing concern. He longed to calm them both so they could have a relaxing, enjoyable evening, but he could not. His hands were tied.

He heard every prayer that Abby sent out into the heavens, but could not give her the answers she wanted, the results she needed. He had witnessed this situation a million times and was sure he would witness it more times than that in the future to come. But no matter how many times the situation had come and gone, Saul still hated the pain and uncertainty it caused.

He watched as Hix ate his dessert, complimenting Abby on the wonderful meal she had prepared for them. He followed the couple as they cleared the table and washed the dishes, almost in silence.

He could feel Abby growing more afraid as the moment of truth drew near, and Hix growing more silent as he dealt with the uncertainty that was rolling off Abby in waves, wondering if Abby had had a change of heart where they were concerned.

Saul could do nothing but stand by and wait. He followed the couple as they moved into the living room, sitting gingerly on the edge of the sofa, acting as if too big a movement would unleash something that neither one was prepared for.

Saul remembered the advice Kendall had given Abby the day before and, as the time was now at hand, he leaned over and whispered into her mortal ear, "Remember Abby, like a band aid. Quick and clean. Do it. Do it NOW!"

Chapter 69

Hix led the way into the living room, having to almost drag Abby behind him the whole way from the kitchen. He parked them both in front of the couch and waited for Abby to sit down. When she didn't move, Hix put his hands on her shoulders and gently pressed down on them, forcing her to bend her legs until she was perched on the edge of the sofa. He lowered himself, with care, to the space beside her, taking her small, cold hand gently into his larger, warm one. He paused for a moment before speaking, feeling that whatever was to come would be of the utmost importance.

"Abby?" he questioned gently, urging her to come out with whatever was bothering her. When she didn't respond, he repeated himself, louder, "Abby? What is it? I know that something has been bothering you all night. I can't help if you don't tell me what it is." His voice had gotten lower and raspier with each word he spoke. He swallowed once, then twice as he waited for her to say something, or to even look at him.

For the longest time she sat still as a statue and as pale as a moon beam. Then, taking a deep breath, she turned her whole body to face Hix. Her eyes remained down cast for one more moment, as the tension in the room built to such a state that Hix could almost taste it.

"What is it, Abby?" Hix asked in desperation "Just spit it out!" He could take the distance between them no longer, as he reached out and pulled Abby's stiff form into his arms and snuggled her head under his chin. He rubbed her arms trying to impart some of his warmth into her cold skin and to let her know that he was there for her if she needed him.

"I have something to tell you," Abby began quietly. "I don't know what you are going to think or do after I tell you, so let me begin by saying I love you," she said as she raised her eyes to look deep into his.

"I love you, too," Hix replied, "and I promise to love you even after you tell me whatever it is that you have to say." Hix felt a shudder run through Abby's body as she huddled against his side.

"I'm pregnant," Abby blurted out, no embellishments, no excuses and no explanations.

Not a breath could be heard in the quiet room, as Abby held hers waiting for Hix to say something, and Hix was unable to draw in air because he felt like someone had just sucker punched him in the gut.

Of all the things he imagined Abby having to say, being pregnant was the last thing he would have guessed.

"Abby," he asked "you're going to have a baby?"

The slight nod of her downcast head was the only answer he got.

Hix sat perfectly still as he struggled to wrap his mind around this information. "Abby was pregnant. Abby was pregnant. Abby was pregnant," was all he seemed to be able to think. It kept going around and around in his head like a hamster on one of those wheels in its cage. Going faster and faster and still getting nowhere.

The food he had eaten just a short time ago sat like a rock in his stomach, and his heart was beating so loud it echoed in his ears.

Hix knew he loved Abby, but starting a family was not even on his near-future radar. When she had been in New York, Hix remembered going into a jewelry shop and looking at rings. He had not meant to, had not planned to, but had felt compelled to, just the same. After that one time, he hadn't even entertained the thought of marriage, or he had pushed it to the back of his mind, not being ready for that step at the time.

"What to do now?" Hix thought.

He knew Abby was waiting for him to say something, but he was unable to get his mouth to work. He felt frozen.

Abby had not moved since she had told him of her condition and he wanted to say the right thing to ease her anxiety, but had no idea what to say.

"Say what's in your heart," a soothing voice inside his head directed. "Do you really love her?" it asked.

"Yes," Hix answered, "at least I think so."

"Does the news of her pregnancy change your feelings for her?" the voice again whispered.

"No, I don't know, maybe. Shit what am I going to do?" Hix replied, feeling at a loss for an answer.

A vision of Abby holding a baby in her arms and him at her side, grew in Hix's mind. He saw himself reaching for the baby and lifting it in his arms to hold it close to his chest, close to his heart. He knew that this small being held his heart in its small hands. Hands that reached for his work roughened fingers and, grasping one, held on with all its might.

A feeling grew in his chest, a tightness that squeezed his heart and brought moisture to his blue eyes. A baby he thought, a small piece of himself and Abby had come together to create an innocent child. Maybe, he thought, it would be a son and he could teach it all about building things, and sports, and fishing, and life.

Maybe, he thought again, it would be a daughter and she would have her mother's good looks and be able to wrap him around her little finger with her smile and her laughter. Reaching small arms up to him, begging to be lifted up and shown the world from his vantage point. Totally safe from harm because of him.

Warmth began to grow in his chest and spread to the farthest reaches of his being, until he was sure he must be glowing with acceptance and happiness. He was going to be a father.

"Holy shit!" he thought. "Can I do this? Do I have a choice?"

"Yes," the soothing voice answered again, "you can, and yes you always have a choice. But chose well," it advised, "the future of more than one is at stake. Ask yourself these questions. Do you love Abby?

Can you be a good father to this child? Do you want to be a father to this child? Will you love this child and accept responsibility for it? If the answers are yes to each question, then be happy with the news of this child coming into your life. You have been given the gift of life and you should always remember the trust this child and the woman beside you are putting in you, to love them always and be there for them. Be strong for them, Hix," the voice said, "and look into your heart for the answers you seek."

Hix waited for more wisdom from the voice, but it was silent, leaving him to chew over what it had said. "Yes," he thought, "I can do this. I do want this and yes, I will love them both. I will be the rock they can cling to when troubles come our way, and I won't let them down."

Hix felt a smile grow on his face and his arm tightened around Abby's shoulders. He felt good about his decision and wanted Abby to be as happy as he was. He opened his mouth to tell Abby that he was more than happy with the news of their coming baby, but paused when he heard a soft laughter in his head.

This laughter was not one of happiness, but one that was sly and mocking. It did not spread warmth like the voice previously, but coldness and doubt.

"Sucker," it whispered, dark and oily. "What makes you think you are the father of the seed riding in this woman's belly? What about Max?" it asked. "Have you forgotten? What if the baby is his? Sucker," it gloated again, before fading away in a swirl of laughter, taking Hix's joy with it.

Chapter 70

Saul had been aware of every thought in Hix's mind, as he was hit with the sledge hammer of knowledge. The knowledge of Abby's pregnancy. He had gently guided Hix through the maze of confusion, helping him lift the burden of his future until it sat upon his shoulders, new, but with ease. He had not told him what to do or what his answer should be, but helped him think and analyze, letting Hix come to his own conclusion.

It was as Destiny had written.

Saul felt good about the way the evening was going, and had decided to leave the couple alone, to talk quietly about the baby, to make promises to love one another and the child. Together to bask in the glow of happiness and celebrate by coming together and deepening their feelings of love for each other. To whisper their plans in the dark between kisses and promises to love and to protect.

Saul had done all he could for Hix and Abby at the moment, and felt satisfaction with his work. Giving a nod of his handsome head, Saul faded away.

But he had left too soon. He left the door open and unprotected, allowing the Dark to ooze its way in, to whisper its poisonous and foul words in mortal ears, and to rend the path of Destiny, steering it to a new and deadly ending. An ending that brought darkness, distrust, hatred and death.

The Dark being, Roman, laughed wildly at his work, was satisfied that the seed of doubt had taken root.

Chapter 71

The seconds ticked by, turning into minutes as Abby waited for Hix to say something. She could almost hear the war he fought in his mind just by the way his body was reacting. When she'd first made her announcement, he'd stiffened in shock and confusion. His body had felt as hard as stone next to hers. He did not move. As time went by, he relaxed, muscle by muscle, until he was more like the Hix she had come to know. His hand had gripped her shoulder and his arm had tightened, pulling her solidly against his side.

Abby heard his heart stutter at first and then begin a deep heavy thump under her ear. She knew when he had worked things out, because his heart picked up speed and she felt warmth move from his skin to hers. She relaxed in anticipation of his words. But as he drew in a deep breath to speak, she again felt him stiffen and cool.

"What now?" she wondered. "*What thought had come to his mind to make him once again doubt and retreat?"* Abby stiffened right along with Hix, and once again waited for him to say something.

"How long?" she wondered. How much longer could she sit and wait without knowing her future? Hix held all the cards. Their futures seemed to be riding on his answer.

"I can do this." she thought. "N*o matter what, I can do this. If Hix rejects us, we will be okay. But I don't want to have to be okay!"* she thought wildly.

Abby's composure started to unravel. She was on the verge of jumping up and running away.

"Hix," Abby said, as she made a desperate attempt at communication, "say something." She pulled out of his arms and turned to face him. "Tell me what you are thinking," she said. "We need to talk this out."

Hix turned his head, his eyes finding Abby's. Stormy blue locked with and held scared brown, as each tried to see inside the other mind without using words. Hix looking for the truth and Abby looking for answers.

"I don't know what to say," Hix finally got out through stiff lips. "I have to take some responsibility for this happening. I just assumed you were on the pill or something. It was foolish of me to not make things safe for you, and me. Were you on the pill Abby?" he asked, trying not to sound accusing. "I thought I saw one of those funny little wheelie things in the bathroom when we first started dating."

Abby's cheeks flamed, as she prepared to answer the question posed to her. "Well, I was," she said, "but then I stopped."

"Why?" Hix asked.

"I don't know." she said. "It just seemed that one night I was throwing them away."

"You should have told me what you were doing," Hix ground out, accusation heavy in his tone. "We should have talked about it together."

"I don't know why I did it," Abby said again, tears beginning to form in her eyes. She had not thought of this as being one of the questions Hix would ask, but she should have. It would now look to Hix like Abby had planned on trapping him all along, when she had not even thought about it that way.

Hix stood up, leaving Abby alone on the couch and he began to pace. He stuffed his fists into his jeans pockets, balling them as he tried to figure out the words to ask Abby about the father of the baby.

"How far along do you think you are?" he finally asked.

"As far as I can tell, maybe a couple of months," Abby said, as truthfully as she could.

"Well, well, well," the voice in Hix's head came back, stopping him in his tracks. Not the good, soothing rational voice, but the other. The one that sounded gleeful and gloating at the situation Hix now found himself in.

"Do the math, Hix," it demanded. "Add up the time it's been since New York and then tell yourself the baby is yours."

Hix wanted to fight the voice, but it had planted the doubt in his head and he could not shake it. He needed to resolve this, and soon. But how?

"Abby," he said, stopping in front of her huddled body on the couch. "I know you need me to say something, but I think I'm going to need a little time to sort this out. I don't mean to leave you hanging, but I think I need to go for a drive. Maybe when I get back I will have my thoughts in order and we can talk it out then. I hope you understand."

He reached down, pulled Abby to her feet, and gathered her against his chest. But the arms that held her were hesitant and different. Not the strong, secure shelter she was relying on.

"I don't blame you, Hix," Abby said, trying for and failing to reassure him with her words. "I've known for a while and you just found out, so I think it's a good idea for you to take some time to sort this out. Then come back and we can talk it through."

Abby clung to Hix for just a moment before backing up and dropping her arms to her sides. She wanted to hang on to him and beg him not to leave until he had told her what was on his mind. But deep down she was afraid to know. Afraid she did not have the answers to lay his doubts to rest. Afraid to hear the question she knew must be on his mind.

Hix gave Abby a quick kiss on the mouth before turning and heading to the door. Without stopping to look back, he opened it and closed it softly behind his retreating back, leaving Abby standing alone in the quiet house.

For a frozen moment she stood there, not knowing what to do next, until her eyes fell on the bag Hix had dropped inside the door when he'd arrived earlier tonight. Moving to the bag, she dropped down to her knees and laid her hands on the top. *"He didn't take his things,"* she thought. Maybe that was a good sign and it meant he was coming back. Or maybe it just meant he didn't think about grabbing his things before making his escape.

Abby opened the bag and ran a hand over the clothing inside. She pulled out a shirt and, lifting it to her face, buried her nose deep in the fabric, breathing in the scent that was Hix. With her face covered and no one to see, Abby did the only thing she could do. She cried.

Chapter 72

Hix made it to his vehicle on rubbery legs, the Dark whispering poison into his ears with every step. He tried to shake the doubts it planted in his mind, but could not. He felt like he was going to explode if he didn't get out of here fast.

He jerked the door handle to open the door, forgetting he had locked it. "*Shit!*" he thought, slapping his palm against the window, reluctantly taking the time to unlock the truck before climbing in. He rammed the keys into the ignition and fired up the engine. In a cloud of dust, he headed nowhere fast.

He rolled down the window, letting the wind blow his hair in wild disarray, breathing in the fresh air in hopes that it would erase the clutter from his mind. But no matter how fast he drove, his troubles clung to him like burrs from a sticker patch. The more he tried to get them out, the deeper they clung.

Deep in thought, Hix jumped as the phone in his pocket rang. He dreaded answering it, knowing it was going to be Abby wanting answers, and realizing he still had none to give her. But as he put it to his ear, the voice he heard wasn't Abby's, but his best friend Andy.

"Hey man," he started out, "what are you doing right now?"

"Hey yourself." Hix responded, relief in his voice, "Just driving. What's up?"

"Well, we need another body for our basketball game tonight and I thought you might be able to step in for us."

Hix latched on to the idea immediately, thankful that for a time he would be able to forget and maybe even work off some of his frustration on the court.

"Sure," Hix said, "What time is tip off?"

"Now!" Andy said, happy that Hix had agreed to play.

"Great," Hix said, "I'll be there in a few minutes." He hung up the phone and turned the truck around, heading back into town.

Ninety minutes later, Hix realized that he had been right. The game had given him a chance to set aside his troubles and work up a good sweat. When the game was over he let himself be talked into going to the local bar to hang with his friends. But as he sat alone, his predicament came back like a bad toothache. He realized that he was going to need to talk to someone before he could come to terms with it. Even though Andy offered to listen if he wanted to talk, Hix decided it was his mother that he needed to get advice from.

He didn't want to tell her everything, but knew if she was going to be able to help him, he would have to do just that. He felt the weight of guilt, knowing he was going to disappoint her with his news, but he had no choice in the matter. He needed his mom to make things better, to tell him what to do, just as she had done his whole life.

With a heavy sigh, Hix got up from the bar stool and said goodnight to his friends. He made his way out to his vehicle and once again started it up. He drove more slowly than he had earlier when he'd all but laid rubber trying to get away from Abby and the situation, but in too short of a time he was standing at his mother's front door, knocking to be let in.

Sarah opened the door with a big smile on her face at the unexpected sight of her son. The smile died a swift death as she took in the look on Hix's face. Grabbing his work roughened hand in her smaller one she pulled him over the threshold saying, "What is it, honey? What happened?"

"Hi mom," Hix said, stepping into the house he had known all his life.

Sarah did not let go of his hand as she led him to the kitchen table and pointed to a chair, "Sit down, Hix," she said.

Hix did as he was told, without saying a word and without looking into his mother's eyes.

"*So*," Sarah thought, "*this is going to be big*." Without asking, she went to the cupboard and pulled out two mugs and, in short order, had hot cocoa with mounds of marshmallows filling the cups. She set one in front of her silent son and took the other for herself, as she made her way around the table so she could see Hix's face as they talked.

Hix looked at the cup of steaming sweetness sitting before him and had to smile a little. He remembered that when he was growing up any serious discussions were always accompanied with a cup of hot cocoa, to make the news go down easier and to give your hands something to hold on to. Nothing had changed.

He picked up his spoon and took a small bite of the melting gooiness. As it slid down his throat, he felt his calm return and was able to take a deep breath without wanting to choke. Hix raised the cup to his lips, blowing gently to cool the liquid and, basically stalling for time, before gathering his courage and finally looking across the table at his mother.

He felt bad. He knew he was about to give her more to worry about and her plate would be heaping with the helping of worry she would be served. That was what mothers did. They worried about their kids, no matter what age they got to be. Right?

"Just say it, Hix," Sarah said into the lengthening silence. "No matter what it is, just spit it out."

Hix looked straight across the table and did as his mother suggested. "Abby's pregnant," he said, no frills attached.

Sarah's eyes widened and suddenly it was her turn to take a sip from her cup, stalling for time. The clock on the wall ticked off the seconds, sounding like a base drum playing in a horror movie, the only sound in the quiet kitchen as Hix waited and Sarah digested.

Sarah gathered her wits and said, "What else? The news of a baby is not all that earth shattering, Hix," she continued when Hix did not reply. "So I am assuming there is more to this story than you have spilled so far. Start from the beginning and fill me in." she gently coaxed. Cocking an eyebrow, with eyes so much like her sons, Sarah gave one final order, "And don't leave anything out."

Chapter 73

Hix did as he was told and, in a slightly unsteady voice, began at the beginning.

"Remember a couple of months ago, when Abby and I were still pretty new, and she had to go to New York for that photo shoot?" Hix asked his mother.

Sarah nodded her head in silence, remembering the time he spoke of. She remembered Hix missing the girl and how he'd spent time at her home to fight off the boredom and loneliness until Abby came back. She remembered being concerned that Hix was going to get hurt. Oh yes, she remembered.

She waited as Hix paused, swallowed, and sat forward, his hands molded to each side of his cup, its warmth soothing his troubled mind. She cupped her hands around his, reading her son's face as he stared at nothing, realizing that whatever was so important that it had brought him to her door, was about to be revealed. His eyes were almost black as he raised them to gaze, unseeing, across the table.

Hix told his mother everything about the photo shoot, about Max, and what he'd claimed had happened after he and Abby had left the bar, stressing to her that this was Max's version, since Abby couldn't remember most of it. With each word that came out, Hix grew angrier, letting the rage he felt boil over into the tone of his voice, as he raked his hands roughly through his thick hair. Ice glazed his eyes, froze his face, and revealed a feeling of helpless anger that dripped blood from his soul.

Sarah saw it all. Felt it all. It was all she could do to keep from reaching across the table to grasp her son's, now fisted, hands in support.

She wanted the entire story, even though she felt sick to her stomach at the evil that had been done to Abby.

Sarah listened without saying a word, as Hix told her how Abby had acted differently when she came back from New York. She pressed her lips tightly together as he explained that he had found out about all of it while standing in line at the grocery store!

Sarah saw a hint of tender sadness cross his face as he explained his confrontation with Abby. How she had tearfully told him everything she remembered, claiming what Max had said was all a lie.

Sarah relived Hix's phone call with Max, sitting quietly as her son told her how he had wanted to reach through the phone lines and tear the lying tongue from the bastard's foul mouth.

Hix paused long enough to take a deep drink of the cooling cocoa, trying to wash the bitterness from his tongue before telling Sarah the rest of the sordid tale. He wanted his mom to know that he didn't blame Abby, explaining his suspicions about Max using drugs on her at the after-shoot party.

He relaxed a little as he told her how the last few months had been good and about the really nice dinner Abby fixed tonight, finishing up with her announcement of her pregnancy after dessert.

"I was shocked at first," he said, "but then I thought about how we were going to have a baby, and I kind of got all warm inside," he confessed.

Hix dropped his eyes, pausing as the warmth of shame crept up his neck as he finished with the question that was put into his mind to fester. "What if the baby isn't mine, Mom? What if Max was telling the truth about sleeping with Abby, and he is the father?" Hix paused for a moment, wrestling with his emotions then fighting back the doubt, he continued, "I don't believe for a minute that Abby crawled into his bed willingly. But what if he took her with the help of drugs and the baby is his?"

With the question hanging in the air between them, both mother and son were quiet. Hix, because he was drained with the purging of his tale. Sarah, with the job of trying to absorb it all and give guidance to her son.

Sarah realized now that this was the reason he had come to her tonight. He was asking her to make the decision for him, to tell him what to do. But she couldn't do that.

"Do you blame Abby at all, Hix?" she finally asked.

"No!" he said, with no hesitation. "I love her Mom. She fits. She's not stuck up, or mean, or thinks she is above anyone who lives here in Nebraska. I built a house for us because I love her, and I want her to marry me."

Sarah nodded her head, hearing the ring of truth in Hix's words and knowing this had been coming all along. She leaned back in her chair and gazed at her son. She saw the happiness that Abby gave him, all mixed up with the war that played within his mind about the baby.

"Hix," she said, after taking a few moments to think, "The baby is totally innocent in all this. If the baby was yours, no questions, would you love it and care for it?"

"Of course I would!" Hix said, without hesitation.

"If you and Abby decide to have this baby together, would you love it any less if at some point you discovered it was not yours?" his mother asked.

Hix thought about it and, as he did, a warmth seemed to seep through him, calming him, pushing the doubts, once again, into a dark corner of his mind.

"I think I could love the baby no matter what, because it will be a part of Abby," Hix said, and knew it to be true.

"Then there is your answer," Sarah said.

Hix sagged against the back of his chair, relief washing through him. He got up from his chair and came around the table to wrap his mother in a huge bear hug.

"Thanks, Mom," he said into the top of her head, giving her a kiss.

"I didn't do anything but listen and ask a few questions," Sarah said, as she wrapped her arms around her boy. Deep inside, her heart filled with pride that she could still bring peace and understanding to her troubled child. "*Ah, the rewards of being a parent*," Sarah thought to herself.

"I need to get back to Abby," Hix said, gently releasing his mother, grinning as he backed towards the door. "I'll call you, and bring Abby by in a day or two, so we can tell you together what we've decided."

Sarah smiled and waved as the door opened and closed, leaving quiet behind to keep her company. Only quiet, until the whispers began.

Chapter 74

Sarah stood, rooted to the floor, as she listened to the buzzing in her head. She tried to make out words, but no matter how hard she tried, she could not. Shaking her head in an attempt to rid herself of the white noise, she gathered up the cups and carried them to the sink, washed them and put them in the rack to dry. She puttered around her cozy kitchen for a few more moments, before turning off the light and heading into the living room.

She felt too restless to go to bed yet. Her mind was on overload with all she had taken in tonight. Sitting down in her favorite recliner, she let her head fall back and closed her eyes. "*Just take a deep breath,*" she told herself, trying to relax. But instead of peace, she found herself replaying the conversation with Hix. She saw, in her mind, the trouble this Max person was causing, and her own anger began to burn.

"This Max is going to hurt Hix even more before this is all done," a voice whispered in her ear.

Sarah's eyes flew open and her fingers clutched the arms of the chair, but the rest of her body remained still. Her eyes moved from side to side, trying to locate the source of the voice, straining to hear more of what this voice had to say.

"You know it's true," it whispered. "His life is going to go to hell in a hand basket because of the questions that will nag him, even in his sleep. You can thank this Max for the hell your son will suffer," the whispers said. "What are you going to do about it? You need to protect your family, Sarah. You're all Hix has. Who will protect him if not you?"

"Hix is a grown man," Sarah replied to the voice only she could hear. "He can take care of himself."

"Not against this Max. Not against a man who will stop at nothing to get what he wants. Are you going to sit back and let him interfere until Hix and Abby's happiness is destroyed? Are you going to let him win?"

The tigress, that was a mother's protection, growled fierce and deep as it came to life within Sarah's breast. It stirred, stretched and grew, until Sarah felt her lips draw back and her fingers curve into claws.

The Dark being, Roman, cackled with glee as he whispered into Sarah's ear, knowing that a mother's instinct for protection was powerful and, when awakened, it unleashed a beast that would fight to the death for her young. He did not rest as he coaxed and goaded and fed that beast with dark words and hints of disaster that was to come.

"This was all the doing of Max," Roman whispered repeatedly in Sarah's ear, never letting up as the night grew long, until he was sure Sarah was on fire with the mother's need to protect.

Over and over he asked the question, "What are you going to do about Max? What are you willing to do?"

He hammered at Sarah until, with heart throbbing, Sarah gave it the answer it was waiting to hear. "Anything!" she vowed, "Anything!"

"Yes!" the Dark hissed. "Yes you will."

Giving one final laugh of wicked glee, Roman left Sarah's mind quiet and dark, having again planted seeds of hate and thoughts of revenge.

With the whispers now silent, Sarah slumped in her chair and, giving out a tired sigh, exhausted from the night's ordeal, she gave in and slept.

Chapter 75

Roman laughed and danced as he drifted lazily through the sleeping town of Winston, being seen as nothing more than a twisting wisp of dark smoke. He was happy with his work so far, as were his Brothers In Darkness who joined him in his celebration.

Humans were so easily influenced! They doubted and hated with the slightest push in that direction. He loved his job. He was good at his job, and he lived to cause hatred and chaos at every turn.

The Guardians could not be everywhere at once and Roman knew how to sneak in when the opportunity presented itself. Saul may be the "big dog" on the side of goodness as the keeper of human destiny, but Roman was the most powerful one for the Dark.

Roman boasted more success than any other Dark being when it came to leading humans to the Dark side. He showed them how lying could get them what they wanted. He let them see how power was a reward when you didn't give a damn who you hurt, or stomped on, or stole from getting to the top.

He taught them the Dark Rule: "Do Whatever It Takes To Get What You Want!"

He had come close to turning the world to darkness many times in the past, but had met with failure because of the Guardians. Nonetheless, history remembered his efforts. Generation after generation talked about the humans he had turned, and the destruction they had caused. They never forgot and, by keeping these memories alive, they made it easier for The Dark to creep back in and influence another to be successful where others had failed. They held up his puppets as examples of what not to be, but in truth, the truth that Roman knew, they fed the imaginations of the weak and made them bow down in secret to the deeds deemed evil. Those were the ones Roman looked for, hunted for, sniffed out and enslaved.

Roman laughed, a gurgle of wet decay, as he licked the thick, black drool from the maw that passed as a mouth, with a tongue that stunk of rot and death. He had one more human to visit before he would sit back and watch. The seeds he had planted in the three humans so far were more than enough, but Roman never left things to chance. He wanted one more player on his side.

He knew that all it would take was for one of the soon to be four to slip over to his side for just a moment, and the deed would be done.

And one of them would.

One of them would then be known only as, murderer.

Chapter 76

Kendall waited all day on pins and needles. Tonight was the night that Abby was going to tell Hix about the baby. Kendall so wanted to be a fly on the wall when she did. She'd never been good at waiting, and tonight was no different.

Trying to focus her mind on something else, she turned on the TV. Most of the channels had stupid reality shows on them that made Kendall want to barf on a good day. So the irritation she usually felt was full blown mad tonight. Did they really think the public was stupid enough to believe all the shit that was supposed to be spontaneous and real life? That anyone on this earth would act like the bimbos and idiots on the screen? Seriously!

Kendall's TV was saved from having something thrown at it by the ringing of her phone. Grabbing it up, she read the caller-ID and, without hesitation, put the phone to her ear.

"Hey woman." she said, keeping her voice light, "What's happening?"

Abby's sob tore through the phone and arrowed straight into Kendall's heart.

"Tell me," Kendall said in a supportive tone.

"I made the dinner like we all talked about," Abby said, thinking she had gotten herself under control after melting on the floor in a puddle of tears.

"And?" Kendall prompted.

"I told Hix about the baby," Abby hiccupped into the phone.

"And?" Kendall asked again, wanting to be in Abby's living room instead of on the phone.

"He left," Abby said, sobbing gently into the phone.

"What do you mean he left? What did he say? When is he coming back?" Kendall prodded.

"He was pretty shocked when I told him," Abby finally began. "I really can't blame him you know. Just when I thought he was going to be okay with it, he kind of stiffened up and said he needed to go for a drive and think. He said he would come back later and we would talk then.

"Okay . . ," Kendall said, ready to be the supportive friend that Abby needed right now. "You're right. He probably had to think about this for a while. And, I'll bet that when he walks in the door, he'll give you a big hug and kiss and you guys will sit down and plan a wedding.

"I don't know," Abby said, sounding doubtful. "He was different when he left. I think he wanted to ask whether he was the baby's father, but he didn't want to bring up Max. I could feel it Kendall. I knew what was going on in his mind. It went through mine when I found out." she said. "Hix is no dummy. So I can't help but think that he is going to ask before all is said and done. What do I tell him Kendall? I don't have an answer for him."

"You tell him the baby is his and you believe it yourself! You and I both know that you did nothing wrong. There isn't a snowball's chance in hell that the baby is Max's! Right?"

When Abby hesitated, Kendall repeated the question, "Right?"

Kendall heard Abby take a deep breath and let it out before she settled her mind and gave her friend the only answer she would accept.

"Yes, yes you're right. Of course you're right."

"Okay," Kendall said, "so stop worrying. Hix will be back soon and things will be great. You guys will be hugging, kissing and doing things we are not going to talk about before the sun rises on another day."

Abby actually giggled, as Kendall meant her to and, after a few more minutes of general conversation she hung up, leaving Kendall to stare at the phone she held tight in her hand. Her fingers felt locked in place as she imagined the phone was Max's neck and she was squeezing the life out of him.

One by one, Kendall loosened her fingers until she was able to let the phone fall onto the couch and her hand drop to her side. As she stood rooted to the spot, Kendall felt the hair on the back of her neck stand on end and a chill crawl up her spine.

"That's right," a whisper of a voice sounded in her head. "Max is to blame for all this trouble. You know he lied about Abby, don't you?" it asked.

"Yes!" Kendall responded fiercely. "He lied and he should pay," she spat out.

"You are so right," the whisper grew stronger. "If he was out of the picture the baby would be good news and your friend, your best friend, would not be crying her eyes out and having her heart broken. This whole mess is because of Max."

"That's right," Kendall said, falling in line with Roman's plan.

The Dark crawled and twisted its way into the deepest, darkest part of Kendall's mind, digging a hole that was deep and dark, planting the seeds of hate and revenge.

"You can't let the slime ball get away with the hurt and destruction he has caused," Roman hissed in her ear.

"No," Kendall agreed, "he can't go scot free without making amends for the trouble he has caused."

"So what are you going to do about it?" the whisper asked, almost dancing with the success it could feel close at hand.

"I don't know," Kendall thought, stopping short of the pit of darkness she wanted to jump into.

"Yes you do," the whisper urged. "You know what needs to be done, and you want to be the one to collect the payback due."

Kendall licked her dry lips, as the plan she had thought of when she first heard Abby's story, grew bright and would not be ignored.

"You can do this," the Dark assured, as it wormed in and out of the ideas in Kendall's head, tweaking here and refining there. "You know what needs to be done. You know no one else is going to do anything about Max. Are you going to step up and do it?" it asked. "Are you going to be the friend Abby needs?"

Kendall fought a war in her mind, knowing what she wanted to do, but fearing that if she acted on this, she would never be able to come back from the blood that would be on her hands.

"Hands can be hidden," the whisper pointed out. "Blood can be washed off. You can be the hero here. The bearer of happiness and peace. All you have to do is commit and act. Can you do this?" it asked, stroking her ego, making Kendall feel powerful and justified. "One moment to plan. One plan to put into play. Are you friend enough?" it goaded. "Or are you going to just sit back and pick up the pieces when everything falls apart?"

The Dark was quiet as Kendall thought, but it did not withdraw. It let her feel its presence as it twisted and wormed around and around in her head. It would not leave her alone until it got what it wanted, and with revenge blossoming into full bloom, it snuck out to dance a dance of victory.

Chapter 77

Saul had been busy with other small problems and could not hurry the guidance he had to give, but he knew he had to be there for Hix and Abby, too. He'd poked his head in long enough to help Hix realize the goodness a new life would bring, leaving him feeling warm and comfortable with the news Abby had delivered.

Feeling confident that everything was under control, Saul left them before the evening was over, returning as soon as he was finished guiding and giving comfort to his many other charges. He was alarmed to find Hix at his mother's house, questioning the baby and not knowing what to do. "What had gone wrong while he was gone?" Saul wondered. He had left Hix feeling warm and confident, only to return to a confused and angry human on the brink of screwing Destiny royally.

Standing behind Hix, Saul laid a gentle hand upon the shoulder that had to heft this new responsibility with love and acceptance. Saul took, into himself, the negative feelings Hix was harboring, and replaced them with happiness and well-being. The path of Destiny had once again been shown, and the mortal had willingly followed the lead.

"What had gone wrong?" Saul wondered again, as he watched Hix exit his mother's home. Something felt wrong about this and Saul was going to have to find out what the problem was before he could rest. He did not like this. Not at all!

Saul was about to enter Sarah's mind to find answers when he felt the Fates summon him into their presence. Another problem had come up which the Fates felt was important enough to call him to them immediately.

With one more troubling thought for Hix and Abby, Saul left to do the Fates bidding. But he was not happy about it. Something was way off here and he had a feeling, deep down, that if he did not attend to it soon, control would be lost and mortal lives would be ruined.

"I'll hurry," Saul told himself. "I cannot neglect my other duties, but I can't leave this one unattended for long, either."

As Saul left to do the Fates bidding, he hoped he had not lied.

Chapter 78

Saul appeared before the Fates, only to find them once again in turmoil. Clouds rolled and the winds howled as Saul stood waiting to be told the reason for his presence.

"Saul," the Fates collective voice rumbled, "We have called on you because we sense a Dark threat to the humans of Earth."

"What kind of threat?" Saul asked, his attention completely focused now.

"A Dark threat!" the Fates repeated.

"Explain!" Saul barked out.

"We feel the Dark has sent at least one of their kind to Earth to cause chaos to the destinies of humans that are in your charge."

"Which ones?" Saul asked, going over in his mind all the mortals he looked after. There were just too many to pinpoint a few in a moment's notice. "Be more specific," he prodded.

"We cannot!" the Fates cried out. "You must go back to your charges and find the ones that have been chosen. Time is short, and your task is great. You must not fail."

"You have no more information than this to give me?" Saul asked, feeling the weight of responsibility riding heavily on his back.

"We do not," groaned the Fates. "We are unable to see all that the Dark has planned. We can only tell you that there is Darkness coming, and it must be stopped. Go now!" they shrieked. "And do not come back until you have righted this wrong!"

Saul remained where he was, but was now alone. Many times in the past, in fact too many to count, Saul had been called to right wrongs and restore order. He had always done so calmly, accepting the part he played, never questioning his role.

But this time he was mad. Mad at the Dark, for once again interfering and taking him away from the mortals that needed him. Saul was angry at the Dark for feeling the need to alter Destiny, to cause chaos, and for being a major pain in his ass.

Saul threw back his handsome head and, with fists clenched and mighty wings spread wide, he let out a roar of such anger that it shook the sky and reached into the very bowels of Darkness, making its hordes cringe in fright.

"Saul is coming," the whispers repeated, until all knew one of theirs was soon to be the prey for the great hunter from above. They scurried and fled to hide in the deep shadows, hoping to bring no attention to themselves.

All but one!

Roman, who stood alone, letting loose his own cackle of glee as he accepted the Guardian's challenge. After all, he knew he already had a head start on bringing Darkness and evil to the mortals. And, as formidable as Saul was, Roman intended to win.

"Come and get me," Roman challenged the Guardian. "Come and get me if you can. But only one of us will survive. And I'm betting on me."

Chapter 79

Hix drove like a man possessed, trying to get to Abby before it was too late. Too late for him to tell her he loved her and the baby, no matter what. He wanted to have a life with her in the house he built for them. He wanted forever with her, and couldn't wait to ask her to be his wife.

Fear rode beside him as he made his way across town and was his companion as he rammed his truck into park and vaulted from the cab, slamming the door behind him. He ran to the door and pounded on it, wanting more than anything for Abby to open the door and her heart, to him again.

"Don't let me be too late," he repeated over and over, until he heard the lock click and saw the door swing wide.

He feasted his eyes on Abby, even though it had only been a few hours since he had left her. He noticed the evidence of tears on her pale face and it broke his heart that he had been the cause of her pain. Reaching out his arms Hix left the choice up to Abby—be with him, choose him or not.

His heart beat twice before his arms were filled with her warm body. She molded herself to him, leaving not a hair's breadth between them. Two hearts beat as one, as Hix drew her head from his shoulder. Cupping her face between his two work-roughened hands, Hix lowered his lips to hers, pressing softly at first until he, tasting her hunger, let himself go and was lost in the kiss.

He felt the rightness as her arms pulled him closer, if that was possible. His heart filled his chest with a love he had never felt before. Hix bent his knees and tightened his arms around Abby, before standing straight and tall. He lifted Abby completely off her feet and stepped into the house, kicking the door closed behind them.

Letting Abby slide down his body until her feet were once again on the floor, Hix leaned back until he could look into the gleaming eyes before him. Letting his feelings show in his eyes and in his smile, Hix did what he had come here to do. "I'm sorry, Abby," he started, his voice strong and sincere. "I never meant to cause you any worry or pain."

Abby started to shake her head in denial, but Hix was having none of it.

"No, Abby," he said. "I need to say this and I need you to listen to it all before you say anything. Okay?"

A nod of her head was all Abby was capable of, as she waited to hear what this man, who held her future in his hands, had to say.

"I love you, Abby. I hope you know that. I hope you can feel it every time I touch you. See it every time I look at you. Hear it every time I say your name. You surprised me tonight when you told me you were pregnant and, as much as I hate to admit it, I wondered if the baby was mine," he said, lowering his head in shame for a moment.

Abby felt sick with the words Hix spoke, and would have pulled away from his arms if he hadn't tightened his grip on her, anchoring her to him.

"No, let me finish," Hix said again, not yet done with what he had to say. "The baby IS mine," he said with conviction. "There will never be a question of who its father is, because I say it's mine and no one will dare say otherwise. I want this baby, Abby. I want it because it is a part of both of us. We made it in love, and I don't think anyone could love their child more than you and I."

"I can't wait to see your belly grow and be able to feel our child as it moves inside you," Hix said, running his hand over Abby's still flat stomach. "I can't wait to hold it in my arms and be able to spoil it rotten, because I have so much love to give. I've never been a father before, but I promise you I will do the best I can."

"I might not have the money you do, but I make a pretty good living, and I'm sure I can provide for our family. We have a beautiful new house to move into, the perfect place to start our family," Hix persuaded.

Then, still holding her but dropping to one knee, Hix laid his soul bare as he uttered the words Abby had been longing to hear. "I want to marry you, Abby. I want to be able to call you my wife and the mother of my children. Make a life with me. I promise you that I will do everything in my power to be a good husband and a good father. I love you, Abby," Hix said again, looking deep into her eyes. "Will you marry me? Will you be my wife?"

Hix stopped talking and breathing at the same time, waiting for Abby to give him her answer. As he watched Abby's face, he felt awe wash over him and tears came to his eyes. The look of wonder and then happiness that came over her face reminded Hix of watching a new sunrise, quiet and still, as its first rays brings light and warmth to a new day. And then the brilliant burst of glory as the sun rises past the horizon and bathes the earth with its life giving energy. Tears once again trailed down Abby's cheeks, but this time they were tears of joy and happiness, not washing away regret and uncertainty.

Abby smiled through her tears and giggled like a school girl, before wrapping her arms around Hix's neck and melting into him.

"I love you, too, Hix," she whispered against his shoulder. "When I found out about the baby, I had questions and doubts about the father, too. But I truly believe that Max was lying about what happened, and feel deep in my heart that we are the parents of this child."

"I've had two months to think about this and what I found out was that my life is empty without you in it. When we're not together, I feel a hole in my chest that aches until I see you again. I wake up in the middle of the night and reach for you. When you're not there, I curl up in a ball to hold in the loneliness," Abby said, remembering the nights spent alone.

"I like touching you, even if it is just holding hands," she said, shyly twining her fingers with his. "Your kisses feed my soul, and when we make love," she said with a deep sigh as she closed her eyes for a moment, "I want to melt into you, to stay that way forever."

Hix waited as Abby fell silent, finally pulling her back until he could see her face. "I need the words, Abby," he said, gripping her upper arms with hope. "I need to hear your answer plain and simple. Will you marry me, Abby? Will you be my wife?"

Abby brought her hands up to rest on Hix's forearms and looked him straight in the eye as she gave her answer with joy and conviction.

"Yes, Hix," she said, "Yes I will marry you. When?"

Chapter 80

Saul watched for a few more minutes, making sure all was as it should be. Abby and Hix had made the choices Destiny had written, and were happy in each other's arms.

It had not taken Saul long to find the ones the Dark had come to earth to gather. Hix and Abby had been their choices, but with Saul's help they were once more where they should be. Still Saul was not completely happy or convinced that the threat was over. He still felt, in each of their minds, a dark spot that he could not reach. It was as if a void had opened up, and when he touched it, there was nothing there. Nothing at all.

Saul did not like that. There was something being hidden from him, and he was going to have to find a way to get to it. Until then, he could do nothing but keep watch.

Saul had touched Hix's shoulder and left his hand resting there as he helped Hix open up and say what he felt to Abby. Men tended to be closed up when it came to their feelings, so a little nudge was needed for it all to come out.

All it had taken for Abby to say 'yes' was for Hix to ask. Saul was not needed there.

Saul left the house, but stayed outside in the quiet night until the lights went out. He could hear the soft sighs of passion coming from inside as Hix and Abby celebrated their love.

Saul looked around, peering into shadows, searching for hidden danger, but all appeared in order. As he began to fade out, he still had an uneasy feeling that all was not quite right. Saul had that itch between his shoulders that usually meant trouble was near.

Unable to ferret out the cause, Saul left to tend to his other mortals. If trouble was still brewing, he was going to have to wait until it revealed itself and deal with it then. He had no doubt that when he did deal with it, the Dark was going to be one more short at roll call. He was going to make sure that one more Dark troublemaker went to hell and never came back.

Chapter 81

Roman stayed hidden in the shadows, far enough away so Saul would not detect him. He stayed in the alleys, flickering and moving with the shadows, blending in but not letting down his guard until all was clear. Saul was a sly one when it came to finding and dispatching unwanted interlopers, and Roman was not done here yet.

He had watched while Saul assisted Hix and Abby, until they had agreed to marry, then leaving them to their happy-ever-after.

Roman couldn't have given a rat's ass if the two got together or not. That was not why he was here. His goal was far more complicated than a mere wedding and an upcoming baby.

He wanted fear and despair and misery and chaos. All the time and effort he had spent whispering in mortal ears and undermining Saul's efforts was going to pay off. All he had to do was be patient and not let opportunity slip by him. The time would come when he would push one of the humans to the edge of reason, to the edge of sanity, and with one swift kick in the ass, topple them over into a pit of darkness there would be no escape from.

Hell was not just a place that stinking, rotting, evil souls went to after they were dead or were killed. Oh no. Hell was a place he could create right here on earth, in the minds of weak mortals. In the plots he encouraged, and the actions it took to carry them out. Guilt was a wonderful tool, and he used it often, letting it eat at their souls until they went mad or, in cases that made him dance in victory, came to enjoy the acts of foulness he lived for. Repeating them over and over until they were caught and their reign of horror ended. No loss to the Dark though. Another weak mortal was found, turned, and chaos began again.

But Roman was not looking for chaos this time. This time he was looking for murder. And the time was fast approaching when he was going to get it.

Chapter 82

Hix and Abby spent the night in each other's arms, reaffirming their love and celebrating their decision to be married. They laughed and giggled like teenagers, making fireworks explode when they touched, burning hot in each other's arms till the wee hours of the morning. When they slept it was a dreamless sleep, putting to rest all the doubts and fears that had been with them for so long.

Noon had come and gone before they woke, each seeking out the other to start the new day with soft kisses and feathery touches. There was no taking turns in the shower, as Hix joined Abby under the hot spray. It was two very clean, very happy people that finally walked out the front door and headed to Sarah's.

Abby gripped Hix's hand tighter as they travelled the short distance to where she would face the mother of the man she loved. Hix had told her how he'd gone to his mother and told her everything. Even though he had reassured her that Sarah was on board with the whole situation, Abby was still nervous and even embarrassed that someone she wanted to love and have love her in return, knew all the awful details.

Hix stopped the truck, got out, and came around to open Abby's door. He saw her hesitation before sliding out to stand beside him. Not knowing what else to do to comfort her, he pulled her close and let her lean against him for just a moment.

"It's going to be okay," he said into her soft hair. Rubbing her back one more time for good measure, he grabbed her hand and led the way up the sidewalk, into the door that his mother held open in welcome for them.

"Hi, Mom," Hix said, bending down and giving her a quick peck on the cheek.

"Come in! Come in!" Sarah said, smiling as she waved them past her before closing the door. She followed them into the kitchen. "Have you guys eaten yet?" she asked, always the mother tending to her children.

"Not yet," Hix admitted with a glint in his eyes. He knew his mom well and anticipated something mouth-watering to fill his belly.

"Sit down," Sarah said as she rummaged through her cupboards for the fixings for cinnamon rolls and fresh bacon.

"You really don't have to go to all this trouble," Abby said, as she watched Sarah make the rolls and, at the same time, put the bacon in the microwave to cook.

"Yes she does," Hix said, eyeing the generous sized sweets as they disappeared into the oven. Hix grunted as Abby's elbow found its way into his side and laughed as his mother threw one of her pot holders at his head.

"It's no trouble at all," Sarah said as she handed Hix a pop and asked Abby what she would like to drink. Placing the beverages on the table, Sarah pulled out a chair and sat down. She took a long drink of her orange juice before turning her full attention on the two sitting across from her.

Her eyes missed nothing. The way Hix sat back relaxed with one arm around Abby and the other hand holding hers loosely. The way Abby sat with her chair moved as close to Hix as possible, and the way her hand squeezed his much more tightly than his did hers. The way her eyes grew dark with nerves and the way she only took small sips of her strawberry milk.

"I won't bite you, Abby," Sarah said kindly. "And I won't give you anything but my full support. I'm not here to blame or judge or rant or rave. I will give you my love, and I will always be here for you," she reassured Abby as she put both her hands around Abby's free one. "Hix told me what happened, that you two are going to be making me a grandmother soon. I can't tell you how happy that makes me! I have no doubt that you both will be wonderful parents!" she said with heartfelt conviction. "And on a more selfish note, I'm sure you will let me babysit whenever you two want some time to yourselves, which I hope will be often."

Abby was thankful that the buzzer on the microwave picked that second to go off, bringing Sarah to her feet as she tended to breakfast, and giving her a moment to wipe her damp eyes.

"Abby and I have decided to get married, Mom," Hix said with pride and love in his voice.

Sarah nodded her head, still with her back to the two, as she laid the crispy meat strips on a paper towel.

"That's wonderful news!" she said, giving them her blessing with those few words, as she opened the oven and removed the rolls.

The mouth-watering smell made Hix's stomach give a deep rumble of anticipation. Sarah laughed as she accepted Abby's offer to help set the table. It took only a few seconds to mix up the frosting and pour the white concoction over the pan of gooey buns. The plate barely hit the table before Hix was reaching for one and taking a man-sized bite before it made its way to his plate. Sarah served Abby one and took one for herself, along with a couple of pieces of bacon. The room fell quiet as they all dug into the food and remained that way until every last morsel was gone.

"Let me help you do the dishes," Abby said, as Sarah shooed Hix into the living room to watch TV.

Sarah smiled and filled the sink with sudsy water. "Have you guys set a date yet?" Sarah asked, taking advantage of the alone time she was getting with her soon-to-be daughter in law."

"Not really," Abby said, "but I would like it to be within the next two months, if we can swing everything."

"Can I suggest you hold the wedding here?" Sarah asked. I don't know too much about your family, but we have friends here and I know they would love to share in Hix's big day."

"That would be great!" Abby said. "It's just me and my mom, too. My friends are here and I think Winston would be a perfect place to get married."

Sarah wiped her hands dry before turning to Abby. "I would like to help if you will let me," she said, letting Abby see that she meant what she said. "It's your wedding, but if there is anything I can do for you please just ask. Hix is my only child, so I will only get to do this once."

Abby reached out and hugged Sarah to her, as again her eyes became damp. "That would be great," she said, her voice quivering slightly, holding tight to the woman who would play an important part in her life from now on. "I have to tell my friends tonight, and then maybe all of us can get together for lunch next week and hash out the details."

"Count me in," Sarah said, as she lifted a hand to brush a strand of hair off Abby's damp cheek. "Now let's go join Hix before you two have to take off."

Abby smiled and led the way, expecting Sarah to follow, but Sarah hesitated for a moment. Abby, her friends, and Sarah would be making plans for the wedding, but Sarah already had the seeds for another plan in her head. Nothing would mess up Abby and Hix's wedding, Sarah vowed. No one had better try to ruin their day, or they would reap the fruit her plan would bear. And its fruit would be death.

Chapter 83

Hix left Abby at her place, saying that he wanted to get his friends together and tell them their news over a couple of cold beers. Abby thought that was an excellent idea, as she was dying to do the same with her friends. After a deep kiss, that promised more to come later, Hix drove away with the phone to his ear.

Abby all but floated up the walk and into her front door. Heading over to her phone, she proceeded to call Mary, Tonia and Kendall, telling them that she needed to see them at her place right away. They all agreed to meet at her place in 15.

Hanging up the phone, Abby scurried around the kitchen setting out sodas to drink and the only things she had to munch on, chips, dip, and a few veggies to make it a small celebration. She had just finished when the anticipated knock sounded on the door. Opening it, Abby was not surprised to see her favorite trio all together on her door step.

"Well?" Kendall asked, not waiting to step inside before posing the question on all their minds.

Abby drug out the moment, casting her eyes down and wringing her hands for good measure. Finally, unable to contain herself any longer, she looked up into three very different faces. All three were dear to her, all three showing different emotions. Mary wore a look of concern, Tonia pity, and Kendall building rage. Abby put them out of their misery by simply throwing her hands in the air as she squealed, "We have a wedding to plan!"

Tonia and Mary screamed their approval and Kendall swallowed her anger, as all three rushed to hug their friend close.

"Let's close the door," Abby said, untangling herself and stepping back so the girls could enter. They piled into the house like puppies let out to play, running into each other, everyone talking at once.

"Come on guys, let's get something to eat and drink and I will tell you all about what happened."

They all grabbed sodas and filled their plates with snacks, before sitting around the kitchen table, eager to hear Abby's tale.

"Well," Abby began her story that took the better part of the next hour to tell. "And so," she said, when she was finally done, "I was really very serious when I said we had a wedding to plan. I hope you are all willing to help me, because I can't do this alone."

Kendall let out a huff of air, "Like we would let you have all the fun? Of course we will help." Reaching into her purse, that was the size of a small suitcase, she pulled out a note pad and pencil. "Ok, first things first, what's the date?" she asked, with pencil poised over the paper.

Abby got up, grabbed a calendar from the wall, and laid it in the middle of the table. "How about two months from today?" she asked them all. "You are going to be my bridesmaid's right?"

Three heads nodded yes and the date was set. They would all clear their schedules for this event, come hell or high water.

And so the afternoon went, with the four friends calling for take-out as they planned well into the dinner hour. They surfed the net for dresses, shoes, and flowers, placing orders for quick shipment, realizing that every second counted if this wedding was going to come off without a hitch. When the plans were completed, they agreed to come to lunch on the following Wednesday to fill Sarah in and finalize the details.

As they put on their coats and prepared to leave, they took turns hugging Abby close as they said their good byes and congratulations.

Kendall was the last to leave, wanting to talk to Abby alone. Plopping her butt on the couch and curling her legs underneath her, she asked Abby, "Have you told your mother yet?"

Abby shook her head no and made a face. "I wanted to tell you guys first and bask in the moment, before calling Cathy and having her bitch at me."

"What do you think she will say?" Kendall asked, even though she thought she already knew the answer.

"She is going to say that Hix is not good enough for me, and that he is only after my money," Abby replied, matter-of-factly.

"Are you going to tell her you are pregnant?" Kendall asked with a raised brow.

Abby pulled on her lower lip as she thought for a moment, and then shrugged her shoulders. "I can't see how I can get around it. By the time the wedding rolls around I will be showing. Better to tell her now, than have her find out that day and ruin it for everyone."

Kendall nodded her head in agreement, "So, call her now," she said, "while I'm still here. Then I can give you moral support and listen to you rant when you hang up.

Abby really did not want to, but she guessed now was as good a time as any, while Kendall was here with her. Closing her eyes, she reached for her phone, gave a big sigh and dialed.

Chapter 84

Cathy had just returned from having a nice dinner with a few of her friends. She was taking off her shoes when her phone rang. Looking at the number, she picked it up, a slight frown creasing her botoxed forehead. She thought about not answering it. Ever since Abby moved to that crappy little town in Nebraska, all they seemed to do was fight. Abby used to listen to her when it came to her career and her life, but not anymore. With a huff, Cathy gave in and clicked on her phone.

"Hello, Abby." she said. "To what do I owe this pleasure?" she asked, her voice dripping with insincerity.

"Hello, Mom," Abby's voice came over the line. "How are you?"

"You didn't call to ask me how I am." Cathy snarked at her. "So, why have you called?"

"I have some news, Mom, and I hope you will be happy about it," Abby answered, her voice eager for her mother's approval.

"You've finally decided to move back to civilization, haven't you?" Cathy asked, getting excited at the idea. "I told you not to move to that shitty little town in the middle of nowhere. I really never thought you would come to your senses, but I am so glad you have, Abby. Do you want me to find you an apartment close to me? I think there might actually be one coming open right in my building. Just think, we would be close enough to go to shoots together again, out for lunch and dinner, and shopping at all our favorite boutiques," she prattled on and on, barely stopping for a breath before she continued. "I was going to surprise you with something, but now that you've called, I'll tell you. I have the perfect guy for you. He is someone you already know. You've worked with him on shoots, so you would have a lot in common. And, I just love him. He is so perfect for you. His name is Max, Max Swift. He's a photographer, do you remember him? I know you don't make it a practice to hang out with people you work with, but I think Max really would be worth your time. I knew you would get bored with that Hix in no time flat and, I hate to say I told you so, but really Abby, I told you so."

Cathy stopped for a second, noticing a small nick in her manicure. "Damn it, how did that happen?" she growled.

The silence at the other end of the phone had Cathy rolling her eyes. "Abby, Abby are you still there? You said you had something to tell me, so what is it? Or did I guess it already?"

"Mrs. Mathews," a voice that was not Abby's said. "This is Kendall, Abby's friend."

"Why am I speaking to you?" Cathy asked. "Where is Abby? I don't want to speak to you. Put my daughter back on the phone or I'm hanging up."

Cathy had no intention of talking to some little nobody from Hicksville. She had never wanted to meet or get to know anyone in that small town, and had no intention of changing that now. Instead of her daughter's voice, she again heard Kendall, only this time she was not so friendly.

"Mrs. Mathews, as I said my name is Kendall, and I am a friend of your daughter's. I don't know what you said to Abby, but she gave me the phone and is sitting here pale as a ghost. So now, evidently I get to tell you the news that should have been Abby's to tell. Abby and Hix are getting married."

Kendall took great pleasure in delivering the news with no frills and no sugar coating. She knew all about Cathy Mathews and how she cared nothing about her daughter, unless it had to do with Abby making her money. She saw Abby as a way to get rich, and pushed her every chance she got to those ends. She was the reason Abby had run from New York and settled in Nebraska.

'Best move ever,' Kendall thought, as she listened to Cathy wheeze into the phone.

"This is a sick joke!" Cathy finally got out. "I don't find it funny at all."

"No it's not funny!" Kendall shot back. "This is big news, and is going to be a major event in Abby's life. She wanted you to know, and maybe even have you tell her you were happy for her. Happy that she found someone that makes her happy, that loves her the way Hix does. The wedding will be held in Winston in two months. You are invited, of course. Abby was hoping you would want to help. If not, that's fine. Her friends here, Hix's mother, and I can handle it with no problem."

Kendall held the phone away from her mouth as she turned to Abby. "What about the rest?" she asked her friend, wondering if she had to be the one to tell Cathy about the baby.

Abby raised dark eyes and shrugged her shoulders. "Would you mind?" she asked, hope and dread mixing in her voice.

Kendall nodded her head in agreement, and even smiled slightly, as she put the phone back to her ear. "Abby has one more piece of news for you," Kendall said, using her best matter of fact tone of voice. "She is pregnant with Hix's baby. She is about two months along. So, by the time the wedding comes, she will probably be showing, just so you know. Oh, by the way, that will make you a grandmother. Nothing to say?" Kendall asked into the silence on the phone. "Well, have a nice day then." And with great satisfaction, Kendall hung up.

Chapter 85

It took Cathy a full thirty seconds before it registered that the only thing on the other end of the phone, that seemed glued to her ear, was a dial tone. In total shock, Cathy finally lowered the phone and hung it up. *"This can't be happening,"* she thought to herself. "*This cannot be happening*!"

In the blink of an eye, she saw her future, and the money she craved, swirling down the drain, out of her control. How could Abby be so stupid, so selfish as to get herself knocked up, having to marry that hick from Nebraska? What was she thinking? For that matter, why was she getting married? Why was she having the baby?

Cathy started pacing. Slow and jerky movements were all she could muster at first, but as her brain began to work faster and faster, her legs followed suit. She spent the better part of an hour burning up the carpet, almost running back and forth across her plush apartment. Every idea she came up with to derail this farce of a wedding, met with a brick wall that she could not figure a way around or over, unless Abby cooperated. And she knew that was not going to happen.

Cathy had tried to teach her daughter the value of fame, and the fortune that came with it, but evidently Abby had turned a deaf ear to all her instructions.

"What to do? What to do?" Cathy asked herself over and over again. She needed a plan but nothing workable came to mind.

Just as she was about to give in to a jag of crying and a full blown pity party, the phone rang again, signaling an incoming call. Cathy grabbed it up, meaning to chuck it against the far wall, but the name caught her eye. Max. Here was the partner she needed.

"Max," she said into the phone, relief washing through her, "I was just thinking about you," she lied.

"That's wonderful to hear, Cathy," Max cooed into her ear. "What were you thinking?"

"Oh, Max," Cathy said, letting a small tremor enter her voice, "I've just had the most awful news given to me. I am just beside myself with the devastation the news has brought into my life." Cathy let a small sob loose, and a delicate sniffle followed.

Max rolled his eyes, and a sneer shaped his lips. Cathy was a snob, and a bitch on top of that, but he needed her to get to Abby. He needed to play her games and feed her ego, until she agreed to help him get what he wanted. Abby.

To that end, Max put just the right amount of concern into his voice as he asked the expected question, "What is it love? Tell me."

Cathy could not wait to tell Max that Abby had called, and then had her friend tell her that her daughter was pregnant and getting married to that small town, money hungry jerk from Nebraska, Hix. She went on to say that she had to do something to save her little girl from certain doom, never noticing that this time she was on the receiving end of a shocked silence.

Max's brain worked faster than Cathy's, and before Cathy could pour any more "poor me" drivel into the phone, Max had a plan.

"Cathy," he said, "I think I can be of help to you."

"Really?" Cathy asked, surprise in her voice. "How?"

"Well," Max began, "as you know, Abby and I had a, shall we say, short interlude the last time she was in New York."

"I remember seeing something in the papers about that," Cathy replied, grabbing on to the idea and hanging on as she waited to see where Max was leading her.

"I believe the baby Abby is carrying is mine," Max said calmly and convincingly.

"Oh my God!" Cathy squealed into the phone. "Are you serious? How can you be so sure?"

"Serious as a heart attack," he said. "Abby may not want to believe anything happened between us that night, but I think I can safely lay claim to the child. Between you and me, we can make her see how much better she would be with me instead of that Hix. Right?'

"You lovely man!" Cathy gushed. "You could marry Abby and move her back to New York where she belongs. We could get a nanny when the baby is born, and Abby could go back to work before the public forgets her face. It would make a great story for the papers, beautiful model and her husband working together, a fairy tale waiting to be sold to the tabloids. We could spin it to our advantage and soon everyone would be drooling to get her to represent their products. What do you think?" she asked, wanting to reach into the phone and plant a big kiss on her future son-in-law's mouth.

She could control Max, she was sure of it. He wanted the same things she did, money, power, the spotlight, and Abby back in the fold with her peers.

"I think we need to get together for lunch tomorrow and talk," Max said. "Say about one?"

"Yes, yes," Cathy said. "Come by my place, darling, and we will make plans."

"Now," Max said, "get some sleep and don't worry. We will make our plans tomorrow, and everything will be fine."

"Yes, alright," Cathy sighed, "good night, Max." And with a bubble of happiness surrounding her, every daughter's worst nightmare hung up the phone.

Chapter 86

Max put down his phone, burning with an awful anger that reached all the way to his soul. He was not going to sit back and watch as Abby made a fool of herself, and him, by hooking up with some unsophisticated moron from the sticks. Everyone was already talking about how she had chosen Hix over him, after the pictures of her leaving his hotel had hit the papers. The press had watched him for weeks, waiting to see a replay of him and Abby together. But all they got was her hanging all over that Hix, reporting that he, the famous, most sought after photographer in the country, had been dumped by a woman he had secretly wanted for ages.

The papers had turned his life into a laughed at affair. He knew everyone was laughing at him behind his back, he heard them. He was not going to forget those that had. He was going to make them crawl back to him and lick his boots when they begged him to take pictures of their ugly faces, to make them famous or keep them in the spot light. He was going to make them pay with ten times the humiliation he had felt.

At the top of the list was Abby herself. He was consumed with wanting revenge on the woman he both wanted and hated. All he had to do was keep her stupid mother close, and find out when and where this wedding was to take place. He was going to crash what he was sure would be the biggest event Winston Nebraska had ever seen, announcing to them and the world that he was the father of Abby's baby.

He had a lot of contacts in the press. Leaking the time and place of the wedding, and even hinting that there was going to be a surprise they would not want to miss, would have them churning the waters like sharks.

And of course, the added bonus of all this would be rubbing Hix's nose in the pile of shit he was going to unleash. His huge ego still stung when he thought of their last conversation. Max remembered the way Hix had talked to him, threatening him over the phone. He would show both Hix and Abby that no one messed with Max Swift and walked away unscathed.

"If anyone has any objections as to why this man and woman should not marry, let them speak now or forever hold their peace," was going to be his cue, and before he was done, he would leave more than one life in ruins.

Max knew without a single doubt that before this wedding day was over, he was going to get what he deserved.

Chapter 87

Kendall hung up the phone and looked at her best friend sitting on her couch, once again shaking and pale.

"What did she say to you?" Kendall asked. "It must have been something pretty bad for you to look the way you do. So just spit it out, because I'm not leaving until you do." And showing every intention of doing just that, Kendall sat down beside Abby.

Abby tried a small smile to reassure her friend, but could not pull it off. Instead she looked white as a corpse, and the hands she gripped together across her stomach were cold and bloodless.

Kendall cocked an eyebrow waiting. Abby cleared her throat and repeated what her mother had said. Kendall's cocked eyebrow lowered until she was frowning, and then gaping in amazement.

Abby sat quietly after she finished, waiting for a response from her friend. When the silence was more than she could take, she raised her eyes and focused on Kendall. What she saw was not what she expected. Instead of the anger, concern, or even pity she had braced herself for, she saw her best friend in the world shaking with laughter.

Kendall could not help it. "Holy crap, Abby!" she gasped, "your mother has balls the size of Texas." Kendall laughed so hard tears ran down her face, and she had to hold her sides tight because they ached.

Abby stared in wonder and confusion. Every time Kendall opened her mouth to explain, she ended up screaming with laughter again. Without meaning to, Abby started to laugh too. She had no idea why, as the whole situation made her want to hurl, but Kendall's laughter was infectious, and in no time at all the two were laughing and crying together.

"I'm sorry, Abby," Kendall finally got out. "I know it's not funny, but dear God, your mother is an ass. She has the nerve to whine because you live here in Nebraska, and then she suggests you hook up with Max again. Is she insane?"

Abby swiped a hand over her eyes as some of the merriment drained from her face. "My mom," Abby began, but Kendall cut her off before she could finish.

"Your mother is a greedy, self-centered bitch who only cares about herself. That's as plain as the pretty little nose on your face."

Abby wanted to defend her mother, but she knew what Kendall said was the truth.

"Maybe she was just saying those things to get back at me for leaving her," Abby ventured.

"That's probably partly true," Kendall conceded, "but the other part is probably that she wanted to hurt you for being happy. She finally realizes she has lost all control over you, and your money that she so heartily craves."

Abby couldn't argue with anything Kendall had said, and she sadly nodded her head in agreement.

Taking a deep cleansing breath, Kendall slapped her hands on her thighs and took control.

"All righty then," she said standing. "We extended the invitation to her, and if she accepts then the more the merrier. But we are not going to hold our breaths. I can see sitting around waiting for her to show up and start playing mommy will be a waste of our time. We are going to do like we planned, and all get together on Wednesday to hash out the details of you wedding. Until then, you need to concentrate on a few details, like location and the guest list. The rest we'll deal with as a group. Operation wedding has begun!" she said with a grin.

Abby was more than happy to let Kendall take the reins. She was mentally exhausted, and needed time to think about all that had happened today. Abby rose to her feet and wrapped her friend in a hug of gratefulness.

"You're a good friend, Kendall," she said. "Thank you from the bottom of my heart."

Kendall returned the hug, and held it for a moment before pulling away. "You're welcome," was all she could get past the lump in her throat. Then, clearing her throat and pulling away from Abby, she turned towards the door saying, "I better get going! There's so much to do and so little time before Wednesday. You try to get a good night sleep and call me tomorrow if you need to talk. Okay?"

"Yes," Abby said, already thinking about the soft bed that waited for her drained body. "I'll talk to you tomorrow."

Abby walked Kendall to the door, closing and locking it behind her friend. Then she drug her tired body into the bedroom and, clothes and all, crawled under the welcoming covers. And she slept. But not alone.

Roman crept in beside her, wrapping his cold, dark arms around her as he led her to his own personal dreamland. Into a nightmare where the blood ran deep and it was Abby's dripping hand that held the knife.

Chapter 88

The minute the door closed at her back and she was alone, Kendall's face went from humorous support to white hot anger. Her legs carried her stiffly to her car, and her hands buckled her in without conscious thought. Her mind was consumed with the hurt her friend once again had to endure because of her mother, the thoughtless bitch, and that slime ball Max.

The mother's actions were easy for Kendall to figure out. She had seen her control over Abby fade and disappear with Abby's exit from the Big Apple, and from under her thumb.

And even though Max was a little harder, Kendall would bet her last dollar that he was sucking up to Cathy in the hopes of forming an alliance with her, to get her to work on Abby on his behalf. She would also bet that Max had never told Cathy all that had happened, or not, the one and only time Abby had been within his sleazy grasp.

Not that it would matter to Cathy, Kendall sneered. She would not put it past good ole mom to pimp her daughter to the highest bidder if it meant more money for her own pockets. Between the two, Kendall was pretty sure they were hatching a plan to get Abby back to New York and away from Winston, NE and Hix.

But they had no idea who they were messing with when they schemed to hurt someone close to Kendall. Not that she had ever been a mean or vindictive person, but lately Kendall had been one hundred percent sure that she would be capable of fighting to the death to protect those she loved. And the death she envisioned was not going to be her own.

Before she knew it, she had made it all the way home without even realizing she had been driving. Mildly surprised, Kendall shut her car off, walked to the front door, unlocked it, and went inside.

The bathroom was the first order of business, but it was not for the usual purpose. Kendall stepped up to the big mirror hanging over the sink and leaning in stared at the familiar reflection. Something was off with her, but what? Her hair was the same, skin, nose, mouth, teeth, all exactly the same as it had been every morning that she could remember.

But as she looked into her own eyes she knew. Knew what was off, what was wrong. It was her eyes. They held no warmth, no emotion, no life in their depths. They just stared back, flat and cold. They were the eyes of a stranger. The eyes of a killer.

Scared, confused, and with a scream begging to be let out, Kendall turned and ran.

Roman laughed!

Chapter 89

Hix made it to Abby's house shortly before midnight, a goofy smile on his face and beer on his breath. He and his friends had drank toast after toast to his future marriage, to his beautiful bride-to-be, and to his soon-to-be lack of freedom. With all the good natured ribbing he took, he still felt the happiness his friends felt for him and the good wishes they gave jokingly, but meant for real.

As good a time as he was having, Hix left well before the bar closed, wanting to get home to Abby. She would probably be asleep when he got there, but as long as he could hold her in his arms, he was okay. His world would be right.

Abby was in bed when he got home. He crept quietly around the room, taking off his clothes before going to the bathroom and brushing his teeth. He turned off the light, opened the door, and made his way to the bed in the dark, until he lay beside the beautiful woman he called his fiancé. He closed his eyes, having every intention of going right to sleep, but want he wanted eluded him.

Instead he felt Abby jerk and jump as she slept, and his worry for her and what she dreamt kept him wide awake. He tried to gently shake her awake, but she only pulled away and moaned with anguish. *"What was wrong?"* he wondered, reaching over and switching on the bedside lamp.

By its soft glow he could see Abby's face, covered with a light film of sweat even as her body felt cool to his touch. "*Maybe getting married was giving her nightmares*," Hix fretted. But no, he thought, she had been so happy when he had asked her to be his wife. Something had to have happened after he left.

Hix wondered if Abby was going to tell him what was bothering her or try to keep it from him like she had with the mess in New York. He'd have to work on her in the morning, he decided. It was better to get things out in the open and deal with them, rather than letting them stew and fester.

Whatever it was, he was sure they could overcome it together. Abby was just going to have to get used to letting him in, to letting him help her.

Gathering her close in his arms, Hix held her until she finally gave in and slept peacefully. His mind continued to churn with possibilities, until his body won out over worry, and he slipped into the sleep he craved.

'Tomorrow,' he thought before going under.' Tomorrow he would get some answers.'

Chapter 90

Saul stood by the bed and watched as Hix succumbed to slumber. With one gentle touch he calmed both of his human's minds, allowing them a night of dreamless sleep. He felt Hix's puzzlement over Abby's behavior, and peered into Abby's dreams to watch her struggle with her own demons. He did not know where all this unrest was coming from, but he used his powers to unravel the distress and replace it with calmness and anticipation of a wonderful future.

Once finished, he stood straight and tall, his work for the moment complete. Still, Saul was puzzled about the origin of their issues. There should be no reason for any of this. It was written that this was to be a time of joy for this couple. But yet there was a worm of doubt and unhappiness that was growing every minute. Every time Saul tried to ferret out where this worm lay in their minds, he was met with a wall of secrecy. Saul saw no way around it. He was going to have to work on these walls, brick by brick, piece by piece, until he could knock them down and reveal what they hid from his sight.

He knew it was the Dark's doing, but not exactly who the Dark's emissary was. It really didn't matter, because Saul feared no one and nothing. He'd battled the Dark more times than he could count, and this time would be no different than the rest. He planned on being victorious and guiding his charges to their destinies. He could not fail, would not fail.

So with his convictions firmly in place, Saul rolled up his sleeves, so to speak, and set to work.

"Damn the Dark," Saul thought as he melded his mind with Hix's. He had to work slowly, so as not to cause damage to this fragile being.

As the night ran towards the next sunrise, Saul was able to make a crack in the wall, and work it until he was able to peer inside the blackness it held.

What he found was the seed of murder, planted by the Dark and tended by evil, until it had grown from that same small seed into a tree, wide of girth and gigantic in height. Its trunk was thick and gnarled, with worms of hatred and revenge crawling in and out of the holes they used for their homes. So many were there, that the bark seemed to be a living being, as it changed with the movement of these foul creatures. Each leaf was black as the deepest night, and the dew that dripped from their pointed tips carried the foul stench of death.

Saul wedged the crack open wide enough that he could creep inside and stand beside the monster the Dark had created. He could not believe he had not known what was going on, and that it had reached this stage of its evolution. It was full grown, with roots going deep. Too deep for Saul to just uproot.

Saul raised his right hand, meaning to lay it on the tree, when he noticed the hand glowing, bringing lightness into the dark. He smiled as he placed his hand on the tree, and felt its trunk shiver and its leaves moan with his touch. Closing his eyes, Saul concentrated, trying to learn the secrets the tree held.

What he learned made his eyes fly open and his beautiful mouth pull back from his teeth with a snarl. It had been left too long to grow, and Saul was not going to be able to stop what the Dark had set in motion.

Saul retreated from Hix's mind and moved on to Abby's. Again, with time running short, he worked his way into the secrets her mind held, finding the same seed planted and growing in unison with Hix's. However, Abby's desire for revenge was stronger. The leaves moaned with hatred, their rustling sending a chill down Saul's spine. The word they repeated over and over grew in volume, until Abby's universe was filled with the need to act on that one word. KILL.

Chapter 91

Hix tried for three days to talk to Abby about what was bothering her. But he got nowhere. He could see how her eyes were haunted, how her mind wandered when she thought she was alone. How her gaiety was not a hundred percent real and her smiles were tinged with nerves. How was he ever going to get her to trust him with her problems? How could they make a life together if she did not trust him? Questions, that Hix had no answers to, nagged him night and day, until he felt ready to explode if he didn't get some answers.

So on Wednesday, he took off work and drove Abby to his mother's house, where she and her friends were going to sit down with his mom and hash out the wedding details. Abby thought Hix's joining them was a great idea. If they had questions for him they could be answered right then and there. After all, it was his wedding too, right?

Hix wasn't really concerned about the details of the ceremony, but rather hoped he would overhear something or be able to ask Kendall what she knew. By the end of the day he hoped to be able to get to the bottom of Abby's troubles.

Hix had never been to one of the girls' get-togethers, and had no idea what to expect. So when he followed Abby inside, he was happy to see just the women, paper and pencils, some magazines, and enough snacks to keep them all feeling fat and happy as they made their plans.

He hung off to the side, enjoying the easy rhythm the friends had with each other. He made himself useful by refilling drinks and filling bowls back up with munchies. He found planning a wedding was way too complicated for his taste, and was amazed how eager they all were to make this day perfect for Abby and himself.

He was not allowed to see the dress they were discussing for Abby, so he made his way out to the back yard and stayed there until Kendall and his mother came to get him.

"The coast is clear," Kendall joked, as Sarah moved past them and stretched her back and legs. Sitting for so long had left Sarah with the need to move for a few moments.

Hix gathered Kendall in his arms and hugged her tight. "Thank you," he said, "you and the rest have been great, helping the way you are."

When his mother moved to his side, he hugged her too. "You too, Mom," he said, a catch to his voice. "Thank you for all you are doing and for being so great about the wedding and the baby and just everything."

Sarah hugged her son back, warmth moving through her heart at his words. "You don't need to thank me," she said, "I do this because I love you and Abby. Everything will be just perfect." She pulled Kendall to her side, and included her in their close group. "We will see to it won't we?"

Kendall looped her arms around Sarah and held on to Hix's hand as she nodded her head. "We will. Your wedding day will be perfect." she said, smiling. But then under her breath she added, "No matter what."

Quiet as she had tried to be, Hix heard her. "What is it, Kendall?" he asked, jumping at the opening he had been waiting for.

Kendall tried to pull off an innocent look, but neither Hix nor Sarah were buying it.

Sarah too chimed in with her concerns, "I can tell something is bothering her, too. She is trying to be normal, but there is something off. Maybe if you tell us, we can all help fix it." Sarah gently coaxed Kendall.

Kendall needed little convincing, as she had been itching to say something all week. '*But this was Abby's story to tell, right?*' she argued with herself.

"Tell them," the voice in her head encouraged. "Tell them and share the secret. Secrets are meant to be told," it whispered. "Tell them."

Kendall moved apart from mother and son, and did as she was told.

"Abby called her mother the other night to tell her the news about the wedding and the baby, but Cathy ruined it."

"How did she do that?" Hix asked, his blood pressure starting to rise.

"First, Cathy butted in and started on Abby about moving back to New York, and finished by saying she had found the perfect man for her. Max. Abby got so upset she handed me the phone and I ended up telling Cathy about the wedding and the baby. Then I hung up on the bitch and spent the next hour trying to calm Abby down, giving her what support I could."

Hix and his mother were left speechless with Kendall's confession.

"Oh my God!" Sarah finally got out. "I can't believe her mother would be so cruel."

"I can." Hix said, his voice flat and cold.

"Those two are going to plan something that will ruin everything," Kendall said out loud what they were all thinking. "They're going to make it big and messy too. I'd bet my life on it. What are we going to do?"

"Protect Abby," Hix said out loud. But he, like Kendall and his mother, was listening to the whispers in his head, telling him he already knew what had to be done. He had known for a long time that there was only one solution to the problem, and the time was coming fast when each one's plan would be put into action.

Roman laughed with glee at his success at getting his four players lined up and ready to go. He danced with the knowledge that he had planted the seeds of revenge and hate, and had only to sit back now and see which one-Abby, Hix, Kendall or Sarah-would claim the title of murderer.

Chapter 92

Cathy made herself walk slowly to the door when the bell sounded. She stopped, fluffed her hair, and arranged her face so that when she opened the door to Max she looked like the poor damsel she wanted him to see. She needed his help and planned on making him feel all-powerful and male.

"Oh, Max," she whined, "come in. I've been so anxious for you to get here. I can't seem to forget what we talked about on the phone. You have to tell me what you have planned. And of course, how I can help," she added.

Max did as he was told, not that he had a choice, as Cathy slipped her arm through his and dragged him inside, holding him captive as she shut the door. She leaned heavily on him as they made their way into the living room.

"Can I offer you anything to drink or eat before we talk?" she asked, waving her arm towards the fully stocked bar in the corner.

"I'll have whatever you are having," Max said, as he untangled his arm from her grip and sat on the overstuffed couch.

Cathy sashayed her way to the bar, and poured each of them a generous glass of whiskey. She took her time crossing the room, swinging her hips and smiling coyly. She was sure she had seen a glint of admiration in Max's eyes, as he had looked her up and down when he had arrived. Of course he would think her beautiful, she reasoned to herself. She was in her prime. She would have to be careful not to lead him on though, as she was planning on him being her son-in-law. Not her lover.

Handing Max his drink, she sat down a short distance from him and took a sip of her drink.

"Thank you again for coming over, Max," she purred. "I must confess, you stunned me when you said Abby's baby was yours. Most men would not have laid claim to a baby, given the circumstances."

"I realize that Abby and I are not together at the moment," Max began, not even pretending to not understand what Cathy meant. "But I was there when it counted," he said, smiling as he gave Cathy a sly wink. "I want, and I am sure you do too, Abby to come to her senses and admit to the world that I am the father of her child. And," he continued, holding up a finger to silence Cathy before she could speak, "for Abby to marry me as soon as possible."

"How?" Cathy asked, sipping her drink in anticipation of the plan finally being revealed to her.

"I'm going to crash the wedding," Max began, "I'm going to stand up and claim the baby is mine, that I love Abby, and I want her to be my wife. It's that simple."

Cathy thought about it, taking a second to picture it in her mind. Max would stand up at the right moment, with cameras flashing of course, and declare his undying love for Abby. He would beg her to stop this farce, to admit the baby was his and marry him.

Cathy clutched her glass to her breast and felt envy stir. She would love to have a man declare himself so publicly.

"You must love my daughter very much," she said, looking at Max out of the corner of her eye. "I mean, to hold yourself up to embarrassment takes devotion."

"What is there to be embarrassed about?" Max countered.

"What if Abby says no," Cathy asked. "I mean, I just want to know what to expect. Just in case things do not go as you would like."

Max shrugged his shoulders, as if it didn't matter one way or another what Abby's answer would be. "Even if Abby says no in front of her guests, Hix will never go through with the wedding, thinking Abby is carrying my child. That will give me the time I need to make Abby see the only option she has is to marry me."

Cathy relaxed back into the soft folds of the couch as she thought about Max's plan. It sounded good on paper, but she was not so sure Abby would fall in line so easily. She had seen the stubborn streak in her daughter grow stronger since she had moved away, and could just picture Abby having the baby on her own and ruining her life for good. Just to spite her of course. Abby would be raked over the coals by the press, who although loved her at the moment, would turn on her just to sell papers, headlining the scandal.

But if Max failed, she would be there to pick up the pieces of her daughter's broken dreams and life, thus making her the hero in her daughter's eyes. She would play the loving mother, waiting until a more opportune time to say, I told you so. '*Win! Win!*" Cathy thought.

Lifting her eyes and her glass, she toasted Max. "I will help any way I can. Oh Max," Cathy said, sweetness dripping from her words, "I truly think you have come up with a wonderful plan, and I can't tell you how much I appreciate the burden you have lifted from my shoulders."

Max sat back, mimicking her gesture as he raised his glass in the air. "All I need from you, Cathy, is the information of where and when the event is to take place. I will take care of the rest."

"Yes, of course," Cathy said. "I will keep in touch, sharing every piece of information as soon as I am made aware."

"Of course I would be grateful if you would talk to Abby between now and the wedding and plead my case," Max said.

"I will do the best I can," Cathy promised, sure that Abby would never listen to her on the matter of her wedding. But whatever it took to keep Max happy and on track to end this unfortunate wedding, Cathy would do.

"Now," Cathy said, taking Max's drink from his hand, "I promised you lunch and, knowing you and I are on the same page when it comes to my daughter and her future, I think I can actually eat,"

Max let his hand rest on Cathy's back, as she led the way out the door. A small celebration was definitely in order, he mused, as everything he wanted so far was falling famously into place. All he needed now was to bide his time and, when the time was right, make his move. 'Yep,' he gloated to himself, as he reached back to close the door, 'I am finally on the road to getting what I so richly deserve.'

The clock was ticking now, and all he had to do was wait for the final buzzer.

Chapter 93

Abby didn't know why she was standing in line at the grocery store with her mouth open in surprise. She should have known this was coming. She should have known her mother would not let an opportunity pass that meant getting her name in the rag papers. She should have known that nothing would make her mother keep even a small morsel of news to herself. And, evidently, this was not small.

Abby snatched the closest paper to her, it didn't matter which one really, as all of them were trumpeting the same head line and, against her better judgment, she began to read. The chicken salad she had enjoyed for lunch only a short time ago, crawled its way up her throat. Only by swallowing many times, did Abby keep it from exploding onto the back of the woman in front of her.

'Super Model Abby Mathews Caught In Scandal As She Plans Quickie Wedding.' Beneath the big, bold print were two pictures, filling up the rest of the front page. One was a picture of Hix and Abby as they shared a kiss in Winston, and the other was of Abby and Max leaving the club in New York. Abby wanted to run from the store, but she stood her ground. She wasn't about to give the gossips in town, that were standing in clumps watching her and whispering, any more to talk about.

Abby was brought back to the present by a polite clearing of the throat from the grocery clerk, indicating she was next up to the register. She pushed her cart forward and, without thought, placed her items on the belt. Including the paper she had been looking at. It seemed an eternity before she was able to grab her bags and, as nonchalantly as possible, walk out to her car.

Abby was able to make it all the way home and into the privacy of her house, before she let herself think. "*Don't read it!*" she told herself. But human nature was strong as she sat down at the kitchen table spreading the paper open before her. It was like coming up on an accident and not being able to look away from the gore all around you. Even though it was going to hurt, Abby began to read the trash written about her.

It said that an inside source, her mother Abby thought again, had revealed to the paper that Abby was getting married in less than two months to a construction worker from Nebraska, named Balthazar Hix. It said that even though Hix was towering and very handsome, the source believed him to be a gold digger and only interested in Abby for her money. It also said that Abby had spent the night with fashion photographer, Max Swift, after a long fashion shoot in New York a couple of months before.

Then Abby's worst nightmare was printed in black and white for the entire world to read. It said how Abby now found herself pregnant, thus the reason for the quick wedding. But, the inside source wondered, as Abby did herself, who the father of her baby actually was.

It finished up by hinting that the wedding was to be a small, intimate affair. Sources hinted that a surprise was in store for the guests, one that would make this wedding an event no one would forget for a very long time.

Abby began to shake as she sat stunned and wondering what the surprise could be.

The pounding at her door did not register, nor did she look up when the door was flung open hard enough to bounce against the wall. Only when she felt her best friend Kendall's arms around her, did she respond.

"I came as soon as I read the article," Kendall said, giving her friend comfort and support by coming to her side.

"I read it," Abby hiccupped, as the tears she'd been holding back were let out to wet Kendall's shoulder.

"You shouldn't have," Kendall said.

"I couldn't help it," Abby replied. "I was standing in line at the market and it jumped up and smacked me in the face."

"You know the crap they write is just that, crap, right?" Kendall urged.

"But it is true," Abby said, her voice husky and rough with her tears. "I AM getting married in a short time. I AM pregnant. AND there is a question in my mind of who the baby's father is. It just sounds so awful when it's splashed all over the papers. It sounds dirty and sordid."

Kendall kept one arm around Abby's shoulder. With her free hand she squeezed and pulled her friends hand until, Abby was forced to face her.

"Stop it! Stop it right now! Everyone who knows what happened knows that Hix is your baby's daddy. And we all know that you and Hix love each other, so a wedding right now is just as it should be. Unless you want to call up the papers and give them an interview and air all the sordid details, I would suggest you throw the paper out and continue like we planned. Focus on the wedding and how happy you and Hix are to be getting married and starting a family." Abby's tears dried up as Kendall, pulling no punches, told her basically to get over it and move on.

"No! Oh poor you," Abby thought. Kendall always shot straight from the hip—no beating around the bush or sugar-coating. And, of course, Kendall was right. Abby was being way too sensitive, letting a silly story sway her and get under her skin.

"Okay," Abby sniffed, squaring her shoulders, "you are absolutely right. Even though there is truth to this story, it is twisted to be sensational and leading. Thanks for coming over, Kendall, I really needed a reality check from my BFF." Abby said. "You know me too well."

"Hey, that's what best friends are for, right?" Kendall responded. "Now, I have to get back to work. I'll call you later," she said, giving Abby a tight hug.

Abby walked Kendall to the door and closed it behind her, meaning to do just as she was told and throw the paper in the trash where it belonged. She picked it up and, with a mind of their own, her eyes found the last line again.

"What was the surprise?" she wondered. She doubted even Kendall could figure that one out, without more information.

Abby knew she should call her mother and find out what she knew but, try as she might, she couldn't make herself pick up the phone. The conversation would end in a fight, her mother berating her for her decisions. Better to wait till the dust settled, Abby decided.

Lifting the lid to the trash can, Abby stuffed the paper way down inside so she would not have to see it or think about it anymore. Dusting off her hands in satisfaction, Abby pulled out her wedding plans and began to look them over, making notes here and a small tweak there. As she worked, the small voice that had become her companion of late whispered and wormed its way around and around in her head.

"It's Max," it said. "He is the one that is going to ruin everything. Are you going to let him ruin your wedding, ruin your life, ruin your happiness?"

Abby's eyes narrowed and her pen dug deep into the paper underneath it. "No!" she whispered fiercely. "He tried once, but he won't get the chance to try again. I'll stop him!" she vowed out loud. "I'll stop him, and this time it will be for good!"

Chapter 94

Time flew by and, before Abby knew it, the wedding was to be the next day. She stood in her bathroom, distractedly gazing in the mirror as she got ready for the rehearsal. Hix would be here shortly to drive them to their home. The home he had built for them would also be the site of their wedding.

Everyone had worked like madmen to get the backyard ready and Abby thought it looked like a dream. Flowers and decorations adorned the newly landscaped lawn and trees. White chairs for the guests formed the aisle she would be walking down. In just a short time she would be walking amidst her friends and family toward Hix, the man she loved. They would exchange their vows that would tie them together as man and wife.

'Wife,' Abby thought, and her hand shook just a little at the big step she was about to take. A step she "Wanted" to take, she assured herself.

After the rehearsal they would all go over to Sarah's house and enjoy a bar-b-que dinner with their wedding party and family. Then Abby intended to head home early and try to get some much-needed sleep before the big day. Her nerves were frazzled, but Abby hid it well.

The town of Winston had been turned into a media circus ever since the story of her wedding had hit the papers. She had paparazzi camping out across the street from her house and they followed her everywhere—to the store, to dinner. There was no doubt in Abby's mind that her mother leaked as many details of their activities as she could. There was never a moment's peace from them.

Or from her mother, who claimed she had shown up a week early to help. Abby knew it was just to be in the camera's range every chance she got. She played the doting mother, giving the false impression she approved of her daughter's wedding to the public, but behind closed doors Cathy wined and picked at Abby about the mistake she was making. She'd even had the nerve to push Max down Abby's throat, by comparing Hix and him against each other.

"One more day," Abby thought. *"I just have to make it through one more day and then everything will get back to normal."*

Putting the lid on her favorite perfume, Abby took a deep breath and went into the living room where her mother waited.

"Oh, Abby," she said, with raised eyebrows. "You're not going to wear that, are you? Why you look so, so ordinary in that. You really have to remember who you are, and that everyone will be looking at you. Why don't you let me pick something out for you that will be more suited to your reputation as a super model?" she said, as she rose from the couch.

Abby opened her mouth to protest, but before she could utter a word the doorbell rang, saving her from, once again, getting into it with Cathy. Abby almost ran to the door. Flinging it open, she saw Hix standing there, looking like a golden god with the sun behind him. She smiled as Hix softly whistled his approval, and moved into his arms for a kiss that set her toes on fire.

"Right back atcha," she said huskily, loving the way Hix looked in his dark suit pants and a dress shirt open at the collar. Dressy and casual at the same time, she noted approvingly. She felt a little in awe that she was the one to call him hers.

"Are you ready?" Hix asked, linking his fingers with Abby's.

"Yes, please," Abby said, squeezing his fingers in return.

Just then, Cathy walked up behind Abby to get a look at Hix before they went outside. She rolled her eyes and sniffed at what she saw. "*Really?"* she thought. "*Couldn't he even wear a tie? And my god, look at that hair. Why it's hanging loose around his shoulders. He could at least have gotten a decent hair cut for the occasion. Oh right,"* she thought. *"Where in this hell-hole of a town was anyone to find a descent hair stylist?"* She forgot herself for a moment.

"Hello, Cathy," Hix said, well aware of the scrutiny he had just been under. "Are you ready to go?"

Cathy turned her back on the couple and walked towards the bathroom. "Actually," she said, "you two go ahead. I'm going to freshen up and then drive myself out. I will only be a few minutes behind you."

Hix looked at Abby and, with a shrug of her shoulders, Abby gathered her purse and a light jacket.

"Okay, mother. We will see you there." she said over her shoulder as they left.

Cathy veered off course as soon as the door had closed and, picking up her purse, got her phone out and dialed the now very familiar number.

"Hello, Cathy," Max said, answering before the first ring finished. "How are you darling?"

"How do you think I am?" Cathy shot back. "My daughter is going to marry that bumpkin tomorrow and I still have not seen you lift a finger to stop it."

"I will be putting my plan into effect starting tonight" Max said slowly, as if he was talking to an idiot. "Now what is the time frame for tonight?"

Cathy was not so stupid that she did not recognize the insult in the tone of Max's voice, but she bit her tongue. She needed him to derail this wedding and then she could tell him, if Abby still said no to his proposal, to get lost. "Abby and Hix just left to go to the house for the rehearsal and then we will be going to Hix's mother's house for, of all things, a bar-b-que."

"I remember the address you gave me for Sarah's house." Max said. "I'll be waiting when you all get there."

"Then what?" Cathy demanded to know.

"You will just have to wait and see like the rest" Max answered mysteriously. "But you will know when I get there I'm sure. Have a good time" and he hung up.

Cathy fumed for a few seconds at not being trusted by Max to be told the whole plan. But maybe she needed to look surprised with the rest when what ever happened, happened. Pacifying herself with this reasoning, Cathy picked up her purse and headed out the door. She strutted to the car she rented, a sassy red corvette and, waving to the shutter bugs still outside, slid gracefully into the soft seat and with a roar of power, drove away leaving them scrambling in her cloud of dust. Every one of them racing to follow her. None of them wanted to miss an opportunity to get a shot of the hottest couple in the news right now.

'Not long now,' Cathy thought as she made the short drive into the country side. '*Not long now and the wedding will be old news and the break-up of Abby Mathews and Balthazar Hix will take center stage.*' "Yummy headlines!" Cathy gloated, "absolutely yummy."

Chapter 95

The rehearsal went off like a well-oiled machine. Everyone was there and the spirit of the group, as a whole, was light-hearted, hovering right below a party. Kendall, Mary, and Tonia acted as Abby's bridesmaids and Dylan, Andrew, and Josh stood up for Hix.

Abby had no one to walk her down the aisle, so she made the journey on her own, keeping her eyes locked with Hix's the whole time. Reaching his side, she placed her hand in his, as Pastor Rod walked them through a quick version of the ceremony that would take place the next day.

The wedding party hung around in a group after all the instructions had been given and they had been cut loose for the time being. They laughed and had a good time just hanging together. Sarah let them be for a few minutes before joining them and herding them all in the direction of their vehicles.

"It's time to head to my house." she declared. "I'm hungry and the grill is your job," she said to Hix and his pals.

Four chests puffed up in manly anticipation, and all agreed that it was time to get the food started. Sarah and the four girls trailed behind, shaking their heads as they witnessed the macho display in front of them.

As the party disappeared around the corner, Sarah came back and searched the area until she found Cathy standing by the altar, tapping her high-heeled foot.

"Are you coming?" she called, wanting to be on her way with everyone else, but not wanting to seem rude not waiting for Abby's mother. Even though Cathy continued to act as if everyone was beneath her notice, and held herself apart from the festivities, Sarah still played the gracious hostess.

Cathy wanted to ignore Sarah, but could find no excuse to snub her as they were alone, and it would have been a waste of time. Pasting on a smile even a blind person could tell was false, she turned around and made her way down the aisle Abby had just graced a few moments before.

"Of course, darling," she sing-songed, "I was just admiring all the effort that went into the wedding preparations."

Sarah thanked her and had to smirk a little as she let the remark slide. She chose to accept Cathy's words as a complement not a put-down. The wedding was going to be beautiful, and Sarah was going to be proud at the end of the day. She was gaining a daughter and a friend.

The two mothers, so different, made their way around the house and into their separate cars. Sarah figured Cathy knew the way to her house, so she did not bother to wait and drive slow so she could follow. She was right.

Cathy lingered until she saw the other car turn onto the highway and head back towards town, before easing her way along the dirt track everyone called a driveway. She took her time, giving everyone else a chance to arrive and get inside. She would casually walk in late and everyone would look at her and know that this was the way to be. If they had any sense at all, they would envy her style, her beauty, her clothes, and everything about her. Her lip turned up in a sneer as she thought to herself that it would actually take very little to out-shine the common folks around this town.

Cathy had to pull the car to a stop several houses down from where the party was due to the fact so many cars lined both sides of the street. 'How rude,' she thought, 'that no one had bothered to save her a space. After all she was special, the mother of the bride.'

Letting the car growl its power one more time before shutting it down, she flipped down the visor and checked her face and hair in the small mirror. As far as she could tell, she was flawless. Fluffing her hair, she made to exit the car but stopped short with her hand on the door handle.

Standing across from Sarah's house, right out in the open, was Max. He was leaning against a car's front fender, looking like he hadn't a care in the world. He didn't bother to look her way, as his focus was on the wide open front door where all were gathered. Cathy still wondered at his plan, but she didn't have to wonder long.

She slid out of her car and began walking towards the house that was to be, for the night, party central. As she turned the corner of the sidewalk, she saw, framed in the doorway, her want-to-be son-in-law, Hix.

He didn't look so loving and gentle at the moment. If fact, he looked like he could do some serious damage. His body was as still as a statue and his fists were clenched into hammers that screamed pain. His lips were pulled back in a snarl, and his eyes, even though narrowed, burned like blue flames, bright and hot with rage.

Cathy's steps faltered as she wondered if Max had made a wise move in letting Hix see him before the wedding.

But that was all Hix was going to get, a look, as Max got into the car he had been leaning on and, with a salute to his rival, drove off down the street.

Cathy thought it best to play dumb and pretend she had seen nothing. As she approached the door, she raised an eyebrow as Hix still blocked the doorway. "I am invited, am I not?" she asked, finally getting Hix's attention.

Hix stepped back and allowed her to pass inside before shutting the door behind her.

"Oh this is going to be fun," she thought, feeling the heat at her back as Hix still burned. "Maybe this night was not going to be a total loss after all," she reasoned and, putting a smile on her face that reeked of secrets, she joined the wedding party.

Chapter 96

There was nothing that could rival a good old-fashioned Nebraska bar-b-que when neighbors and friends got together to relax and have fun. Having one for a wedding was extra special.

Everything on the groaning tables was made with home-grown ingredients from local farmers and personal gardens. From the newly dug potatoes and farm-fresh eggs for the salad, to the big fat ears of corn-on-the-cob and the home-churned butter that would be slathered on the kernels when they came off the grill. From the pies made from fresh-picked fruit, to the deviled eggs fresh from farm chickens, and the mouth-watering beef that came from a local farmer for the grill.

Juicy, fat steaks of all kinds smoked and sizzled on the grill, and people hastened to line up when Hix and his groomsmen called out, "They're done!" There were hamburgers for those who wanted something smaller than a steak, but just as tasty, garnished with pickles, onions, tomatoes and lettuce, all fresh-picked or canned from Sarah's own garden.

Sarah wandered from group to group, playing the perfect hostess, making sure everyone had drinks of their choice and no one went hungry. Along with Abby's bridesmaids, she kept the dishes on the table full and the trash picked up. When everyone had filled their bellies to bursting, the food was cleared from the table and put in the kitchen to be brought out if anyone wanted to snack later.

Sarah stood off to one side, content that all had gone well and that everyone was having a good time. The only glitch in the evening was the way Cathy separated herself from the locals. The only person she really talked to was Abby. And every time she cornered her daughter, Sarah had tried to ease her way in and rescue Abby.

As the festivities began to wind down, Sarah noticed that Abby was looking a little tired. She was going to have to tell Hix to take his bride home and put her to bed, so she would be fresh and rested for the wedding.

It was still a couple of hours later before the guests and wedding party started to leave. Sarah walked them out, making sure that everyone took some food home to enjoy. She did not want to have to try to eat the leftovers by herself and she was glad when the food disappeared, leaving her with a small bit she could send with Hix and Kendall, who were the last two to leave.

"Where's Abby?" Sarah asked, joining Hix and Kendall in the now quiet back yard.

"She walked her mother to her car," Hix said.

Sarah picked up on the tone of his voice right away and asked only, "What is it?"

Hix looked around and motioned Kendall and his mother to come closer. "There's something going on," he said, putting his hands in his pockets to hide their clenching.

"What do you mean?" Kendall asked, instantly on alert.

Again Hix looked over his shoulder to make sure they were alone.

"When I was at the front door letting people in, I saw Max standing across the street," he told them.

"What!?!" Kendall ground out "What was he doing? Where did he go? What did he want? Did he say anything?" She fired questions fast at Hix, not giving him time to answer any of them.

Hix held up his hands, before running them through his hair in frustration. "He was just leaning on his car, staring at the house. Then he gave me a wave, got in his car, and drove off. He didn't say a word, just stared at me with a damn smile on his face."

"What do you think he wants?" Sarah asked.

Looking at his mother, Hix noticed she had paled and her expression was grim.

"I don't know," Hix said, shaking his head, "but the timing is too convenient for it to be anything else but to stir up trouble at the wedding."

"I'm sure of it," Kendall said. "I don't know if either of you read the rag papers a couple of months ago. Right when they got wind of the wedding, each reported that an inside source said there may be a surprise at the wedding that would have people talking for a long time afterwards."

"Any clues as to what they might have been eluding to?" Sarah asked.

Kendall felt two sets of eyes boring into her, but she had no answers for them. "Not a clue," she said, adding to the frustrations of being in the dark.

"Well," Sarah started, "I assume that he is staying in town somewhere right?"

"That sounds logical," Kendall agreed. "Why? Are we, or at least one of us, going to try talking to him and finding out what he wants?"

"I'll talk to him," Hix offered, but one look at his face and it was clear to Kendall and Sarah that talking was the one thing Hix did not want to do with Max. Violence was more apt to be on the agenda.

"I don't think any of us should talk to him," Kendall said. "Why should we play his game and let him get to us when we should be focusing on the wedding tomorrow?"

"You want to just ignore him?" Hix asked, disbelief written all over his face.

"I want us to not jump to conclusions and to not let this butthead interfere with what should be a very happy occasion tomorrow. I think we could drive ourselves crazy wondering what Max is planning next. And whether we like it or not, we are going to have to just go on like normal and deal with whatever when it happens," Kendall replied.

"You're right," Sarah said, nodding her head reluctantly. "He may not be planning anything except what he just pulled. We don't know."

"Well I know one thing," Hix said, "we need to keep this quiet. I don't think Abby needs to find out about this right now. Actually, ever."

Hix was not finished, but he noticed the look of horror on Kendall and his mother's face and he knew. Turning slowly, Hix found Abby, white as a sheet and clutching the back of a chair for support. He rushed to her side as her legs began to buckle, catching her in his arms and feeling her body tremble against his as he held her tight. All he wanted was to protect her from any more hurt. But how could he, with that jerk showing up on the eve of their wedding to cause trouble?

Something had to be done. Done and done tonight!

Chapter 97

Roman watched as Kendall and Sarah crowded around Hix and Abby, worry etched on their faces. His dark tongue crawled out of the black hole that passed as a mouth, licking his dried out lips and leaving behind thick yellow slime that dropped in globs onto the lush green of Sarah's back yard, making the grass wither and brown instantly.

When Sarah took notice of the spot, Roman laughed because he knew that she would think, what all the humans thought, that a dog had gotten into her yard and peed on the lawn, killing it. "Stupid humans," he mused. "They wouldn't know the super natural even if it jumped up and bit them in the ass." And he was super, if he did say so himself. After all, his plan was working perfectly and was going to continue to work perfectly because he had all his bases covered. He had his brothers working to keep Saul busy so he would not interfere, would not suspect until it was too late to stop what was so close to being finished.

Roman listened as three of the four of his pawns discussed the thorn in their sides, Max. He listened as they tried to figure out what to do, but he, Roman, had already told them what to do, must do, would do.

He lurked in the shadows until Kendall, Sarah, and Hix calmed Abby down, having no choice but to tell her Max was in town. He skulked and squirmed, wishing they would hurry up and get done, so he could take over and lead this final charge to the finish line. But humans were so dramatic and loved to prolong their pain. He was quiet until each had had their say.

Each voicing their opinion, that they should do nothing. Hix suggesting that they just post men at all the entrances and tell them to be friendly and polite, but to be on the look-out for Max and to deny him entrance to the wedding. Then there would be no trouble and they could all be assured the wedding would go smoothly. All had agreed and, after hugs, kisses and promises not to worry, went their separate ways for the night.

But Roman was not done!

Reaching into all four minds, he destroyed the black walls hiding the seeds he had planted long ago, bringing their monstrous growth into the light. He unleashed the rage, the need for revenge, the need to protect, and the need to provide safety, security and happiness for loved ones, to pour through the four humans. When each was seeped with these emotions, Roman let loose his final Dark Whisper that was heard by the four as one.

"It's time," he commanded, swelling with power until his voice rang in the minds of his pawns, blocking all else from their minds. "There is no tomorrow, there is only tonight. It must be tonight. Remember your plan. Do it. DO IT NOW!!"

Chapter 98

Saul had been busy helping his many charges, leading them back to their Destinies, cleaning up the hundreds of small issues that, of late, seemed never-ending. Nothing earth-shattering, but still problems that needed his guidance and his time.

He had not forgotten Abby and Hix, but felt sure that he had steered them back to the paths they were to follow and that the wedding that was to take place tomorrow would go exactly as planned.

Saul dusted off his hands in satisfaction as he finished with the last of his charges. He wanted to make one last stop before the Window to the World for a final peek, before attending the wedding of Abby and Hix. He loved weddings. The feelings of love and hope reigned supreme at these events. The happiness he shared with the lucky couple made his work seem very rewarding, allowing him to feel what they felt and find joy in his Immortal life.

But he never made it to the Window.

He was stopped cold as he felt the swell of the dark power. Black clouds gathered and thick ropes of lightning forked, making the skies shriek with the pain of chaos unleashed.

Saul ground his teeth in anger as he knew he had been duped. He was kept busy enough so as not to notice the true plan of the Dark, until it was too late.

Saul stretched his mighty wings, threw back his head, and with arched back and clenched fists, let loose a roar of rage that made the shrieking of the skies seem but a small annoyance. With all his might, Saul thrust his wings, sending him into flight. Each beat propelled him faster and faster, until the fire that burned in his eyes left a trail behind him that resembled a comet in the sky.

He knew of the plan now, knew what he had to do, and knew that time was against him. He had to destroy the seeds of hate and death planted by the Dark in not one mind, but four.

Saul made it to Winston and started to work, having to be careful as he worked with the fragile humans. To hurry too fast would damage their minds beyond repair. Carefully, Saul pushed to save the destinies and lives of the ones the Dark had infected—Abby, Hix, Kendall and Sarah. Four innocents that had done nothing to deserve the meddling and interference of the Dark, but singled out just the same.

But Saul failed.

He saved three, but the fourth, the fourth got away.

The Dark's plan was carried out.

Roman laughed in victory.

Chapter 99

Max drove away, as if in no hurry, but in truth his heart was beating like a jack hammer, wondering if Hix was going to come after him. Checking his rearview mirror every few seconds, Max didn't relax until he was safely locked inside his hotel room, both locks in place and the flimsy chain across the door. "*Yeah like that would keep Hix out*," Max thought, swallowing hard. If that giant of a man wanted to get to him, Max doubted there would be much a few locks could do to keep him safe. And after tomorrow Max felt sure that Hix was going to want his head on a platter. All he had to do was make it through this one night and then tomorrow, tomorrow all this would be over. The tabloids would be screaming to get a story about what happened at the big wedding. "*Big wedding my ass*," Max thought. He was going to make the news of Abby's wedding old hat before it even got a chance to be news.

Max pulled off his shirt and kicked off his shoes before going into the small bathroom. Wetting a wash cloth, he attempted to wash the stink of fear from his body without taking a complete shower. The last thing he wanted was to be in the shower, naked, if Hix decided to pay him a visit. If he had to run for his life, he didn't want to be bare-assed naked with his junk dangling, risking the chance that a photographer would get a picture of him like that and turn it into the story that hit the front pages, instead of the one he had planned.

Abby, embarrassed and in tears, was what he was gunning for. Followed by pictures of Hix with his mouth open in shock, and of course himself looking cool and calm as he stood before the packed house, delivering the news that he was the father of Abby's baby. They would have to rerun the story with pictures of Abby leaving the club with him, and then of her leaving his hotel room the next morning. He had it all figured out.

Cathy had given him the information of where and when the wedding was to take place. She told him where the rehearsal dinner was to be, also.

"Dinner," Max thought, "*yeah right. Only in this small town would a bar-b-que be thought of as good enough for a rehearsal dinner.*"

How could Abby choose this bumpkin over him? If they were getting married, or rather when, Max smirked, he would have the best wedding planner in New York slaving away to make their day one that no one could rival.

He was going to look so good standing at the alter waiting for Abby to make her way to him and begin their new life together. Yes, that was exactly the way things should be, and would be after tomorrow. Of course he was going to have to insist that they either get married as soon as possible, or wait until the baby was born. He did not think it would be very photo-worthy if Abby came plodding down the aisle with a belly the size of a beach ball, drawing everyone's attention away from how good the two of them looked together as they focused on her damn baby bump! That would never due!

Max lay down on the bed with his arms behind his head and let his imagination run wild as he went over what he had planned for the next day. He loved the way it played out in his head, perfect in every way. Max let his eyes close and before long he dropped off into a light doze, relaxed as only sleep would allow.

It seemed only a few seconds before his eyes flew open as his phone, on the beside table, began to ring. Looking over at the red digital numbers shining from the cheap hotel clock, Max frowned. It showed almost eleven o'clock. The only one that knew this number was Cathy. But why would she be calling at this hour? Maybe something had come up, gone wrong, or maybe right for a change. Max didn't know, and wouldn't know, unless he actually picked up the phone.

Picking up the phone, he again frowned, as the read out showed an unfamiliar number. Who the hell was this and how did they get his number? Max rubbed a hand over his eyes in irritation, before he gave in and answered the phone.

"Hello," he said, letting the anger creep into his voice. "Who is this and how did you get this number?"

He waited, but no one spoke back. All he could hear was the proverbial heavy breathing.

"I said, who is this?" he demanded, giving it one more try. "Fine," he said, "I'm hanging up."

Before Max could follow through on his threat, a voice, which was more of a harsh whisper, started to speak. Max pressed the phone tight against his ear, trying to catch what it said.

"I can't hear a thing you're saying, so if you can't speak up, asshole, I'm going to hang up."

"I can help you," the voice said, this time loud enough that Max jerked his head back in surprise.

"Help me with what?" Max asked.

"With the plan you have for tomorrow."

"I don't know what you're talking about," Max bluffed.

"Of course you do," the harsh voice said, carrying the hint of a shared secret in its tone.

"What do you want?" Max asked, choosing to let the caller's last statement die away without acknowledging it.

"I want to help you get what you deserve."

"Which is?" Max questioned.

"Do you want my help or not?" the voice asked. "I can promise you that without it, you will fail. Without it you will be the butt of every joke the paparazzi, that you so love to give information to, can come up with for the next month. Maybe even longer, depending on how slow the gossip is at print time."

Max ground his teeth in frustration, but curiosity and ego got the better of him. "Fine!" he said, giving in. "What do I have to do?"

"Meet me tonight," the caller said.

"Where, and why can't you just tell me over the phone?" Max whined.

"This has to be face to face. I want to meet the famous Max Swift, and I want you to meet me."

"Oh for shit sake," Max thought. "*This was going to turn out to be some hick that thought he was going to take one look at them and want to make them famous by taking their picture. Did this slow-witted person really think he was going to be in awe of anyone from Winston? That anyone here could compete with the people that already begged him to take their pictures? Really? Were they that stupid?"*

'Yea okay,' he thought, '*this was going to be fun.*' It was just what he needed tonight. To grind someone's dreams into the dirt, at the same time he showed everyone in this po-dunk town that they were no match for him.

"Alright," Max said, deciding on the spur of the moment to have a little fun. "Where and when?"

"Midnight," the voice rasped.

"Okay I got the when, now how about the where?" Max repeated.

"Ten miles west of town there is a road, County Rd 669, turn there. Go until you see the first turn on you right. Take that. Keep driving until you see a car. I'll be in it. Follow me from there."

"Why all the cloak and dagger shit?" Max asked.

"I don't want anyone to see us talking and put two and two together, and realize I helped you. Are you going to be there or not?" the voice asked, impatient now.

"Okay," Max said, "I'll meet you, but this better be worth my time."

"Count on it," the voice said. "It'll be to die for!"

Chapter 100

Max got dressed again, leaving nothing behind in the hotel room. He'd traveled light, leaving what he did bring in his car just in case he needed to make a run for it to escape Hix. Getting in his car and driving away in the middle of the night was just too corny!

He laughed out loud as he made his way out of the sleeping town, following the directions given by the voice on the phone. He was surprised the directions had not been "turn right at the one and only tree, follow the cow trail to the big weed clump, and then go a tad until you get to the leaning barn." That would fit the situation better.

Max found his way to the first turn with no problem, aided by the bright moon that had risen in the midnight sky. He slowed to make sure he did not miss the next turn and, feeling fairly sure he had gotten on the right road, stepped down harder on the gas. He had to admit he was curious as to the identity of the person he was to meet. He checked his watch and was satisfied that he was right on time.

He drove for another five minutes with nothing to keep him company but the bright eyes in the ditch that watched him unblinkingly as he passed by. He swallowed hard and tried turning on the radio, but the music was too loud no matter the volume and seemed out of place with the total quiet. "No, not total quiet," Max amended, "the sounds of crickets, frogs and even a coyote could be heard over the rush of air coming in through the rolled down window." '*Creepy*,' Max thought. The sounds of the plains were foreign to him. They made him grip the steering wheel with sweaty hands and goose bumps were crawling up and down his spine. He would have been much more comfortable meeting in a crowd or even in a bar, instead of out in the open on some cow shit ridden ground.

Just when Max was ready to turn around, almost certain he was being sent on a wild goose chase, his head lights picked up the reflection of tail lights off to the side of the road up ahead. He slowed and was preparing to pull in behind and park, when the small pickup's lights came on and he was forced to follow in the cloud of dust it kicked up, off the road and over some rough ground for another mile or so. His teeth clacked together more than once as he bounced over holes and ruts other drivers had made, until finally his follow-the-leader master came to a stop and turned its lights out.

Max inched up beside the pickup and did the same, sitting for just a few seconds while the quiet made his ears ring and his mouth go dry. The time had arrived to see just who his secret helper was.

Max got out of his car, pausing a few seconds for his eyes to readjust from the dome light to the eerie dark. The only source of light was the moon, as he made his way around the car, trailing his hand along the hood, needing something solid to anchor his racing mind and settle his nerves.

Max peered at the small, dark pickup truck, trying to see if anyone was inside. But he could see nothing. Where was the driver? He finally spotted a darker shadow standing next to the passenger side door. As it separated itself from the other shadows, Max knew who it was and his mouth dropped open in surprise.

"Oh this is rich," he said, laughter and gloating in his voice. "I thought this was what you wanted?" Max shrugged his shoulders as he made his way, with a swagger, to stand before his partner in crime. "What went wrong he asked? Why the change of heart?"

Max got no answer, but that did not stop his gloating.

"This is going to look so good in the papers," he said, throwing back his head and bellowing his laughter to the sky. "Tell me how you are going to help me?" he said, finally getting himself under control. "I already have a plan, and I think it's pretty good. So how can you make it better?"

"By giving you what you need, what you so richly deserve," the voice said all harsh and raspy.

"You can drop the voice," Max said. "I'm standing right here and I can see you. Don't you think you're carrying this a little too far?"

"Let's walk," the voice said, still low, still raspy. "Let's walk and get this over with."

Chapter 101

Max followed close behind, not wanting to get lost in the dark. Once again the night sounds grew, until they were so loud they drowned out the crunching of the two people walking through the knee high grasses and weeds.

"Where are we going?" Max asked the retreating back in front of him.

"Nowhere," the voice said, "right here is fine." Turning to face Max the voice started to speak, quiet at first, almost as if it were talking to itself.

"This should be a time of happiness, weddings usually are. All the love that everyone wishes for the bride and groom is taken away with each guest as they leave. For a time everyone is happy, everyone wishes only good things for themselves and their neighbors. Life is hard enough without our enemies trying to undermine our small moments of happiness."

"What are you talking about?" Max demanded. "If you have some information for me that will help put a stop to this farce, then tell me right now!" he demanded. "If not, I'm leaving. I knew this was going to be a waste of my time," he sneered. "What did you hope to gain by bringing me here? Did you think you could persuade me to just leave town without telling everyone that the baby is mine? Without getting some pay-back for making me look like an ass in front of the whole world? Well guess again. None of you know me at all. But after tomorrow you will, you all will. I'm leaving."

And with that, Max backed up two steps. But that was all he could manage, as the figure in front of him turned to face him. As it did,

Max caught the glint of cold moonlight on even colder steel. Long and wicked was the blade that the hand held pointing straight at him.

"I was hoping it would not come to this," the voice ground out, "but you leave me no choice."

"This is bullshit," Max said, his voice losing its sneer, having been replaced with squeakiness brought on by fear. His face in the moonlight looked like death already had come to call, pale and waxy. "You cannot be serious!" he said, his hands now coming up to keep the figure out of striking distance as it advanced towards him. He tried to move his feet, but could only manage a halting shuffle. Nothing like the speed his mind was screaming for him to achieve.

"What do you think you are going to do with that?" Max asked, pointing an accusing finger at the pointed bringer of death. "You can't kill me. People will miss me. They will ask questions and you will be caught. Do you want to spend the rest of your life in jail?"

"Look! Look!" he repeated louder, "I'm leaving! Okay? I won't be back. I give you my word that I won't say anything and I won't bother any of you again. Just let me leave." he begged, but he knew deep down it was to no avail.

"You have proven yourself to be a slimy snake that cannot be trusted," the harsh voice accused. "You will never leave us alone! You will always return to cause trouble!" the voice came in low, deadly tones. "I am so sorry to say I cannot allow that."

"Please," was all Max got out before the blade was swung through the air with deadly speed and accuracy. It bit deep into the side of Max's throat, and laid him open from ear to breast bone.

Max grabbed his neck, staring into the eyes of the killer standing in front of him. He saw his blood splash on his murders face and clothes. He was surprised to see how black it looked in the moonlight, not red at all. His vision began to narrow as he dropped to his knees and let his hand, dripping with his own blood, fall to his side. He felt hands on the back of his neck as he was helped to lie on his back. The sky in shadow from a form he could no longer make out.

It moved away and Max could see the millions of stars that shone so brightly when there were no other lights to interfere. No street lights were out here to obstruct the beauty of the night sky. With his last breath he marveled at how pretty they looked and how they seemed to fall to earth to blanket him until he could see nothing except their bright whiteness.

The Nebraska soil greedily drank the blood that poured into it, until it slowed and ran no more, becoming only a death bed for the late Max Swift.

Chapter 102

Saul arrived too late to stop the blades blow and could only watch for the few moments it took for the life to run out of Max. He did not mourn the passing of the damaged soul, nor did he interfere when the Dark came to claim it as their own. He turned a deaf ear as Max pleaded with him to go with him, instead of the dark monster that grabbed him with its cold claw-like hands and pulled him down into the earth to his new home.

He stood still as the cries of the damned faded away, leaving only the silence of the plains. He watched as the one known now as murderer drove away without looking back at the body left to rot.

Saul watched as the scent of a fresh kill carried on the wind and brought the scavengers out to feed. He did not scare them away, but let nature takes its course. Only when they had had their fill, did he stand over the now ravaged unrecognizable body. He lifted his hands to hover in the air above the carcass, letting his power flow from them, until what was left, bones and clothing, turned to dust, leaving no evidence of the crime committed.

He could not condone the act, but he understood the human need to seek vengeance for loved ones wronged.

The Dark had succeeded in causing a death that was not meant to be at this time. It would have changed the destinies of everyone involved. The effects would have been as the ripples of a stone dropped into water, ever growing, ever widening. But Saul stopped the ripples by removing any trace of the deed.

There would be questions, but there would never be proof of wrong doing. Max would be listed as a missing person, and would soon be pushed to the bottom of the cold case files. Never to be solved! Never to be missed!

Saul watched as Roman appeared, ready to do battle with him over what the Dark had caused. But Saul remained still.

"I will not fight you over this one," Saul said to his Dark counterpart. "It should not have happened this way, but it has saved much pain and heartache to innocent humans. So I will give you this one, but do not expect me to be so lenient the next time we meet."

"You are weak," Roman said, feeling strong and invincible with his victory.

"Are you so anxious to have your existence come to an end tonight that you would taunt me until I respond by fighting you?" Saul asked, muscles beginning to tighten in readiness, should Roman attack.

Roman hated to lose this opportunity to try to best the great Saul, but he was no fool. He knew that to strike at the Guardian when he was expecting it could very well bring his existence to the end Saul had warned him of.

"Very well," Roman said, "we will meet again."

"Yes," Saul agreed, "we will. Now leave my sight before I regret my decision to let you live."

Roman left, but not before he shrieked out the news of the Darks victory, making the wind moan as it carried the sound across the waving grasses.

A lone coyote, feeling full and sated, heard the Dark's cries and, lifting its nose into the air, wailed long and eerily, warning those creatures that listened of the evil walking the earth this night.

"Beware!" it warned. "Beware and hide!"

For now the Dark's whispers were silent, silent but not gone.

Chapter 103

The next day dawned with the promise of clear skies and cool temperatures, perfect for Hix and Abby's wedding. The guests gathered, in joy, to help celebrate the couple's joining together as one.

Hix stood straight and tall as he watched his bride walk towards him. His throat tightened and his heart swelled with the feelings of love he had for this woman. She looked like an angel. The delicate white dress shimmered with sequins and crystals, with only a small veil atop her honey blonde tresses, curled to perfection, hanging long and silky down her back. He pledged with all of his being to take care of her, to love her, and to be faithful as long as they lived.

Abby walked down the aisle alone, her destination the giant of a man standing, waiting for her at the altar. She smiled as if eager to join him, but on the inside she quaked with the step they were taking. What ifs and should haves would not be silent as she too stood and promised to love this man, making her voice tremble and her words stumble. But she made it through, lifting her mouth for the first kiss from her husband, smiling with him as their friends and family cheered and wished them a long and happy life together.

Saul watched with tears in his eyes, calming Abby's fears by taking them into himself, so she could enjoy this special moment without regrets and worries. All too soon Destiny would be enacted and his powers would be needed to help his humans cope with the trials sent to them. To live their lives according to Destiny's plan.

Saul stayed until Abby and Hix jumped into a car, amidst a shower of bird seed, and drove off to spend their honeymoon in a place they had kept secret from the public and the reporters. He would be the last to leave, and the one to make sure no pain was too great this day.

Sarah watched them drive away, with tears in her eyes and trickling softly down her cheeks. She waved until they were out of sight. She put her arm around Kendall's shoulders, giving them a squeeze, letting her know she was not alone in her feelings of loss.

"I'm not sad, really," Sarah told her, dabbing at her face with a tissue. "It's just he will never be mine again, like he was. He belongs to Abby now. I know that sounds selfish and bad, but I guess all mothers of sons have to face this day and let go."

"He will always be your son and you will always be his mother," Kendall said in a soft, comforting tone. "But you will have a daughter too now, and she needs you. Look at what she has to call mother. I am hoping that you will take her into your heart and show her the love she never had from her own mother, but the love Hix has had his whole life."

"I know Abby," Kendall continued, "and I know she is desperate for a friend like you. She is going to be looking to you for advice. From what I've seen and know of you, you are going to be everything and more to her, and when she calls you Mom, she will mean it with all her heart."

Sarah slapped at Kendall. "Darn it girl! I just got the water works shut off and here you go turning them on full blast again."

Kendall laughed. "Come on," she said, "let's go get us something to eat and pig out on that great cake. We will worry about our butts getting bigger tomorrow."

Sarah nodded her head in agreement and, arm in arm, she went with Kendall to enjoy herself and to send her wishes for a happy life to her son and her new daughter-in-law.

"Please find happiness," she wished, as she took a bite of cake. "*Be happy with each other and never say mean and hurtful things that can never be taken back.*" She wished for nothing else but that for them. She had already given this advice to Hix, but she still sent her wishes to the ones

guarding and guiding them.*" Let them be happy,"* she wished,*" let them always love each other above all else*." Taking a bite of the special cake, she knew she could do no more. Well, except help with the clean-up, which she did with pleasure, as it kept her busy and the loneliness at bay.

Kendall, Tonia, and Mary changed their clothes and stayed until all evidence of the wedding was cleaned up. Tonia poured a glass of wine for each of them and, along with Sarah, they sat and enjoyed each other's company and the peaceful quiet after the long day. They laughed together when Kendall suggested they open just a few of the gifts, because she was dying to find out what everyone gave them for presents.

Saul made sure no more tears fell as they all said good night. He gave Sarah and Kendall only sweet dreams, as they slept with little pieces of cake under their pillows.

He made sure no one gave even one thought to Max.

No one but Cathy.

Chapter 104

Cathy took special care with her looks and her clothing the morning of the wedding. She wanted to look fabulous when the cameras started to go off like 4th of July fireworks. Every reporter would be trying to get a shot of the bride walking down the aisle. They didn't know it yet, but when Max stood up and played his trump card, they were going to go into a wild frenzy. When the crowd sat stunned, Cathy knew she would be the center of many shots.

As she stood in front of the mirror, she practiced her look of shock, her look of horror, and her look of sadness. Shock for when Max first broke his news, horror as she realized the implications and sadness as she thought of her daughters' pain and total embarrassment. She even went so far as to lay her hands on her cheeks as she practiced her look of shock and reached out her hand towards the mirror, as if reaching to reassure her daughter, to ease her pain. Cathy did this over and over until she felt she had it just right. Smiling to herself, Cathy blew a kiss to her image in the mirror and left the bathroom.

She opted to drive herself to the site of the wedding, rather than ride with all the bridesmaids and Abby in a limo that had been rented for the girls. She was sure she was going to want to hoot with joy after the day was over, and she did not want to have to contain herself any longer than she had to. She wanted to be able to turn up the radio and sing along in celebration of the non-marriage of her daughter to Hix. Just thinking the name Hix made Cathy want to gag, but after today she would be able to erase it from her memory.

Cathy left the house after Abby and her friends had departed. Once again she gave the reporters a wave and even stopped for a few seconds to pose for their cameras, playing it up as if it was a red carpet event and she, of course, was the center of attention.

"It took less time to get to the house where the wedding was to be held than it did to brush her teeth." Cathy thought. It was just not normal that there not be a string of traffic carrying important guests to the front door for Abby's wedding. She could not get over Abby's lack of respect for her position in the fashion industry, and how she was going to piss off a lot of people by not inviting them to her wedding. Abby should have issued invitations, if for no other reason than to get some pricey gifts out of them. Maybe Cathy should have insisted that she be in charge of the guest list so these things were not over looked, but it was too late now. It was all going to be a mute-point in a few minutes any way.

Cathy parked her car, no valets here she sneered, and made her way into the house. She made her way to the back door and looked out on the gathering. Most of the guests were seated already, and the ones who were not, gathered in small clumps, talking and laughing. Ushers were busy escorting groups to their seats, then hurrying back down the aisle to get the next bunch started. They did not want to be the reason for the wedding getting started late.

Cathy glanced at her watch, covered in diamonds of course, and found she still had a few moments before everything started. So she made her way to the kitchen, found a tall, fluted crystal glass, and poured herself a healthy amount of champagne. She promptly downed it, trying to calm her nerves before heading back to the festivities.

A tall, good looking young man approached her and, offering his arm, asked, "May I escort you to your seat Ms. Mathews?" Cathy looked at the front row of chairs and noticed that Sarah had not been seated yet. There was no way she was going to be seated before Hix's mother, letting herself be the last one in and the one everyone would remember.

"I think I will wait for just a few more minutes," she said, giving this young hunk a big smile. *"Good God!"* Cathy thought. "W*as everyone in this state as tall as a house and good looking enough to make your mouth water with thoughts barely legal popping unbidden into your head?"* With so many choices, she wondered why Abby had limited herself to only one of the corn-fed men this boring state had to offer, instead of playing the field and enjoying as many as she could get her hands on. That's what she would have done. Played the field!

Cathy let her eyes wander over the crowd and swallowed a lump in her throat as she took in the male sights that were everywhere. They made her pulse jump up more than a notch and she wondered if she might not take a little time in this town before going back to civilization. There certainly wouldn't be any harm if she took some time to sample a small mouthful of the beef cake so temptingly on display. Cathy let a small smile play about her lips as she thought of the favor she would be doing for the women of this town by, shall we say, educating a few of the young men in the ways of sophistication and love. "Maybe there's some fun to be had here after all," Cathy decided.

Cathy's musings were interrupted by the arrival of Sarah. They nodded to each other before Hix appeared out of the house and, offering his arm to his mother, escorted her to her place of honor on the groom's side of the aisle. The crowd sighed in appreciation as Hix bent down and hugged his mother tight, before drawing back enough to kiss her cheek. A hush fell as everyone strained to hear the tender words Hix murmured into his mother's ear.

"Thanks Mom," he said, with a catch in his deep voice. "Thank you for everything you have done for me. I love you so much."

Sarah did not wipe at the tear that fell from her eye and traveled down her rosy cheek. "I love you too, Hix," she said, looking into his eyes so much like her own. "I want you to know how proud of you I am, have always been, and will always be." Both mother and son stood for one more moment as they fought emotions that threatened to over whelm them, before, with a smile, Sarah sent Hix back down the aisle so the ceremony could get under way.

Cathy ground her teeth together as she was escorted to her seat, not with any of the fanfare and admiration she should have received. Hix had made sure that his mother was the center of attention instead of her.

"*That's fine.*" Cathy thought to herself. "*Enjoy this while you can, because before long you are going to be crying for another reason and this one's not going to be so enjoyable. No not so enjoyable for them,*" she gloated. "B*ut for me.*"

"Me? I'm going to be having the time of my life!"

Chapter 105

Cathy stood with the rest of the guests as the wedding march began to play. She turned and, for just a moment, she felt pride in her daughter as she watched her walk down the aisle, looking breathtakingly beautiful. But the feeling only lasted an instant, as Cathy still could not understand why she had not been allowed to walk beside Abby down the aisle. After all she did not have a father to do the chore. Cathy felt she had been more than generous in offering herself as a substitute. But she had taken the rejection of the offer in stride, reasoning that Abby had said no because she did not want to share the lime light with her mother. Maybe even knowing she would probably be upstaged, as everyone would have seen how glamorous and beautiful she, the mother of the bride, still was.

Cathy sat back down with the others as the ceremony began. She tried not to fidget as the time neared for Max to stand up and protest this farce and declare himself the father of her grandchild. Cathy gave a delicate shudder as she thought of being a grandmother. She would definitely have to think of something else to be called other than grandmother! But the time came and went with no Max. Cathy sat stunned as Pastor Rod declared them husband and wife. She did not join in as the crowd clapped and cheered for the new Mr. and Mrs. Balthazar Hix. She did stand up and scan the crowd trying to find the rat who had assured her the marriage would never take place. She should never have trusted anyone but herself to take care of anything so important. Now it was too late.

The guests filed out in a noisy mass to shake the hands of the bride and groom. For the women, it was a final excuse to kiss the one that got away, and for the men to kiss a rare beauty the likes of which they had never seen before.

No one noticed that Cathy stayed in her seat, pale and shaking. No one noticed when she pulled her phone from her sassy little purse and speed dialed an unknown number. And no one gave a rats ass when, getting no answer, she threw her phone onto the ground and, in a fit of temper, stomped on it with her two thousand dollar pair of snooty heels.

No one noticed except the reporters that smelled something off and captured the tantrum in vivid color. They lived for family drama when the rich and beautiful got together and rarely were they disappointed. Today was just such an occasion, as they were allowed to take pictures of the wedding as long as they agreed to the conditions set down by the bride and groom. No crowding out the guests, no using a flash, and all pictures had to be approved by Abby and Hix before they were given the okay to be printed. Everything was pretty boring, lovely and sweet, but boring, until the wedding was over and Cathy became the center of attention as she threw a star-sized hissy fit. They laughed together as they caught it all on film. They could just see the headlines now: 'Not Everyone Happy as Super Model Abby Mathews Weds.'

Cathy realized, too late, that she had made a huge error by venting her feelings in public. She was cringing inside at the pictures she was sure would be in the next week's publications. Damn Max any way! This was all his fault!

With as much dignity as she could muster, Cathy took a deep breath and bent over to pick up the pieces of her mangled phone, hiding it in her purse before walking into the house and straight out the front door. She got into her car and, showing restraint, drove slowly away from the biggest horror of her life. The biggest mistake of her daughter's life! What was Abby thinking? Letting herself get knocked up and then having to marry the first man who asked her. Her career was not even at its peak yet and now it very well might be over.

Cathy needed time to think and to plan, by herself. Deciding this, she drove to Abby's house, packed her bags, and drove to the nearest airport. Flashing enough money could get you whatever you wanted and Cathy wanted on the first flight out of this hell hole and back to New York.

She got it, and within the next hour was on her way back home.

Having no phone and nothing to do, Cathy tried to read a magazine. But as she turned the pages, pictures of Abby selling beauty seemed to be everywhere, taunting her, rubbing her nose in what she had lost. She did not see the wedding as her gaining a son, but as her losing millions.

Snapping the magazine shut and giving it a toss across the cabin, Cathy spent the rest of the flight drinking herself into a sloppy stupor. She was going to find Max when she got back to New York and, when she did, she was going to kick his scrawny ass.

As she sat and drank the flight away, Cathy had an idea that made her sit up in shock and awe. Awe at how smart and clever she was. 'Why had she not thought of this before?' she wondered. The answer to her problem came to her in a glorious flash of booze induced wisdom. Tomorrow she was going to go see the head of every network and pitch them her brilliant idea and, by tomorrow night, everything was going to be just fine. In fact it would be better than before, because she was not going to have to share the money with anyone else. By this time tomorrow she was going to have a deal in hand for her very own reality show.

The show would be about the mother of a famous daughter and how she copes with the mess her life had become because of her daughter's selfishness. How the daughter never gave her mother a second thought when she turned her back on her.

But the mother, Cathy, would come out on top and the cameras would follow her every step of the way on her epic journey. Cathy had seen enough bad acting by every boring family that they currently had on TV to know she could do as well, if not better. All she had to do was run around with half her clothes off, get drunk, cuss and act like a slut to make the show a hit. Not so far-fetched that she couldn't pull it off with her eyes closed.

"Oh my God!" Cathy marveled. *"I am so smart!"* Raising her half-empty glass, Cathy toasted to her future. "*To me,"* she said, half under her breath. *"To always coming out on top and to hell with the rest of the world."*

Cathy got so caught up in her own importance that she forgot about Max and her intentions to do him bodily harm when she got back to New York. Nope, Max did not even rate a passing blip on her to do list as she planned her future. The last thought he did get from Cathy was a wish she made that she could send him to hell. But she was too late. He was already there.

Chapter 106

Abby and Hix spent a week driving around the country, seeing the sights and enjoying each other without anyone interrupting or interfering. They turned their phones off every morning and did not turn them back on until they were in for the night. They may be tired but they were full of excitement from the adventures they had experienced that day.

Hix even talked Abby into camping for a few days, as they explored the Rocky Mountains. She never looked as good to him as she did waking up in the cool mountain air, no make-up on her face and her hair in a loose pony tail. He loved the way the dancing light from the campfires they built played over her features, making them dark and mysterious one minute and bathed in golden glows the next. If Hix was not in love with her already, he would have been by the end of their honeymoon.

Hix showed Abby places he already knew, but discovering them all over again through her eyes was wonderful and he loved it. They visited new places, making them their own by creating memories that they would be able to talk about for the rest of their lives. And, of course, they took pictures, hundreds of them, with every intention of making their friends and family sit through the "slide" show when they got home.

The week flew by on wings of total happiness, and they both were sad when their time alone came to an end. But arriving home held its own rewards. They were able to move into their new house as man and wife, where they had fun planning the small details that would make their home uniquely their own.

Their days soon fell into a routine, Hix going to work every morning and Abby busy fixing up the house and planning a nursery. Hix loved what he did, but he loved coming home every night even more. Seeing Abby as he walked into the house, having her show him each night what she had been doing that day, and falling asleep every night in each other's arms made his life more than he had ever dreamt he would have.

Abby kept herself busy putting together the nursery and putting special touches on their home. She liked spending a few hours every day just browsing through stores, seeking out special treasures that she sprinkled throughout the house, making it come alive, reflecting the personalities of the two people that lived there.

Abby transformed one of the back bedrooms into a sitting room that was girly, a perfect place for Kendall, Mary, Tonia, and herself to sit and visit when they all got together.

And, of course, Hix had his Husker room that he retreated to when Dylan, Andrew, and Josh came over to shoot the breeze and drink a few beers. At first Abby left them alone to watch their sports on the big screen TV, rubbing her growing belly when cheers and groans echoed throughout the house. She found herself hoping that she was carrying a girl, so she would have someone to hang with when the guys got together. But she had doubts that even having a daughter would help there, as the women in Winston were as big of fans as the men when it came to the University of Nebraska sports.

Eventually Abby decided when in Rome . . . and began to join in on the game day festivities. She even went so far as to invite her friends to join her and the guys, until it became the norm that everyone gathered at their house and made a day of it by eating and watching the games together.

Abby knew she was doomed when the baby she carried began to join in on the fun and kicked vigorously whenever the Huskers scored. "Another fan in the making." Abby thought, and smiled with approval.

When it came time to clean up, Hix never left it to the girls to do alone. He pitched in and, in doing so, shamed the other guys into helping.

After all, if Hix could do it, so could they. No matter the occasion, when everyone got together they all had a blast.

Sarah was always invited to join in the fun, but sometimes she left the young people to kick up their heels without her, but she never felt left out. She was so pleased with Hix's obvious happiness, and the way Abby seemed to fit so well into her new role of wife and mother-to-be.

Sarah helped when asked, but did not butt in, even when she began to notice the strain on Abby's face, when she thought no one was looking. Abby was pretty good at faking her enthusiasm and happiness, but Sarah saw, with a mother's eyes, the way the shadows grew more pronounced in those beautiful brown eyes each time she saw Abby. She noticed how some unknown demon had made her jumpy, and she sat back and watched as everyone, even her son, passed off her behavior as part of the pregnancy.

Sarah tried to bring up the subject of Abby every time she talked to Hix, asking how she was, hoping Hix would eventually ask why she was concerned. But Hix was in his own happy world, being married to Abby and having a child on the way. He didn't get the hint and he did not see the signs Sarah wanted so desperately to point out.

So finally Sarah went straight to the source, asking Abby "How are you doing?" She was hoping Abby would need some advice and confide in her. But Abby drew back every time, saying nothing was wrong. So Sarah dropped it.

She dropped it, but she did not forget it. She could only guess that Abby was having trouble coping with her new life as wife and soon-to-be mother. So she stayed back and watched, doing nothing, as her mother's instinct kicked into over drive. It was warning her that something was about to explode and life was about to get messy.

But whose?

Chapter 107

Saul watched over his charges and knew sadness as he witnessed Destiny unfold. He wanted to take all the suffering into himself and spare them the future, but he was not allowed. He wanted to touch Sarah and tell her that her instincts were correct and to force the issue, but he could not. All things were as they should be which, by his way of thinking, really sucked.

He made sure that all memories of the doubts and trouble Max caused were kept in the deepest part of their minds. Even when the police came and questioned everyone, none could give them any information that would point them in the direction of the missing photographer.

Saul shielded the killer from harm and detection, taking the secret of the death into himself, to keep it safe and guard it for eternity. Max had done enough damage when he was alive, and Saul could see no reason to give him the satisfaction in death to continue.

Saul never let down his guard, as he kept tabs on the Dark being that Max had become, keeping him away from Abby, Hix, and all those close to them. He even went as far as to protect the new soul of the baby Abby carried. There would be no Dark influences creeping in to taint the life Destiny had planned for the baby.

Saul took care to watch over his other charges, but he stayed close to Abby and Hix, as the time for the birth was drawing ever closer. He took as much of Abby's anxieties into himself as he could, until he could take no more. He was trying to let them enjoy the last few months of being a couple alone before the baby came into their lives to make them a family of three.

He watched as Abby stood alone in front of the full length mirror in the bathroom and turned from side to side each day, assessing the growth of her belly. Until one day, not being able to see her feet for her belly, she crumpled to the floor sobbing. Saul felt his heart ache right along with hers, and he felt her confusion at not knowing why she cried. The need to continue overwhelmed them both and Abby did not stop until she was limp with exhaustion. When Abby was finished, Saul knelt down beside her and, unknown to Abby, wrapped his arms and wings around her until she was enclosed in a cocoon of healing and warmth. He held her close to his breast until she was strong enough once again to make it through another day.

"Not much longer now." he whispered into her ear. *"Not much longer until you get to meet your baby and take it into your heart to love as only a mother can. Be strong Abby, and when you cannot, use your friends and your husband to help you. There is no shame in asking for support and in needing those you love to be there for you. No one stands alone in life, and you are among the few that have many who love you. Don't worry Abby, and don't forget, all is as it should be."*

With a final stroke to Abby's bowed head, Saul left her to stand on her own, to find the strength to live her life as the Fates had written. He could step in no more. It would be up to Hix and Abby's close friends and Sarah to provide the shoulders to cry on and the arms to hold her when she needed it.

With shoulders bowed from the weight he had to carry, Saul left the mortal realm and watched the future unfold from his vantage point in front of the Window to the World. 'Not long now.' he told himself. 'Not long now until he would once again visit his humans, but the next time he would not be acting as a Guardian.'

Not a Guardian, but a Guide.

Chapter 108

As the days grew shorter and the weather much colder, Abby spent more and more time at home alone. She did not want to risk driving on the snowy roads with the baby due in less than a month, so she tried to keep herself busy at the house. But there was really nothing left to do. She had taken great pleasure in creating a beautiful home. All her love went into making the nursery one that would be welcoming to their new baby. She loved picturing herself or Hix sitting in the comfy rocking chair, singing and rocking their baby until it fell asleep. Or imagining them standing over the crib, arms wrapped around each other, watching as the small chest rose and fell with the breaths of innocent slumber.

She folded and refolded the tiny clothes, burying her face in them, imagining how they would smell when worn by their son or daughter.

When she could play in the room no more, Abby would call one of her friends and they would talk with her or come out to the house to take Abby out to lunch or just for a drive to relieve her boredom.

Kendall had the most flexible schedule, so it fell to her most often to try and make Abby as comfortable and content as she could, while Hix was a work. She never once begrudged her friend the time or her company when she needed it. And, when the baby came, she would be right there at the hospital with Hix and Abby, to help however she could.

Kendall noticed the paleness that rode Abby's cheeks, and the way she became almost desperate when it was time for Kendall to leave after each visit. She felt helpless to solve the mystery of what was going on in Abby's mind, and got no clues from her friend. She asked often but was always being told that everything was fine. It was just being so close to delivering that had Abby on edge, and the normal fears that all new mothers-to-be go through. No matter how Kendall probed, she was met with a wall of stubbornness that Abby threw up and hid behind, until Kendall was forced to change the subject when Abby became agitated or weepy. Kendall was at a loss as to how to help, so each time she let it go, figuring Abby would confide in her when she felt the time was right.

As November drew to a close, Kendall once again came out at Abby's request. They bundled up to take a short walk in the cold air. Abby was tired of being cooped up inside, and she wanted out! Kendall made Abby laugh as she commented on the way Abby waddled as they made their way down the driveway and back. Taking their time and enjoying each other's company.

When they returned to the house, they sat outside and watched the grey clouds build and talked of the snow storm that had been predicted for that night. It was not long before big snowflakes, the size of quarters, began to fall in ever increasing amounts, signaling the arrival of the storm. The wind followed, making the snow swirl and dance with hypnotic and deceptive beauty. So beautiful to watch, yes, but so deadly for the ones that did not give the snowstorms the respect they deserved. They took toes, noses, fingers, and even lives, in the blink of an eye, for those stupid enough to be caught outside without shelter.

When Abby's cheeks and nose became rosy with the cold, Kendall insisted they go in and warm up. Abby made them both a cup of hot cocoa, and they spent the next half hour watching out the front window, until visibility worsened and Kendall had to head back to town.

Kendall made sure Abby had everything she needed before getting in her car and pointing it away from the house as she headed towards town. Before the snow obscured the house, Kendall looked once more in her rearview mirror and saw Abby as only a dark shadow, standing in the window with her hand planted against the cold pane. Maybe waving good bye? Kendall could not tell. All she could tell was that she looked so alone. Kendall got a bad feeling. A really bad feeling! It felt like she was seeing her friend for the last time. But that was crazy, right? Hix would be home in less than an hour and Abby would be fine by herself in that short of time.

Kendall shook her dark head and gave her attention to the road that was now snow-covered and slick. She made a mental note to call Hix and make sure he had made it home and that Abby was okay, when she reached her own house. With worry still nagging at her mind, Kendall drove away until the snow swallowed up the red tail lights, leaving nothing but the fast approaching dark.

Abby stood at the window until her friend disappeared from sight into the thick snow. As she turned from the window, meaning to go into the kitchen and put something on for supper, she felt the first pains low in her belly. What started out as a small ache, grew until Abby was left breathless and holding on to the counter for support.

"It's the baby!" Abby thought. "I*t's the baby coming!"*

She made her way carefully into the living room, and reached for her phone to call Hix. But the next pain made her scream as black dots blurred her vision. This was not right. Everything her doctor, Sarah, and others had told her indicated that it was supposed to start out with twinges, and then grow until the baby was born. Not this pain that ran over her like a freight train out of control. Abby felt sweat bead up on her brow, as fright at the unknown and worry for her unborn child occupied her every thought.

"Hix," she said out loud, just to hear her voice, "I have to call Hix. He needs to come home now." Abby once again reached for her phone, and this time was able to dial the number. But before she heard Hix's voice, she screamed, unable to stop herself as another pin ripped her apart. This time the dots in front of her eyes grew until all she could see was black, before, with a thump, she hit the floor and knew no more.

Chapter 109

Hix put away his tools and gathered up his belongings, as he prepared to call it a day. On a job site, they tried to do the outside work when the weather was warm, leaving the inside details until the late fall and winter temperatures made working in the cold painful and miserable. But today had him out in the biting wind and he was bone tired from it. His hands still tingled as they tried to warm up and his nose had seen the folds of more tissues than he cared to remember. His muscles were tired from being held tight and shivering, as he tried to keep himself warm while he worked.

But all that was behind him for another day, as he got into his truck and cranked the heat on high. All he wanted now was to get home. Get home to Abby and feel her heat surround him as he took her into his arms and kissed her hello. He treasured each day as he watched her belly grow with his child. He smiled as he sat for a moment in the warming cab of his truck and remembered how he would feel their baby move against his body when he held Abby close, as if it too were wanting attention. The first time he had felt the tiny thump of movement he had been speechless with wonder, and his heart had grown ten times its size in his chest, until he had almost burst with the wonder of the life they had created, the reality of it. He loved to take out that memory and marveled at the same feelings it never failed to produce, no matter how many times he thought about it. He would never forget, never wanted to forget.

Hix put his truck in gear and, as he was on the other side of town, thought that he would stop at the store on his way through and pick up the stuff for the hot fudge sundaes that Abby seemed to be craving lately.

He liked to get her anything she wanted and many nights had seen him making a trip into town to pick up some treat for her that she assured him could wait until morning. But Hix never minded. It made him feel a part of the pregnancy and it was the least he could do for those he loved. Mama and baby.

Pulling up in front of the grocery store, Hix called Sarah and asked if there was anything she needed as it was already snowing and he would be happy to drop whatever off at her house on his way home, not wanting her to have to go out in the storm. Sarah assured him she needed nothing and, after asking about Abby and the baby, let Hix go so he could get his shopping done and get home

Hix was not the only one who had the same idea, it seemed. The store was crowded with late shoppers as people in town stocked up on essentials, just in case the weather report was right and they ended up with the foot of predicted snow. He was stopped more than once by people wanting to say hi, asking after his family, and telling him about their latest adventures or about the newest gossip in town. It took Hix half an hour to make it back to the freezer section, pick out a tub of rich ice cream, and find the jar of thick chocolate sundae topping he had come in for.

As he turned to head back to the front and the cash registers, his phone began to sing. Hix transferred his items into one arm and pulled the phone from his pocket. He smiled as Abby's face appeared on the screen and, for a second, thought what good timing it was, her calling while he was at the store. He was sure she needed him to pick up something and he was right here to do it. Hix pushed the button to answer the call and smiling, raised it to his ear. But before he could say a word, Abby's scream blew through the phone line and arrowed straight into his guts, freezing his blood and stealing his breath.

Just one scream, a crash, and then nothing. Hix stood frozen for just an instant as the blood drained from his face and his world tilted off center. "*No!*" his soul screamed, "*NO!*"

Without a second thought, Hix let the groceries fall to the floor and ran.

Chapter 110

Hix dodged the other shoppers that had stopped to stare at him, mouths agape and eyes opened wide, like a professional football player heading for the end zone with the winning score. He hit the doors on a dead run, sliding past his truck on the icy parking lot. Only by grabbing the door handle, did he stop himself from ending up in the gutter on his butt. In one motion he had the door open and vaulted inside, fumbling in his pocket as he tried to make his stiff hands obey his brain that was screaming for him to hurry. He turned over the motor and jammed his foot down hard on the gas, but all he succeeded in doing was make the tires spin on the ice and the ass end of his truck come within a hands breadth of the car parked next to him, as it slid sideways instead of going straight. Hix cussed like a sailor as he realized he was not going to be able to speed all the way home. Instead he was going to have to go slow and careful as he navigated the snow packed streets and the icy roads outside of town.

"Its okay," Hix told himself, as he finally made it out of the parking lot and headed towards home. *"I'm going to get home and everything will be okay."* Still he drove with his hands gripping the steering wheel and his heart thumping like a bass drum, so loud he could hear nothing but the boom, boom, boom in his ears. But he did not need to hear the words in his head to know what he was thinking, praying. Abby was in trouble and she needed him to be home now, not in the twenty minutes it was going to take to get home safely before he could help his wife. Hix grew up in Nebraska and knew how to drive in the snow, but nothing had ever prepared him for the eternity it seemed to take before he pulled into their driveway and slid to a stop in front of the house. Hix made it

up the steps in one leap and had the door open before he started yelling for Abby.

"Abby, Abby where are you? Abby!" he shouted. He looked in the kitchen, but found nothing, so he ran into the living room and his heart leapt into his throat as he saw her lying crumpled up on the floor, her phone still in her hand. "Abby," Hix whispered, as he fell to his knees beside her and gently gathered her up in his arms. He brushed the hair out of her eyes and tipped her face up so he could look at her. Her eyes were open and looking at him, but not at him. She seemed so pale, and those brown eyes, that Hix knew as well as he knew his own, were dazed and unfocused.

"Hix?" Abby said her voice weak and confused, "What happened?"

Before Hix could answer, Abby was rocked with another strong contraction and she doubled over in pain, not even having the breath to scream out. Hix did not wait for the pain to end before he lifted her and stood up. He went to the couch and got a blanket to wrap around Abby, before heading to the door with her again in his arms. His footsteps faltered for just one stride as his eyes were drawn to the floor where Abby had been lying. There was a large wet spot, but Hix did not want to see if it was just her water that had broken, or if it was her blood that had pooled beneath her. "*Not now!*" he thought. "N*o time.*"

Hix was careful but quick as he managed the steps and got to the passenger side of his truck. He pulled it open and, as gently as he could, set Abby in the seat.

"Hang on baby," he said to her, as he got her comfortable. "We will be at the hospital in just a few minutes."

Abby grabbed Hix's hand and squeezed hard. "I'm scared, Hix," she said, her voice reflecting the fear that drenched her soul.

"I'm here, Honey," Hix reassured her as best he could, while trying to hide his own fears. "I won't let anything happen to either of you. I promise."

"Okay," Abby said, placing her faith in her rock of a husband.

Hix gave Abby a quick hard kiss before slamming the door and getting in behind the wheel. Once again he navigated the bad roads as he headed into town and to the only hospital in the county.

"I'll be right back," Hix told Abby, before leaving her to run into the emergency entrance. He reappeared in less than thirty seconds with four nurses and a gurney for Abby. He lifted her out and placed her on the bed, before half running at her side as the staff wheeled her into the hospital. He had no intention of being left behind as they made their way inside. Abby was wheeled into an examination room, but as Hix tried to follow, he was barred from entering.

"We have to check your wife out, Mr. Hix," the nurse said, "and you need to wait here until we are done."

"Bull shit!" Hix growled out, as he had every intention of muscling his way past anyone who tried to keep him from his wife.

"I'm serious," the nurse said, placing both hands on the mile-wide chest to stop Hix's forward progress. "You need to give us time to do our jobs and take care of your wife. The doctor is on his way and I suggest you get the paperwork filled out and make some calls if you want anyone to be here with you. Now, someone will be out to talk to you when we have an idea what is going on."

With that, she turned her back on Hix, entered the examination room, and shut the door in his face.

Hix stood where he was, his nose almost touching the door that he wanted to be on the other side of. His fists balled and his muscles stood out like thick ropes, as it took everything he had to do as he was told and wait. Swallowing hard, Hix pulled out his phone and called his mother, telling her what happened and where they were.

"I'm on my way." Sarah told Hix, and hung up on him before he could say okay. Next he called Kendall and told her to get to the hospital because Abby was there and he needed her. Kendall too hung up on him, as she was out the door before Hix was done talking.

Hix had just finished with the damn paperwork when Doctor Sigg finally strolled in.

"Hey, Hix," the Doctor said, coming over to shake his hand.

"Hi, Brody," Hix said, stamping down the urge to grab his friend by the collar and the seat of his pants and toss him into the room with Abby. In a small town like Winston everyone pretty much knew everyone else and it was the same with Hix and the Doctor. They played on the same basketball team and had hung out many times, downing a few beers while shooting the breeze. But Hix was in no mood to visit as a friend right now. Right now, he wanted to be told what was going on and to be reassured that Abby and the baby were going to be okay.

Brody recognized the signs of anger and fear that Hix was struggling to hold back. The flat eyes that bored into him, the flared nostrils, and the handshake that almost crushed his bones, were a dead give-away that Hix was not in the mood to exchange pleasantries.

"Tell me what happened," Brody said, wanting to get what he could out of Hix before heading in to see his patient.

Hix told him what he knew and, with a nod of his head, the Doctor turned and entered where Hix was not allowed. Hix looked at his watch and then back at the door that was keeping Abby from him.

"Five minutes," he growled, talking out loud as if there was someone to hear him. "Five minutes and then you better call in the National Guard because I'm coming in!"

Chapter 111

Hix had only made two trips as he paced up and down the hallway before his mother and Kendall came barreling through the door, latching on to his arms and wanting to know what happened. Hix told them what he could, but had no real answers for their questions.

"I was with her this afternoon," Kendall confessed to Hix. "I shouldn't have left her alone. I would have waited until you got home, but the snow started getting bad, so I left. Abby was fine, really, when I left. I swear."

"I don't blame you, Kendall," Hix assured her. "Something just happened, and it would have happened whether you were there or not."

"Let's go sit over by the door so we can catch the Doctor when he comes out," Sarah said, leading the way back down the hall. Each of them took a seat, but Hix found it hard to sit still, his leg giving him away as it started jumping up and down like a jack hammer.

"Hix," Sarah said in a soothing voice, "calm down. We'll know something soon, I'm sure." She, herself, wanted to go see what was taking so long, but she knew that if Hix caught a whiff of her anxiety, no one was going to be able to control him. He would fight his way to Abby's side, come hell or high water.

It was another half hour before the door opened and Brody came out. Hix swallowed hard, noticing right away that the friendly, relaxed Doctor that went into the examination room was nowhere to be found.

Brody stopped in front of Hix and waited until he rose to his full height before beginning. Looking Hix straight in the eye, he began to give news about Abby.

"As you've probably guessed, Abby is in labor. Both she and the baby are in distress, so we are going to do a C-section right away."

"What do you mean 'in distress'?" Hix demanded. "Are they okay or not?"

"Yes they are fine for now, but we don't have a lot of time to waste here. Abby has started to hemorrhage, so we need to go in and get the baby out and stop the bleeding. I need you to sign the release form now."

A nurse appeared at the Doctor's side, shoving a clipboard with the papers on it at Hix. "Sign here," she said, pointing to the bottom of the page. When Hix just stood there in shock, she jammed them into his stomach to get his attention.

"Now, Hix," Brody said, hovering over Hix until he scribbled his name where he was told. "We are going to take her back now and someone will be out to get you when we're done."

"I want to come in now," Hix said.

"Not until we get the baby delivered. Then you can come in." Brody replied.

"But . . ." was all Hix got out, and then he was left talking to the door swinging closed.

Hix started forward with a growl deep in his chest, having every intention of going to his wife, and God help anyone who tried to stop him.

"Hix, no," Sarah said, as she grabbed his arm and pulled him back. "I know it's hard to wait, but you will just be in the way, taking up time and attention that needs to be focused on Abby and the baby."

Hix's jaw balled over and over as he ground his teeth together in frustration.

Turning his head, he looked down at his mother. She pursed her lips as she saw the storm raging in the deep blue orbs, until they became almost black with his emotions.

"It won't be long. These things go very fast," she reassured him, rubbing his back as her arm encircled him in a fierce motherly hug.

Hix finally nodded his head, but he was far from happy with his decision. And Sarah was right, it only took forty five minutes before a nurse came and asked Hix to follow her.

Hix disappeared with her, leaving Sarah and Kendall to, once again, wait for news. Now that Hix was not around, they could let the fear and worry show on their faces, moving closer to each other and clasping hands. Sarah had just risen to go in search of something to drink for both of them when the door opened again, but this time their anxiety was met with good news.

Hix stood in the open door holding a pink bundle in his arms, tears of joy running unchecked down his face. Looking at his mother, Hix stated the obvious, "It's a girl." His voice was rough with emotion as he cradled his daughter with tenderness and total love for the life he and Abby had created.

Both Sarah and Kendall rushed forward to get a better look, reaching out their hands to greet this new addition with touches of love. As if by magic, a nurse appeared at Hix's elbow and barred the way. "No touching unless you wash your hands."

Sarah and Kendall both rushed for the door seeking out the nearest place to wash, no protests or questions asked.

Hix stood where he was, marveling at his perfect daughter until both women came back. They were allowed to touch the soft cheeks and to peer under the tiny pink hat, trying to look at everything at once.

Hix stood proud, as he too took in the pink cheeks, the thick cap of brown hair, the impossible small hands, and the tiny feet, never tiring of the thought, "*I have a daughter!*"

"Okay," Sarah finally said, "first congratulations, and second give me the details." At Hix's confusion, Sarah poked him in the arm. "Hix," she said laughing, "length, weight, and time please."

Hix looked at the nurse for help and she stepped in. "This young lady was born on November 24th at one thirty two in the morning, weighing in at seven pounds five and one half ounces, and measuring twenty inches long."

"How is Abby?" Kendall asked, her finger being gripped by the soft newborns hand.

"Mother is doing just fine. The Doctor is still with her, but they stopped the bleeding and everything looks really good."

Kendall wiped her damp eyes and gave a watery sigh. "Good," she said, "that's good. When can we see her?"

"Not until afternoon, I would say," the nurse replied, looking at the clock on the wall. "She will be in recovery for a little while and she needs some rest. It's time we take this little one back to her mother," she said, as she gently took the baby from Kendall. "I would suggest you go home and get some rest yourselves. Come back this afternoon," she said, motioning Hix to follow her back through the door.

"I'm going to stay here, Mom," Hix said. He gave both his mother and Kendall a hug of thanks and saying, "I love you," he disappeared with his precious cargo, behind the door once more.

Chapter 112

Hix stayed with Abby and their new baby girl until they were settled in a room and both were sleeping before he took a break himself. He looked at his watch and saw that it was just past four a.m., but he wasn't tired. Leaving the room he walked out of the hospital and sat on a bench, pulled out his phone, and dialed Cathy's number. He didn't even give it a second thought, figuring it was never too early to call and tell Abby's mother that she was a grandmother. He let the phone ring until it finally went to voice mail.

"Hi, Cathy," he said, "this is Hix. I just thought I would call and tell you that, as of one thirty two this morning, you are a grandmother of a seven pound, five and one-half ounce baby girl. Abby and I have decided to call her Peyton Elizabeth Hix. Nice huh? Any way you can call Abby at the hospital. She and the baby are in room 221. She and Peyton just got to sleep, so wait until this afternoon, okay? Hope you get this message. Okay, good-bye then."

Hix was slightly disappointed that Cathy had not picked up, but he really shouldn't have expected any more from her. She hadn't called or talked to Abby since the wedding. Hix felt sad for her. She had missed all the opportunities to share Abby's pregnancy with her, and give advice when Abby had questions. Hix put his phone away while shaking his head. His family meant everything to him, and he would never cut them out of his life, not for anyone or anything.

Hix walked around the block a couple of times before going back into the room and pulling the recliner close to the bed. Finally he settled. He closed his eyes but they kept opening on their own, as they were drawn time and again to his wife and their daughter. He watched both sleep in the quiet hours of the new day, taking these moments for himself. As his eyes finally closed, Hix reached out a hand and found his wife, letting his fingers rest on her thigh, needing the contact with her.

"Thank you, Abby," he whispered. "Thank you for our daughter. I love you so very much." And with that he slept.

Chapter 113

Hix took a week off work to help Abby with the baby, letting her rest and recover from her surgery. Both parents enjoyed feeding times, bath times, and Hix even got in on some diaper duty. Not that it was his favorite thing to do, but he never shirked his duty. It never failed to amaze him how something so small and cute could poop so much and so often. Abby and Hix would look at each other and laugh as Peyton would screw up her face and make it turn red with her efforts to fill her diapers to over-flowing. So far they were not at the stage where they would pay the other one to take their turn, like on TV. They just rolled up their sleeves and got it done as quickly as possible, before the smell made their hair fall out!

Both parents marveled each day at how fast Peyton was growing and how she seemed to always have a smile for everyone who talked to her. She was just a very happy baby. Love tended to do that.

Sarah tried to not come over too much, but she couldn't help herself. Being a proud grandmother, she would call and ask if it would be okay to come for a visit at least every other day. Abby loved having her over. It gave her someone to talk to and Sarah would watch her granddaughter while Abby caught a short nap or ran errands. Whatever Abby needed to do, even if it was just taking a long hot bath and a little "me" time for mommy was okay with Sarah.

Hix would walk in the door from work, give Abby a big hug and kiss, get cleaned up, and then hog his daughter until it was time to put her down for the night. He loved hearing how their day went, laughing along with Abby as she described something the baby had done that day.

The first time Peyton rolled over on her own, they celebrated by calling all their friends and Sarah, bragging as if she had just won a gold medal in the Olympics. They even went so far as to invite them all out for lunch on the weekend, which turned into staying for supper that night, so everyone had plenty of time to watch Peyton perform her new skill.

Time seemed to fly by, with things going smoothly. Except for the week that Cathy came to stay. Peyton was already six months old before her MIA grandmother came to the house to be introduced to her one and only grandchild, and ended up staying for a week. It was one of the longest weeks of Abby's life.

Cathy was distant, but pleasant in her own way when others, besides herself and Abby, were in the house. When they were alone she changed, never letting an opportunity pass where she wasn't cutting Abby down by telling her how haggard and plain she looked.

"Why can't you put some make up on and fix your hair, Abby?" she would say. "I would say that motherhood definitely does not agree with you. You really should be going to the gym and trying to get your figure back, since it has been over six months since the baby came." She always referred to Peyton as "the baby" instead of by her name. "Has anyone even called you lately to ask you to work?" she badgered. When Abby shook her head no and shrugged, Cathy curled her lip and said she was not surprised, as Abby was doing nothing to get herself ready to go back to work.

"You've stayed home long enough, don't you think?" she would ask, over and over during the week. "Is Hix the reason you are falling into this rut and not trying to get back into your career?"

"No," Abby would assure her, "I like staying home and taking care of Peyton and Hix. I like taking care of the house and doing things to make this a good and happy home."

"Oh, for the love of God!' Cathy sneered, "What has happened to you? Where is the daughter I raised, because the housewife in front of me is not her. You've lost your edge and pretty soon, if you continue the way you are, you will loose your body and your looks. Do you think Hix will love you then?" With that parting blow she would leave the room, with Abby brow-beaten and her esteem in tatters.

"Was her mother right?" Abby began to wonder. "Was she turning into a frumpy, unexciting, drab, dime-a-dozen housewife? Would Hix get tired of what she was turning into, the routine she had fallen into? Maybe her mother was right. Maybe she should start paying more attention to her looks and get back to her career." She just didn't know what to think.

All it took was one week with her mother and Abby's contentment began to waver. Abby loved her daughter and Hix above all else, but she wondered if making them the center of her world was going to be enough for her in the future. Would it be enough for them?

Abby began to have doubts about her life and the direction it was heading. She hid her feelings of confusion from Hix and her closest friends, instead of talking to them, listening to their advice and accepting their support.

The only one that knew what she was thinking and feeling was her mother, who never gave up her plan to undermine the marriage she was so opposed to. The more Cathy talked to her, the more confused Abby became.

Cathy had never told Abby about her plan to have her own TV show, or that she had been rejected at every turn, making her bitter and looking for someone to blame for her failure. If she had, Abby would not have fallen so easily into the pit of bitterness and despair that her mother had dug for her and pushed her into.

But fall she did, down, down, down with no bottom in sight.

Roman laughed softly as he, once again, watched his work in play. He could not resist one last push to interfere in Abby's life. It was not big enough to attract the attention of Saul, but enough to cause pain and turmoil to these humans. Abby in particular.

Cathy was his perfect pawn, already cruel and self-serving by nature. It had taken just a tickle from Roman to get her to resent Abby's happiness, and the bitterness that she felt poured out in her words and actions towards her daughter. Abby had everything Cathy wanted, youth, beauty, money, success and love. Roman had just peeled back a few layers to let all Cathy was feeling pour out. All Roman had to do now was sit back and enjoy the show, until the final curtain fell.

Chapter 114

Cathy's visit had shed a definite dark cloud over Abby's new life but, like an ominous tornado, she touched down, then passed without tearing anything down, all except for Abby's self-esteem. But under the umbrella of love that Hix and Peyton provided, she was able to push the negative thoughts to the back of her mind and enjoy her new role as wife and mother.

The next year was filled with happiness for Abby and Hix, as they watched their daughter go from infant to toddler in what seemed like only a day. They marveled as her coos turned into Dada's and Mama's, her rolling over progressed to crawling, and the legendary first steps. The first tentative steps gave way to confidence on two little legs that never seemed to stop moving until bath time. Then a story calmed her and let her slip into a dreamland that held ponies, puppies and kittens. All for Peyton Elizabeth Hix.

Each day Abby woke with Hix, spending precious time with him in the quiet of the early mornings, talking quietly so as not to wake Peyton. Today was no different. Abby made Hix a lunch to take to work, giggling as Hix moved up behind her and wrapped his arms around her waist.

"Have I told you I love you today?" Hix purred, as he nuzzled her warm neck. "That I love you every day?"

Abby sighed as the warm breath and soft kisses from her husband made goose bumps jump up her arms and roll down her legs till her toes curled.

"If you did, it would still be fine by me if you wanted to say it again," Abby assured him. She could feel her stomach muscles jump and heat up as Hix let his hand drop from her waist to her belly, his fingers spreading out to cover her below her belly button.

"I used to love feeling your belly when you were carrying Peyton. How she would move inside you and how I could feel the changes each day," Hix confessed.

"Mmmmmm," was all Abby could say, as she was immersed in an erotic whirl pool created by the heat of Hix's body, the sweetness of his words, and the magic of his hands. Hix's lovemaking could turn her inside out and leave her aquiver, unable to breathe until the feelings slowed to a simmer, never dying out, just being banked, to await the next opportune moment to flare up again.

"You know, I've been thinking," Hix said, letting his hot breath dry the moisture on Abby's neck where he had let his lips kiss and his tongue taste.

"About what?" Abby asked, having trouble drawing a decent breath.

"Maybe we could start trying to give Peyton a little brother or sister," he said letting his fingers trace small circles on Abby's belly that he pictured, once again, growing large with their baby.

It took Abby a few heartbeats for the words Hix had said to sink in and make sense. Her eyes flew open and her fingernails dug into Hix's forearms, where only a couple of seconds ago she had been caressing with slow, soft touches imagining touching his body in the same silky way.

"Really?" she squeaked out.

"Yeah, why not?" Hix said matter-of-factly. "If we have them within a couple of years, we can have plenty of time for us to enjoy ourselves when they go off to college. I mean we did such a good job with Peyton, another one should be just as good. It would give Peyton someone to play with and, you know, I was just throwing the idea out there for us to talk about."

Abby swallowed hard and pasted on a smile that she hoped would fool Hix as she turned in his arms and gave him a quick kiss. "You better head out baby and we will talk about this when you get home tonight."

Sensing now was not the time to push the issue Hix gave Abby's butt a playful pat as he stole one last kiss, before out the door he went.

Abby was frozen to the kitchen floor as her mind boiled with the thought of having another child. She had just gotten her figure back and had been toying with the idea of bringing up to Hix that she start back to work. She'd never told him that she had been talking to her mother, who had told Abby that she was in the process of lining up work for her in the near future. Abby kind of liked the idea of going back to work, for the simple fact it would give her a break from mommy-hood, some adult time for a change. Not that she didn't love Peyton and thoroughly enjoyed spending time with her, but after almost a year and a half she was just ready for a change and work might be just what she needed. As much as she hated to admit it, her mother was right. It was time to get back into the swing of things.

Abby's phone rang before she could get her thoughts sorted out and, of course, on the other end was her mother. "Not now," Abby groaned out loud. But the phone kept ringing and Abby had to answer it before it woke Peyton.

"Hello mother," Abby said, keeping her voice low. "Why are you calling so early?"

"Hello to you, too," Cathy said, slightly miffed that her daughter was not happier to hear from her. "I just had such good news that I just could not wait to tell you."

Controlling her sigh, Abby pulled out a chair from the table and made herself comfortable, knowing that when her mother started talking about herself the call could turn into a marathon.

"What's your good news mom?" she prompted.

"Well it's not my good news really, but yours," Cathy said, actually sounding happy.

"Go on," Abby said cautiously.

"Well I have been talking to some of my people. In fact, I just got off the phone with the head of marketing for your favorite perfume and they want you to be the new face for their campaign that will be launched this summer!" Not pausing for Abby to respond, she continued, "The money is even more than you were getting before you got married and had the baby, so it is a very good offer. Of course I told them, as your manager, I could speak for you, and that you would be happy to work with them to make this their most successful campaign ever. Well?" Cathy demanded when her big announcement was met with silence form Abby. "Say something," she said, impatience dripping from her voice.

"I wish you had asked me first," Abby finally said. "Now may not be the best time for me."

"What do you mean?" Cathy fairly shouted. "What is the matter with now? Can't your poor husband get along without you for a few weeks? Are you so busy doing his dirty laundry that you can't get away to make some serious money and get your career back on track?"

"It's not that," Abby said, hoping that her mother would just take no for an answer, but she was delusional if she thought that would ever happen.

"Then tell me what it is and maybe you can convince me why I should turn down this peach of a job I got for you," Cathy said, wanting to reach through the phone and choke some sense into her daughter.

"Well if you must know," Abby started, trying for nonchalance but failing, "Hix and I were talking about having another baby."

The scream that Cathy funneled into the phone echoed all the way to Saul, making him draw in a deep breath and wince as he knew it had started.

Chapter 115

Abby pulled her car into Sarah's driveway and shut off the motor. She sat clutching the steering wheel in a death grip as she fought with herself and what she was about to do. She had to, she must, she argued with herself, she just had to.

Abby got out of the car, closed her door, and opened the back one. She reached in and lifted Peyton out of her car seat, holding her close for just a second, as if memorizing her smell and the way she felt in her arms, before grabbing the bag she had put together and heading for the front door.

Sarah stood in the doorway waiting for Abby, curious as to what had brought her two favorite girls to her doorstep unannounced.

"Hi, Abby," she said, at the same time reaching out her arms for Peyton, hugging her close, always glad to see her. "This is a nice surprise! What's up?"

"Hi, Sarah," Abby said, "I was wondering if you could watch Peyton for a little while? I have an errand to run, so could you? I mean, watch her?"

Sarah looked closer at Abby, as she heard the shaking in her voice and saw the residual signs of crying on her face.

"Why sure honey, you know I love having my granddaughter here. Are you okay? Would you like to come in and talk for a few minutes?" Sarah replied, smiling as she tried to see what might be bothering Abby.

"No, no, that's okay," Abby said, panic in her voice and in her eyes. "I just have to take care of something and I can't take Peyton with me."

"Sure I'll keep her," Sarah said, "you just go do what you have to and don't worry about us. We'll be fine."

"Okay, thanks," Abby said. She moved in and gave Peyton a hug and kiss without taking her from Sarah's arms and, when she pulled back, there were tears in her haunted brown eyes. "Mommy loves you baby," she whispered into her daughter's tiny ear. "Don't ever forget that. I love you so much."

"Okay, Abby, what gives?" Sarah asked. "You're starting to scare me. You know you can talk to me and I will keep it between us, if that is what you are worried about. Just talk to me."

"I can't," Abby said, backing up. "I just can't." And with that, she whirled and ran to her car. She dove in and drove away. But as she was leaving Sarah caught one last glance of her daughter-in-law as she turned her head for one last look.

What Sarah saw made her heart thump and sorrow wash through her from head to toe. She knew without a doubt that Abby was never coming back.

Chapter 116

Hix pulled into his driveway and breathed a sigh of relief. It had been a long hard day and he was glad it was over. He had been thinking that since it was going to be a nice evening that maybe he could throw some steaks and burgers on the grill so Abby would not have to cook and they could just relax tonight.

He had been uneasy all day, knowing that by bringing up the subject of another baby, he had shocked and maybe even upset Abby. He was going to have to assure Abby that this was not something they would do unless they were both on board with it and it did not have to be right away. There really was no hurry.

Hix opened the door and as he stepped inside. He was met with silence. An empty house. 'Okay,' he thought, 'Abby must be out running an errand, or visiting with Kendall, or his mother, or something like that. No need to panic. Right?' So why did he have a bad feeling? A feeling that he needed to find Abby, that Abby was in trouble.

Hix made a quick circuit of every room, but he had been right, no one was home. He pulled out his phone and checked, but he had not missed any calls. He dialed his mother to see if maybe Abby was there or his mother knew where she was.

"Hey, mom," Hix said when she answered, "Is Abby there?"

"No," Sarah said, "but she came by a few hours ago and dropped Peyton off."

"Did she say where she was going?" Hix asked, his gut starting to roll with fear.

"Come over and we will talk," Sarah said, not wanting to tell Hix her fears and what she had seen in Abby's eyes over the phone.

"Mom," Hix said, intending to say more but was cut off by Sarah.

"Just get over here," she said and hung up the phone.

Hix dialed Abby's phone and waited for her to answer. But his heart stopped as he heard the familiar ring coming from the bedroom. Letting the phone drop from his ear, Hix followed the sound and found her phone on top of the dresser. That was not like Abby. She carried her phone, as everyone did, with her always. He ran back out to his truck and, only then did he notice that Abby's car was not in the garage. "*Don't panic*," he told himself as he drove the short distance to his mothers. "*Don't panic!*"

Sarah had the door open, waiting for her son, before Hix stopped his truck.

"What is it, Mom?" Hix asked, making short work of the distance to the house.

"Inside," his mother said, moving aside so Hix could pass.

Sarah shut the door and waited, as Peyton, hearing her father's voice, came running, making a flying leap into her father's protecting arms.

"Hi, sweetie," Hix said, as he held his daughter close to his chest and kissed her hair that was so much like his own.

Sarah went to the fridge and got Hix a pop, while he said hello to his daughter. She opened it and sat it on the table, taking a seat herself and waiting until Hix sat down with Peyton on his lap. Hix looked at the pop waiting for him and then at his mother.

"No cocoa?" he asked, always remembering that serious talks were done over the sweet drink.

"Would you like a cup?" Sarah asked, confirming Hix's fear that what she had to say was not going to be good.

"No just tell me what's going on. Where's Abby?" he asked, fearing the answer.

"Like I said, she came over a few hours ago and asked if I would watch Peyton while she ran an errand."

"Seems pretty harmless, what else," Hix asked, because just babysitting was not going to make his mother call him to her house for a face to face.

"Something was wrong," Sarah said, looking her son straight in the eye. "She looked like she had been crying and she was jumpy. I asked her if she needed to talk and tried to get her to come inside, but she refused. She didn't look good, Hix."

"What do you mean, she didn't look good? How did she look?" he asked, alarmed at what his mother was telling him.

"It was her eyes," Sarah said, "They looked desperate and scared. As she was driving away she looked over at Peyton and I just got a bad feeling, like she was not coming back."

"Why would she leave?" Hix asked looking to his mother for answers she did not have. Answers she could not even guess at.

"Did you fight, or was she upset about something this morning," Sarah prodded, hating to pry but needing to try to find some reason for Abby's behavior.

"I brought up the idea that maybe we could think about having another baby. I think I kind of shocked her, but she was okay when I left. I don't think that was it. But, at the same time, that was the only thing that made today different from any other day. Do you think that was what upset her?" Hix asked, as guilt and his own shock was rocking his soul.

"I doubt it," Sarah said. "I mean I don't know, but that does not seem earth-shattering enough to make her run."

Hix set Peyton down. "Why don't you go into the living room and watch some cartoons while Grandma and I talk for a minute," Hix told his daughter. He watched as she ran off, feeling his chest squeeze as he realized she might never see her mother again.

When Peyton was out of earshot, Hix reached into his pants pocket and pulled out Abby's phone. "She left her phone, Mom," Hix said, starting to panic.

"Take a look and see who she talked to today," Sarah prompted. "I'm sure Abby wouldn't mind. It may give us a clue as to what happened today."

Hix wasted no time pulling up her phone log and as he read the name of the only person she had talked to, his blood began to boil.

Sarah watched as Hix's face turned stony and his eyes shot fire.

"What is it, Hix?" she asked, wanting to know.

"She talked to her mother this morning," Hix said, and Sarah knew what he was feeling. If there was one person that could upset Abby, it was Cathy.

"What do you want to do now?" Sarah asked, wanting Hix to make the decision where they would go from here.

Hix did not hesitate, as he punched in the number and waited to find out his future.

Chapter 117

Cathy had just walked into her home, closing the door and putting her keys in the expensive little dish, when her phone rang. She really did not feel like talking to anyone until she had taken a nice hot shower. But looking at the caller ID, she changed her mind. She couldn't pass up another chance to pressure her daughter into going back to work, and, in doing so, making her some money.

Maybe Abby was calling to tell her that she had changed her mind about becoming a breeding cow for her hick of a husband. God knows that Cathy had told her in no uncertain terms exactly what she thought of that idea. How, with a decision like that, she would be throwing away a career that had given her everything in her life. She ranted about how disappointed she was in Abby for moving to a hick town and getting involved with the first man who showed interest in her. Pointing out how she had let herself become pregnant by, don't forget, one of two men.

She had not let up, even when Abby started to cry and begged her to stop.

Cathy's stroke of brilliance had come when she suggested that maybe she could start working on a career for Abby's daughter. After all, she told her, she was pretty in a blonde-haired, blue-eyed sort of way that played well with the cameras.

Cathy had just laughed when Abby had cried harder and told her, between hiccups, to leave Peyton out of all of this. That she would never let Cathy push her daughter like she had pushed her. She warned her mother that Hix would never allow Peyton to be used by her.

Threatening, that he would stop her from abusing their daughter the way she did Abby.

Cathy had dismissed Abby's threats, telling her to make up her mind about the shoot she had booked for her, adding that she would pick her up at the airport in a week. She hung up the phone before Abby could protest any further.

Smiling as she relived the earlier conversation, Cathy arched an eyebrow and pushed the button on her phone.

"Unless you are calling to tell me that you will be in New York in a week and are ready to get back to work, I don't want to hear it. I don't want to hear how Hix is going to stand in my way if I decide to introduce my granddaughter to the world of modeling. And, if you even think about telling me you are actually thinking about having another brat, I will come to Nebraska and knock some sense into your stubborn head myself! Really, Abby, have you lost all sense of how to get ahead in life, and especially the business of modeling? Do you care nothing for all the hard work I've had to endure to get you to the top and keep you there? Well?" she demanded. "You called me, so talk or let me get back to my evening."

The voice that came through the line was not the timid one she was expecting, but instead one that was deep and growled with anger and unforgiving hate. A chill raced down Cathy's spine, knowing she had gone too far and given herself away. All it took was three little words delivered with no fanfare, and her world changed forever.

Hix almost melted the phone, so hot was his rage. All he wanted to know was, "WHERE'S MY WIFE!?"

Chapter 118

Hix got nothing from Cathy except stuttering, as she told him she did not know where Abby was. He refused to listen to any of Cathy's lame attempts at concern as to Abby's whereabouts, and hung up on her before she could drag him under with her unending drivel. He didn't care if he ever talked to her or saw her again.

Sarah waited impatiently as Hix sat with the phone to his ear, not saying a word then asking one question. Hanging up the phone, he was rigid with anger.

She let him be until his eyes refocused on her. Then all he said was "She doesn't know."

"That's not all she said, was it? What did she say, Hix?" Sarah pushed. She sat in disbelief as Hix, through gritted teeth, told her what Cathy had said.

"Oh my God," Sarah groaned, stunned that any mother could talk to or treat her child that way. "What are you going to do now?" she finally asked, as they had both sat in silence trying to digest what they had learned.

"I'm going to call the police and file a missing person's report, so we can find Abby and bring her back. I have to find her and tell her that I love her. That I am happy with our life just the way it is. I didn't mean to put any pressure on her to have another baby, Mom. I didn't mean to add to her troubles. If she would just have told me what was going on, I would have done anything to help her," Hix said, as his chest began to heave and his eyes filled with tears.

"Shhhh," Sarah said, as she got up and came around the table to hold her son, to let him draw from her strength. "Let's get that call made, shall we?" she asked, and picked up the phone, giving Hix time to gather himself for the ordeal of repeating the story to the police when they arrived.

It was only a few minutes before a knock on the door had Sarah on her feet, opening it and thanking the officer for coming as she welcomed him inside. She motioned for him to make himself comfortable while she got him something to drink.

Hix knew Officer Hayes, as he pretty much knew everyone in town, and talked to Jace comfortably, as he was a friend. He told him that he needed to file a report on Abby, giving him as many details as he could, leaving nothing out. It was hard, but he understood when he was told that most missing person's reports were not even considered until the person was missing for twenty four hours.

"I'm going to pull the friend card," Hix told Jace, "and ask that you start looking now. I have a feeling that I need to get to Abby as soon as I can."

Jace sat for a minute thinking. "I think I can do that for you," he said, standing up. "I'll head back to the station and get a BOLO out yet tonight."

"Thanks, man," Hix said as they shook hands and he walked his friend to the door.

"I've got your number, so I'll call when I know anything." Jace said and turned to leave.

Hix nodded his head and stood for a minute, looking out at the rain that had started to fall sometime after he had arrived. He watched as lightning forked through the black sky, white hot bolts, one right after another, not giving the eyes time to adjust. They just kept coming. Hix wanted to be out there doing something, not just sitting in his mother's kitchen, feeling helpless.

As Hix stood in the open door way he felt a small tug on his leg. Looking down he saw his daughter standing close to his leg. She lifted her arms to be picked up and Hix scooped her up high in his arms. Peyton wrapped her arms around her father's neck and together they watched the rain come down harder. It seemed as if the sky had opened up, sharing their pain as it helped in the only way it could, by washing the slate clean so a new day could start fresh.

The mortals on earth had to make it through the night. If they could do that, then a new day would dawn and new hope would be given.

They just had to survive the night.

Chapter 119

Abby drove away from not only Sarah's house, but her daughter and her husband too. The feelings of fear, helplessness, and failure flooded her mind, so she bolted, trying to out-run her demons. She loved her life with Hix, her daughter, and all her close friends in Winston, but did she really belong there? Her mother did not think so. It was hard when you had to listen to someone that said they loved you, cut you so deep that you bled on the inside. The only thing holding in all the hurt was your skin and knowing that each time you talked to her that skin got thinner and thinner, until you feared it would rip and your pain and insecurities would fall out and lay there in the open for everyone to see.

Abby did not want things to get that far and, knowing that if she didn't do something soon, all her worst fears would be realized. All she could think to do after talking to her mother today was to get away. Get away and think things through.

Abby knew she shouldn't have taken off without telling Hix what was going on first, but she needed to get away and couldn't wait. If she'd stayed, she knew she would have broken down and told Hix everything. His shoulders were wide and she knew he would have taken on her problems, trying to fix them so she would be happy and content. But it would have made her feel worse because she was not strong enough to handle things on her own. She would have caused trouble for him, and she loved him too much to intentionally do that.

Abby wasn't totally selfish in her leaving. She had written Hix a letter. And, as she pulled over and dropped it in the mail slot at the post office, she found herself hoping that she had explained herself well enough for him to know she was safe and that she would be coming back soon.

As the letter left her hand, it began to rain. It was just a few drops at first, not enough to cause her concern and definitely not enough to slow her escape. It was miles down the road before she noticed the rain had gotten a lot worse, her mind still churning as she drove. Her wipers blurred in the dark as they tried to keep up with the downpour, but the rain was coming down so hard that what the slim blades were able to push away was replaced faster than they could handle.

It wasn't long before Abby became concerned. '*Not afraid*,' she told herself. After all, she only had to make it to the next hotel and she could stop for the night. Maybe after getting some sleep she would be able to see things more clearly.

She bent forward in the seat, trying to see the road signs through the deluge, but they only appeared as wavy green squares that passed all too quickly and were gone before she could read them.

Abby had just decided to pull off at the next exit and wait the rain out, when she felt the wheels jerk to the right and, although she had never hydroplaned before, she was sure that was what was happening now. She jerked the wheel to the left and stomped on the brake, but the car acted as if it had a mind of its own as it headed for the ditch.

Abby's world spun around and around, and her ears were filled with screams and shrieks as metal met the road. The windshield blew inward, as it was filled with the trunk of a cottonwood tree that did not give as the car slammed into it.

Abby lay stunned, waiting for her mind to finally stop spinning. *"It's not so bad."* Abby thought. "I*t's not so bad*." She wasn't in any pain and the total quiet was soothing. Where the front window had been was now only a big jagged hole, and the roof had been rolled back like a tin of sardines. Abby did not feel the cold rain as it beat down on her. In fact, all she felt was warmth. Not the warmth of her blood as it stopped flowing from her wounds, or the warmth from the motor that still pinged and hissed. But the warmth that comes from peace and well-being.

For the first time in a long while now, Abby was at peace.

Chapter 120

Hix had left his mother's house with his daughter in the car seat beside him, Sarah following in her own car right behind. She had insisted on coming to stay the night, or at least until Abby came home, not wanting Hix to be alone.

The small convoy pulled into Hix's driveway, as Hix, hoping against hope, scanned the yard for signs of Abby's return. But he found nothing. Grabbing Peyton in his arms and covering her head with his shirt, Hix made a mad dash towards the door. He made it inside, but not before he was soaked to the bone. Sarah followed, just as wet and just as unconcerned with something so small when bigger issues loomed over them.

"I'll get Peyton ready for bed," Sarah said, as she took Peyton from Hix's arms. "Why don't you give Kendall a call and ask her if Abby is there or if she knows anything, okay?"

Hix gave his mother a kiss on the cheek for trying to give him something to do to keep busy. "Thanks, mom," he said gently, making his way into the kitchen to make his call and start the fixings for something hot to drink. All he could think of was hot cocoa, and his gut rolled with the meaning of the yummy beverage. Trouble.

Hix had hoped Kendall would be able to shed some light on Abby's whereabouts, but she had no idea. Hix talked her out of coming out in the rain, telling her he would call as soon as he found out anything.

Sarah brought out a bathed, sweet-smelling, and tired Peyton, turning her care over to her father as she went to stand at the front window. She looked out at the rain, thinking that usually she would have been thrilled with the moisture, but tonight it just seemed to bring a feeling of dread. She hoped that wherever Abby was, she was safe and dry.

She turned from her musings as Hix came into the room, having tucked Peyton into her bed, and gave her a half smile. "We really will be fine, mom," he said, giving his mother permission to return to her own home now that she was sure that he and Peyton were home and safe.

"I think I'll just stay in the spare bedroom tonight," she said, "if that's alright with you."

"That's fine," he said. They retrieved their cups of now-cool cocoa and went to sit in the living room, staring at the TV, but not really seeing it. It wasn't long before Hix drifted off to sleep.

Hix was brought awake by a knocking on the front door. He rubbed his tired eyes as he stumbled to the door and jerked it open. The sunlight that greeted him seemed overly bright and it took him a moment to focus. When he did, he found Jace on the front step with his hat in his hand, his face haggard and grey.

"Hey, Jace," Hix said, his mouth dry. "Come on in."

"Sure," the officer said, stepping past Hix and coming face to face with Sarah.

One look at his face and Sarah knew. Hix walked around him and stood by his mother's side, not asking what the Police had found out, not wanting to know. Scared.

"We found her, Hix," Jace began. "About an hour ago a motorist was driving about a hundred miles from here and they called in an accident. They said a car had gone off the road and rolled over. I am very sorry to tell you this Hix," Jace said relying on words he had used in the past to deliver the hardest news of all to loved ones, "but Abby was killed in that accident."

Hix sank to his knees and cried.

Epilogue

Hix quietly opened the front door and walked into the home he had built for his family, carrying his sleeping daughter in his arms. Her head rested on his shoulder as she slept, having fallen asleep on the drive home from the funeral, not waking as he lifted her from the car. Peyton was too young, at a year and a half, to realize what was happening. She had no idea how her world was going to change. She trusted the big man she knew as her daddy to take care of her and keep her from harm.

Hix passed a mirror in the hall and stopped to look at their reflection. A strand of his golden hair had become mixed with the feathery soft strands of the same color on the small head. He could not tell which was hers and which was his, so close was the color and softness of their hair. He raised his free hand to place it on her sleeping back and only then realized that he still held the mail that he had picked up on his way inside. He turned to toss it on the kitchen table, but froze as the mail spread across the smooth surface, recognizing the writing on a letter that separated from the rest.

As if in a trance, he picked up the envelope and stared at his name and address in Abby's handwriting. Lowering himself into a chair, Hix opened the letter with hands that shook. Lifting out the single page, he began to read, hearing Abby's now silent voice speak to him in his head.

My love,

By now you know that I have left, and are probably half out of your mind with worry. I know I took the coward's way out by leaving without telling you first, but I need some time alone to get my head on straight. Please do not, for one minute, think that I do not love you and our beautiful daughter, Peyton, because I do. It is just hard to explain in words what I am feeling right now. Everything seems to be building up inside me and I don't feel like myself right now. I need time. Time to be by myself and sort things out.

If I'd have told you how I'm feeling, I know you would have tried to fix things and it would have just made me feel more confused, more like a failure. I will be better when I return, I promise.

Please do not look for or try to find me. If you love me, which I know in my heart that you do, let me have this time apart from our family. I'll be back.

Until then always remember that I love you both.

Abby

Hix read the letter one more time, as pain roared through his body and soul. Abby had no way of knowing that her flight from them would lead to an accident, and that she would never be back. Not alive. Only cold, broken and dead. The letter had given him the answers he needed about why she had left, easing the guilt he had been left to shoulder. It also brought all the grief and the loneliness that he had tried to lock away inside back into the glaring bright light, and he broke under its weight.

Crumpling the letter he still held in his hand, he buried his face in the warm soft neck of his daughter and silently sobbed.

Abby's pale form stood across the table from Hix, as he sobbed out his grief into their daughter's neck. Turning her head, she looked at the beautiful man standing at her side. "Who are you?" she asked, her voice sounding weak in her ears.

"I am Saul," the man said, his voice covering her like honey, making her feel warm and calm. "I am your Guardian, here to help you as you continue your journey."

"I don't understand," she said, "I don't remember what happened. Why am I here? Why can't Hix see me?"

Saul looked into the still beautiful eyes and, with regret for the news he had to give, told her about the accident. "You died," he said gently. "I am here to guide you on the next leg of your soul's journey."

"What have I done?" she asked, guilt riding heavy in her voice as she looked longingly at her husband and child.

"You fulfilled your destiny as it was written," Saul explained. "No more and no less. It was meant to be."

"What happens now?" Abby asked, being afraid of the unknown.

"You will be reborn into a human body and continue your search for your true soul mate." At Abby's startled glance Saul nodded his head saying, "It is true. Even though you both found love at this time, it was not the love of soul mates. Your journey must continue."

"Will they be okay?" Abby asked, as she felt herself begin to rise into the air.

"Yes," Saul replied as he began to lead Abby on her next journey. "I will watch over them and keep them safe."

Abby raised her hand to her mouth and blew one last kiss to Hix and her daughter before she was pulled away by Saul.

In the kitchen, for just a second in time, Hix could have sworn that he smelled Abby's perfume, as if she was standing beside him. But they were alone, he and Peyton. Alone with nothing but the ticking of the clock in an otherwise silent house.